DEATH AND THE DANCING FOOTMAN

The Critics say of Ngaio Marsh

D1347455

NGAIO MARSH

Death and the
Dancing Footman

Collins

FONTANA BOOKS

First published 1942
First issued in Fontana Books 1958
Second Impression January 1965
Third Impression September 1968
Fourth Impression March 1969
Fifth Impression December 1969

For
Mivie and Greg
with my love

Printed in Great Britain
Collins Clear-Type Press
London and Glasgow

CONTENTS

Part One

Part Two

CAST OF CHARACTERS

JONATHAN ROYAL	*of Highfold Manor, Cloudyfold, Dorset*
CAPER	*his butler*
AUBREY MANDRAKE	*born Stanley Footling, poetic dramatist*
SANDRA COMPLINE	*of Penfelton Manor*
WILLIAM COMPLINE	*her elder son*
NICHOLAS COMPLINE	*her younger son*
CHLORIS WYNNE	*William's fiancée*
DR. FRANCIS HART	*a plastic surgeon*
MADAME ELISE LISSE	*a beauty specialist, of the Studio Lisse*
LADY HERSEY ABLINGTON	*Jonathan's distant cousin; beauty specialist, of the Salon Hersey*
THOMAS	*a dancing footman*
MRS. POUTING	*Jonathan's housekeeper*
JAMES BEWLING	*an outside hand at Highfold*
THOMAS BEWLING	*his brother*
RODERICK ALLEYN	*Chief Detective-Inspector, C.I., New Scotland Yard*
AGATHA TROY ALLEYN	*his wife*
WALTER COPELAND	*Rector of Winton St. Giles*
DINAH COPELAND	*his daughter*
FOX	*Detective-Inspector C.1, New Scotland Yard*
DETECTIVE-SERGEANT THOMSON	*a photographic expert*
DETECTIVE-SERGEANT BAILEY	*a finger-print expert*
A HOUSEMAID	
SUPERINTENDENT BLANDISH	*of the Great Chipping Constabulary*

Part One

CHAPTER I

PROJECT

I

ON the afternoon of a Thursday early in 1940, Jonathan Royal sat in his library at Highfold Manor. Although daylight was almost gone, curtains were not yet drawn across the windows, and Jonathan Royal could see the ghosts of trees moving in agitation against torn clouds and a dim sequence of fading hills. The north wind, blowing strongly across an upland known as Cloudyfold, was only partly turned by Highfold woods. It soughed about the weathered corners of the old house, and fumbled in the chimneys. A branch, heavy with snow, tapped vaguely at one of the library windows. Jonathan Royal sat motionless beside his fire. Half of his chubby face and figure flickered in and out of shadow, and when a log fell in two and set up a brighter blaze, it showed that Jonathan was faintly smiling. Presently he stirred slightly and beat his plump hands lightly upon his knees, a discreetly ecstatic gesture. A door opened, admitting a flood of yellow light, not very brilliant, and a figure that paused with its hand on the door-knob.

"Hallo," said Jonathan Royal. "That you, Caper?"

"Yes, sir."

"Lighting-up time?"

"Five o'clock, sir. It's a dark afternoon."

"Ah," said Jonathan, suddenly rubbing his hands together, "that's the stuff to give the troops."

"I beg your pardon, sir?"

"That's the stuff to give the troops, Caper. An expression borrowed from a former cataclysm. I did not intend you to take it literally. It's the stuff to give my particular little troop. You may draw the curtains."

Caper adjusted Jonathan's patent black-out screens and drew the curtains. Jonathan stretched out a hand and switched on a table lamp at his elbow. Fire and lamplight were now reflected in the glass doors that protected his books, in the dark surfaces of his desk, in his leather saddle-back chairs, in his own spectacles, and in the dome of his bald pate. With a quick movement he brought his hands together on his belly and began to revolve his thumbs one over the other sleekly.

"Mr. Mandrake rang up, sir, from Winton St. Giles rectory. He will be here at 5.30."

"Good," said Jonathan.

"Will you take tea now, sir, or wait for Mr. Mandrake?"

"Now. He'll have had it. Has the mail come?"

"Yes, sir. I was just——"

"Well, let's have it," said Jonathan eagerly. "Let's have it."

When the butler had gone, Jonathan gave himself a little secret hug with his elbows, and, continuing to revolve his thumbs, broke into a thin falsetto, singing:

> "Il était une bergère
> Qui ron-ton-ton. Petit pat-a-plan."

He moved his big head from side to side, in time with his tune and, owing to a trick of the firelight on his thick-lensed glasses, he seemed to have large white eyes that gleamed like those of the dead drummer in the *Ingoldsby Legends*. Caper returned with his letters. He snatched them up and turned them over with deft, pernickety movements, and at last uttered a little ejaculation. Five letters were set aside and the sixth opened and unfolded. He held it level with his nose, but almost at arm's length. It contained only six lines of writing, but they seemed to give Jonathan the greatest satisfaction. He tossed the letter gaily on the fire and took up the thin tenor of his song. Ten minutes later, when Caper brought in his tea, he was still singing, but he interrupted himself to say:

"Mr. Nicholas Compline is definitely coming to-morrow. He may have the green visitors' room. Tell Mrs. Pouting, will you?"

"Yes, sir. Excuse me, sir, but that makes eight guests for the week-end?"

"Yes. Yes, eight." Jonathan ticked them off on his plump fingers. "Mrs. Compline. Mr. Nicholas and Mr. William

Compline. Dr. Francis Hart. Madame Lisse. Miss Wynne. Lady Hersey Amblington. and Mr. Mandrake. Eight. Mr. Mandrake to-night, the rest for dinner to-morrow. We'll have the Heidsiek '28 to-morrow, Caper, and the Courvoisier."

"Very good, sir."

"I am particularly anxious about the dinner to-morrow, Caper. Much depends upon it. There must be a warmth, a feeling of festivity, of anticipation, of—I go so far—of positive luxury. Large fires in the bedrooms. I've ordered flowers. Your department now. Always very satisfactory, don't think there's an implied criticism, but to-morrow "—he opened his arms wide—" Whoosh! Something quite extra. Know what I mean? I've told Mrs. Pouting. She's got everything going, I know. But your department—— Ginger up that new feller and the maids. Follow me?"

"Certainly, sir."

"Yes. The party "—Jonathan paused, hugged his sides with his elbows and uttered a thin cackle of laughter—" the party may be a little sticky at first. I regard it as an experiment."

"I hope everything will be quite satisfactory, sir."

"Quite satisfactory," Jonathan repeated. " Yes. Sure of it. Is that a car? Have a look."

Jonathan turned off his table-lamp. Caper went to the windows and drew aside their heavy curtains. The sound of wind and sleet filled the room.

"It's difficult to say, sir, with the noise outside, but—yes, sir, there are the head-lamps. I fancy it's coming up the inner drive, sir."

"Mr. Mandrake, no doubt. Show him in here, and you can take away these tea things. Too excited for 'em. Here he is."

Caper closed the curtains and went out with the tea things. Jonathan switched on his lamp. He heard the new footman cross the hall and open the great front door.

"It's beginning," thought Jonathan, hugging himself. " This is the overture. We're off."

II

Mr. Aubrey Mandrake was a young poetic dramatist and his real name was Stanley Footling. He was in the habit of telling himself, for he was not without humour, that if it had been a little worse; if, for instance, it had been Albert Muggins, he would have clung to it, for there would have been a kind of distinction in such a name. Seeing it set out in the programme, under the titles of his " Saxophone in Tarleton," the public would have enclosed it in mental inverted commas. But they would not perform this delicate imaginary feat for a Stanley Footling. So he became Aubrey Mandrake, influenced in his choice by such names as Sebastian Melmoth, Aubrey Beardsley and Peter Warlock. In changing his name he had given himself a curious psychological set-back, for in a short time he grew to identify himself so closely with his new names that the memory of the old ones became intolerable, and the barest suspicion that some new acquaintance had discovered his origin threw him into a state of acute uneasiness, made still more unendurable by the circumstance of his despising himself bitterly for this weakness. At first his works had chimed with his name, for he wrote of Sin and the Occult, but as his by no means inconsiderable talent developed, he found his subject in matters at once stranger and less colourful. He wrote, in lines of incalculable variety, of the passion of a pattern-cutter for a headless bust, of a saxophonist who could not perform to his full ability unless his instrument was decked out in tarleton frills, of a lavatory attendant who became a gentleman of the bed-chamber (this piece was performed only by the smaller experimental theatre clubs), and of a chartered accountant who turned out to be a reincarnation of Thäis. He was successful. The post-surrealists wrangled over him, the highest critics discovered in his verse a revitalising influence on an effete language, and the philistines were able to enjoy the fun. He was the possessor of a comfortable private income derived from his mother's boarding-house in Dulwich and the fruit of his father's ingenuity—a patent suspender clip. In appearance he was tall, dark, and suitably cadaverous; in manner, somewhat sardonic, in his mode of dressing, correct, for he had long since passed the stage when unusual cravats and strange shirts seemed to be a necessity for his æsthetic development. He was lame and extremely sensitive about the deformed foot which caused this disability. He wore a heavy boot on his left foot and always tried as far as possible to hide it under the chair on which he was sitting. His acquaintance with Jonathan Royal was some five years old. Late in the nineteen-thirties Jonathan had backed one of Mandrake's plays, and though it had not made a fortune for either of them it had unexpectedly paid its way and had established their liking for one another.

Mandrake's latest play, "Bad Black-out" (finished since the
outbreak of war but, as far as the uninstructed could judge,
and in spite of its title, not about the war), was soon to go into
rehearsal with an untried company of young enthusiasts. He
had spent two days at Winton St. Giles rectory with his leading
lady and her father, and Jonathan had asked him to come on
to Highfold for the week-end.

His entrance into Jonathan's library was effective, for he had
motored over Cloudyfold bareheaded with the driving-window
open, and the north wind had tossed his hair into elf-locks. He
usu lly did the tossing himself. He advanced upon Jonathan
with his hand outstretched, and an air of gay hardihood.

" An incredible night," he said. " Harpies and warlocks
abroad. Most stimulating."

" I trust," said Jonathan, shaking his hand and blinking up
at him, " that it hasn't stimulated your Muse. I cannot allow
her to claim you this evening, Aubrey——"

" O God!" said Mandrake. He always made this ejaculation
when invited to speak of his writing. It seemed to imply
desperate æsthetic pangs.

"—because," Jonathan continued, " I intend to claim your
full attention, my dear Aubrey. Our customary positions are
reversed. For to-night, yes, and for to-morrow and the next
day, I shall be the creator and you the audience." Mandrake
darted an apprehensive glance at his host.

" No, no, no," Jonathan cried, steering him to the fireside,
" don't look so alarmed. I've written no painful middle-aged
belles-lettres, nor do I contemplate my memoirs. Nothing of
the sort."

Mandrake sat opposite his host by the fire. Jonathan rubbed
his hands together and suddenly hugged them between his
knees. " Nothing of the sort," he repeated.

" You look very demure," said Mandrake. " What are you
plotting?"

" Plotting! That's the word! My dear, I am up to my ears
in conspiracy." He leant forward and tapped Mandrake on the
knee. " Come now," said Jonathan, " tell me this. What do
you think are my interests?"

Mandrake looked fixedly at him. " Your *interests*?" he
repeated.

" Yes. What sort of fellow do you think I am? It is not only
women, you know, who are interested in the impressions they
make on their friends. Or *is* there something unexpectedly

feminine in my curiosity? Never mind. Indulge me so far. Come now."

"You skip from one query to another. Your interests, I should hazard, lie between your books, your estate, and—well, I imagine you are interested in what journalists are pleased to call human contacts."

"Good," said Jonathan. "Excellent. Human contacts. Go on."

"As for the sort of fellow you may be," Mandrake continued, "upon my word, I don't know. From my point of view a very pleasant fellow. You understand things, the things that seem to me to be important. You have never asked me, for instance, why I don't write about real people. I regard that avoidance as conclusive."

"Would you say, now, that I had a sense of the dramatic?"

"What is the dramatic? Is it merely a sense of theatre, or is it an appreciation of æsthetic climax in the extroverted sense?"

"I don't know what that means," said Jonathan impatiently. "And I'm dashed if I think you do."

"Words," said Mandrake. "Words, words, words." But he looked rather put out.

"Well, damnit, it doesn't matter two ha'po'th of pins. I maintain that I have a sense of drama in the ordinary un-classy sense. My sense of drama, whether you like it or not, attracts me to your own work. I don't say I understand it, but for me it's got *something*. It jerks me out of my ordinary reactions to ordinary theatrical experiences. So I like it."

"That's as good a reason as most."

"All right. But wait a bit. In me, my dear Aubrey, you see the unsatisfied and inarticulate artist. Temperament and no art. That's me. Or so I thought until I got my Idea. I've tried writing and I've tried painting. The results have on the whole been pitiable—at the best negligible. Music—out of the question. And all the time, here I was, an elderly fogey plagued with the desire to create. Most of all have I hankered after drama, and at first I thought my association with you, a delightful affair from my point of view, I assure you, would do the trick; I would taste, at second-hand as it were, the pleasures of creative art. But no, the itch persisted and I was in danger of becoming a disgruntled restless fellow, a nuisance to myself and a bore to other people."

"Never that," murmured Mandrake, lighting a cigarette.

"It would have been the next stage, I assure you. It threatened. And then, in what I cannot but consider an inspired moment, my dear Aubrey, I got My Idea."

With a crisp movement Jonathan seized his glasses by their nose-piece and plucked them from his face. His eyes were black and extremely bright.

"My Idea," he repeated. "One Wednesday morning four weeks ago, as I was staring out of my window here and wondering how the devil I should spend the day, it suddenly came to me. It came to me that if I was a ninny with ink and paper, and brush and canvas, and all the rest of it, if I couldn't express so much as a how-d'ye-do with a stave of music, there was one medium that I had never tried."

"And what could that wonderful medium be?"

"Flesh and blood!"

"What!"

"Flesh and blood!"

"You are *not*," said Mandrake, "I implore you to say you are *not* going in for social welfare."

"Wait a bit. It came to me that human beings could, with a little judicious arrangement, be as carefully ' composed ' as the figures in a picture. One had only to restrict them a little, confine them within the decent boundaries of a suitable canvas, and they would make a pattern. It seemed to me that, given the limitations of an imposed stage, some of my acquaintances would at once begin to unfold an exciting drama; that, so restricted, their conversation would begin to follow as enthralling a design as that of a fugue. Of course the right, how shall I put it, the right ingredients must be selected, and this was where I came in. I would set my palette with human colours and the picture would paint itself. I would summon my characters to the theatre of my own house and the drama would unfold itself."

"Pirandello," Mandrake began, "has become quite——"

"But this is *not* Pirandello," Jonathan interrupted in a great hurry. "No. In this instance we shall see, not six characters in search of an author, but an author who has deliberately summoned seven characters to do his work for him."

"Then you mean to write, after all?"

"Not I. I merely select. As for writing," said Jonathan, "that's where you come in. I make you a present of what I cannot but feel is a golden opportunity."

Mandrake stirred uneasily. "I wish I knew what you were up to," he said.

" My dear fellow, I'm telling you. Listen. A month ago I decided to make this experiment. I decided to invite seven suitably chosen characters for a winter week-end here at High-fold, and I spent a perfectly delightful morning compiling the list. My characters must, I decided, be, as far as possible, antagonistic to each other."

" O God!"

" Not antagonistic each one to the other seven, but there must at least be some sort of emotional intellectual tension running like a connecting thread between them. Now a very little thought showed me that I had not far to seek. Here, in my own corner of Dorset, here in the village and county under-currents, still running high in spite of the war, I found my seven characters. And since I must have an audience, and an intelligent audience, I invited an eighth guest—yourself."

" If you expect me to break into a pæan of enraptured gratitude——"

" Not just yet, perhaps. Patience. Now, in order to savour the full bouquet of the experiment you must be made happily familiar with the dramatis personæ. And to that end," said Jonathan cosily, " I propose that we ring for sherry."

III

" I propose," said Jonathan, filling his companion's glass, " to abandon similes drawn from painting or music, and to stick to a figure that we can both appreciate. I shall introduce my characters in terms of dramatic art and, as far as I can guess, in the order of their appearance. You look a little anxious."

" Then my looks," Mandrake rejoined, " do scant justice to my feelings. I feel terrified."

Jonathan uttered his little cackle of laughter. " Who can tell?" he said. " You may have good cause. You shall judge of that when I have finished. The first characters to make their unconscious entrances on our stage are a mother and two sons. Mrs. Sandra Compline, William Compline, and Nicholas Compline. The lady is a widow and lives at Penfelton, a charming house some four miles to the western side of Cloudyfold village. She is the grand dame of our cast. The Complines are an old Dorset family and have been neighbours of ours for many generations. Her husband was my own contemporary. A rackety, handsome fellow, he was, more popular perhaps with women than with men, but he had his own set in London and a very fast set I fancy it was. I don't know where he met his wife, but I'm afraid it was an ill-omened encounter for her, poor thing. She was a pretty creature and I suppose he fell in love with her looks. His attachment didn't last as long as her beauty, and that faded pretty fast under the sort of treatment she had to put up with. When they'd been married about eight years and had these two sons, a ghastly thing happened to Sandra Compline. She went to stay abroad somewhere and, I suppose with the idea of winning him back, she had something done to her face. It was more than twenty years ago, and I dare say these fellows weren't as good at their job as they are nowadays. Lord knows what the chap she consulted did with Sandra Compline's face. I've heard it said (you may imagine how people talked) that he bolstered it up with wax and that the wax slipped. Whatever happened, it was quite disastrous. Poor thing," said Jonathan, shaking his head while the lamplight glinted on his glasses, " she was a most distressing sight. Quite lop-sided, you know, and, worst of all, there was a sort of comical look. For a long time she wouldn't go out or receive anyone. He began to ask his own friends to Penfelton, and a very dubious lot they were. We saw nothing of the Complines in those days, but local gossip was terrific. She used to hunt, wearing a thick veil and going so recklessly that people said she wanted to kill herself. Ironically, though, it was her husband who came a cropper. Fell with his horse and broke his neck. What d'you think of that?"

" Eh?" said Mandrake, rather startled by this sudden demand. " Why, my dear Jonathan, it's quite marvellous. Devastatingly Edwardian. Gloriously county. Another instance of truth being much more theatrical than fiction, and a warning to all dramatists to avoid it."

" Well, well," said Jonathan. " I dare say. Let's get on. Sandra was left with her two small sons, William and Nicholas. After a little she seemed to take heart of grace. She began to go about a bit; this house was the first she visited. The boys had their friends for the holidays, and all that, and life became more normal over at Penfelton. The elder boy, William, was a quiet sort of chap, rather plain on the whole, not a great deal to say for himself; grave, humdrum fellow. Well enough liked, but the type that—well, you can never remember whether he was or was not at a party. That sort of fellow, do you know?"

" Poor William," said Mandrake unexpectedly.

" What? Oh yes, yes, but I haven't quite conveyed William to you. The truth is," said Jonathan, rubbing his nose, " that William's a bit of a teaser. He's devoted to his mother. I think he remembers her as she was before the tragedy. He was seven when she came back, and I've heard that although he was strangely self-possessed when he saw her, he was found by their old nurse in a sort of hysterical frenzy, remarkable in such a really rather commonplace small boy. He *is* quiet and hum-drum, certainly, but for all that there's something not quite—well, he's a little *odd*. He's usually rather silent, but when he does talk his statements are inclined to be unexpected. He seems to say more or less the first thing that comes into his head, and that's a sufficiently unusual trait, you'll agree."

" Yes."

" Yes. Odd. Nothing wrong really, of course, and he's done very well so far in this war. He's a good lad. But sometimes I wonder . . . However, you shall judge of William for yourself. I want you to do that."

" You don't really like him, do you?" asked Mandrake suddenly.

Jonathan blinked. " What can have put that notion into your head?" he said mildly. He darted a glance at Mandrake. " You mustn't become *too* subtle, Aubrey. William is merely rather difficult to describe. That is all. But Nicholas!" Jonathan continued. " Nicholas was his father over again. Damned good-looking young blade, with charm and gaiety, and dash, and all the rest of it. Complete egoist, bit of a showman, and born with an eye for a lovely lady. So they grew up and so they are to-day. William's thirty-two and Nick's twenty-nine. William (I stress this point) is concentrated upon his mother, morbidly so, I think, but that's by the way. Gives up his holidays for no better reason than she's going to be alone. Watches after her like an old Nanny. He's on leave just now, and of course rushed home to her. Nick's the opposite, plays her up for all she's worth, never lets her know when he's coming or what he's up to. Uses Penfelton like a hotel and his mother like the proprietress. You can guess which of these boys is the mother's favourite."

" Nicholas," said Mandrake. " Of course, Nicholas."

" Of course," said Jonathan, and if he felt any disappointment he did not show it. " She dotes on Nicholas and takes William for granted. She's spoilt Nicholas quite hopelessly from the day he was born. William went off to prep-school and Eton; Nick, if you please, was pronounced delicate, and led a series of tutors a fine dance until his mother decided he was old enough for the Grand Tour and sent him off with a bear-leader like some young regency lordling. If she could have cut William out of the entail I promise you she'd have done it. As it is she can do nothing. William comes in for the whole packet, and Nick, like the hero of Victorian romance, must fend for himself. This, I believe, his mother fiercely resents. When war came she moved heaven and earth to find a safe job for Nicholas, and took it in her stride when William's regiment went to the front. Nick has got some department job in Great Chipping. Looks very smart in uniform, and his duties seem to take him up to London pretty often. William, at the moment, as I have told you, is spending his leave with his mamma. The brothers haven't met for some time."

"Do they get on well?"

"No. Remember the necessary element of antagonism, Aubrey. It appears, splendidly to the fore, in the Compline family. William is engaged to Nicholas's ex-fiancée."

"Really? Well done, William."

"I need scarcely tell you that the lady is the next of my characters, the ingénue, in fact. She will arrive with William and his mamma, who detests her."

"Honestly, my dear Jonathan——"

"She is a Miss Chloris Wynne. One of the white-haired kind."

"A platinum blonde?"

"The colour of a light Chablis, and done up in plaster-like sausages. She resembles the chorus of my youth. I'm told that nowadays the chorus looks like the county. I find her appearance startling and her conversation difficult, but I have watched her with interest and I have formed the opinion that she is a very neat example of the woman scorned."

"Did Nicholas scorn her?"

"Nicholas wished to marry her, but being in the habit of eating his cake in enormous mouthfuls, and keeping it, he did not allow his engagement to Miss Chloris to cramp his style as an accomplished philanderer. He continued to philander with the fifth item in our cast of characters—Madame Lisse."

"O God!"

"More in anger than in sorrow, if Sandra Compline is to be believed, Miss Chloris broke off her engagement to Nicholas.

After an interval so short that one suspects she acted on the ricochet, she accepted William, who had previously courted her and been cut out by his brother. My private opinion is that when William returns to the front, Nicholas is quite capable of recapturing the lady, and, what's more, I think she and William both know it. Nicholas and William had quarrelled in the best tradition of rival brothers and, as I say, have not met since the second engagement. I need not tell you that Mrs. Compline, William, and his betrothed, none of them knows I have invited Nicholas, nor does Nicholas know I have invited them. He knows, however, that Madame Lisse will be here. That, of course, is why he has accepted."

"Go on," said Mandrake, driving his fingers through his hair.

"Madame Lisse, the ambiguous and alluring woman of our cast, is an Austrian beauty specialist. I don't suppose Lisse is her real name. She was among the earliest of the refugees, obtained naturalisation papers, and established a salon at Great Chipping. She had letters to the Jerninghams at Pen Cuckoo, and to one or two other people in the county. Diana Copeland at the rectory rather took her up. So, as you have gathered, did Nicholas Compline. She is markedly a dasher. Dark-auburn hair, magnolia complexion, and eyes—whew! Very quiet and composed, but undoubtedly a dasher. Everybody got rather excited about Madame Lisse . . . everybody, that is, with the exception of my distant cousin, Lady Hersey Amblington, who will arrive for dinner to-morrow evening."

The spectacles glinted in Mandrake's direction, but he merely waved his hands.

"Hersey," said Jonathan, "as you may know, is also a beauty specialist. She took it up when her husband died and left her almost penniless. She did the thing thoroughly and, being a courageous and capable creature, made a success of it. The mysteries of what I believe is called 'beauty culture' are as a sealed book to me, but I understand that all the best complexions and coiffures of Great Chipping and the surrounding districts were, until the arrival of Madame Lisse, Hersey's particular property. Madame Lisse immediately began to knock spots out of Hersey. Not, as Hersey explained, that she now has fewer customers, but that they are not quite so smart. The smart clientele has, with the exception of a faithful few, gone over to the enemy. Hersey considers that Madame used unscrupulous methods and always alludes to her as 'The Pirate.' You haven't met my distant cousin, Hersey?"

"No."

"No. She has her own somewhat direct methods of warfare, and I understand that she called on Madame Lisse with the intention of giving her fits. I'm afraid Hersey came off rather the worse in this encounter. Hersey is an old friend of the Complines and, as you may imagine, was not at all delighted by Nicholas's attentions to her rival. So you see she is linked up in an extremely satisfactory manner to both sides. I have really been extraordinarily fortunate," said Jonathan, rubbing his hands. "Nothing could be neater. And Dr. Hart fills out the cast to perfection. The 'heavy,' I think, is the professional term for his part."

"Doctor——?"

"Hart. The seventh and last character. He, too, is of foreign extraction, though he became a naturalised Briton some time after the last war. I fancy he is a Viennese, though whether I deduce this conclusion subconsciously from his profession I cannot tell you." Jonathan chuckled again and finished his sherry.

"What, in Heaven's name, is his profession?"

"My dear Aubrey," said Jonathan, "he is a plastic surgeon. A beauty specialist *par excellence*. The male of the species."

IV

"It seems to me," said Mandrake, "that you have invited stark murder to your house. Frankly, I can imagine nothing more terrifying than the prospect of this week-end. What do you propose to do with them?"

"Let them enact their drama."

"It will more probably resemble some disastrous vaudeville show."

"With myself as compère. Quite possibly."

"My dear Jonathan, you will have no performance. The actors will either sulk in their dressing-rooms or leave the theatre."

"That is where we come in."

"We! I assure you——"

"It is where I come in, then. May I, without exhibiting too

much complacency, claim that if I have a talent it lies in the direction of hospitality?"

"Certainly. You are a wonderful host."

"Thank you," said Jonathan, beaming at his guest. "It delights me to hear you say so. Now, in this party I have set myself, I freely admit, a stiff task."

"I'm glad you realise it," said Mandrake. "The list of opponents is positively ghastly. I don't know if I have altogether followed you, but it appears that you hope to reconcile a rejected lover both to his successor and to his late love, a business woman to her detested rival, a ruined beauty to an exponent of the profession that made an effigy of her face, and a mother to a prospective daughter-in-law who has rejected her favourite son for his brother."

"There is another permutation that you have not yet heard. Local gossip rings with rumours of some secret understanding between Dr. Hart and Madame Lisse. It appears that Madame recommends Dr. Hart's surgery to those of her clients who have passed the stage when Lisse creams and all the rest of it can improve their ageing faces."

"A business arrangement?"

"Something more than that if Hersey, a prejudiced witness, certainly, is to be believed. Hersey's spies tell her that Dr. Hart has been observed leaving Madame Lisse's flat at a most compromising hour; that he presented to an exciting degree the mien of a clandestine lover, his hat drawn over his brows, his cloak (he wears a cloak) pulled about his face. They say that he has been observed to scowl most formidably at the mention of Nicholas Compline."

"Oh, no," said Mandrake, " it's really a little too much. I boggle at the cloak."

"It's a Tyrolean cloak with a hood, a most useful garment. Rainproof. He has presented me with one. I wear it frequently. You shall see it to-morrow."

"What's he like, this face-lifter?"

"A smoothish fellow. I find him amusing. He plays very good bridge."

"We are *not* going to play bridge?"

"No. No, that, I feel, would be asking for trouble. We *are* going to play a round game, however."

"O God!"

"You will enjoy it. A stimulating game. I hope that it will go far towards burying our little armoury of hatchets. Imagine what fun, Aubrey, if on Monday morning they all go gaily away, full of the milk of human kindness."

"You're seeing yourself in the detestable rôle of uplifter. I've got it! This is not Pirandello, nor is it vaudeville. Far from it. But it *is*," cried Mandrake with an air of intense disgust, " it *is* ' The Passing of the Third Floor Back.' "

Jonathan rose and stood warming his hands at the fire. He was a small man, very upright, with a long trunk and short legs. Mandrake, staring at him, wondered if it was some trick of firelight that lent a faintly malicious tinge to Jonathan's smile; it was merely his thick-lensed glasses that gave him that air of uncanny blankness.

" Ah, well," said Jonathan, " a peacemaker. Why not? You would like to see your room, Aubrey. The blue room, as usual, of course. It is no longer raining. I propose to take a look at the night before going up to change. Will you accompany me?" ·

" Very well."

They went out, crossing a wide hall, to the entrance. The wind had fallen, and as Jonathan opened his great outer doors the quiet of an upland county at dusk entered the house, and the smell of earth still only lightly covered with snow. They walked out on the wide platform in front of Highfold. Far beneath them, Cloudyfold village showed dimly through tree-tops, and beyond it the few scattered houses down in the Vale, four miles away. In the southern skies the stars were out, but northward above Cloudyfold Top there was a well of blackness. And as Jonathan and his guest turned towards the north they received the sensation of an icy hand laid on their faces.

" That's a deathly cold, sir," said Mandrake.

" It's from the north," said Jonathan, " and still smells of snow. Splendid! Let's go in."

CHAPTER II

ASSEMBLY

I

ON the following day Mandrake observed his host to be in a high state of excitement. In spite of his finicky mannerisms and his somewhat old-maidish pedantry, it would never have occurred to his worst enemy to call Jonathan effeminate. Nevertheless he had many small talents that are unusual in a man. He took a passionate interest in the appointments of his house. He arranged flowers to perfection, and on the arrival of three boxes from a florist in Great Chipping, darted at them like a delighted ant. Mandrake was sent to the Highfold glasshouses for tuberoses and gardenias. Jonathan, looking odd in one of his housekeeper's aprons, buried himself in the flower-room. He intended, he said, to reproduce bouquets from the French prints in the boudoir. Mandrake, whose floral tastes ran austerely to dead flowers, limped off to the library and thought about his new play, which was to represent twelve aspects of one character, all speaking together.

The morning was still and extremely cold. During the night there had been another light fall of snow. The sky was leaden and the countryside seemed to wait ominously for some portent from the north. Jonathan remarked several times, and with extraordinary glee, that they were in for a severe storm. Fires were lit in all the guest-rooms, and from the Highfold chimneys rose columns of smoke, lighter in tone than the clouds they seemed to support. Somewhere up on Cloudyfold a farmer was moving his sheep, and the drowsy sound of their slow progress seemed uncannily near. So dark was the sky that the passage of the hours was seen only in a stealthy alteration of shadows. Jonathan and Mandrake lunched by lamplight. Mandrake said that he felt the house to be alive with anticipation, but whether of a storm without or within he was unable to decide. " It's a grisly day," said Mandrake.

" I shall telephone Sandra Compline and suggest that she brings her party for tea," said Jonathan. " It will begin to

22

snow again before six o'clock, I believe. What do you think of the house, Aubrey? How does it feel?"

"Expectant and luxurious."

"Good. Excellent. You have finished? Let us make a little tour of the rooms, shall we? Dear me, it's a long time since I looked forward so much to a party."

They made their tour. In the great drawing-room, seldom used by Jonathan, cedar-wood fires blazed at each end. Mrs. Pouting and two maids had put glazed French covers on the arm-chairs and the bergere sofas.

"Summer-time uniforms," said Jonathan, "but they chime with the flowers and are gay. Admire my flowers, Aubrey. Don't they look pleasant against the linen-fold walls? Quite a tone-poem, I consider."

"And when seven furious faces are added," said Mandrake, "the harmony will be complete."

"You can't frighten me. The faces will be all smiles in less than no time, you may depend on it. And, after all, even if they are not to be reconciled, I shall not complain. My play will be less pretty but more exciting."

"Aren't you afraid that they will simply refuse to stay under the same roof with each other?"

"They will at least stay to-night, and to-morrow, I hope, will be so inclement that the weather alone will turn the balance."

"Your courage is amazing. Suppose they all sulk in separate rooms?"

"They won't. I won't let 'em. Confess now, Aubrey, aren't you a little amused, a little stimulated?"

Mandrake grinned. "I feel all the more disagreeable sensations of first-night nerves, but—all right, I'll admit to a violent interest."

Jonathan laughed delightedly and took his arm. "You must see the bedrooms and the boudoir and the little smoking-room. I've allowed myself some rather childish touches, but they may amuse you. Elementary symbolism. Character as expressed by vegetation. As the florists' advertisements would have it, I have said it with flowers."

"Said what?"

"What I think of every one."

They crossed the hall to the left of the front door and entered the room that Jonathan liked to call the boudoir, an Adams' sitting-room painted a light green and hung with French brocades whose pert garlands were repeated in nosegays which Jonathan had set in the window and upon a spinet and a writing-desk.

"Here," said Jonathan, "I hope the ladies will forgather to write, gossip and knit. Miss Chloris, I should explain, is a 'Wren,' not yet called up, but filling the interim with an endless succession of indomitable socks. My distant cousin, Hersey, is also a vigorous knitter. I feel sure poor Sandra is hard at work on some repellent comfort."

"And Madame Lisse?"

"The picture of Madame in close co-operation with strands of khaki wool is one which could be envisaged only by a surrealist. No doubt you will find yourself able to encompass it. Come along."

The boudoir opened into the small smoking-room where Jonathan permitted a telephone and a radio set, but which, he explained, had in other respects remained unaltered since his father died. Here were leather chairs, a collection of sporting prints flanked by a collection of weapons and by fading groups of Jonathan and his Cambridge friends in the curious photographic postures of the nineties. Above the mantelpiece hung a trout rod complete with cast and fly.

"Sweet-scented tobacco plants, you see," said Jonathan, "in pots. A trifle obvious, but I couldn't resist them. Now the library."

The library opened out of the smoking-room. It had an air of being the most-used room in the house, and indeed it was here that Jonathan could generally be found among a company of books that bore witness to generations of rather freakish taste and to the money by which such taste could be gratified. Jonathan had added lavishly to the collection. His books ranged oddly from translations of Turkish and Persian verse to the works of the most inscrutable of the moderns, and textbooks on criminology and police detection. He had a magpie taste in reading, but it was steadied by a constancy of devotion to the Elizabethans.

"Here," he said, "I was troubled by an embarrassment of riches. A Shakespearian nosegay seemed a little *vieux jeu*, but on the other hand it had the advantage of being easily recognised. I was tempted by Leigh Hunt's conceit of 'saying all one feels and thinks in clever daffodils and pinks; in puns of tulips and in phrases, charming for their truth, of daisies.' Unfortunately the glass-houses were not equal to Leigh Hunt in mid-winter, but here, you see, is the great Doctor's ensign of supreme command, the myrtle, and here, after all, is most of poor Ophelia's rather dreary little collection. The sombre note predominates. But upstairs I have let myself go again. A riot of snowdrops for Chloris (you take the allusion to William Stone's charming conceit?), tuberoses and even some orchids for Madame Lisse, and so on."

" And for Mrs. Compline?"

" A delightful arrangement of immortelles."

" Aren't you rather cruel?"

" Dear me, I don't think so," said Jonathan, with a curious glance at his guest. " I hope you admire the really superb cactus on your window-sill, Aubrey. John Nash might pause before it, I believe, and begin to plan some wonderful arrangement of greys and elusive greens. And now I must telephone to Sandra Compline, and after that to Dr. Hart. I am making the bold move of suggesting he drives Madame Lisse. Hersey has her own car. Will you excuse me?"

" One moment. What flowers have you put in your own room?"

" Honesty," said Jonathan.

II

Mrs. Compline, her son William, and his fiancée Chloris Wynne, arrived by car at four o'clock. Mandrake discovered himself to be in almost as high a state of excitement as his host. He was unable to decide whether Jonathan's party would prove to be disastrous, amusing, or merely a bore, but the anticipation, at least, was enthralling. He had formed a very precise mental picture of each of the guests. William Compline, he decided, would present the most interesting subject-matter. The exaggerated filial devotion hinted at by Jonathan, brought him into the sphere of Mandrake's literary interest. And, muttering " Mother-fixation " to himself, he wondered if indeed he should find William the starting-point for a new dramatic poem. Poetically, Mrs. Compline's disfigurement might best be conveyed by a terrible mask, seen in the background of William's spoken thought. " Perhaps in the final scene," thought Mandrake, " I should let them turn into the semblance of animals. Or would that be a little banal?" For not the least of a modern poetic dramatist's problems lies in the distressing truth that where all is strange nothing escapes the imputation of banality. But in William Compline, with his dullish appearance, his devotion to his mother, his dubious triumph over his brother, Mandrake hoped to find matter for his art. He was actually picturing an opening scene in which William, standing between his mother and his fiancée, appeared against a sky composed of cubes of greenish light, when the drawing-room door opened and Caper announced them.

They were, of course, less striking than the images that had grown so rapidly in Mandrake's imagination. He had seen Mrs. Compline as a figure in a sombre robe, and here she was in Harris tweeds. He had envisaged a black cowl, and he saw a countrified hat with a trout fly in the band. But her face, less fantastic than his image, was perhaps more distressing. It looked as if its maker had given it two or three vicious tweaks. Her eyes, large and lack-lustre, retained something of their original beauty, her nose was short and straight, but the left corner of her mouth drooped and her left cheek fell into a sort of pocket, so that she looked as though she had hurriedly stowed a large mouthful into one side of her face. She had the exaggerated dolorous expression of a clown. As Jonathan had told him, there was a cruelly comic look. When Jonathan introduced them, Mandrake was illogically surprised at her composure. She had a cold, dry voice.

Miss Chloris Wynne was about twenty-three, and very, very pretty. Her light-gold hair was pulled back from her forehead and moulded into cusps so rigidly placed that they might have been made of any material rather than hair. Her eyes were wide apart and beautifully made-up, her mouth was large and scarlet and her skin flawless. She was rather tall and moved in a leisurely fashion, looking gravely about her. She was followed by William Compline.

In William, Mandrake saw what he had hoped to see—the commonplace faintly touched by a hint of something that was disturbing. He was in uniform and looked perfectly tidy but not quite smart. He was fair, and should have been good-looking, but the lines of his features were blunted and missed distinction. He was like an unsuccessful drawing of a fine subject. There was an air of uneasiness about him, and he had not been long in the room before Mandrake saw that whenever he turned to look at his fiancée, which was very often, he first darted a glance at his mother, who never by any chance returned it. Mrs. Compline talked easily and with the air of an old friend to Jonathan, who continually drew the others into their conversation. Jonathan was in grand form. " A nice start," thought Mandrake, " with plenty in reserve." And he turned to Miss Wynne with the uneasy feeling that she had said something directly to him.

" I didn't in the least understand it, of course," Miss Wynne was saying, " but it completely unnerved me, and that's always rather fun."

" Ah," thought Mandrake, " one of my plays."

" Of course," Miss Wynne continued, " I don't know if you were thinking when you wrote it, what I was thinking when I saw it, but if you were, I'm surprised you got past the Lord Chamberlain."

" The Lord Chamberlain," said Mandrake, " is afraid of me, and for a similar reason. He doesn't know whether it's my dirty mind or his, so he says nothing."

" Ah," cried Jonathan, " is Miss Wynne a devotee, Aubrey?"

" A devotee of what?" asked Mrs. Compline in her exhausted voice.

" Of Aubrey's plays. The Unicorn is to reopen with Aubrey's new play in March, Sandra, if all goes well. You must come to the first night. It's called ' Bad Black-out ' and is enormously exciting."

" A war play?" asked Mrs. Compline. It was a question that for some reason infuriated Mandrake, but he answered with alarming politeness that it was not a war play but an experiment in two-dimensional formulism. Mrs. Compline looked at him blankly and turned to Jonathan.

" What does that mean?" asked William. He stared at Mandrake with an expression of offended incredulity. " Two-dimensional? That means flat, doesn't it?"

Mandrake heard Miss Wynne give an impatient sigh, and guessed at a certain persistency in William.

" Does it mean that the characters will be sort of unphotographic?" she asked.

" Exactly."

" Yes," said William heavily, " but *two-dimensional*. I don't quite see——"

Mandrake felt a terrible apprehension of boredom, but Jonathan cut in neatly with an amusing account of his own apprenticeship as an audience to modern drama, and William listened with his mouth not quite closed and an anxious expression in his eyes. When the others laughed at Jonathan's facetiæ, William looked baffled. Mandrake could see him forming with his lips the offending syllables " two-dimensional."

" I suppose," he said suddenly, " it's not what you say but the way you say it that you think matters. Do your plays have plots?"

" They have themes."

" What's the difference?"

" My darling old Bill," said Miss Wynne, " you mustn't browbeat famous authors."

William turned to her and his smile made him almost handsome. " Mustn't you?" he said. " But if you do a thing, you like talking about it. I like talking about the things I do. I mean the things I did before there was a war."

It suddenly occurred to Mandrake that he did not know what William's occupation was. " What do you do?" he asked.

" Well," said William, astonishingly, " I paint pictures."

Mrs. Compline marched firmly into the conversation. " William," she said, " has Penfelton to look after in peace time. At present, of course, we have our old bailiff, who manages very well. My younger son, Nicholas, is a soldier. Have you heard, Jonathan, that he did *not* pass his medical for active service? It was a very bitter blow to him. At the moment he is stationed at Great Chipping, but he longs so much to be with his regiment in France. Of *course*," she added. And Mandrake saw her glance at the built-up shoe on his club-foot.

" But you're on leave from the front, aren't you?" he asked William.

" Oh, yes," said William.

" My son Nicholas . . ." Mrs. Compline became quite animated as she spoke of Nicholas. She talked about him at great length, and Mandrake wondered if he only imagined there was a sort of defiance in her insistence on this awkward theme. He saw that Miss Wynne had turned pink and William crimson. Jonathan drew the spate of maternal eulogy upon himself. Mandrake asked Miss Wynne and William if they thought it was going to snow again, and all three walked over to the long windows to look at darkening hills and vale. Naked trees half-lost their form in that fading light and rose from the earth as if they were its breath, already frozen.

" Rather menacing," said Mandrake, " isn't it?"

" Menacing?" William repeated. " It's very beautiful. All

black and white and grey. I don't believe in seeing colour into things. One should paint them the first colour they seem when one looks at them. Yes, I suppose it is what you'd call menacing. Black and grey and white."

"What is your medium?" Mandrake asked, and wondered why everybody looked uncomfortable when William spoke of his painting.

"*Very* thick oil paint," said William gravely.

"Do you know Agatha Troy?"

"I know her pictures, of course."

"She and her husband are staying with the Copelands at Winton St. Giles, near Little Chipping. I came on from there. She's painting the rector."

"Do you mean Roderick Alleyn?" asked Miss Wynne. "Isn't he her husband? How exciting to be in a house-party with the handsome Inspector. What's he like?"

"Oh," said Mandrake, "quite agreeable."

They had turned away from the windows, but a sound from outside drew them back again. Only the last turn of the drive as it came out of the Highfold woods could be seen from the drawing-room windows.

"That's a car," said William. "It sounds like——" he stopped short.

"Is any one else coming?" asked Miss Wynne sharply, and caught her breath.

She and William stared through the windows. A long and powerful-looking open car, painted white, was streaking up the last rise in the drive.

"But," stammered William, very red in the face, "that's—that's——"

"Ah!" said Jonathan from behind them. "Didn't you know? A pleasant surprise for you. Nicholas is to be one of our party."

III

Nicholas Compline was an extremely striking version of his brother. In figure, height, and colouring they were alike. Their features were not dissimilar, but the suggestion of fumbled drawing in William was absent in Nicholas. William was clean-shaven, but Nicholas wore a fine blond moustache. Nicholas had a presence. His uniform became him almost too well. He glittered a little. His breeches were superb. His face was not unlike a less dissipated version of the best-known portrait of Charles II, though the lines from nose to mouth were not so dominant, and the pouches under the eyes had only just begun to form.

His entrance into the drawing-room at Highfold must have been a test of his assurance. Undoubtedly it was dramatic. He came in smiling, missed his brother and Miss Wynne, who were still in the window, shook hands with Jonathan, was introduced to Mandrake, and, on seeing his mother, looked surprised but greeted her charmingly. Jonathan, who had him by the elbow, turned him towards the window.

There was no difficult silence, because Jonathan talked briskly, but there was, to a degree, a feeling of tension. For a moment Mandrake wondered if Nicholas Compline would turn on his heel and walk out, but after checking, with Jonathan's hand still at his elbow, he merely stood stock-still and looked from William to Chloris Wynne. His face was as pale as his brother's was red, and there was a kind of startled sneer about his lips. It was Miss Wynne who saved the situation. She unclenched her hands and gave Nicholas a coster's salute, touching her forehead and spreading out her palm towards him. Mandrake guessed that this serio-comic gesture was foreign to her and applauded her courage.

"Oi," said Miss Wynne.

"Oi, oi," said Nicholas, and returned her salute. He looked at William and said in a flat voice: "Quite a family party."

His mother held out her hand to him. He moved swiftly towards her and sat on the arm of her chair. Mandrake saw adoration in her eyes and mentally rubbed his hands together.

"The Mother-fixation," he thought, "is *not* going to let me down." And he began to warn himself against the influence of Eugene O'Neil. William and his Chloris remained in the window. Jonathan, after a bird-like glance at them, embarked on a comfortable three-cornered chat with Mrs. Compline and Nicholas. Mandrake, sitting in the shadow, found himself free to watch the lovers, and again he gloated. At first William and Chloris stared out through the windows and spoke in undertones. She pointed to something outside, but Mandrake felt certain the gesture was a bluff and that they discussed hurriedly the arrival of Nicholas. Presently he observed a small incident that he thought curious and illuminating. It was a sort of dumb-show, an interplay of looks subdued to the exigencies of polite behaviour, a quarter of glances. William had turned from the window and was staring at his mother. She had been talking, with an air that almost approached gaiety, to Nicholas. She looked into his face and a smile, painful in its intensity, lifted the drooping corners of her mouth. Nicholas's laugh was louder than the conversation seemed to warrant, and Mandrake saw that he was looking over his mother's head full at Chloris Wynne. Mandrake read a certain insolence in this open-eyed direct stare of Nicholas. He turned to see how the lady took it, and found that she returned it with interest. They looked steadfastly and inimically into each other's eyes. Nicholas laughed again, and William, as if warned by this sound, turned from his sombre contemplation of his mother and stared first at Nicholas and then at Miss Wynne. Neither of them paid the smallest attention to him, but Mandrake thought that Nicholas was very well aware of his brother. He thought Nicholas, in some way that was clearly perceived by the other two, was deliberately baiting William. Jonathan's voice broke across this little pantomime.

"—a long time," Jonathan was saying, " since I treated myself to one of my own parties, and I don't mind confessing that I look forward enormously to this one."

Miss Wynne joined the group round the fire and William followed her.

" Is this the party?" she asked, " or are we only the beginning?"

" The most important beginning, Miss Chloris, without which the end would be nothing."

" Who else have you got, Jonathan?" asked Nicholas, with his eyes still on Miss Wynne.

" Well, now, I don't know that I shall tell you, Nick. Or shall I? It's always rather fun, don't you think," Jonathan said, turning his glance towards Mrs. Compline, " to let people meet without giving them any preconceived ideas about each other? However, you know one of my guests so well that it doesn't matter if I anticipate her arrival. Hersey Amblington."

" Old Hersey's coming, is she," said Nicholas, and he looked a little disconcerted.

" Don't be too ruthless with your adjectives, Nick," said Jonathan mildly. " Hersey is ten years my junior."

" You're ageless, Jonathan."

" Charming of you, but I'm afraid people only begin to compliment one on one's youth when it is gone. But Hersey, to me, really does seem scarcely any older than she was in the days when I danced with her. She still dances, I believe."

" It will be nice to see Hersey," said Mrs. Compline.

" I don't think I know a Hersey, do I?" This was the first time Chloris had spoken directly to Mrs. Compline. She was answered by Nicholas.

" She's a flame of Jonathan's," Nicholas said. " Lady Hersey Amblington."

" She's my third cousin," said Jonathan sedately. " We are all rather attached to her."

" Oh," said Nicholas, always to Chloris. " She's a divine creature. I adore her."

Chloris began to talk to William.

Mandrake thought that if anybody tried to bury any hatchets in the Compline armoury it would not be William. He decided that William was neither as vague nor as amiable as he seemed. Conversation went along briskly under Jonathan's leadership, with Mandrake himself as an able second, but it had a sort of substratum that was faintly antagonistic. When inevitably, it turned to the war, William, with deceptive simplicity, related a story about an incident on patrol when a private soldier uttered some comic blasphemy on the subject of cushy jobs on the home front. Mrs. Compline immediately told Jonathan how few hours sleep Nicholas managed to get, and how hard he was worked. Nicholas himself spoke of pulling strings in order to get a transfer to active service. He had, he said, seen an important personage. " Unfortunately, though, I struck a bad moment. The gentleman was very liverish. I understand," said Nicholas, with one of his bright stares at Chloris, " that he has been crossed in love."

" No reason, surely," said Chloris, " why he shouldn't behave himself with comparative strangers."

Nicholas gave her the shadow of an ironical bow.

Jonathan began an account of his own activities as chairman of the local evacuation committee, and made such a droll affair of it that with every phrase his listeners' guardedness seemed to relax. Mandrake, who had a certain astringent humour of his own, followed with a description of a member of the chorus who found himself in an ultra-modern play. Tea was announced and was carried through on the same cheerful note of comedy. " Good Lord," Mandrake thought, " if he should bring it off after all!" He caught Jonathan's eye and detected a glint of triumph.

After tea Jonathan proposed a brisk walk, and Mandrake, knowing his host shared his own loathing for this sort of exercise, grinned to himself. Jonathan was not going to risk another session in the drawing-room. With any luck there would be more arrivals while they were out, and the new set of encounters would take place in the propitious atmosphere of sherry and cocktails. When they assembled in the hall Jonathan appeared in a sage-green tyrolese cape. He looked a quaint enough figure, but Chloris Wynne, who had evidently decided to like her host, cried out in admiration, and Mandrake, who had decided to like Chloris Wynne, echoed her. At the last moment Jonathan remembered an important telephone message, and asked Mandrake to see the walking-party off. He flung his cape over Nicholas's shoulders. It hung from his shoulder-straps in heavy folds, and turned him into a Ruritanian figure.

" Magnificent, Nick," said Jonathan, and Mandrake saw that Mrs. Compline and Chloris agreed with him. The cloak neatly emphasised the touch of bravura that seemed an essential ingredient of Nicholas's character. They went out of doors into the cold twilight of late afternoon.

IV

" But," said Dr. Hart in German, " it is an intolerable position for me—for *me*, do you understand."

" Don't be ridiculous," said Madame Lisse in English. " And please, Francis, do not speak in German. It is a habit of which you should break yourself."

" Why should I not speak in German? I am a naturalised Austrian. Everybody knows that I am a naturalised Austrian and that I detest and abhor the Nazi régime with which we— *we* British—are in conflict."

" Nevertheless, the language is unpopular."

" Very well, very well, I now speak in English. In plain English I tell you that if you continue your affair with this Captain Nicholas Compline I shall take the strongest possible steps to——"

B

"To do what? You are driving too fast."

"To put an end to it."

"How will you do that?" asked Madame Lisse, settling down into her furs with an air of secret enjoyment.

"By taking you up to London next week."

"With what object? Here is Winton. I beg that you do not drive so fast."

"On our return," said Dr. Hart, shifting his foot to the brake, "we shall announce our marriage. It will have taken place quietly in London."

"Are you demented? Have we not discussed it already a thousand times? You know very well that it would injure your practice. A woman hideous with wrinkles comes to me. I see that I can do nothing, cannot even pretend to do anything. I suggest plastic surgery. She asks me if I can recommend a surgeon. I mention two or three, of whom you are one. I give instances of your success, you are here in Great Chipping, the others are abroad or in London. She goes to you. But can I say to my client with the same air of detached assurance: 'Certainly. Go to my husband. He is marvellous!' And can you, my friend, whose cry has been the utter uselessness of massage, the robbery of foolish women by beauty specialists, the fatuity of creams and lotions; can you produce as your wife Elise Lisse of the Studio Lisse, beauty specialist *par excellence*? The good Lady Hersey Amblington would have something to say to that, I promise you, and by no means to our advantage."

"Then give up your business."

"And halve my income, in effect *our* income? And, besides, I enjoy my work. It has amused me to win my little victories over the good Lady Hersey. The Studio Lisse is a growing concern, my friend, and I propose to remain at the head of it."

Dr. Hart accelerated again as his car mounted the steep road that climbed from the Vale of Pen Cuckoo up to Cloudyfold.

"Do you see the roofs of the large house up in those trees?" he asked suddenly.

"That is Pen Cuckoo. It is shut up at present. What of it?"

"And you know why it is shut up? I shall remind you. Two years ago it housed a homicidal lunatic, and her relatives have not returned since her trial."

Madame Lisse turned to look at her escort. She saw a sharp profile, a heavy chin, light-grey eyes, and a complexion of extreme though healthy pallor.

"Well," she murmured. "Again, what of it?"

"You have heard of the case, of course. She is said to have murdered her rival in love. They were both somewhere between forty-five and fifty-five. The dangerous age in both sexes. I am myself fifty-two years of age."

"What conclusions am I supposed to draw?" asked Madame Lisse tranquilly.

"You are to suppose," Dr. Hart rejoined, "that persons of a certain age can go to extremes when the safety of their—shall I call it love-life?—is in jeopardy."

"But, my dear Francis, this is superb. Am I to believe that you will lie in ambush for Nicholas Compline? What weapon shall you choose? Does he wear his sword? I believe that it is not extremely sharp, but one supposes that he could defend himself."

"Are you in love with him?"

"If I answer no, you will not believe me. If I answer yes, you will lose your temper."

"Nevertheless," said Doctor Hart calmly, "I should like an answer."

"Nicholas will be at Highfold. You may observe us and find out."

There followed a long silence. The road turned sharply and came out on the height known as Cloudyfold. For a short distance it followed the snow-covered ridge of the hills. On their right, Madame Lisse and Dr. Hart looked down on the frozen woods of Pen Cuckoo; on cold lanes, on slow columns of chimney-smoke, and, more distantly, towards a long dark mass that was the town of Great Chipping. On their left the powdered hills fell away smoothly into the Vale of Cloudyfold. Under clouds that hung like a pall from horizon to horizon, the scattered cottages of Dorset stone looked almost black, while their roofs glistened with a stealthy reflected light. A single flake of snow appeared on the windscreen and slid downwards.

"Very well," said Dr. Hart loudly, "I shall see."

Madame Lisse drew a gloved hand from under the rug and with one finger touched Dr. Hart lightly behind his ear. "I am really devoted to you," she said.

He pulled her hand down, brushing the glove aside with his lips.

"You know my temperament," he said. "It is a mistake to play the fool with me."

" Suppose I am only playing the fool with Nicholas Compline?"

" Well," he said again, " I shall see."

V

Through the office window of the Salon Cyclamen Hersey Amblington watched two of her clients walk off down the street with small steps and certain pert movements of their sterns. They paused outside the hated windows of the Studio Lisse, hesitated for a moment, and then disappeared through the entrance.

" Going to buy Lisse Foundation Cream," thought Hersey. " So that's why they wouldn't have a facial." She turned back into her office and was met by the familiar drone of driers, by the familiar smells of hot hair, setting lotion, and the sachets used in permanent waving, and by the familiar high-pitched indiscretions of clients in conversation with assistants.

"——long after the milk. I look like death warmed up and what I feel is nobody's business."

"——much better after a facial, Moddam. Aye always think a facial is marvellous, what it does for you."

"——can't remember his name so of course I shall never see them again."

" Common woman," thought Hersey. " All my clients are common women. Damn that Lisse. Blasted pirate."

She looked at her watch. Four o'clock. She'd make a tour of the cubicles and then leave the place to her second-in-command. " If it wasn't for my snob-value," she thought grimly, " I'd be living on the Pirate's overflow." She peered into the looking-glass over her desk and automatically touched her circlet of curls. " Greyer and greyer," said Hersey, " but I'll be shot if I dye them," and she scowled dispassionately at her face. " Too wholesome by half, my girl, and a fat lot of good 'Hersey's Skin Food' is to your middle-aged charms. Oh, well."

She made her tour through the cubicles. With her assistants she had little professional cross-talk dialogues, calculated to persuade her clients that the improvement in their appearance was phenomenal. With the clients themselves she sympathised, soothed and encouraged. She refused an invitation to dinner from the facial, and listened to a complaint from a permanent wave. When she returned to the office she found her second-in-command at the telephone.

" Would Madam care to make another appointment? No? Very good."

" Who's that?" asked Hersey wearily.

" Mrs. Ainsley's maid to say she wouldn't be coming for her weekly facial to-morrow. The girls say they've seen her coming out of the Studio Lisse."

" May she grow a beard," muttered Hersey, and grinned at her second-in-command. " To hell with her, anyway. How's the appointment book?"

" Oh, we're full enough. Booked up for three days. But they're not as smart as they used to be."

" Who cares! I'm going now, Jane. If you should want me to-morrow, I'll be at my cousin Jonathan Royal's, Highfold, you know."

" Yes, Lady Hersey. It looked as if the Lisse was going away for the week-end. I saw her come out of the shop about half an hour ago and get into Dr. Hart's car. I wonder if there's anything in those stories. She had quite a big suitcase."

" I wish she'd had a pantechnicon," said Hersey. " I'm sick of the sound of the wretched woman's name. She may live in sin all over Dorset as long as she doesn't include Highfold in the tour."

The second-in-command laughed. " *That's* not very likely, Lady Hersey, is it?"

" No, thank the Lord. Good-bye, Jane."

CHAPTER III

CONTACT

I

"NOT very propitious weather for looking at a bathing-pool," said Mandrake, "but I insist on showing it to you."

He had sent the guests off at a round pace to go through Highfold woods, where the rides were heavy with sodden leaves, down to Jonathan's model farm, and back up a steep lane to the north side of the house, where he limped out to meet them. Here they came on a wide terrace. Beneath them, at the foot of a flight of paved steps flanked by bay trees, was a large concrete swimming-pool set in smooth lawns and over-looked by a charming eighteenth-century pavilion, now trimmed, like a Christmas card, with snow. The floor of the pool had been painted a vivid blue, but now the water was wrinkled, and in the twilight of late afternoon reflected only a broken pattern of repellent steely greys flecked by dead leaves. Mandrake explained that the pavilion had once been an aviary, but that Jonathan had done it up in keeping with its empire style, and that when summer came he meant to hold *fêtes galantes* down there by his new swimming-pool. It would look very Rex Whistlerish, Mandrake said, and would have just the right air of formalised gaiety.

"At the moment," said Chloris, "it has an air of formalised desolation, but I see what you mean."

"Wouldn't you like to come for a nice bracing plunge with me, Chloris, before breakfast to-morrow?" asked Nicholas. "Do say yes."

"No, thank you," said Chloris.

"It would have been awkward for you," said William, "if Chloris *had* said yes." It was the first remark William had addressed directly to his brother.

"Not at all," rejoined Nicholas, and he made his stiff little bow to Chloris.

"I'll bet ten pounds," William said to nobody in particular, "that nothing on earth would have got him into that water before or after breakfast."

38

" Would you?" asked Nicholas. " I take you. You've lost."

Mrs. Compline instantly protested. She reminded Nicholas of the state of his heart. William grinned derisively, and Nicholas, staring at Chloris, repeated that the bet was on. The absurd conversation began to take an unpleasant edge. Mandrake felt an icy touch on his cheek and drew attention to a desultory scatter of snowflakes.

" If that was our brisk walk," said Chloris, " I consider we've had it. Let's go in."

" Is it a bet?" Nicholas asked his brother.

" Oh, yes," said William. " You may have to break the ice, but it's a bet."

To the accompaniment of a lively torrent of disapprobation from Mrs. Compline they walked towards the house. Mandrake's interest in William mounted with each turn of the situation. William was as full of surprises as a lucky-bag. His sudden proposal of this ridiculous wager was as unexpected as the attitude which he now adopted. He looked hang-dog and frightened. He hung back and said something to his mother, who set that tragically distorted mouth and did not answer. William gave her a look strangely compounded of malice and nervousness, and strode after Chloris who was walking with Mandrake. Nicholas had joined them, and Mandrake felt sure that Chloris was very much aware of him. When William suddenly took her arm she started and seemed to draw back. They returned to the accompaniment of an irritating rattle of conversation from Nicholas.

As soon as they came out on the platform before the house, they found that someone else had arrived. Nicholas's car had been driven away, and in its place stood a very smart three-seater from which servants were taking very smart suitcases.

" That's not Hersey Amblington's car," said Mrs. Compline.

" No," said Nicholas. And he added loudly: " Look here; what's Jonathan up to?"

" What do you mean, darling?" asked his mother quickly.

" Nothing," said Nicholas. " But I think I recognise the car." He hung back as the others went into the house, and waited for Mandrake. He still wore Jonathan's cape over his uniform, and it occurred to Mandrake that since Nicholas allowed himself this irregularity he must be very well aware of its effectiveness. He put his hand on Mandrake's arm. The others went into the house.

" I say," he said. " *Is* Jonathan up to anything?"

"How do you mean?" asked Mandrake, wondering what the devil Jonathan would wish him to reply.

"Well, it seems to me this is a queerly assorted house-party."

"Is it? I'm a complete stranger to all the other guests, you know."

"When did you get here?"

"Last night."

"Well, hasn't Jonathan said anything? About the other guests, I mean?"

"He was very pleased with his party," said Mandrake, carefully. "He's longing for it to be an enormous success."

"Is he, by God!" said Nicholas. He turned on his heel and walked into the house.

Mrs. Compline and Chloris went up to their rooms; the three men left their overcoats in a downstairs cloakroom, where they noticed the twin of Jonathan's cape. When they came back into the hall they could hear voices in the library. As if by common consent they all paused. There were three voices—Jonathan's, a masculine voice that held a foreign suggestion in its level inflections, and a deep contralto.

"I thought as much," said Nicholas, and laughed unpleasantly.

"What's up?" William asked Mandrake.

"Nothing, so far as I know."

"Come on," said Nicholas. "What are we waiting for? Let's go in."

He led the way into the library.

Jonathan and his new arrivals stood before a roaring fire. The man had his back turned to the door, but the woman was facing it with an air of placid anticipation. Her face was strongly lit by a wall lamp, and Mandrake's immediate reaction to it was a sort of astonishment that Jonathan could have forgotten to say how spectacular she was. In Mandrake's world women were either sophisticated and sleek or hideous and erratic. "Artificiality," he was in the habit of saying, "is a fundamental in all women with whom one falls in love, and to so exquisite an extreme has artifice been carried that it sometimes apes nature with considerable success." This subtlety of grooming appeared in Madame Lisse. Her hair was straight and from a central parting was drawn back and gathered into a knot at the nape of her neck. It lay close to her head like a black satin cap with blue high-lights. Her face was an oval, beautifully pale, her lashes needed no cosmetic to darken them, her mouth alone proclaimed her art, for it was sharply painted a dark red. Her dress was extremely simple, but in it her body seemed to be gloved rather than clothed. She was not very young, not as young as Chloris Wynne, not perhaps as pretty as Chloris Wynne either, but she had to the last degree the quality that Mandrake, though he knew very little French, spoke of and even thought of as *soignée*. And, in her own vein, she was exceedingly beautiful.

"Madame Lisse," Jonathan was saying, "you know Nicholas, don't you? May I introduce his brother, and Mr. Aubrey Mandrake? Hart, do you know——?" Jonathan's introductions faded gently away.

Dr. Hart's bow was extremely formal. He was a pale dark man with a compact paunch and firm white hands. He was clad in the defiant tweeds of a firmly naturalised ex-Central European. Mandrake gathered from his manner that either he had not met Nicholas Compline and didn't wish to do so, or else that he had met him and had taken a firm resolve never to do so again. Nicholas, for his part, acknowledged the introduction by looking at a point some distance beyond Dr. Hart's left ear, and by uttering the words "How do you do?" as if they were a malediction. Madame Lisse's greeting to Nicholas was coloured by that particular blend of composure and awareness with which Austrian women make Englishmen feel dangerous and delighted. With something of the same air, but without a certain delicate underlining, she held out her hand to William and to Mandrake. Mandrake remembered that Nicholas had known Madame Lisse was coming to the party, and saw him take up a proprietory position beside her. "He's going to brazen it out," thought Mandrake. "He's going to show us the sort of dog he is with the ladies, by heaven."

Mandrake was right. Nicholas, with a sort of defiant showmanship, devoted himself to Madame Lisse. He stood beside her in an attitude reminiscent of a Victorian military fashion-plate, one leg straight and one flexed. Occasionally he placed one hand on the back of her chair, while the other went to his blond moustache. Whenever Dr. Hart glared at them, which he did repeatedly, Nicholas bent towards Madame Lisse and uttered a loud and unconvincing laugh calculated, Mandrake supposed, to show Dr. Hart how vastly Nicholas and Madame Lisse entertained each other. Madame was the sort of woman whose natural habitat was the centre of a group of men and, with the utmost tranquillity, she dominated the conversation and even, in spite of Nicholas, contrived to instil into it an air of genuine gaiety. In this she was ably supported by Jonathan and by Mandrake himself. Even William, who watched his brother pretty closely, responded in his own odd fashion to Madame's charm. He asked her abruptly if anybody had ever painted her portrait. On learning that this had never been done, he started to mutter to himself, and Nicholas looked irritated. Madame Lisse began to talk to Mandrake about his plays, Jonathan chimed in, and once again the situation was saved. It was upon a conversation piece, with Madame Lisse very much in the centre of vision, that Mrs. Compline and Chloris made their entrances. Mandrake thought that Mrs. Compline could not be aware of the affair between Nicholas and Madame Lisse, so composedly did she acknowledge the introduction. But, if this was the case, what reason had Chloris given for the broken engagement with Nicholas? "Is it not impossible that everybody but his mother should be aware of *l'affaire Lisse*?" Mandrake speculated. " Perhaps she sees him as a sort of irresistible young god, choosing where he will, and, without resentment, accepts Madame as a votaress." There was no doubt about Chloris's reaction. Mandrake saw her stiffen and go very still when Jonathan pronounced Madame Lisse's name. For perhaps a full second neither of the women spoke, and then, for all the world as if they responded to some inaudible cue, Chloris and Madame Lisse were extremely gracious to each other. " So they're going to take *that* line," thought Mandrake, and wondered if Jonathan shared his feelings of relief. He felt less comfortable when he saw Mrs. Compline's reaction to Dr. Hart. She murmured the conventional greeting, looked casually and then fixedly into his face, and turned so deadly white that for a moment Mandrake actually wondered if she would faint. But she did not faint. She turned away and sat in a chair farthest removed from the light. Caper brought in sherry and champagne cocktails.

II

The cocktails, though they did not perform miracles, helped considerably. Dr. Hart in particular became more sociable. He continued to avoid Nicholas, but attached himself to Chloris Wynne and to William. Jonathan talked to Mrs. Compline;

Mandrake and Nicholas to Madame Lisse. Nicholas still kept
up his irritating performances, now, apparently, for the benefit
of Chloris. Whenever Madame Lisse spoke he bent towards
her, and whether her remark was grave or gay, he broke out
into an exhibition of merriment calculated, Mandrake felt
certain, to arouse in Chloris the pangs proper to the woman
scorned. If she suffered this discomfort she gave no more
evidence of her distress than might be discovered in an occasional thoughtful glance at Nicholas, and it seemed to Mandrake that if she reacted at all to the performance it was
pleasurably. She listened attentively to Dr. Hart, who became
voluble and bland. Chloris had asked if any one had heard
the latest wireless news. Hart instantly embarked on a description of his own reaction to radio. " I cannot endure it. It
touches some nerve. It creates a most disagreeable—an unendurable *frisson*. I read my papers and that is enough. I am
informed. I assure you that I have twice changed my flat because of the intolerable persecution of neighbouring radios.
Strange, is it not? There must be some psychological explanation."

" Jonathan shares your dislike," said Mandrake. " He has
been persuaded to install a wireless next door in the smoking-
room, but I don't believe he ever listens to it."

" My respect for my host grows with everything I hear of
him," said Dr. Hart. He became expansive, enlarged upon his
love of nature, and spoke of holidays in the Austrian Tyrol.

" When it was still Austria," said Dr. Hart. " Have you
ever visited Kaprun, Miss Wynne? How charming it was at
Kaprun in those days! From there one could drive up the
Gross Glockner, one could climb into the mountains above
that pleasant wein-stube in the ravine, and on Sunday morn-
ings one went into Zelleum-Zee. Music in the central square.
The cafés! and the shops where one might secure the best
shoes in the world."

" And the best cloaks," said Chloris with a smile.

" Hein? Ah, you have seen the cloak I have presented to
our host."

" Nicholas," said Chloris, " wore it when we went for a walk
just now."

Dr. Hart's eyelids, which in their colour and texture a little
resembled those of a lizard, half closed over his rather prominent eyes. " Indeed," he said.

"I hope," said Jonathan, "that you visited my swimming-pool on your walk."

"Nicholas is going to bathe in it to-morrow," said William, "or hand over ten pounds to me."

"Nonsense, William," said his mother. "I won't have it. Jonathan, please forbid these stupid boys to go on with this nonsense." Her voice, coming out of the dark corner where she sat, sounded unexpectedly loud. Dr. Hart turned his head and peered into the shadow. When Chloris said something to him it appeared for a moment that he had not heard her. If, however, he had been startled by Mrs. Compline's voice, he quickly recovered himself. Mandrake thought that he finished his cocktail rather rapidly, and noticed that when he accepted another it was with an unsteady hand.

"That's odd," thought Mandrake. "He's the more upset of the two, it appears, and yet they've never met before. Unless—but no! That would be too much. I'm letting the possibilities of the situation run away with me."

"Lady Hersey Amblington, sir," said Caper in the doorway.

Mandrake's first impression of Hersey Amblington was characteristic of the sort of man his talents had led him to become. As Stanley Footling of Dulwich, he would have been a little in awe of Hersey. As Aubrey Mandrake of the Unicorn Theatre, he told himself she was distressingly wholesome. Hersey's face, in spite of its delicate make-up, wore an out-of-doors look, and she did not pluck her dark brows, those two straight bars that guarded her blue eyes. She wore Harris tweed and looked, thought Mandrake, as though she would be tiresome about dogs. A hearty woman, he decided, and he did not wonder that Madame Lisse had lured away Hersey's smartest clients.

Jonathan hurried forward to greet his cousin. They kissed. Mandrake felt certain that Jonathan delayed the embrace long enough to whisper a warning in Lady Hersey's ear. He saw the tweed shoulders stiffen. With large, beautifully shaped hands, she put Jonathan away from her and looked into his face. Mandrake, who was nearer to them than the rest of the party, distinctly heard her say: "Jo, what are you up to?" and caught Jonathan's reply: "Come and see." He took her by the elbow and led her towards the group by the fire.

"You know Madame Lisse, Hersey, don't you?"

"Yes," said Hersey, after a short pause. "How do you do?"

"And Dr. Hart?"

" How do you do? Sandra, darling, how nice to see you,"
said Hersey turning her back on Dr. Hart and Madame Lisse,
and kissing Mrs. Compline. Her face was hidden from Mandrake, but he saw that her ears and the back of her neck were
scarlet.

" You haven't kissed me, Hersey," said Nicholas.

" I don't intend to. How many weeks have you been
stationed in Great Chipping, and never a glimpse have I had
of you? William, my dear, I didn't know you had actually
reached home again. How well you look."

" I feel quite well, thank you, Hersey," said William gravely.
" You've met Chloris, haven't you?"

" Not yet, but I'm delighted to do so, and to congratulate
you both," said Hersey, shaking hands with Chloris.

" And Mr. Aubrey Mandrake," said Jonathan, bringing Hersey a drink.

" How do you do? Jonathan told me I should meet you.
I've got a subject for you."

" O God," thought Mandrake, " she's going to be funny
about my plays."

" It's about a false hairdresser who strangles his rival with
three feet of dyed hair," Hersey continued. " He's a male hairdresser, you know, and he wears a helmet made of tin waving
clamps and no clothes at all. Perhaps it would be better as a
ballet."

Mandrake laughed politely. " A beguiling theme," he said.

" I'm glad you like it. It's not properly worked out yet, but
of course his mother had long hair, and when he was an infant
he saw his father lugging her about the room by her pigtail,
and it gave him convulsions, because he hated his father and
was in love with his mother, and so he grew up into a hairdresser and worked off his complexes on his customers. And I
must say," Hersey added, " I wish I could follow his example."

" Do you dislike your clients, Lady Hersey?" asked Madame
Lisse. " I do not find in myself any antipathy to my clients.
Many of them have become my good friends."

" You must be able to form friendships very quickly," said
Hersey sweetly.

" Of course," Madame Lisse continued, " it depends very
much upon the class of one's clientele."

" And possibly," Hersey returned, " upon one's own class,
don't you think?" And then, as if ashamed of herself, she
turned again to Mrs. Compline.

" I suppose," said William's voice close to Mandrake, " that Hersey was making a joke about her subject, wasn't she?"

" Yes," Mandrake said hurriedly, for he was startled, " yes, of course."

" Well, but it *might* be a good idea, mightn't it? I mean, people do write about those things. There's that long play—I saw it in London about four years ago—where the brother and sister find out about their mother and all that. Some people thought that play was a bit thick, but I didn't think so. I thought there was a lot of reality in it. I don't see why plays should say what people feel in the same way as pictures ought to. Not what they do. What they do in their thoughts."

" That is my own contention," said Mandrake, who was beginning to feel more than a little curious about William's pictures. William gave a rather vapid laugh, and rubbed his hands together. " There you are, you see," he said. He looked round the circle of Jonathan's guests, and lowered his voice. " Jonathan has played a trick on all of us," he said unexpectedly. Mandrake did not answer, and William went on: " Perhaps you planned it together."

" No, no. This party is entirely Jonathan's."

" I'll bet it is. Jonathan is doing in the ordinary way what he does in his thoughts. If you wrote a play of him what would it be like?"

" I really don't know," said Mandrake hurriedly.

" Don't you? If I painted his picture I should make him egg-shaped, with quite a merry smile, and a scorpion round his head. And then, you know, for eyes he would have the sort of windows you can't see through. Clouded glass."

In Mandrake's circles this sort of thing was more or less a commonplace. " You are a surrealist, then?" he murmured.

" Have you ever noticed," William continued placidly, " that Jonathan's eyes are quite blank. Impenetrable," he added, and a phrase from *Alice through the Looking Glass* jigged Mandrake's thoughts.

" It's his thick glasses," he said.

" Oh," said William, " is that it? Has he told you about us? Nicholas and Chloris and me? And, of course, Madame Lisse?" To Mandrake's intense relief William did not pause for an answer. " I expect he has," he said. " He likes talking about people, and of course he would want somebody for an audience. I'm quite glad to meet Madame Lisse, and I must say it doesn't surprise me about her and Nicholas. I should like to make a picture of her. Wait a moment. I'm just going to get another drink. My third," added William, with the air of chalking up a score.

Mandrake had had one drink and was of the opinion that Jonathan's champagne cocktails were generously laced with brandy. He wondered if in this circumstance lay the explanation of William's astonishing candour. The rest of the party had already responded to the drinks, and the general conversation was now fluent and noisy. William returned, carrying his glass with extreme care.

"Of course," he said, "you will understand that Chloris and I haven't seen Nicholas since we got engaged. I went to the front the day after it was announced, and Nicholas has been conducting the war in Great Chipping ever since. But if Jonathan thinks his party is going to make any difference . . ." William broke off and drank a third of his cocktail. "What was I saying?" he asked.

"Any difference," Mandrake prompted.

"Oh, yes. If Jonathan, or Nicholas for that matter, imagine I'm going to lose my temper, they are wrong."

"But surely if Jonathan has any ulterior motive," Mandrake ventured, "it is entirely pacific. A reconciliation. . . ."

"Oh, no," said William, "that wouldn't be at all amusing." He looked sideways at Mandrake. "Besides," he said, "Jonathan doesn't like me much, you know."

This chimed so precisely with Mandrake's earlier impression that he gave William a started glance. "Doesn't he?" he asked helplessly.

"No. He wanted me to marry a niece of his. She was a poor relation, and he was very fond of her. We were sort of engaged but I didn't really like her so very much, I found, so I sort of sloped off. He doesn't forget things, you know." William smiled vaguely. "She died," he said. "She went rather queer in the head, I think. It was very sad, really."

Mandrake found nothing to say and William returned to his theme. "But I shan't do anything to Nicholas," he said. "Let him cool his ardour in the swimming pool. After all, I've won, you know. Haven't I?"

"He is tight," thought Mandrake, and he said with imbecile cheerfulness: "I hope so."

William finished his drink. "So do I," he said thoughtfully.

He looked across to the fireplace where Nicholas, standing by Madame Lisse's chair, stared at Chloris Wynne.

" But he always *will* try," said William, " to eat his cake and keep it."

III

Madame Lisse fastened three of Jonathan's orchids in the bosom of her wine-coloured dress, and contemplated herself in the looking-glass. She saw a Renaissance picture smoothly painted on a fine panel. Black, magnolia, and mulberry surfaces, all were sleek and richly glowing. Behind this magnificence, in shadow, was reflected the door of her room, and while she still stared at her image this door opened slowly.

" What is it Francis?" asked Madame Lisse without turning her head.

Dr. Hart closed the door, and in a moment his figure stood behind hers in the long glass.

" It was unwise to come in," she said, speaking very quietly. " That woman has the room next to yours, and Mrs. Compline is on the other side of this one. Why have you not changed? You will be late."

" I must speak to you. I cannot remain in this house, Elise. I must find some excuse to leave immediately."

She turned and looked fixedly at him.

" What is it now, Francis? Surely you cannot be disturbed *à cause de* Nicholas Compline. I assure you . . ."

" It is not solely on his account. Although . . ."

" What, then?"

" His mother's!"

" His *mother's*!" she repeated blankly. " That unfortunate woman? Have you ever seen a more disastrous face? What do you mean? I wondered if perhaps Mr. Royal had thought that by inviting her he might do you a service."

" A service," Dr. Hart repeated. " *A service. Gott in Himmel!*"

" Could you not do something?"

" What you have seen," said Dr. Hart, " I did."

" *You!* Francis, she was not——?"

" It was in my early days. In Vienna. It was the Schmitt-Lipmann treatment—paraffin wax. We have long ago aban-

doned it, but at that time it was widely practised. In this case
—as you see——"

"But her name. Surely you remembered her name?"

"She did not give her own name. Very often they do not.
She called herself Mrs. Nicholas, after her accursed son, I suppose. Afterwards, of course, she made a great scene. I
attempted adjustments, but in those days I was less experienced, the practice of plastic surgery was in its infancy. I
could do nothing. When I came to England my greatest dread
was that I might one day encounter this Mrs. Nicholas." Dr.
Hart uttered a sort of laugh. "I believe my first suspicions of
that young man arose from the associations connected with
his name."

"Obviously she did not recognise you."

"How do you know?"

"Her manner was perfectly calm. How long ago was this
affair?"

"About twenty-five years."

"And you were young Doktor Franz Hartz, of Vienna?
Did you not wear a beard and moustache then? Yes. And you
were slim in those days. Of course she did not recognise you."

"Franz Hartz and Francis Hart; it is not such a difference.
They all know I am a naturalised Austrian, and a plastic surgeon. I cannot face it. I shall speak, now, to Royal. I shall
say I must return urgently to a case——"

"And by this behaviour invite her suspicion. Nonsense, my
friend. You will remain and make yourself charming to Mrs.
Compline and, if she now suspects, she will say to herself: 'I
was mistaken. He could never have faced me.' Come now,"
said Madame Lisse, drawing his face down to hers, "you will
keep your head, Francis, and perhaps to-morrow, who knows,
you will have played your part so admirably, that we shall
change places."

"What do you mean?"

Madame Lisse laughed softly. "I may be jealous of Mrs.
Compline," she said. "No, no, you are disarranging my hair.
Go and change and forget your anxiety."

Dr. Hart moved to the door and paused. "Elise," he said,
"suppose this was planned."

"What do you mean?"

"Suppose Jonathan Royal knew. Suppose he deliberately
brought about this encounter."

" What next! Why in the world should he do such a thing?"
" There is something mischievous about him."
" Nonsense," she said. " Go and change,"

IV

" Hersey. I want to speak to you."

From inside the voluminous folds of the dress she was haul-
ing over her head Hersey said : " Sandra, darling, come in.
I'm longing for a gossip with you. Wait a jiffy. Sit down."
She tugged at the dress and her head, firmly tied up in a strong
net, came out at the top. For a moment she stood and stared
at her friend. That face, so painfully suggestive of an image in
some distorting mirror, was the colour of parchment. The lips
held their enforced travesty of a smile, but they trembled and
the large eyes were blurred by tears.

" Sandra, my dear, what is it?" cried Hersey.

" I can't stay here. I want you to help me. I've got to get
away from this house."

" Sandra! But why?" Hersey knelt by Mrs. Compline.
" You're not thinking of the gossip about Nick and the Pirate?
blast her eyes."

" What gossip? I don't know what you mean? What about
Nicholas?"

" It doesn't matter. Nothing. Tell me what's happened."
Hersey took Mrs. Compline's hands between her own, and,
feeling them writhe together in her grasp, was visited by an
idea that the distress which Mrs. Compline's face was incapable of expressing had flowed into these struggling hands.
" What's happened?" Hersey repeated.

" Hersey, that man, Jonathan's new friend. I can't meet
him again."

" Aubrey Mandrake?"

" No, no. The other."

" Dr. Hart?"

" I can't meet him."

" But why?"

" Don't look at me. I know it's foolish of me, Hersey, but
I can't tell you if you look at me. Please go on dressing and
let me tell you."

Hersey returned to the dressing-table, and presently Mrs.
Compline began to speak. The thin, exhausted voice, now well

controlled, lent no colour to the story of despoiled beauty. It
trailed dispassionately through her husband's infidelities, her
own despair, her journey to Vienna, and her return. And
Hersey, while she listened, absently made up her own face,
took off her net, and arranged her hair. When it was over she
turned towards Mrs. Compline, but came no nearer to her.

"But can you be sure?" she said.

"It was his voice. When I heard of him first, practising in
Great Chipping, I wondered. I said so to Deacon, my maid.
She was with me that time in Vienna."

"It was over twenty years ago, Sandra. And his name——"

"He must have changed it when he became naturalised."

"Does he look at all as he did then?"

"No. He has changed very much."

"Then——"

"I am not positive, but I am almost positive. I can't face
it, Hersey, can I?"

"I think you can," said Hersey, "and I think you will."

V

Jonathan stood in front of a blazing fire in the drawing-
room. Brocaded curtains hung motionless before the windows,
the room glowed with reflected light and, but for the cheerful
hiss and crackle of burning logs, was silent. The night outside
was silent too, but every now and then Jonathan heard a
momentary sighing as if the very person of the North Wind
explored the outer walls of Highfold. Presently one of the
shutters knocked softly at its frame and then the brocaded
curtains stirred a little, and Jonathan looked up expectantly.
A door at the far end of the room opened and Hersey Amblington came in.

"Hersey, how magnificent! You have dressed to please me,
I believe. I have a passion for dull green and furs. Charming
of you, my dear."

"You won't think me so charming when you hear what I've
got to say," Hersey rejoined. "I've got a bone to pick with
you, Jo."

"What an alarming phrase that is," said Jonathan. "Will
you have a drink?"

"No, thank you. Sandra Compline has been threatening to
go home."

" Indeed? That's vexing. I hope you dissuaded her?"

" Yes. I did."

" Splendid. I'm so grateful. It would have quite spoiled my party."

" I told her not to give you the satisfaction of knowing you had scored."

" Now, that really *is* unfair," cried Jonathan.

" No, it's not. Look here, did you know about Sandra and your whey-faced boy-friend?"

" Mandrake?"

" Now, Jo, none of that nonsense. Sandra confides in her maid, and she tells me the maid is bosom friends with your Mrs. Pouting. You've listened to servants' gossip, Jo. You've heard that Sandra thought this Hart man might be the Dr. Hartz who made that appalling mess of her face."

" I only wondered. It would be an intriguing coincidence."

" I'm ashamed of you, and I'm furious with you on my own account. Forcing me to be civil to that blasted German."

" Is she a German?"

" Whatever she is, she's a dirty fighter. I've heard on excellent authority she's started a rumour that my Magnolia Food Base grows beards. But never mind about that. I can look after myself."

" Darling Hersey! If only you had allowed me to perform that delightful office!"

" It's the cruel trick you've played on Sandra that horrifies me. You've always been the same, Jo. You've a passion for intrigue, wedded to an unholy curiosity. You lay your plans, and when they work out and people are hurt or angry, nobody is more sorry or surprised than you. It's a sort of blind patch in your character."

" Was that why you refused me, Hersey, all those years ago?"

Hersey caught her breath, and for a moment was silent.

" Not that I agree with you, you know," said Jonathan. " One of my objectives is a lavish burial of hatchets. I hope great things of this week-end."

" Do you expect the Compline brothers to become reconciled because you have given Nicholas an opportunity to do his barn-yard strut before Chloris Wynne? Do you suppose Hart, who is obviously in love with The Pirate, will welcome the same performance with her, or that The Pirate and I will wander up and down your house with our arms round each other's waists, or that Sandra Compline will invite Hart to have another cut at her face? You're not a fool, Jo."

" I *had* hoped for your co-operation," said Jonathan wistfully.

" *Mine!*"

" Well, darling, to a certain extent I've had it. You made a marvellous recovery from your own encounter with Madame Lisse, and you tell me you've persuaded Sandra to stay."

" Only because I felt it was better for her to face it."

" Don't you think it may be better for all of us to face our secret bogey-men? Hersey, I've collected a group of people each one of whom is in a great or small degree hag-ridden by a fear. Even Aubrey Mandrake has his little bogey-man."

" The poetic dramatist? What have you nosed out from his past?"

" Do you really want to know?"

" No," said Hersey, turning pink.

" You are sitting beside him at dinner. Say, in these exact words, that you understand he has given up footling, and see what sort of response you get."

" Why should I use this loathsome phrase to Mr. Mandrake?"

" Why, simply because, although you won't admit it, darling, you have your share of the family failing—curiosity."

" I *don't* admit it. And I won't do it."

Jonathan chuckled. " It is an amusing notion. I shall make the same suggestion to Nicholas. I believe it would appeal to him. To return to our cast of characters. Each of them, Sandra Compline to an extreme degree, has pushed his or her fear into a cupboard. Chloris is afraid of her old attraction to Nicholas, William is afraid of Nicholas's fascination for Chloris and for his mother, Hart is afraid of Nicholas's fascination for Madame Lisse, Sandra is afraid of a terrible incident in her past, Madame Lisse, though I must say she does not reveal her fear, is perhaps a little afraid of both Hart and Nicholas. You, my dearest, fear the future. If Nicholas has a fear it is that he may lose prestige, and that is a terrible fear."

" And you, Jo?"

" I am the compère. Part of my business is to unlock the cupboards and show the fears to be less terrible in the light of day."

"And you have no bogey-man of your own?"

"Oh, yes, I have," said Jonathan, and the light gleamed on his spectacles. "His name is Boredom."

"And therein am I answered," said Hersey.

CHAPTER IV

THREAT

I

WHILE he was dressing, Mandrake had wondered how Jonathan would place his party at dinner. He actually tried to work out, on several sheets of Highfold notepaper, a plan that would keep apart the most bitterly antagonistic of the guests. He found the task beyond him. The warring elements could be separated, but any such arrangement seemed only to emphasise friendships that were in themselves infuriating to one or another of the guests. It did not enter his head that Jonathan, with reckless bravado, would choose the most aggravating and provocative arrangement possible. But this was what he did. The long dining-table had been replaced by a round one. Madame Lisse sat between Jonathan and Nicholas, Chloris between Nicholas and William. Sandra Compline was on Jonathan's right, and had Dr. Hart for her other partner. Hersey Amblington was next to Dr. Hart, and Mandrake himself, the odd man, sat between Hersey and William. From the moment when they found their places it was obvious to Mandrake that the success of the dinner-party was most endangered by Mrs. Compline and Dr. Hart. These two had been the last to arrive, Mrs. Compline appearing after Caper had announced dinner. Both were extremely pale and, when they found their place-cards, seemed to flinch all over: "Like agitated horses," thought Mandrake. When they were all seated, Dr. Hart darted a strange glance across the table at Madame Lisse. She looked steadily at him for a moment. Jonathan was talking to Mrs. Compline; Dr. Hart, with an obvious effort, turned to Hersey Amblington. Nicholas, who had the air of a professional diner-out, embarked upon a series of phrases directed equally, Mandrake thought, at Madame Lisse and Chloris Wynne. They were empty little phrases, but Nicholas delivered them

with many inclinations of his head, this way and that, with
archly masculine glances, punctual shouts of laughter, and
frequent movements of his hand to his blond moustache. " In
the 'nineties," Mandrake thought, " Nicholas would have been
known as a masher. There is no modern word to describe
his gallantries." They were successful gallantries, however,
for both Chloris and Madame Lisse began to look alert and
sleek. William preserved a mulish silence, and Dr. Hart, while
he spoke to Hersey, glanced from time to time at Madame
Lisse.

Evidently Jonathan had chosen a round table with the object
of keeping the conversation general, and in this project he was
successful. However angry Hersey may have been with her
cousin, she must have decided to pull her weight in the rôle
of hostess for which he had obviously cast her. Mandrake,
Madame Lisse, and Nicholas all did their share, and presently
there appeared a kind of gaiety at the table. " It's merely going
to turn into a party that is precariously successful in the teeth
of extraordinary obstacles," Mandrake told himself. " We have
made a fuss about nothing." But this opinion was checked
when he saw Dr. Hart stare at Nicholas, when on turning to
William he found him engaged in what appeared to be some
whispered expostulation with Chloris, and when, turning away
in discomfort, he saw Mrs. Compline with shaking hands hide
an infinitesimal helping under her knife and fork. He emptied
his glass and gave his attention to Hersey Amblington, who
seemed to be talking about him to Jonathan.

" Mr. Mandrake sniffs at my suggestion," Hersey was saying. " Don't you, Mr. Mandrake?"

" Do I?" Mandrake rejoined uneasily. " What suggestion,
Lady Hersey?"

" There! He hasn't even heard me, Jo. Why, the suggestion I made before dinner for a surrealist play."

Before Mandrake could find an answer Nicholas Compline
suddenly struck into the conversation.

" You mustn't be flippant with Mr. Mandrake, Hersey," he
said. " He's looking very austere. I'm sure he's long ago given
up footling."

Mandrake experienced the sensation of a violent descent in
some abandoned lift. His inside seemed to turn over, and
the tips of his fingers went cold. " God!" he thought. " They
know. In a moment they will speak playfully of Dulwich."
And he sat with his fork held in suspended animation, half-

way to his mouth. " This atrocious woman," he thought, " this atrocious woman. This loathsome, grinning young man." He turned to Hersey and found her staring at him with an expression that he interpreted as knowing. Mandrake shied away and, looking wildly round the table, encountered the thick-lensed glasses of his host. Jonathan's lips were pursed, and in the faint creases at the corners of his mouth Mandrake read complacency and amusement. " So that's it," thought Mandrake furiously. " He knows and he's told them. It's the sort of thing that would delight him. My vulnerable spot. He's having a tweak at it, and he and his cousin and his bloody friend will laugh delicately and tell each other they were very naughty with poor Mr. Stanley Footling." But Jonathan was speaking to him, gently carrying forward the theme of Hersey's suggestion for a play.

" I have noticed, Aubrey, that the layman is always eager to provide the artist with ideas. Do you imagine, Hersey darling, that Aubrey is a sort of æsthetic scavenger?"

" But mine was such a *good* idea."

" You must excuse her, Aubrey. No sense of proportion, I'm afraid, poor woman."

" Mr. Mandrake *does* excuse me," said Hersey, and her smile held such a warmth of friendliness that it dispelled Mandrake's panic. " I was mistaken," he thought. " Another false alarm. Why must I be so absurdly sensitive? Other people have changed their names without experiencing these terrors." The relief was so great that for a time he was lost in it, and heard only the gradual quieting of his own heart-beats. But presently he became aware of a lull in the general conversation. They had reached dessert. Jonathan's voice alone was heard, and Mandrake thought that he must have been speaking for some little time.

II

" No one person," Jonathan was saying, " is the same individual to more than one other person. That is to say, the reality of individuals is not absolute. Each individual has as many exterior realities as the number of encounters he makes."

" Ah," said Dr. Hart, " this is a pet theory of my own. The actual ' he ' is known to nobody."

" Does the actual ' he ' even exist?" Jonathan returned.

" May it not be argued that ' he ' has no intrinsic reality since different selves arise out of a conglomeration of selves to meet different events?"

" I don't see what you mean," said William, with his air of worried bafflement.

" Nor do I, William," said Hersey. " One knows how people will react to certain events, Jo. We say : ' Oh, so-and-so is no go when it comes to such-and-such a situation.' "

" My contention is that this is exactly what we do not know."

" But, Mr. Royal," cried Chloris, " we *do* know. We know, for instance, that some people will refuse to listen to gossip."

" We know," said Nicholas, " that one man will keep his head in a crisis where another will go jitter-bug. This war——"

" Oh, don't let's talk about this war," said Chloris.

" There are some men in my company——" William began, but Jonathan raised his hand and William stopped short.

" Well, I concede,." said Jonathan, " that the same ' he ' may make so many appearances that we may gamble on his turning up under certain circumstances, but I contend that it *is* a gamble and that though under these familiar circumstances we may agree on the probability of certain reactions, we should quarrel about theoretical behaviour under some unforeseen, hitherto un-experienced circumstances."

" For example?" asked Madame Lisse.

" Parachute invasion——" began William, but his mother said quickly : " No, William, not the war." It was the first time since dinner that Mandrake had heard her speak without being addressed.

" I agree," said Jonathan. " Let us not draw our examples from the war. Let us suppose that—what shall I say——?"

" That the Archangel Gabriel popped down the chimney," suggested Hersey, " and blasted his trumpet in your ear."

" Or that Jonathan told us," said Nicholas, " that this was a Borgia party and the champagne was lethal and we had but twelve minutes to live."

" *Not* the Barrie touch, I implore you," said Mandrake, rallying a little.

" Or," said Jonathan, peering into the shadows beyond the candle-lit table, " that my new footman, who is not present at the moment, suddenly developed homicidal mania and was possessed of a lethal weapon. Let us, at any rate, suppose ourselves shut up with some great and impending menace." He paused, and for a moment complete silence fell upon the company.

The new footman returned. He and Caper moved round the table again. " So he's keeping the champagne going," thought Mandrake, " in case the women won't have brandy or liqueurs. Caper's being very judicious. Nobody's tight, unless it's William or Hart. I'm not sure of them. Everybody else is nicely, thank you."

" Well," said Jonathan, " under some such disastrous circumstance, how does each of you believe I would behave? Come now, I assure you I shan't cavil at the strictest censure. Sandra, what do you think I would do?"

Mrs. Compline raised her disfigured face. " What you would do?" she repeated. " I think you would talk, Jonathan." And for the first time that evening there was a burst of spontaneous laughter. Jonathan uttered his high-pitched giggle.

" *Touché*," he said. " And you, Madame Lisse?"

" I believe that for perhaps the first time in your life you would lose your temper, Mr. Royal."

" Nick?"

" I don't know. I think——"

" Come on, now, Nick. You can't insult me. Fill Mr. Compline's glass, Caper. Now, Nick?"

" I think you might be rather flattened out."

" I don't agree," said Chloris quickly. " I think he'd take us all in hand and tell us what to do."

" William?"

" What? Oh, ring up the police, I suppose," said William, and he added in a vague mumble only heard by Mandrake: " Or you might go mad, of course."

" I believe he would enjoy himself," said Mandrake quickly.

" I agree," said Hersey, to Mandrake's surprise.

" And Dr. Hart?"

" In a measure, I too agree. I think that you would be enormously interested in the behaviour of your guests."

" You see?" said Jonathan in high glee. " Am I not right? So many Jonathan Royals. Now shall we go further. Shall we agree to discuss our impressions of each other, and to keep our tempers as we do so? Come now."

" How clever of Jonathan," thought Mandrake, sipping his brandy. " Nothing interests people so much as the discussion of their own characters. His invitation may be dangerous, but at least it will make them talk." And talk they did. Mrs.

Compline believed that Nicholas would suffer from extreme
sensibility, but would show courage and resource. Nicholas,
prompted, as Mandrake considered, by a subconscious memory
of protective motherhood, thought his mother would console
and shelter. William, while agreeing with Nicholas about their
mother, hinted that Nicholas himself would shift his respon-
sibilities. Chloris Wynne, rather defiantly, supported William.
She suggested that William himself would show up very well
in a crisis, and her glance at Nicholas and at Mrs. Compline
seemed to say that they would resent his qualities. Mandrake,
nursing his brandy-glass, presently felt his brain clear, miracu-
lously. He would speak to these people in rhythmic, perfectly-
chosen phrases, and what he said would be of enormous importance. He heard his own voice telling them that Nicholas, in
the event of a crisis, would treat them to a display of pyro-
technics, and that two women would applaud him and one
man deride. " But the third woman," said Mandrake solemnly,
as he stared at Madame Lisse, " must remain a shadowed
figure. I shall write a play about her. Dear me, I am afraid
I must be a little drunk." He looked anxiously round, only
to discover that nobody had been listening to him, and he
suddenly realised that he had made his marvellous speech in
a whisper. This discovery sobered him. He decided to take
no more of Jonathan's brandy.

III

Jonathan did not keep the men long in the dining-room, and
Mandrake, who had taken stock of himself and had decided
that he would do very well if he was careful, considered that
his host had judged the drinks nicely as far as he and the
Complines were concerned, but that in the case of Dr. Hart,
Jonathan had been over-generous. Dr. Hart was extremely
pale, there were dents in his nostrils and a smile on his lips.
He was silent and fixed his gaze, which seemed a little out of
focus, on Nicholas Compline. Nicholas was noisily cheerful.
He moved his chair up to William's, and subjected his brother
to a kind of banter that made Mandrake shudder and caused
William to become silent and gloomy. Jonathan caught Mandrake's eye and suggested that they should move to the drawing-room.

" By all means," said Nicholas. " Here's old Bill as silent

as the grave, Jonathan, longing for his love. And Dr. Hart not much better, though whether it's from the same cause or not we mustn't ask."

"You are right," said Dr. Hart thickly. "It would not be amusing to ask such a question."

"Come along, come along," said Jonathan quickly, and opened the door. Mandrake hurriedly joined him, and William followed. At the door Mandrake turned and looked back. Nicholas was still in his chair. His hands rested on the table, he leant back and smiled at Dr. Hart, who had risen and was leaning heavily forward. Mandrake was irresistibly reminded of an Edwardian problem picture. It was a subject for the Hon. John Collier. There was the array of glasses, each with its highlight and reflection, there was the gloss of mahogany, of boiled shirt-fronts, of brass buttons. There was Dr. Hart's face, so violently expressive of some conjectural emotion, and Nicholas's, flushed, and wearing a sneer that dated perfectly with the Hon. John's period: all this unctuously lit by the candles on Jonathan's table. "The title," thought Mandrake, " would be 'The Insult.' "

"Come along, Nick," said Jonathan, and when it appeared that Nicholas had not heard him, he murmured in an undertone: " You and William go on, Aubrey. We'll follow."

So Mandrake and William did not hear what Nicholas and Dr. Hart had to say to each other.

IV

Mandrake had suspected that if Jonathan failed it would be from too passionate attention to detail. He feared that Jonathan's party would die of over-planning. Having an intense dislike of parlour-games, he thought gloomily of sharpened pencils and pads of paper neatly set out by the new footman. In this he misjudged his host. Jonathan introduced his game with a tolerable air of spontaneity. He related an anecdote of another party at which the game of Charter had been played. Jonathan had found himself with a collection of six letters and one blank. When the next letter was called it chimed perfectly with his six, but the resulting word was one of such gross impropriety that even Jonathan hesitated to use it. A duchess of formidable rigidity had been present. " I encountered her eye. The glare of a basilisk, I assure you. I could not venture.

But the amusing point of the story," said Jonathan, " is that I am persuaded her own letters had fallen in the same order. We played for threepenny points, and she loathes losing her money. I hinted at my own dilemma, and saw an answering glint. She was in an agony."

" But what is the game?" asked Mandrake, knowing that somebody was meant to ask this question.

" My dear Aubrey, have you never played Charter? It is entirely *vieux jeu* nowadays, but I still confess to a passion for it."

" It's simply a crossword game," said Hersey. " You are each given the empty crossword form and the letters are called one by one from a pack of cards. The players put each letter, as it is read out, into a square of the diagram. This goes on until the form is full. The longest list of complete words wins."

" You score by the length of the words," said Chloris. " Seven-letter words get fifteen points, three-letter words two points, and so on. You may not make any alterations, of course."

" It sounds entertaining," said Mandrake with a sinking heart.

" Shall we?" asked Jonathan, peering at his guests. " What does everybody think? Shall we?"

His guests, prompted by champagne and brandy to desire, vaguely, success rather than disaster, cried out that they were all for the game, and the party moved to the smoking-room. Here, Jonathan, with a convincing display of uncertainty, hunted in a drawer where Mandrake had seen him secrete the printed block of diagrams and the requisite number of pencils. Soon they were sitting in a semicircle round the fire with their pencils poised and with expressions of indignant bewilderment on their faces. Jonathan turned up the first card:

" X," he said, " X for Xerxes."

" Oh, *can't* we have another," cried Madame Lisse, " there aren't any—— Oh, no, wait a moment. I see."

" K for King."

Mandrake, finding himself rather apt at the game, began to enjoy it. With the last letter he completed his long word, " extract," and with an air of false modesty handed his Charter to Chloris Wynne, his next-door neighbour, to mark. He himself took William's Charter, and was embarrassed to find it in a state of the strangest confusion. William had either failed to understand the game, or else had got left so far behind that he could not catch up with the letters. Many of the spaces were blank, and in the left-hand corner William had made a singular little drawing of a strutting rooster, with a face that certainly bore a strong resemblance to his brother Nicholas.

"Anyway," said William, looking complacently at Mandrake, "the drawing is quite nice. Don't you think so?"

Mandrake was saved from making a reply by Nicholas, who at that moment uttered a sharp ejaculation.

"What's up, Nick?" asked Jonathan.

Nicholas had turned quite pale. In his left hand he held two of the Charter forms. He separated them and crushed one into a wad in his right hand.

"Have I made a mistake?" asked Dr. Hart softly.

"You've given me two forms," said Nicholas.

"Stupid of me. I must have torn them off the block at the same time."

"They have both been used."

"No doubt I forgot to remove an old form, and tore them off together."

Nicholas looked at him. "No doubt," he said.

"You can see which is the correct form by my long word. It is ' threats.' "

"I have not missed it," said Nicholas, and turned to speak to Madame Lisse.

v

Mandrake went to his room at midnight. Before switching on his light he pulled aside the curtains and partly opened the window. He saw that at last the snow had come. Fleets of small ghosts drove steeply forward from darkness into the region beyond the window-panes, where they became visible in the firelight. Some of them, meeting the panes, slid down their surface and lost their strangeness in the cessation of their flight. Though the room was perfectly silent, this swift enlargement of oncoming snowflakes beyond the windows suggested to Mandrake a vast nocturnal whispering. He suddenly remembered the black-out and closed the window. He let fall the curtain, switched on the light, and turned to stir his fire. He was accustomed to later hours and felt disinclined for sleep. His thoughts were busy with memories of the evening. He was filled with a nagging curiosity about the second Charter form, which had caused Nicholas Compline to turn pale and to look so strangely at Dr. Hart. He could see Nicholas's hand thrusting the crumpled form down between the seat and the arm of his chair. "Perhaps it is still there," Mandrake thought. "Without a doubt it is still there. Why should it have upset him so much? I shall never go to sleep. It is useless to undress and get into bed." And the prospect of the books Jonathan had chosen so carefully for his bedside filled him with dismay. At last he changed into pyjamas and dressing-gown, visited the adjoining bathroom, and noticed that there was no light under the door from the bathroom into William's bedroom at the farther side. "So William is not astir." He returned to his room, opened the door into the passage, and was met by the indifferent quiet of a sleeping house. Mandrake left his own door open and stole along the passage as far as the stairhead. In the wall above the stairs was a niche from which a great brass Buddha, indestructible memorial to Jonathan's Anglo-Indian grandfather, leered peacefully at Mandrake. He paused here, thinking. "A few steps down to the landing, then the lower flight to the hall. The smoking-room door is almost opposite the foot of the stairs." Nicholas had sat in the fourth chair from the end. Why should he not go down and satisfy himself about the crumpled form? If by any chance someone was in the smoking-room he could get himself a book from the library next door and return. There was no shame in looking at a discarded paper from a round game.

He limped softly to the head of the stairs. Here, in the diffused light, he found a switch and turned it on. A wall-lamp half-way down the first flight came to life. Mandrake descended the stairs. The walls sighed to his footfall, and near the bottom one of the steps creaked so loudly that he started and then stood rigid, his heart beating hard against his ribs. "This is how burglars and illicit lovers feel," thought Mandrake, "but why on earth should I?" Yet he stole cat-footed across the hall, pushed open the smoking-room door with his fingertips, and waited long in the dark before he groped for the light-switch and snapped it down.

There stood the nine arm-chairs in a semicircle before a dying fire. They had an air of being in dumb conclave, and in their irregular positions were strangely eloquent of their late occupants. There was Nicholas Compline's chair, drawn close to Madame Lisse's and turned away contemptuously from Dr. Hart's saddle back. Mandrake actually fetched a book from

a sporting collection in a revolving case before he moved to
Nicholas's chair, before his fingers explored the crack between
the arm and the seat. The paper was crushed into a tight wad.
He smoothed it out on the arm of the chair and read the
five words that had been firmly pencilled in the diagram.

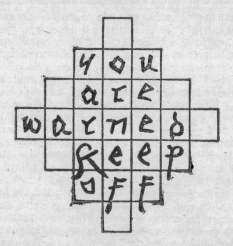

The fire settled down with a small clink of dead embers, and
Mandrake, smiling incredulously, stared at the scrap of paper
in his hand. It crossed his mind that perhaps he was the victim
of an elaborate joke, that Jonathan had primed his guests, had
invented their antipathies, and now waited maliciously for
Mandrake himself to come to him, agog with this latest find.
" But that won't wash," he thought. " Jonathan could not have
guessed I would return to find the paper. Nicholas *did* change
colour when he saw it. I must presume that Hart *did* write this
message and hand it to Nicholas with the other. He must have
been crazy with fury to allow himself such a ridiculous gesture.
Can he suppose that Nicholas will be frightened off the lady?
No, it's too absurd."

But, as if in answer to his speculations, Mandrake heard a
voice speaking behind him: " I tell you, Jonathan, he means
trouble. I'd better get out."

For a moment Mandrake stood like a stone, imagining that
Jonathan and Nicholas had entered the smoking-room behind

his back. Then he turned, and found the room still empty, and realised that Nicholas had spoken from beyond the door into the library, and for the first time noticed that this door was not quite shut. He was still speaking, his voice raised hysterically.

"It will be better if I clear out now. A pretty sort of party it'll be! The fellow's insane with jealousy. For her sake—don't you see—for her sake——"

The voice paused, and Mandrake heard a low murmur from Jonathan, interrupted violently by Nicholas.

"I don't give a damn what they think." Evidently Jonathan persisted, because in a moment Nicholas said: "Yes, of course I see that, but I can say . ." His voice dropped, and the next few sentences were half-lost. ". . . it's not that . . . I don't see why . . . urgent call from headquarters. . . . Good Lord, of course not! . . . Miserable fat little squirt. I've cut him out and he can't take it." Another pause, and then: "*I* don't mind if *you* don't. It was more on your account than . . . But I've told you about the letter, Jonathan . . . not the first . . . Well, if you think . . . Very well, I'll stay." And for the first time Mandrake caught Jonathan's words: "I'm sure it's better, Nick. Can't turn tail, you know. Good-night." "Good-night," said Nicholas, none too graciously, and Mandrake heard the door from the library to the hall open and close. Then from the next room came Jonathan's reedy tenor:

> "*Il était une bergère*
> *Qui ron-ton-ton, petit pat-a-plan.*"

Mandrake stuck out his chin, crossed the smoking-room, and entered the library by the communicating door.

"Jonathan," he said, "I've been eavesdropping."

VI

Jonathan was sitting in a chair before the fire. His short legs were drawn up, knees to chin, and he hugged his shins like some plump and exultant kobold. He turned his spectacles towards Mandrake, and, by that familiar trick of l ght, the thick lenses obscured his eyes and glinted like two moons.

"I've been eavesdropping," Mandrake repeated.

"My dear Aubrey, come in, come in. Eavesdropping? Non-

sense. You heard our friend Nicholas? Good! I was coming
to your room to relate the whole story. A diverting complication."

"I only heard a little of what he said. I'd come down to the
smoking-room." He saw Jonathan's spectacles turned on the
book he still held in his hand. "Not really to fetch a book,"
said Mandrake.

"No? One would seek a book in the library, one supposes.
But I am glad my choice for your room was not ill-judged."

"I wanted to see this."

Like a small boy in disgrace, Mandrake extended his right
hand and opened it, disclosing the crumpled form.

"Ah," said Jonathan.

"You have seen it?"

"Nick told me about it. I wondered if anyone else would
share my own curiosity. May I have it? Ah—— Thank you.
Sit down, Aubrey." Mandrake sat down, tortured by the suspicion that Jonathan was laughing at him.

"You see," said Mandrake, "that I am badly inoculated
with your virus. I simply could not go to bed without knowing what was on that form."

"Nor I, I assure you. I was about to look for it myself. As
perhaps you heard, Nick is in a great tig. It seems that before
coming here he had had letters from Hart warning him off
the lady. According to Nick, Hart is quite mad for love of
her and consumed by an agonising jealousy."

"Poor swine," said Mandrake.

"What? Oh, yes. Very strange and uncomfortable. I must
confess that I believe Nick is right. Did you notice the little
scene after dinner?"

"You may remember that you gave me to understand very
definitely that my cue was to withdraw rapidly."

"So I did. Well, there wasn't much in it. He merely glared
at Nick across the table, and said something in German which
neither of us understood."

"You'll be telling me next he's a fifth columnist," said
Mandrake.

"Not at all. He gives himself away much too readily. But
I fancy he has frightened Nick. I have observed, my dear
Aubrey, that of the two Complines, William catches your attention more than Nicholas. I have known them all their lives,
and I suggest that you turn your eyes on Nicholas. Nicholas
is rapidly becoming the—not perhaps the *jeune premier*—but

the central character of our drama. In Nicholas we see the vain man, frightened. The male flirt who finds an agreeable stimulant in another man's jealousy, and suddenly realises that he has roused the very devil in his rival. Would you believe it, Nicholas wanted to leave to-night? He advanced all sorts of social and gallant reasons, consideration for me, for the lady, for the success of the party; but the truth is Nick had a jitter-bug and wanted to make off."

"How did you prevent him?"

"I?" Jonathan pursed his lips. "I have usually been able to manage Nicholas. I let him see I understood his real motive. He was afraid I would make a pleasing little anecdote of his flight. His vanity won. He will remain."

"But what does he think Hart will do?"

"He used the word 'murderous.'"

There was a long silence. At last Mandrake said: "Jonathan, I think you should have let Nicholas Compline go."

"But why?"

"Because I agree with him. I have watched Hart to-night. He did look murderous."

"Gorgeous!" Jonathan exclaimed, and hugged his hands between his knees.

"Honestly, I think he means trouble. He's at the end of his tether."

"You don't think he'll go for Nick with a dinner-knife?"

"I don't think he's responsible for his behaviour."

"He was a little tipsy, you know."

"So was Compline. While the champagne and brandy worked he rather enjoyed baiting Hart. Now, evidently, he's not so sure. Nor am I."

"You disappoint me, Aubrey. Our æsthetic experiment is working beautifully and your only response——"

"Oh, I'm absorbingly interested. If *you* don't mind—after all, it's your house."

"Exactly. And my responsibility. I assembled the cast, and, my dear fellow, I offered you a seat in the stalls. The play is going too well for me to stop it at the close of the first act. It falls very prettily on Nick's exit, and I fancy the last thing we hear before the curtain blots out the scene is a sharp click."

"What?"

"Nicholas Compline turning the key in his bedroom door."

"I hope to God you're right," said Mandrake.

CHAPTER V

ATTEMPT

I

THE next morning Mandrake woke at the rattle of curtain rings to find his room penetrated by an unearthly light, and knew that Highfold was under snow. A heavy fall, the maid said. There were patches of clear sky, but the local prophets said they'd have another storm before evening. She rekindled his fire and left him to stare at his tea-tray and to remember that, not so many years ago, Mr. Stanley Footling, in the attic-room of his mother's boarding-house in Dulwich, had enjoyed none of these amenities. Stanley Footling always showed a tendency to return at the hour of waking, and this morning Mandrake asked himself for the hundredth time why he could not admit his metamorphosis with an honest gaiety; why he should suffer the miseries of unconfessed snobbery. He could find no answer, and, tired of his thoughts, decided to rise early.

When he went downstairs he found William Compline alone at the breakfast-table.

"Hallo," said William. "Good-morning. Jolly day for Nick's bath, isn't it?"

"What!"

"Nick's bath in the pool. Have you forgotten the bet?"

"I should think *he* had."

"I shall remind him."

"Well," said Mandrake, "personally I should pay a good deal more than ten pounds to get out of it."

"Yes, but you're not my brother Nicholas. He'll do it."

"But," said Mandrake uncomfortably, "hasn't he got something wrong with his heart? I mean——"

"It won't hurt him. The pool's not frozen. I've been to look. He can't swim, you know, so he'll just have to pop in at the shallow end and duck." William gave a little crow of laughter.

"I'd call it off, if I were you."

"Yes," said William, "but you're not me. I'll remind him

of it, all right." And on this slightly ominous note they continued with their breakfast in silence. Hersey Amblington and Chloris Wynne came in together, followed by Jonathan, who appeared to be in the best of spirits.

"We shall have a little sunshine, I believe," said Jonathan. "It may not last long, so doubtless the hardier members of the party will choose to make the most of it."

"I don't propose to build a snow-man, Jonathan, if that's what you're driving at," said Hersey.

"Don't you, Hersey?" said William. "I rather thought I might. After Nick's bath, you know. Have you heard about Nick's bath?"

"Your mother told me. You're not going to hold him to it, William?"

"He needn't if he doesn't want to."

"Bill," said Chloris, "*don't* remind him of it. Your mother——"

"She won't get up for ages," said William, "and I don't suppose there'll be any need to remind Nick. After all, it *was* a bet."

"I think you're behaving rather badly," said Chloris uncertainly. William stared at her.

"Are you afraid he'll get a little cold in his nose?" he asked, and added: "I was up to my waist in snow and slush in France not so long ago."

"I know, darling, but——"

"Here *is* Nick," said William placidly. His brother came in and paused at the door.

"Good-morning," said William. "We were just talking about the bet. They all seem to think I ought to let you off."

"Not at all," said Nicholas. "You've lost your tenner."

"*There!*" said William. "I said you'd do it. You mustn't get that lovely uniform wet, Nick. Jonathan will lend you a bathing suit, I expect. Or you could borrow my uniform. It's been up to——" Mandrake, Chloris, Hersey, and Jonathan all began to speak at once, and William, smiling gently, fetched himself another cup of coffee. Nicholas turned away to the sideboard. Mandrake had half-expected Jonathan to interfere, but he merely remarked on the hardihood of the modern young man and drew a somewhat tiresome analogy from the exploits of ancient Greeks. Nicholas suddenly developed a sort of gaiety that set Mandrake's teeth on edge, so falsely did it ring.

" Shall you come and watch me, Chloris?" asked Nicholas, seating himself beside her.

" I don't approve of your doing it."

" Oh, Chloris! Are you angry with me? I can't bear it. Tell me you're not angry with me. I'm doing it all for your sake. I must have an audience. Won't you be my audience?"

" Don't be a fool," said Chloris. " But, damn it," thought Mandrake, " she's preening herself, all the same." Dr. Hart arrived, and was very formal with his greetings. He looked ghastly and breakfasted on black coffee and toast. Nicholas threw him a glance curiously compounded of malice and nervousness, and began to talk still more loudly to Chloris Wynne of his bet with William. Hersey, who had evidently got sick of Nicholas, suddenly said she thought it was time to cut the cackle and get to the 'osses.

" But everybody isn't here," said William. " Madame Lisse isn't here."

" Divine creature!" exclaimed Nicholas affectedly, and showed the whites of his eyes at Dr. Hart. " She's in bed."

" How do you know?" asked William, against the combined mental opposition of the rest of the party.

" I've investigated. I looked in to say good-morning on my way down."

Dr. Hart put down his cup with a clatter and walked quickly out of the room.

" You are a damned fool, Nick," said Hersey softly.

" It's starting to snow again," said William. " You'd better hurry up with your bath."

II

Mandrake thought that no wager had ever fallen as inauspiciously as this one. Even Jonathan seemed uneasy, and when they drifted into the library made a half-hearted attempt to dissuade Nicholas. Lady Hersey said flatly that she thought the whole affair extremely boring and silly. Chloris Wynne at first attempted an air of jolly house-party waggishness, but a little later Mandrake overheard her urging William to call off the bet. Mrs. Compline somehow got wind of the project and sent down a message forbidding it, but this was followed by a message from Madame Lisse saying that she would watch from her bedroom window. Mandrake tried to get up a party to play badminton in the barn, but nobody really listened to him. An atmosphere of bathos hung over them like a pall, and through it William remained complacent and Nicholas embarrassingly flamboyant.

Finally it was resolved by the Complines that Nicholas should go down to the pavilion, change there into a bathing suit, and, as William put it, go off at the shallow end. William was to watch the performance, and Nicholas, rather offensively, insisted upon a second witness. Neither Hersey nor Chloris seemed able to make up her mind whether she would go down to the pool. Jonathan had gone out, saying something about Dr. Hart. It appeared that Mandrake would be obliged to witness Nicholas's ridiculous antics, and, muttering to himself, he followed him into the hall.

The rest of the party had disappeared. Nicholas stood brushing up his moustache and eyeing Mandrake with an air half-mischievous, half-defiant. "Well," he said, "this is a pretty damn-fool sort of caper, isn't it?"

"To be frank," said Mandrake, "I think it is. It's snowing like hell again. Don't you rather feel the bet's fallen flat?"

"I'll be damned if I let Bill take that tenner off me. Are you coming?"

"I'll go up and get my coat," said Mandrake unwillingly.

"Take one out of the cloakroom here. I'm going to. The Tyrolese cape."

"Jonathan's?"

"Or Hart's!" Nicholas grinned. "Hart's mantle may as well fall across my shoulders, what? I'll go down now and change in that bloody pavilion. You follow. Bill's running down from the west door when he's given me time to undress."

Nicholas went into the cloakroom and reappeared wearing one Tyrolese cape and carrying another. "Here you are," he said, throwing it at Mandrake. "Don't be long."

He pulled the hood of his cape over his head and went out through the front doors. For a moment Mandrake saw him, a fantastic figure caught in a flurry of snow. Then Nicholas lowered his head to the wind and ran out of sight.

Mandrake's club-foot prevented him from running. It was some distance from the front of the house to the pool, and he remembered that the west door opened directly on a path that led to the terrace above the pool. He decided that, like William, he would go down that way. He would go at once, before William started. He loathed people to check their

steps to his painful limp. Imitating Nicholas, he pulled the
hood of the second cape over his head and made his way
along a side passage to the west door, and as he opened it
heard somebody call after him from the house. He ignored the
call and, filled with disgust at the whole situation, slammed
the door behind him and limped out into the storm.

The north wind drove against him, flattening the cloak
against his right side and billowing it out on his left. He felt
snow on his eyelids and lips and pulled the hood farther over
his brows so that he could see only the ground before him. As
he limped forward, snow squeaked under his steps. It closed
over his sound foot above the rim of his shoe. The path was
still defined, and he followed it to the edge of the terrace.
Below him lay the pool and the pavilion. The water was a
black hole in a white field, but the pavilion resembled a light-
hearted decoration, so well did the snow become it. Mandrake
was tempted to watch from the terrace, but the wind was so
violent there that he changed his mind and crept awkwardly
down the long flight of steps, thinking to himself that it would
be just like this party if he slipped and broke his good leg.
At last he reached the rounded embankment that curved
sharply above the pool, hiding the surface of the water from
anybody who did not climb its steps. Mandrake reached the
top of this bank with difficulty and descended the far side to
the paved kerb, now covered in snow. He glanced at the
pavilion and saw Nicholas wave from one of the windows.
Mandrake walked to the deep end of the pool, where there was
a diving platform, and stood huddled in his cloak watching
fleets of snow die on the black surface of the water. He looked
back towards the terrace steps, but the embankment hid the
bottom flight. There was nobody on the top flight. Perhaps,
after all, none of the others would come. "Damn!" said
Mandrake. "Damn Nicholas, damn William, and damn Jonathan for his filthy party. I've never been so bored or cold or
angry in my life before." He staggered a little against a sudden
gust of wind and snow.

The next moment something drove hard against his shoulders. He took a gigantic stride forward into nothingness and
was torn from head to foot with the appalling shock of icy
water.

III

The fabric of the cape was in his eyes and mouth and clamped about his arms and legs. The cold cut him with terrible knives of pain. As he sank he thought: " This is disgusting. This is really bad. A terrible thing has happened to me." Water rushed in at his nose and ears. His heavy boot pulled at his leg. His arms fought the cape, and after a timeless interval it rose above his head, free of his face, and he saw a green prison about him. Then with frozen limbs he struggled and fought, and at last, feeling the bottom of the pool, struck at it with his feet and rose into the folds of the cape. His lungs were bursting, his body dying of cold. His hands wrenched at the fastening about his throat and broke it, his arms fought off the nightmare cape, and after an age of suffocating despair he reached the surface. He drew a retching gasp and swallowed air. For a moment he felt and saw snow, and heard, quite close by, a voice. As he sank again, something slapped the water above his head. " But I can swim a little," he thought, as wheels clashed and whirred behind his brain, and he made frog-like gestures with his arms and legs. Immediately the fingers of his right hand touched something smooth that slipped away from them. He made a more determined effort and, after three violent strokes, again reached the surface. As he gasped and opened his eyes, he was confronted by a scarlet face, beaked, on the end of a long scarlet neck. He flung his arms round this neck, fell backwards and was half-suffocated with another in-drawn jet of water. Then he found himself lying on the pond, choking into the face of a monstrous bird. Again he heard voices, but they now sounded unreal and very far away.

" Are you all right? Kick. Kick out. You're coming this way."

" But that is *my* cloak."

" Kick, Aubrey, kick."

He kicked, and, after an æon of time, floated into the view of five faces, upside down with their mouths open. His head struck against hardness.

" The rail. There's a rail here. Get hold of it."

" You're all right now. Here!"

He was drawn up. His arms scraped against stone. He was lying on the edge of the pool clasping an inflated india-rubber bird to his bosom. He was turned so that his face hung over the edge of the pond. His jaws had developed an independent life of their own, and his teeth chattered like castanets. His skin, too, leapt and jerked over the surface of his frozen muscles. When he tried to speak he made strange ugly noises. Acrid water trickled from his nostrils over his lips and chin.

" How the devil did it happen?" somebody—William—was asking.

" The edge is horribly slippery," said Chloris Wynne. " I nearly fell in myself."

" I didn't fall," Mandrake mouthed out with great difficulty. " I was pushed." Nicholas Compline burst into a shout of laughter and Mandrake wondered dimly if he could make a quick grab at his ankle and overturn him into the pool. It was borne in on Mandrake that Nicholas was wearing bathing drawers under his cape.

" Did he fall or was he pushed?" shouted Nicholas.

" Shut up, Nicholas." That was Chloris Wynne.

" My dear fellow," Jonathan made a series of little dabs at Mandrake, " you must come up at once. My coat. Take my coat. Ah, yours too, William, that's better. Help him up, now. A hot toddy and a blazing fire, eh, Hart? There never was anything more unfortunate. Come now."

Mandrake was suddenly torn by a violent retching. " Disgusting," he thought. " *Disgusting!*"

" That will be better," said a voice. Dr. Hart's! " We should get him up quickly. Can you walk, Mr. Mandrake?"

" Yes."

" Your arm across my shoulders. So, come now."

" I'll just get into my clothes," said Nicholas.

" Perhaps, Mr. Compline, as you are in bathing dress, you will be good enough to retrieve my cape."

" Sorry, I can't swim."

" We'll fish it out somehow," said Chloris. " Take Mr. Mandrake in."

Jonathan, William, and Dr. Hart took him back. Over the embankment, up the terrace steps, through a mess of footprints left by the others. The heavy boot on his club-foot dragged and hit against snow and sodden turf. Half-way up he was sick again. Jonathan ran ahead and, when at last they reached the house, could be heard shouting out orders to the servants. " Hot-water bottles. All you can find. His bath—quickly. Brandy, Caper. The fire in his room. What are you doing, all of you! God bless my soul, Mrs. Pouting, here's Mr. Mandrake, half-drowned."

If only his teeth would stop chattering he would enjoy being in bed, watching flames mount in the fireplace, feeling the toddy set up a little system of warmth inside him. The hot bath had thawed his body, the hot bottles lay snug against his legs. Jonathan again held the glass to his lips.

"What happened?" asked Mandrake.

"After you fell, you mean? Nick looked out from the window of his dressing-room. He saw you and ran out. He can't swim, you know, but he snatched up the inflated pelican— there are several in the pavilion—and threw it into the pond. By that time I fancy William and Hart were there. They arrived before Miss Wynne and myself. It appears that William had stripped off his overcoat and was going after you when you seized the improvised lifebuoy. When we arrived your arms were wreathed about its neck and you were fighting your way to the side. My dear Aubrey, I can't tell you how distressed I am. Another sip, now, do."

"Jonathan, somebody came behind me and thrust me forward."

"But my dear fellow——"

"I tell you they did. I can still feel the impact of their hands. I did *not* slip. Good God, Jonathan, I'm not romancing! I tell you I was deliberately thrown into that water."

"Nicholas saw nobody," said Jonathan uncomfortably. He primmed his lips and gave a little cough.

"When did he look out?" Mandrake said. "I know he saw me when I first got there. But afterwards?"

"Well—the first thing he saw was your cape—Dr. Hart's cape, unhappily—on the surface of the water."

"Exactly. Whoever pushed me in, had by that time hidden himself. He had only to dodge over the embankment and duck down."

"But we should have seen him," said Jonathan.

"Hart and William Compline were already there when you arrived?"

"Yes, but——"

"Did they go down together to the pond?"

"I—no, I think not. Hart left by the front door and came by the other path, past the pavilion. William came by the west door."

"Which of them arrived first? Thank God I've stopped chattering."

"I don't know. I persuaded Hart to go out. I managed to calm him down after that *most* unfortunate passage with Nicholas at breakfast. I suggested he should go out for a—for a sort of breather, do you know—and I supposed he followed the path to the pavilion, and was arrested by Nicholas's shouts for help. I myself heard Nicholas as I went to the west door. I overtook Miss Wynne who was already on the terrace. When I reached the edge of the terrace, Hart and the two Complines were all by the pond. My dear Aubrey, I shall tire you if I go on at this rate. Finish your drink and try to go to sleep."

"I don't in the least want to go to sleep, Jonathan. Somebody has just tried to drown me, and I do not find the experience conducive to slumber."

"No?" murmured Jonathan unhappily.

"No. And don't, I implore you, look as though I was mentally unhinged."

"Well, you *have* had a shock. You may even have a slight fever. I don't want to alarm you——"

"If you try to fob me off, I shall certainly run a frightful temperature. At the moment I assure you I am perfectly normal, and I tell you, Jonathan, somebody tried to drown me in your loathsome pond. I confess I should like to know who it was."

"A thoughtless piece of foolery, perhaps," mumbled Jonathan. Mandrake suddenly pointed a trembling finger at the mound in the bedclothes made by his left foot.

"Does any one but a moron play that sort of prank on a cripple?" he asked savagely.

"Oh, my dear fellow, I know, but——"

"Madame Lisse!" Mandrake cried. "She was to watch from her window. She must have seen."

"You can't see that end of the pool from her window," said Jonathan quickly. "It's hidden by the yew trees on the terrace."

"How do you know?"

"I do know. Yesterday, when I did her flowers, I noticed. I assure you."

Mandrake looked at him. "Then whoever did it," he said, "must have also known that she could not see him. Or else——"

There was a tap on the door.

" Come in," cried Jonathan in a loud voice. " Come in."

IV

It was Nicholas Compline. " Look here," he said. " I hope
you don't mind my butting in. I had to see Jonathan. Are you
all right?"

" Thanks to you," said Mandrake, " I believe I am."

" Look here; I'm damn sorry I laughed."

" It was infuriating, but I can't quarrel with you. As we say
in the provinces, you quite literally gave me the bird. Not the
first time I have been so honoured, but certainly the first time
I have welcomed it with both arms."

" Jonathan," said Nicholas, " you realise the significance of
this business?"

" The significance, Nick?"

" It was done deliberately."

" Just what I've been trying to tell Jonathan, Compline. My
God, I was literally hurled into that water. I'm sorry to dwell
on a tiresome subject, but somebody tried to drown me."

" No, they didn't."

" What!"

" They tried to drown *me*."

" Here!" shouted Mandrake, " what the hell d'you mean!"

" Jonathan," said Nicholas, " we'd better tell him about me
and Hart."

" Oh, that," said Mandrake. " I know all about that."

" May I ask how?"

" Need we go into it?"

" My dear Nick," began Jonathan in a great hurry, " Mandrake noticed all was not well between you. The scene at the
dinner-table. The game of Charter. He asked me if I—if
I——"

" Well, never mind," Nicholas interrupted impatiently.
" You know he's been threatening me? All right. Now, let
me tell you that as I went down to the pond I glanced up at the
front of the house. You know the window on the first floor
above the front door?"

" Yes," said Jonathan.

" All right. He was watching me through that window."

" But my dear Nick——"

"He was watching me. He saw me go down wearing that cape. He didn't see Mandrake go down wearing the other cape, because Mandrake went out at the west door. Don't interrupt me, Jonathan, this is serious. When Mandrake was shoved overboard, he was standing up to his hocks in snow on the kerb of the pool, with that embankment hiding his legs from anybody that came up from behind. You had the hood pulled over your head, I suppose, Mandrake?"

"Yes."

"Yes. Well, it was Hart shoved you overboard, and Hart thought he was doing me in, by God!"

"But, Nick, we must keep our heads and not rush impetuously into conclusions. . . ."

"See here," said Nicholas, always to Mandrake. "Had anybody in this party reason to wish you any harm?"

"I'd never met one of them in my life before. Except Jonathan, of course."

"And I can assure you, my dear Aubrey, that I entertain only the kindest——"

"Of course."

"Well, then?" said Nicholas.

"I believe you're right," cried Mandrake.

The door opened and Dr. Hart came in.

Nicholas, who had been sitting on the edge of the bed, sprang up and walked out of the room. Jonathan uttered a series of little consolatory noises, and moved to the window. Hart went to the bed and laid his fingers on Mandrake's wrist.

"You are better," he said. "That is right. It will be well to remain in bed to-day, perhaps. There has been a little shock." He looked placidly at Mandrake and repeated: "Just a little shock."

"Yes," said Mandrake.

Hart turned to Jonathan. "If I might speak to you, Mr. Royal."

"To me?" Jonathan gave a little start. "Yes, of course. Here?"

"I was about to suggest—somewhere else. But, perhaps—— I remember, Mr. Mandrake, that as we brought you to the house, you declared repeatedly that you had been deliberately pushed into this swimming pool."

Mandrake looked at that large pale face, surely more pale than ever since it's owner began to speak, and thought: "This may be the face of a potential murderer." Aloud, he said: "I am quite convinced of it."

"Then perhaps it would be well to set your mind at ease on this matter. No attempt was made wittingly upon you, Mr. Mandrake."

"How do you know?"

"It was a case of mistaken identity."

"Good God!" said Jonathan with violence.

Dr. Hart tapped the palm of one hand with the fingers of the other. "The person who made this attack," he said, "believed that he was making it upon me."

v

Mandrake's first reaction to this announcement was a hysterical impulse to burst out laughing. He looked at Jonathan, who stood with his back to the light, and wondered if he only imagined that an expression of mingled relief and astonishment had appeared for a moment on his host's face. Then he heard his voice, pedantic and high-pitched as usual.

"But, my dear Hart," Jonathan said, "what can have put such a strange notion into your head?"

"The fact that there is, among your guests, a man who wishes most ardently for my death."

"Surely not," said Jonathan, making a little purse of his lips.

"Surely, yes. I had not intended to go so far. I merely wished to reassure Mr. Mandrake. Perhaps if we withdrew . . .?"

"For pity's sake," Mandrake ejaculated, "don't withdraw. I'm all right. I want to get this thing straight. After all," he added peevishly, "it *was* me in the pond."

"True," said Jonathan.

"And I think I should tell you, Doctor Hart, that as I came down the steps, Compline saw me through the pavilion window and waved. He must have recognised me."

"It was snowing very heavily. Your face, no doubt, was in shadow, hidden by the hood of my cape."

"I hope you got your cape," said Jonathan anxiously.

"Thank you, yes. There must be a considerable amount of weed in your pond. It is to me quite evident, Mandrake, that Compline mistook you for myself. He came out of the pavilion and ran up quickly behind you, giving you a sharp thrust on the shoulder-blades."

"It *was* a sharp thrust on the shoulder-blades. But you forget that there is one thing about me that is quite distinctive." Mandrake spoke rapidly, with an air of jeering at himself. "I am lame. I wear a heavy boot. I use a stick. You can't mistake a man with a club foot, Doctor Hart."

"Your foot was hidden. One does not walk evenly in snow, and I assure you that while I, as a medical man, would not make such a mistake, Compline, glancing out through heavy sheets of falling snow, might easily do so."

"I don't agree with you. And didn't Compline see you looking from an upper window as he went to the pond? He could hardly imagine you would spirit yourself down there as quickly as that."

"Why not? I could have done so. A matter of a few moments. In actual fact I did go down a few minutes later. Mr. Royal saw me leave."

"Is it altogether wise to stress that point, do you think?"

"I do not understand you, Mr. Mandrake."

Jonathan began to talk very quickly, stuttering a little, and making sharp gestures with both hands.

"And, my dear Hart, even if, as you suggest, any one could mistake Mandrake for yourself; even supposing, and I cannot suppose it, that any one could entertain the idea of thrusting you into that water, surely, *surely* it would be preposterous to suggest that it was with any—any—ah—murderous intent. Can you not swim, my dear Doctor?"

"Yes, but——"

"Very well, then. I myself cannot help thinking that Mandrake is mistaken, that a sudden gust of wind caught him . . ."

"No, Jonathan."

"Or that at the worst it was a stupid and dangerous practical joke."

"A *joke*!" shouted Dr. Hart. "A *joke*."

Mandrake suppressed a nervous giggle. Hart stared sombrely at him, and then turned to Jonathan. "And yet I do not know," he said heavily. "Perhaps with an Englishman it is possible. Perhaps he did not mean to kill me. Perhaps he wished to make me a foolish figure, shivering, dripping stagnant water, my teeth chattering—yes, I can accept that possibility. He recognised the Tyrolese cape and thought——"

"Wait a moment," Mandrake interrupted, "before we go

any further I must put you right about the cape. It is impossible that Nicholas should have thought you were inside your own Tyrolese cape."

" And why?"

" Because he himself gave it to me to wear to the pond."

Dr. Hart was silent. He looked from Mandrake to Jonathan, and those little dents appeared in his nostrils. " You are protecting him," he said.

" I assure you I am speaking the truth."

" There is one explanation that seems to have occurred to nobody." Jonathan raised his hand to his spectacles and adjusted them slightly. " I myself wear a Tyrolese cape, your own gift, my dear Hart, and a delightful one. Is it not at least possible that somebody may have thought it would be amusing to watch me flounder in my own ornamental pool?"

" But who the hell?" Mandrake objected.

" It might be argued," said Jonathan, smiling modestly, " almost every member of my house-party."

VI

When they had left him alone, Mandrake surrendered himself to a curious state of being, engendered by exhaustion, brandy, speculation, and drowsiness. His thoughts floated in a kind of hinterland between sleep and wakefulness. At times they were sharply defined, at times nebulous and disconnected, but always they circled about the events leading to his plunge into the swimming-pool. At last he dozed off into a fitful sleep from which he was roused, as it seemed, by a single, clear inspiration. " I must see William Compline," he heard himself say. " I must see William Compline." He was staring at the ridge of snow that had begun to mount from the sill up the window-pane when his door moved slightly, and Chloris Wynne's beautifully groomed head appeared in the opening.

" Come in."

" I thought you might be asleep. I called to inquire."

" The report is favourable. Sit down and have a cigarette. I haven't the remotest idea of the time."

" Nearly lunch-time."

" Really. What are you all doing?"

" I've known house-parties go with a greater swing. Nicholas is sulking by the radio in the smoking-room. Lady Hersey and

Mr. Royal seem to be having a quarrel next door, in the library, and when I tried the boudoir on the other side of the smoking-room I ran into Dr. Hart and Madame Lisse both quite green in the face, and obviously at the peak of an argument. My ex-future mother-in-law has developed a bad cold, and I have had a snorter of a row with William."

" Here!" said Mandrake. " What *is* all this?"

" I ticked him off for harping on about the bet with Nicholas, and then he said some pretty offensive things about Nicholas and me, and I said he was insane, and he huffed and broke off our engagement. I don't know why I tell you all this, unless it's to get in first with the news bulletin."

" It's all very exciting, of course, but I consider the human interest really centres about me."

" Because you fell in the pool?"

" Because I was pushed in "

" That's what we're quarrelling about, actually. So many people seem to think it was all a mistake."

" The fact remains, I was pushed in."

" Oh, they've dropped saying it was an *accident*. But each of the men seems to think you were mistaken for him."

" Does William think that?"

" No. William confines himself to saying he wishes it had been Nicholas. He's made Nicholas pay him the ten pounds."

" I suppose," said Mandrake, " *you* didn't push me in?"

" No, honestly, I didn't. When I got to the top of the steps William and Nicholas and Dr. Hart were all down by the pool screaming instructions to you. I got a frightful shock. I thought you were Mr. Royal drowning in his own baroque waters."

" Why?"

" I don't know. Oh, because of the cloak, I suppose. It was floating about like a large water-lily leaf, and I said to myself: ' Crikey, that's Jonathan Royal.' "

Mandrake sat up in bed and bent his most austere gaze upon Miss Wynne. " How did you feel," he asked, " when you knew it was I?"

" Well, when Mr. Royal came up behind me, I knew it was thee, if that's the right grammar. And then I saw you clinging to that bathing-bird, and your hair was over your face like seaweed, and your tie was round at the back of your neck, and so on, and "—her voice quivered slightly—" and I was terribly sorry," she said.

" No doubt I was a ludicrous figure. Look here, from what you tell me it seems that you were the last to arrive."

" No, Mr. Royal came after me. He'd been round at the front of the house, I think. He overtook me on the steps."

" Will you tell me something? Please try to remember. Did you notice the footprints on the terrace and the steps?"

" I *say*," said Miss Wynne, " are we going to do a bit of 'teckery? Footprints in the snow!"

" Do leave off being gay and inconsequent, I implore you, and try to remember the footprints. There would be mine, of course."

" Yes. I noticed yours. I mean I——"

" You saw the marks of my club-foot. You needn't be so delicate about it."

" You needn't be so insufferably on the defensive," said Chloris with spirit, and immediately added: " Oh, gosh, I'm so sorry. At least let there not be a quarrel up here by your bed of sickness. Yes, I saw your footprints, and I think I saw— no, I can't remember, except that there were others. William's, of course."

" Any coming back to the house?"

" No, I'm sure not. But——"

" Yes?"

" Well, you're wondering, aren't you, if somebody could have gone down and shoved you overboard and then come back up the steps and then sort of pretended they were going down for the first time? I'd thought of that. You see, as I went down I stepped in your footprints because it was easier going. Anybody else might have done that. It was snowing so hard nobody would have noticed the steps within the steps."

" Hart came by a different path from the front of the house, William came down the terrace steps, then you, then Jonathan. I don't think William would have had time unless he came hard on my heels. I'd only just got there when it happened. Nicholas didn't do it, because he gave me the cloak and therefore couldn't have mistaken me for any one else. I believe Nicholas is right. I believe Hart did it. He saw Nicholas, wearing his cloak, go by the front way, and followed him. Then he skulked round the corner of the pavilion, saw a figure in a cloak standing on the kerb, darted out through the snow and did his abominable stuff. Then he darted back and reappeared, all surprise and consternation, when he heard Nicholas yell. By that time William was coming down the steps, no doubt, and you, followed by Jonathan, were leaving the house. Hart's our man."

" Yes, but *why*?"

" My dear girl——"

" All right, all right. Because of Madame Lisse. We only met last night and you talk as if I were a congenital idiot."

" There's nothing like attempted murder to bring people together."

" Nicholas *is* a fool."

" You ought to know. I thought you still seemed to get a flutter out of him."

" Now *that*," said Chloris warmly, " I do consider an absolutely insufferable remark."

" It's insufferable because it happens to be true. Nicholas Compline is the sort of person that all females get self-conscious about, and all males instinctively wish to award a kick in the pants."

" Barnyard jealousy."

" You know," said Mandrake, " you've got more penetration than I first gave you credit for. All the same," he said, after a long pause, " there's one little thing that doesn't quite fit in with my theory. It doesn't exactly contradict it, but it doesn't fit in."

" Well, don't mumble about it. Or aren't you going to tell me?"

" When they brought me back up those unspeakable steps, I was sick."

" You don't have to tell me that. I was looking after you."

" I'm damned if I know how I came to notice them, but I did notice them. At the top of the terrace, leading out from the house, coming round from the front door and stopping short at the edge of the terrace. You didn't see them when you went down. Neither did I. Which proves——"

" Do you mind," Chloris interrupted, " breaking the thread of your narrative just for a second? Surrealism may be marvellous in poetic drama, but it's not so good in simple conversation. What didn't we see going down that you saw coming back, sick and all as you were?"

" A row of footprints in the snow coming out from the house as far as the top of the terrace, and turning back again."

" Oh."

" They were small footprints."

CHAPTER VI

FLIGHT

I

THE afternoon was remarkable for an increasing heaviness in the snowfall, the state of Mandrake's feelings, and the behaviour of William Compline. Snow mounted from the window-sill in a tapering shroud, light diminished stealthily in Mandrake's bedroom, while he felt too relaxed and too idle to stretch out his hand to the bedside lamp. Yet though his body was fatigued, his brain was active and concerned itself briskly with the problem of his immersion and with speculations on the subject of Chloris Wynne's strange relations with the Compline brothers. He was convinced that she was not in love with William, but less sure that she did not still hanker after Nicholas. Mandrake wondered testily how a young woman who did not try the eyes and was by no means a ninny, could possibly degrade her intelligence by falling for the brummagen charms of Nicholas Compline. "A popinjay," he muttered, "a stock figure of dubious gallantry." And he pronounced the noise usually associated with the word " Pshaw." He had arrived at this point when he received a visit from William and Lady Hersey.

"We hear you're better," Hersey said. "Everybody's being quite frightful downstairs, and William and I thought we'd like a little first-hand information, so we've come to call. They're all saying you think somebody tried to drown you. William's afraid you might suspect him, so I've brought him up to come clean."

"Do you suspect me?" asked William anxiously. "Because I didn't, you know."

"I don't in the least suspect you. Why should I? We've had no difference of opinion."

"Well, they seem to think I might have mistaken you for Nicholas."

"Who suspects this?"

"My mama, principally. Because I stuck to the bet, you see.

So I thought I'd like to explain that when I got there you were already in the pool."

" Was Hart there? "

" No. No, he turned up a minute or so later."

" Did you notice the footprints on the terrace steps? "

" Yes, rather," said William unexpectedly. " There were your footsteps. I noticed them because one was bigger than the other."

" William ! " Hersey murmured.

" Well, Hersey, he'd know about that, wouldn't he? And then, you know, Chloris and Jonathan arrived."

" Perhaps you'd like my alibi, Mr. Mandrake," said Hersey. " It's not an alibi at all, I'm afraid. I sat in the smoking-room and listened to the wireless. The first intimation I had about your adventure was provided by Jonathan, who came in shouting for restoratives. I *could* tell you about the wireless programme, I think."

Hersey went to the window and looked out. When she spoke again her voice fell oddly on the silence of the room. " It's snowing like mad," she said. " Has it struck either of you that in all probability, whether we like it or not, we are shut up together in this house with no chance of escape? "

" Dr. Hart wanted to go after lunch," William said. " I heard him say so to Jonathan. But Jonathan said they've had word that you can't get over Cloudyfold, and, anyway, there's a drift inside the front gates. Jonathan seemed pleased about that."

" He would be." Hersey turned and rested her hands behind her on the sill. Her figure appeared almost black against the hurried silence of the storm beyond the window. " Mr. Mandrake," she said, " you know my cousin quite well, don't you? "

" I've known him for five years."

" But that doesn't say you know him well," she said quickly. " You arrived before all of us. He was up to something, wasn't he? No, that's not a fair question. You needn't answer. I know he was up to something. But, whatever his scheme was, it didn't involve *you* unless—yes, William, that must be it, of course. Mr. Mandrake was to be the audience."

" I don't like performing for Jonathan," William said. " I never have."

" Nor do I, and, what's more, I won't. The Pirate can register fatal woman in heaps all over the house, but she won't get a rise out of me."

" I suppose I *have* performed, Hersey. Chloris and I broke off our engagement before lunch."

" I thought something had happened. Why?"

William hunched his shoulders and drove his hands into his trousers pockets. " She ticked me off about the bet," he said, " and I ticked her off about Nicholas, so what have you?"

" Well, William my dear, I'm sorry, but, honestly, *is* she quite your cup of tea?" Hersey confronted Mandrake. " What do you think?" she demanded abruptly. He was not very much taken aback. For some reason that he had never been able to understand, Mandrake was a man in whom his fellow-creatures confided. He was by no means obviously sympathetic and he seldom asked for confidences, but, perhaps, because of these very omissions, they came his way. Sometimes he wondered if his lameness had something to do with it. People were inclined to regard a lame man as an isolated being, set apart by his disability, as a priest is set apart by his profession. He usually enjoyed hearing strange confessions, and was surprised, therefore, at discovering in himself a reluctance to receive William's explanations of his quarrel with Chloris Wynne. He was profoundly glad that the engagement was broken, and quite determined to make no suggestions about mending it.

" You must remember," he said, " that we met for the first time last night."

Hersey fixed him with a bright blue eye. " How guarded!" she said. " William, I believe Mr. Mandrake has——"

" Since we are being so frank," Mandrake interrupted in a great hurry, " I should like to know whether you believe somebody pushed me into that loathsome pond, and if so, who."

" Nick says it was Hart," said Hersey. " He's gone and thrown his mother into a fever by telling her Hart has tried to drown him. He's behaving like a peevish child."

" Mightn't you have been blown in?" William asked vaguely.

" Does a gust of wind hit you so hard on the shoulder-blades that you can feel the bruises afterwards? Damn it, I *know*. They're my shoulder-blades."

" So they are," Hersey agreed, " and I for one think it was Dr. Hart. After all, we know he was gibbering with rage at Nicholas, and it seems he saw Nicholas go down wearing a cape. I don't suppose he meant to drown him. He simply couldn't resist the temptation. I rather sympathise. Nicholas has bounded like a tennis ball, I consider, from the time he got here."

" But Hart must have known Nick couldn't swim," said William. " He kept explaining that was why he wouldn't go in at the deep end."

" True. Well, perhaps he meant to drown him."

" What does Madame Lisse say about it?" Mandrake asked.

" The Pirate?" Hersey helped herself to a cigarette. " My dear Mr. Mandrake, she doesn't say anything about it. She dressed herself up in what I happen to know is a Chanel model at fifty guineas, and came down for lunch looking like an orchid at a church bazaar. Nicholas and William and Dr. Hart curvet and goggle whenever they look at her."

" Well, you know, Hersey, she is rather exciting," said William.

" Does Jonathan goggle?"

" No," said Hersey. " He looks at her as he looks at all the rest of us—speculatively, from behind those damned glasses."

" I've always wanted," William observed, " to see a really good specimen of the *femme fatale*." Hersey snorted, and then said immediately: " Oh, I grant you her looks. She's got a marvellous skin, thick and close. You can't beat 'em."

" And then there's her figure, of course."

" Yes, William, yes. I suppose you and your girl didn't by any chance quarrel over the Pirate?"

" Oh, no. Chloris isn't jealous. Not of me, at any rate. It is I," said William, " who am jealous. Of course you know, don't you, that Chloris broke her engagement to Nick because or Madame Lisse?"

" Is Madame at all in love with your brother, do you suppose?" Mandrake asked.

" I don't know," said William, " but I think Chloris is."

" Rot!" said Hersey. Mandrake suddenly felt abysmally depressed. William walked to the fireplace and stood with his back to them and his head bent. He stirred the fire rather violently with his heel, and through the splutter and rattle of coals they heard his voice.

" . . . I think I'm glad. It's always been the same. . . . *You* know, Hersey. Second best. For a little while I diddled myself into thinking I'd cut him out. I thought I'd show them. My mother knew. At first she was furious, but pretty soon she saw it was me that was the mug as usual. My mother thinks it's all as it should be, Nick having strings of lovely ladies fall-ing for him—*le roi s'amuse* sort of idea. By God!" said William with sudden violence, " it's not such fun having a brother like Nick. By God, I wish Hart *had* shoved him in the pond."

" William, don't."

" Why not? Why shouldn't I say for once what I think of my lovely little brother? D'you suppose I'd blame Hart, if he was after Nicholas? Not I. If I'd thought of it myself, be damned if I wouldn't have done it."

" Stop!" Hersey cried out. " Stop! Something appalling is happening to all of us. We're saying things we'll regret for the rest of our lives."

" We're merely speaking the truth."

" It's the sort that shouldn't be spoken. It's a beastly lop-sided exaggerated truth. We're behaving like a collection of neurotic freaks." Hersey moved to the window. " Look at the snow," she said, " it's heavier than ever. There's a load on the trees, they're beginning to droop their branches. It's creeping up the sides of the house, and up the window-panes. Soon you'll hardly be able to see out of your window, Mr. Man-drake. What are we going to do, shut up in the house together, hating each other? What are we going to do?"

II

At half-past four that afternoon, Nicholas Compline sud-denly announced in a high voice that he must get back to his headquarters at Great Chipping. He sought out Jonathan and with small regard for plausibility informed him that he had received an urgent summons by telephone.

" Strange!" said Jonathan, smiling. " Caper tells me that the telephone is out of commission. The lines are down."

" The order came through some time ago."

" I'm afraid you can't go, Nick. There's a six-foot drift in Deep Bottom at the end of the drive, and it'll be worse up on Cloudyfold."

" I can walk over Cloudyfold to Chipping and get a car there."

" Twelve miles!"

" I can't help that," said Nicholas loudly.

"You'll never do it, Nick. It'll be dark in an hour. I can't allow you to try. It's a soft fall. Perhaps to-morrow, if there's a frost during the night——"

"I'm going, Jonathan. You used to have a pair of Canadian snowshoes, usen't you? May I borrow them? Do you know where they are?"

"I gave them away years ago," said Jonathan blandly.

"Well, I'm going."

Jonathan hurried up to Mandrake's room with this piece of news. Mandrake had dressed and was sitting by his fire. He still felt extremely shaky and bemused, and stared owlishly at Jonathan, who plunged straight into his story.

"He's quite determined, Aubrey. Perhaps I had better remember that after all I didn't give away the snowshoes. And yet, even with snowshoes, he will certainly lose his way in the dark, or smother in a drift. Isn't it too tiresome?" Jonathan seemed to be more genuinely upset by this turn of events than by anything else that had happened since his party assembled. "It will ruin everything," he muttered, and when Mandrake asked him if he meant that the death of Nicholas Compline from exposure would ruin everything, he replied testily: "No, no, his *departure*. The central figure! The whole action centres round him. I couldn't be more disappointed."

"Honestly, Jonathan, I begin to think you are suffering from some terrible form of insanity. The *idée fixe*. People may drown in your ornamental waters or perish in your snowdrifts, and all you can think of is your hell-inspired party." Jonathan hastened to protest, but in a moment or two he was looking wistfully out of the window and declaring that surely even Nicholas could not be so great a fool as to attempt the walk over Cloudyfold in such a storm. As if in answer to this speech there came a tap on the door, and Nicholas himself walked in. He wore his heavy khaki waterproof and carried his cap. He was rather white about the mouth.

"I'm off, Jonathan," he said.

"Nick, my dear fellow—I implore——"

"Orders is orders. There's a war on. Will you let me leave my luggage. I'll collect the car as soon as possible."

"Do I understand," said Mandrake, "that you are walking over Cloudyfold?"

"Needs must."

"Nick, have you considered your mother?"

"I'm not telling my mother I'm going. She's resting. I'll leave a note for her. Good-bye, Mandrake. I'm sorry you had the rôle of my stand-in forced upon you. If it's any satisfaction you may be quite certain that in a very short space of time I shall be just as wet and possibly a good deal colder than you were."

"If you persist, I shall come as far as Deep Bottom with you," said Jonathan wretchedly. "We'll have some of the men with shovels, and so on."

"Please don't bother, Jonathan. Your men can hardly shovel a path all the way over Cloudyfold."

"Now listen to me," said Jonathan. "I've talked to my bailiff, who came in just now, and he tells me that what you propose is out of the question. I told him you were determined, and he's sending two of our men——"

"I'm sorry, Jonathan. I've made up my mind. I'm off. Don't come down. Good-bye."

But before Nicholas got to the door, it burst open and William, scarlet in the face, strode in and confronted his brother.

"What the hell's this nonsense I hear about your going?" he demanded.

"I don't know what you've heard, but I'm going. I've got orders to report at——"

"Orders my foot! You've got the wind up and you're doing a bolt. You're so damn' frightened, you'd rather die in a snow-drift than face the music here. You're not going."

"Unusual solicitude!" Nicholas said, and the lines from his nostrils to the corners of his mouth deepened.

"Don't imagine I care what happens to you," said William, and his voice broke into a higher key. He used the clumsy, vehement gestures of a man who, unaccustomed to violence of speech or action, suddenly finds himself consumed with rage. He presented a painful and embarrassing spectacle. "You could drown yourself and welcome, if it weren't for Mother. D'you want to kill her? You'll stay here and behave yourself, my bloody little Lothario."

"Oh, shut up, you fool," said Nicholas, and made for the door. "No you don't!" William said, and lurched forward. His brother's elbow caught him a jolt in the chest, and the next moment Nicholas had gone.

"William!" said Jonathan sharply. "Stay where you are."

"If anything happens to him, who do you suppose she'll blame for it? For the rest of her life his damned dead sneer will tell her that but for me—— *He's not going.*"

"You can't stop him, you know," said Mandrake.

"*Can't* I! Jonathan, please stand aside."

"Just a moment, William." Jonathan's voice had taken an unaccustomed edge. He stood, an unheroic but somehow rather menacing figure, with his plump fingers on the door-knob and his back against the door. "I cannot have you fighting with your brother up and down my house. He is determined to go and you can't stop him. I am following him to the first drift in the drive. I am quite convinced that he will not get through it, and I do not propose to let him come to any grief. I shall take a couple of men with me. If you can behave yourself you had better accompany us." Jonathan touched his spectacles delicately with his left hand. "Depend upon it," he said, "your brother will not leave Highfold to-night."

III

Mandrake's bedroom windows overlooked the last sweep of the drive as it passed the west wing of Highfold and turned into the wide sweep in front of the house. Through the white-leopard mottling on his window-pane he saw Nicholas Compline, head down, trudge heavily through the snow and out of sight. A few moments later, Jonathan and William appeared, followed at some distance by two men carrying long-handled shovels. "Nicholas must have delayed a little, after he left here," Mandrake thought. "Why? To say good-bye to Madame Lisse? Or to Chloris?" And at the thought of a final interview between Nicholas and Chloris Wynne he experienced an unaccustomed and detestable sensation, as if his heart sank with horrid speed into some unfathomable limbo. He looked after the trudging figures until they passed beyond the range of his window, and then suddenly decided that he could no longer endure his own company but would go downstairs in search of Chloris Wynne.

"The difference," Jonathan observed, "between a walk in an ordinary storm and a walk in a snowstorm is the difference between unpleasant noise and even more unpleasant silence.

One can hear nothing but the squeak of snow under one's feet. I'm glad you decided to come, William."

"It's not for love of dear little Nicholas, I promise you," William muttered.

"Well, well, well," said Jonathan equitably.

They plodded on, walking in Nicholas's steps. Presently Highfold wood enclosed them in a strange twilight where shadow was made negative by reflected whiteness, and where the stems of trees seemed comfortless and forgotten in their naked blackness. Here there was less snow and they mended their pace, following the drive on its twisting course downhill. At first they passed between tall banks and heard the multiple voices of tiny runnels of water, then they came out into open spaces where the snow lay thick over Jonathan's park. It stretched away before their eyes in curves of unbroken pallor and William muttered: "White, grey, and black. I don't think I could paint it." When they entered the lower wood, still going downhill, they saw Nicholas, not far ahead, and Jonathan called to him a shrill "Hallo!" that set up an echo among the frozen trees. Nicholas turned and stood motionless, waiting for them to overtake him. With that air of self-conciousness inseparable from such approaches, they made their way towards him, the two farm-hands still some distance behind.

"My dear Nick," Jonathan panted, "you should have waited a little. I told you I'd see you as far as the first obstacle. See here, I've brought two of the men. They know more about the state of affairs than I do. My head shepherd and his brother. You remember James and Thomas Bewling?"

"Yes, of course," said Nicholas. "Sorry you've both been dragged out on my account."

"If there is a way through Deep Bottom," said Jonathan, "the Bewlings will find it for you. Eh, Thomas?"

The older of the two men touched his cap and moved nearer. "I do believe, sir," he said, "that without us goes at it hammer and tongs with these yurr shovels for an hour or so, they bain't *no* way over Deep Bottom."

"There, you see, Nick. And in an hour or so it'll be dark."

"At least I can try," said Nicholas stiffly.

Jonathan looked helplessly at William, who was watching his brother through half-closed eyes. "Well," said Jonathan on a sudden spurt of temper, "it's beginning to snow quite abominably hard. Shall we go on?"

"Look here," William said, "you go back, Jonathan. I

don't see why you should be in this. Nor you two Bewlings.
Give me your shovel, Thomas."

"I've said I'll go alone, and I'm perfectly ready to do so,"
said Nicholas sulkily.

"Oh damn!" said Jonathan. "Come on."

As they moved off downhill, the snow began to fall even
more heavily.

Deep Bottom was at the foot of a considerable slope beyond
the wood, and was really a miniature ravine extending for some
two miles inside Jonathan's demesnes. It was crossed by the
avenue, which dipped and rose sharply to flatten out on the
far side with a level stretch of some two hundred yards ending
at the entrance gates. As they approached it, the north wind,
from which they had hitherto been protected, drove full in
their faces with a flurry of snow. Thomas Bewling began a
long roaring explanation: "She comes down yurr proper blus-
tracious like, sir. What with being druv by the wind and what
with being piled up be the natural forces of gravitation, like,
she slips and she slides in this yurr bottom till she's so thick as
you'd be surprised to see. Look thurr, sir. You'd tell me there
was nothing but a little tiddly bit of a slant down'ill, but
contrariwise. She's deceptive. She's-a-laying out so smooth
and sleek enough to trap you into trying 'er, but she's deep
enough and soft enough to smother the lot on us. You won't
get round her and you won't make t'other side, Mr. Nicholas,
as well you ought to know, being bred to these parts."

Nicholas looked from one to another of the four faces, and
without a word turned and walked on. Half a dozen strides
brought him up to his knees in snow. He uttered a curious
inarticulate cry and plunged forward. The next second he was
floundering in a drift, spreadeagled and half-buried.

"And over he goes," William observed mildly. "Come on."

He and the two Bewlings joined hands, and by dint of extending the shovel-handle brought Nicholas out of his predica-
ment. He had fallen face first into the drift, and presented a
ridiculous figure. His fine moustache was clotted with snow,
his cap was askew, and his nose was running.

"Quite the little snow-man," said William. "Ups-a-daisy."

Nicholas wiped his face with his gloved hands. It was
blotched with cold. His lips seemed stiff, and he rubbed them
before he spoke.

"Very well," Nicholas whispered at last. "I give up. I'll
come back. But, by God, I tell you both I'd have been safer

crossing Cloudyfold in the dark than spending another night at Highfold."

IV

" Francis," said Madame Lisse, " we may not be alone to- gether again this evening. I cannot endure this ridiculous and uncomfortable state of affairs any longer. Why do Nicholas and William Compline and the Wynne girl all avoid you? Why, when I speak of Mr. Mandrake's accident, do they look at their feet and mumble of other things? Where have they all gone? I have sat by this fire enduring the conversation of Mrs. Compline and the compliments of our host until I am ready to scream, but even that ordeal was preferable to suffer- ing your extraordinary gloom. Where is Nicholas Compline?"

Dr. Hart stood inside the boudoir door, which he had closed behind him. In his face was reflected the twilight of the snow- bound world outside. This strange half-light revealed a slight tic in his upper lip, a tic that suggested an independent life in one of the small muscles of his face. It was as if a moth fluttered under his skin. He raised his hand and pressed a finger on his lip, and over the top of his hand he looked at Madame Lisse.

" Why do you not answer me? Where is Nicholas?"

" Gone."

" Gone? Where?"

Without shifting his gaze from her face, Hart made a move- ment with his head as much as to say: " Out there." Madame Lisse stirred uneasily. " Don't look at me like that," she said. " Come here, Francis."

He came and stood before her with his hands clasped over his waistcoat and his head inclined forward attentively. There was nothing in his pose to suggest anger, but she moved back in her chair almost as if she was afraid he would strike her.

" Ever since we came here," said Hart, " he has taken pains to insult me by his attentions to you. Your heads together, secret jokes, and then a glance at me to make sure I have not missed it. Last night after dinner he deliberately baited me. Well, now he is gone, and immediately I enter the room you, *you* ask for him."

" Must there be another of these scenes? Can you not understand that Nicholas is simply a type? It is as natural to him to pay these little attentions as it is for him to draw breath."

"And as natural for you to receive them? Well, you will not receive them again, perhaps."

"What do you mean?"

"Look out there. It has been snowing all day. In a little while it will be dark and your friend will be on those hills we crossed yesterday. Do not try to seem unconcerned. Your lips are shaking."

"Why has he gone?"

"He is afraid."

"Francis," cried Madame Lisse, "what have you done? Have you threatened him? I see that you have, and that they all know. This is why they are avoiding us. You fool, Francis. When these people go away from here they will lunch and dine on this story. You will be a figure of fun, and what woman will choose to have a pantaloon with a violent temper to operate on her face? And my name, *mine,* will be linked with yours. The Amblington woman will see to it that I look as ridiculous as you."

"Do you love this Compline?"

"I have grown very tired of telling you. I do not."

"And I am tired of hearing your lies. His behaviour is an admission."

"What has he done? What are you trying to suggest?"

"He mistook Mandrake for me. He tried to drown me."

"What nonsense is this! I have heard the account of the accident. Nicholas saw Mr. Mandrake through the pavilion window and recognised him. Nicholas told me that he recognised Mandrake and that Mandrake himself realises that he was recognised."

"Then you have seen Compline. When did you see him?"

"Soon after the affair at the swimming-pool."

"You did not appear until nearly lunch-time. He came to your room. You had forbidden me, and you received him. Is that true? Is it?"

"Cannot you see——" Madame Lisse began, but he silenced her with a vehement gesture and, stooping until his face was close to hers, began to arraign her in a sort of falsetto whisper. She leant away from him, pressing her shoulders and head into the back of her chair. The movement suggested distaste rather than fear, and all the time that he was speaking her eyes looked over his shoulder from the door to the windows. Once she

raised her hand as if to silence him, but he seized her wrist and
held it, and she said nothing.

". . . you said I should see for myself, and, *Lieber Gott*,
have I not seen? I have seen enough, and I tell you this. He
was wise to go when he did. Another night and day of his
insolence would have broken my endurance. It is well for
him that he has gone."

He was staring into her face and saw her eyes widen. He
still had her by the wrist, but with her free hand she pointed
to the window. He turned and looked out.

He was in time to see Jonathan Royal and William Compline trudge past laboriously in the snow. And three yards
behind them, sullen and bedraggled, trailed Nicholas Compline.

V

Hersey Amblington, Mrs. Compline, Chloris Wynne, and
Aubrey Mandrake were in the library. They knew that Dr.
Hart and Madame Lisse were in the boudoir, separated from
them by the small smoking-room. They knew, too, that Jonathan and William had gone with Nicholas on the first stage
of his preposterous journey. Hersey was anxious to have a
private talk with Sandra Compline, Mandrake was anxious to
have a private talk with Chloris Wynne; but neither Mandrake
nor Hersey could summon up the initiative to make a move.
A pall of inertia hung over them all, and they spoke, with an
embarrassing lack of conviction, about Nicholas's summons to
his headquarters in Great Chipping. Mrs. Compline was in
obvious distress, and Hersey kept assuring her that if the road
was unsafe Jonathan would bring Nicholas back. "Jonathan
shouldn't have let him go, Hersey. It was very naughty of him.
I'm extremely displeased with William for letting Nicholas go.
He should never have allowed it."

"William did his best to dissuade him," said Mandrake
dryly.

"He should have come and told me, Mr. Mandrake. He
should have used his authority. He is the elder of my sons."
She turned to Hersey. "It's always been the same. I've always
said that Nicholas should have been the elder."

"I don't agree," said Chloris quickly.

"No," Mrs. Compline said, "I did not suppose you would,"
and Mandrake, who had thought that Mrs. Compline's face

could express nothing but its own distortion, felt a thrill of alarm when he saw her look at Chloris.

"I speak without prejudice," said Chloris, and two spots of colour started up in her cheeks. "William and I have broken off our engagement."

For a moment there was silence, and Mandrake saw that Mrs. Compline had forgotten his existence. She continued to stare at Chloris, and a shadow of a smile, painful and acrid, tugged at her distorted mouth. "I am afraid you are too late," she said.

"I don't understand."

"My son Nicholas——"

"This has nothing whatever to do with Nicholas."

"Hersey," Mrs. Compline said, "I am terribly worried about Nicholas. Surely Jonathan will bring him back. How long have they been gone?"

"*It has nothing whatever to do with Nicholas,*" Chloris said loudly.

Mrs. Compline stood up. "Hersey, I simply cannot sit here any longer. I'm going to see if they're coming."

"You can't, Sandra. It's snowing harder than ever. There's no need to worry, they're all together."

"I'm going out on the drive. I haven't stirred from the house all day. I'm stifled."

Hersey threw up her hands and said: "All right. I'll come with you. I'll get our coats. Wait for me, darling."

"I'll wait in the hall. Thank you, Hersey."

When they had gone, Mandrake said to Chloris: "For God's sake, let's go next door and listen to the news. After this party, the war will come as a mild and pleasurable change."

They moved into the smoking-room. Mrs. Compline crossed the hall and entered the drawing-room, where she stood peering through the windows for her son Nicholas. Hersey Amblington went upstairs. First she got her own raincoat, and then she went to Mrs. Compline's room to fetch hers. She opened the wardrobe doors and stretched out her hand to a heavy tweed coat. For a moment she stood stock-still, her fingers touching the shoulders of the coat.

It was soaking wet.

And through her head ran the echo of Sandra Compline's voice: "I haven't stirred from the house all day."

VI

In the days that followed that week-end Mandrake was to trace interminably the sequence of events that in retrospect seemed to point so unmistakably towards the terrible conclusion. He was to decide that not the least extraordinary of these events had been his own attitude towards Chloris Wynne. Chloris was not Mandrake's type. If, in the midst of threats, mysteries, and mounting terrors, he had to embark upon some form of dalliance, it should surely have been with Madame Lisse. Madame was the sort of woman to whom Aubrey Mandrake almost automatically paid attention. She was dark, sophisticated, and—his own expression—immeasurably *soignée*. She was exactly Aubrey Mandrake's cup of tea. Chloris was not. Aubrey Mandrake was invariably bored by pert blondes. But—and here lay the reason for his curious behaviour—Stanley Footling adored them. At the sight of Chloris's shining, honey-coloured loops of hair and impertinent blue eyes, the old Footling was roused in Mandrake. Bloomsbury died in him and Dulwich stirred ingenuously. He was only too well aware that in himself was being enacted a threadbare theme, a kind of burlesque, hopelessly out of date, on Jekyll and Hyde. It had happened before but never with such violence, and he told himself that there must be something extra special in Chloris so to rouse the offending Footling that Mandrake scarcely resented the experience.

He followed her into the smoking-room and tuned in the wireless to the war news, which in those almost forgotten days largely consisted of a series of French assurances that there was nothing to report. Chloris and Mandrake listened for a little while, and then he switched off the radio, leant forward and kissed her.

"Ah!" said Chloris. "The indoor sport idea, I see."

"Are you in love with Nicholas Compline?"

"I might say: 'What the hell's that got to do with you?'"

"Abstract curiosity."

"With rather un-abstract accompaniments."

"When I first saw you I thought you were a little nitwit." Chloris knelt on the hearthrug and poked the fire. "So I am," she said, "when it comes to your sort of language. I'm quite smartish, but I'm not at all clever. I put up a bluff, but you'd despise me no end if you knew me better."

She smiled at him. He felt his mouth go dry, and with a sensation of blank panic he heard his own voice, distorted by embarrassment, utter the terrible phrase.

" My real name," said Mandrake, " is Stanley Footling."

" Oh, my dear, I'm so sorry," said Chloris. He knew that for a moment, when she recovered from her astonishment, she had nearly laughed.

" *Stanley Footling,*" he repeated, separating the detestable syllables as if each was an offence against decency.

" Sickening for you. But, after all, you've changed it, haven't you?"

" I've never told any one else. In a squalid sort of way it's a compliment."

" Thank you. But lots of people must know, all the same."

" No. All my friendships occurred after I changed it. I got a hideous fright last night at dinner."

Chloris looked up quickly. " Why, I remember! I noticed. You went all sort of haywire for a moment. It was something Nicholas said, something about——"

" My having given up footling."

" Oh Lord!" said Chloris.

" Go on—laugh. It's screamingly funny, isn't it?"

" Well it *is* rather funny," Chloris agreed. " But it's easily seen that you don't get much of a laugh out of it. I can't quite understand why. There are plenty of names just as funny as Footling."

" I'll tell you why. I can't brazen it out because it's got no background. If we were the Footlings of Fifeshire, or even the Footlings of Furniture Polish, I might stomach it. I'm a miserable snob. Even as I speak to you I'm horrified to hear how I give myself away by the very content of what I'm saying. I'm committing the only really unforgivable offence. I'm being embarrassing."

" It seems to me you've merely gone Edwardian. You're all out of focus. You say you're a snob. All right. So are we all in our degree, they say."

" But don't you see it's the *degree* I'm so ashamed of. Intellectual snob I may be; but I don't care if I am. But to develop a really bad social inferiority complex—it's so degrading."

" It seems a bit silly, certainly. And, anyway, I don't see, accepting your snobbery, what you've got to worry about. If it's smartness you're after, isn't it smart to be obscure nowadays? Look at the prizefighters. Everybody's bosoms with them."

"That's from *your* point of view. *De haut en bas.* I want to be the *haut*, not the *bas*," Mandrake mumbled.

"Well, intellectually you are." Chloris shifted her position and faced him squarely, looking up, her pale hair taking a richness from the fire "I say," she said, "Mr. Royal knows all about it, doesn't he? About your name?"

"No. *Why?*"

"Well, I thought last night . . . I mean after Nicholas dropped that brick, I sort of felt there was something funny and I noticed that he and Lady Hersey and Mr. Royal looked at each other."

"By God, he put them up to it! I wondered at the time. By God, if he did that, I'll pay him for it!"

"For the love of Heaven, why did I go and say that! I thought you and I were going to remain moderately normal. Nobody else is. Do snap out of being all Freudian over Footling. Who cares if you're called Footling? And, anyway, I must say I think 'Aubrey Mandrake' is a bit thick. Let's talk about something else."

The invitation was not immediately accepted, and in the silence that followed they heard Hersey Amblington come downstairs into the hall and call Mrs. Compline:

"Sandra! Where are you? Sandra!" They heard an answering voice, and in a moment or two the front doors slammed.

Mandrake limped about the room inwardly cursing Jonathan Royal, Chloris Wynne, and himself. Most of all, himself. Why had he given himself away to this girl who did not even trouble to simulate sympathy, who did not find even so much as a pleasing tang of irony in his absurd story, who felt merely a vague and passing interest, a faint insensitive amusement? He realised abruptly that it was because she made so little of it that he wanted to tell her. An attitude of sympathetic understanding would have aggravated his own morbid speculations. She had made little of his ridiculous obsession, and for the first time in his life, quite suddenly, he saw it as a needless emotional extravaganza.

"You're perfectly right, of course," he said. "Let's talk about something else."

"You needn't think I'll shrink from you on account of your name, and I won't tell any one else."

"Not even Nicholas Compline?"

"Certainly not Nicholas Compline. At the moment I never want to see a Compline again. You needn't think you're the only one to feel sick at yourself. What about me and the Complines? Getting engaged to William on the rebound from Nicholas."

"And continuing to fall for Nicholas's line of stuff?"

"Yes. All right! I'll admit it. Up to an hour ago I knew Nicholas was faithless, horrid-idle, a philanderer, a he-flirt— all those things, and not many brains into the bargain. But, as you say, I fell for his line of stuff. Why? I don't know. Haven't you ever fallen for a little bit of stuff? Of course you have. But when *we* do it, you hold up your hands and marvel."

Through Mandrake's mind floated the thought that not so long ago he had considered himself in much the same light as regards Chloris. He began to feel ashamed of himself.

"What *does* attract one to somebody like Nicholas?" Chloris continued. "I don't know. He's got 'It,' as they say. Something in his physical make-up. And yet I've often gone all prickly and irritated over his physical tricks. He does silly things with his hands and he's got a tiresome laugh. His idea of what's funny is too drearily all on one subject. He's a bit of a cat, too, and bone from the eyes up if you try to talk about anything that's not quite in his language. And yet one more or less went through one's paces for him; played up to his barn-door antics. Why?"

"Until an hour ago, you said."

"Yes. I met him in the hall when he was going. He was in a blue funk. That tore it. I suppose the barn-door hero loses his grip when he loses his nerve. Anyway, I'm cured of Nicholas."

"Good."

"You know, I'm quite certain that Dr. Hart *did* think you were Nicholas and shoved you in the pond. I think Nicholas was right about that. We ought to be making no end of a hullabaloo, staying in the same house with a would-be murderer, and all we do is let down our back hair and talk about our own complexes. I suppose it'll be like that in the air-raids."

"Nicholas was making a hullabaloo, anyway."

"Yes. I'm afraid he's a complete coward. If he'd brazened it out and stayed, I dare say I shouldn't have been cured, but he scuttled away and that wrecked it. I wonder if The Lisse feels the same."

"Pool Nicholas," said Mandrake. "But I'm glad he didn't stay."

"What's that?"

Chloris scrambled to her feet. She and Mandrake stood stock-still gaping at each other. The hall was noisy with voices, Mrs. Compline scolding, Jonathan explaining, Hersey Amblington asking questions. It went on for some seconds, and then Mandrake limped to the door and threw it open.

Outside in the hall was a group of five—Jonathan, Mrs. Compline, Hersey, William, and, standing apart, bedraggled, patched with snow, white-faced and furtive, Nicholas. Mandrake turned and stared at Chloris.

"So now, what?" he asked.

CHAPTER VII

BOOBY-TRAP

I

WITH the return of Nicholas the house-party entered upon a new phase. From then onwards little attempt was made by anybody to pretend there was nothing wrong with Jonathan Royal's week-end. Jonathan himself, after a half-hearted effort to treat the episode as a mere inconvenient delay, fluttered his hands, surveyed the apprehensive faces of his guests, and watched them break away into small groups. Nicholas muttered something about a bath and change, and followed his mother upstairs. Dr. Hart and Madame Lisse, who had come out of the boudoir on the arrival of the outdoors party, returned to it. Mandrake and Chloris returned to the smoking-room. The others trailed upstairs to change.

Darkness came with no abatement of the storm. A belated pilot of the Coastal Command, who had flown off his map, battled over Cloudyfold through a driving misery of snow, and for a fraction of time passed through the smoke from Jonathan's chimneys. Peering down, he discerned the vague shapes of roofs, and pictured the warmth and joviality of some cheerful week-end party. Just about cocktail time, he thought, and was gone over the rim of Cloudyfold.

It was cocktail time down in Highfold. Jonathan ordered

the drinks to be served in the drawing-room. Mandrake joined him there. He was filled with a strange lassitude, the carry-over, he supposed, from half-drowning. His thoughts clouded and cleared alternately. He was glad of the cocktail Jonathan brought him.

"After all," Jonathan said as they waited, "we've got to meet at dinner, so we may as well assemble here. What am I to do with them, Aubrey?"

"If you can prevent them from getting at each other's throats, you will have worked wonders. Jonathan, I insist on your telling me. Who do you suppose tried to drown me, and who do you suppose they thought I was?"

"It's an interesting point. I must confess, Aubrey, that I am now persuaded that an attack *was* made."

"Thank you. If you had felt——"

"I know, I know. I agree that you could not have been mistaken. I also agree that whoever made the attempt believed it to be made upon someone other than yourself. Now let us, perfectly cold-bloodedly, examine the possibilities. You wore a cloak, and for this reason might have been taken for Nicholas, for Hart, or for myself. If you were mistaken for Nicholas then we must suppose that the assailant was Hart, who resents his attentions to Madame Lisse, and who had threatened him; or William, who resents his attentions to Miss Chloris; or possibly Miss Chloris herself, whose feelings for Nicholas——"

"Don't be preposterous!"

"Eh? Ah, well, I don't press it. If you were mistaken for Hart, then, as far as motive goes, the assailant might have been Nick himself——"

"Nicholas knew Hart was indoors. He saw him looking out of the bedroom window."

"He might have supposed Hart had hurried down by the shorter route."

"But I swear Nicholas recognised me through the pavilion window, and, over and above all that, he knew I had the cloak."

"I agree that Nicholas is unlikely. I am examining motive only. Who else had motive, supposing you were thought to be Hart?"

"Madame Lisse?"

"There we cannot tell. What are their relations? Could Madame have risen from her bed and picked her way down to the pavilion without being seen by anybody? And why, after all should she do so? She, at least, could not have known any one was going down, singly or otherwise."

" She might have seen me from her window."

" In which case she would have realised that you were yourself, and not Hart. No, I think we may dismiss Madame as a suspect. There remains Sandra Compline."

" Good God, why Mrs. Compline?"

Jonathan blinked and uttered an apologetic titter. " A little point which I could not expect you to appreciate. My housekeeper, the excellent Pouting, is a sworn crony of Sandra's maid. It seems that when Hart first arrived in our part of the world, this maid, who was with Sandra at the time of the catastrophe in Vienna, thought she recognised him. She said nothing to her mistress, but she confided her news to Pouting. And I, in my turn, did a little gleaning. The Viennese surgeon was a Doktor Franz Hartz, I learnt, and I knew that Hart, when he changed his nationality, also changed his name. The temptation was too great for me, Aubrey. I brought them together."

" It was a poisonous thing to do."

" You think so? Perhaps you are right. I am quite ashamed of myself," said Jonathan, touching his spectacles.

" There's one thing I'd rather like to hear from you, Jonathan. How did you find out my name was Stanley Footling?" Mandrake watched his host and saw him give a little inward start.

" My dear fellow!" Jonathan murmured.

" It's only a point of curiosity. I should be amused to know."

A pink flush mounted from Jonathan's chin up into his bald pate. " I really forget. It was so long ago. In the early days of our delightful association. Somebody connected with your theatre. I quite forget."

" Ah, yes," said Mandrake. " And is Lady Hersey in the joke?"

" No. No, I assure you. Word of honour."

" What about Nicholas Compline? He knows. You've told him."

" Well, I—I—really, Aubrey—I——"

" You put him up to saying what he did at dinner."

" But without any intention of hurting you, Aubrey. I had no idea your secret——"

" You asked me the other night what sort of man I considered you to be. I didn't know then, and I'm damned if I know now."

The light flickered on Jonathan's spectacles. " In a sense," he said, " you might call me an unqualified practitioner."

" Of what?"

" The fashionable pursuit, my dear Aubrey. Psychology."

II

Madame Lisse dressed early that evening, and got rid of the maid Mrs. Pouting had sent to help her. She sat by her fire listening intently. She heard a delicate sound as if someone tapped with his fingernails at her door. She turned her head quickly but did not rise. The door opened and Nicholas Compline came in.

" Nicholas! Are you certain——?"

" Quite certain. He's in his bath. I listened outside the door."

He stooped swiftly and kissed her. " I had to see you," he said.

" What has happened? He's furious."

" You needn't tell me that. I suppose you realise that he tried to kill me this morning. They won't listen to me. Elise, I can't put up with this any longer. Why can't we——?"

" You know very well. I cannot risk it. A scandal would ruin me. He would make scenes. God knows what he would not do. You should have gone away."

" Damn it, I did my best! Did you want me to do myself in? I tell you I *couldn't* get away. I assure you I don't enjoy the prospect of another attack."

" Quiet! Are you mad, to make such a noise? What is the matter with you? You've had too much to drink."

" I came in half-dead with cold," he said. " Do you suppose he'll have another go at me? Pleasant, isn't it, waiting?"

She looked at him attentively.

" I cannot believe he would go to such lengths, and yet one can find no other explanation. You must be careful, Nicholas. Devote yourself again to the Wynne child. You deliberately baited Francis by your behaviour. I warned you. You should have refused the invitation; it was madness to come here."

" I wanted to see you. God, Elise, you seem to forget that I love you."

"I do not forget. But we must be careful."

"Careful! Listen here. For the last time, will you make a clean break? We could meet in London. You could write and——"

"I have told you, Nicholas. It is impossible. How could I continue my work? And when this war ends, my friend, what then? How should we live?"

"I could find something——" He broke off and looked fixedly at her. "You're very mercenary, Elise, aren't you?"

"All my life I have had to fight. I have known the sort of poverty that you have never dreamed of. I will not endure such poverty again, no, nor anything approaching it. Why can you not be content? I love you. I give you a great deal, do I not?"

He stooped down to her, and behind them on the far wall their fire-shadows joined and moved only with the movement of the fire itself. From this embrace Nicholas was the first to draw back. His shadow started from hers, and in the silence of the room his whisper sounded vehemently:

"*What's that?*"

"*What do you mean?*"

"*Ssh!*"

He stepped back quickly towards a screen near her bed. It was the serio-comic movement of a surprised lover in some Restoration play, and it made a foolish figure of Nicholas. Madame Lisse looked at him, and in response to his gesture moved to the door, where she stood listening, her eyes on Nicholas. After a moment she motioned him to stand farther aside, and with a shamefaced look he slipped behind the screen. The door was opened and closed again, and her voice recalled him.

"There is nobody."

"I swear I heard somebody at that door," Nicholas whispered.

"There is nobody there. You had better go."

He crossed to the door and paused, staring at her, half hang-dog, half-glowering. Nicholas did not cut a brave figure at that moment, but Madame Lisse joined her hands behind his neck and drew his face down to hers. There was an urgency, a certain rich possessiveness in her gesture.

"Be careful," she whispered. "Do go, now."

"At least *you* believe he means trouble. *You* know it's he that's at the back of this."

" Yes."

" I feel as if he's behind every damn door in the place. It's a filthy feeling."

" You must go."

He looked full in her face, and a moment later slipped through the door and was gone.

Madame Lisse seemed to hesitate for a moment and then she too went to the door. She opened it a very little and looked through the crack after Nicholas. Suddenly she flung the door wide open and screamed. Immediately afterwards came the sound of a thud, a thud so heavy that she felt its vibration and heard a little glass tree on her mantelpiece set up a faint tinkling. And a second later she heard the shocking sound of a man screaming. It was Nicholas.

III

Mandrake and Jonathan heard the thud. The drawing-room chandelier set up a little chime, and immediately afterwards, muffled and far away, came the sound of a falsetto scream. With no more preface than a startled exclamation, Jonathan ran from the room. Mandrake, swinging his heavy boot, followed at a painful shamble. As he toiled up the stairs, the quick thump of his heart reminded him of his nocturnal prowl. He reached the guest-wing passage and saw, half-way down it, the assembled house-party, some in dressing-gowns, some in evening clothes. They were gathered in Nicholas's doorway; William, Chloris, Dr. Hart, Madame Lisse, and Hersey Amblington. From inside the room came the sound of Mrs. Compline's voice, agitated and emphatic, punctuated by little ejaculations from Jonathan, and violent interjections from Nicholas himself. As he came to the doorway, Mandrake was dimly aware of some difference in the appearance of the passage. Without pausing to analyse this sensation he joined the group in the doorway. William, who was scarlet in the face, grabbed his arm. " By gum!" said William, " it's true after all. Somebody's after Nick, and, by gum, they've nearly got him."

" Bill, *don't*!" cried Chloris, and Hersey said fiercely: " Shut up, William."

" No, but isn't it extraordinary, Mandrake? He didn't want to come back, you know. He said . . ."

" What's happened?"

" Look."

William stepped aside and Mandrake saw into the room.

Nicholas sat in an arm-chair nursing his left arm. He was
deadly pale, and kept turning his head to look first at Jonathan
and then at his mother who knelt beside him. Between this
group and the door, lying on its back on the carpet and leering
blandly at the ceiling, was an obese brass figure, and when
Mandrake saw it he knew what it was he had missed from the
passage. It was the Buddha that had watched him from its
niche when he stole downstairs in the night.

" . . . it all seemed to happen at once," Nicholas was saying
shakily. " I went to push open the door—it wasn't quite shut
—and it felt as if someone were resisting me on the other side.
I gave it a harder shove and it opened so quickly that I sort of
jumped back. I suppose that saved me, because at the same
time I felt a hell of a great thud on my arm, and Elise
screamed."

From down the passage, Madame Lisse said: " I saw something fall from the door and I screamed out to him."

" A booby-trap," said William. " It was a booby-trap, Mandrake. Balanced on the top of the door. We used to do it with
buckets of water when we were kids. It *would* have killed him,
you know. Only, of course, its dead weight dragged on the
door, and when it overbalanced the door shot open. That's
what made him jump back."

" His arm's broken," said Mrs. Compline. " Darling, your
arm's broken."

" I don't think so. It was a glancing blow. It's damn' sore,
but, by God, it might have been my head. Well, Jonathan,
what have you to say? Was I right to try and clear out?"
Nicholas raised his uninjured arm and pointed to the crowded
doorway. " One of them's saying to himself: ' Third time
lucky.' Do you realise that, Jonathan?"

Jonathan said something that sounded like " God forbid."
Mrs. Compline began again:

" Let me look at your arm, darling. Nicky, my dear, let me
see it."

" I can't move it. Look out, Mother, that hurts."

" Perhaps you would like me . . ." Dr. Hart came through
the door and advanced upon Nicholas.

" No, thank you, Hart," said Nicholas. " You've done
enough. Keep off."

Dr. Hart stopped short, and then, as though growing slowly conscious of the silence that had fallen upon his fellow-guests, he turned and looked from one face to another. When he spoke it was so softly that only a certain increase in foreign inflexions in the level stressing of his words, gave any hint of his agitation.

"This has become too much," he said. "Is it not enough that I should be insulted, that Mr. Compline should insult me, I say, from the time that I arrived in this house? Is that not enough to bear without this last, this fantastic accusation? I know well what you have been saying against me. You have whispered among yourselves that it was I who attacked Mr. Mandrake thinking he was Compline, I who goaded by open enmity as well as by secret antagonism, have plotted to injure, to murder Compline. I tell you now that I am not guilty of these outrages. If, as Compline suggests, anything further is attempted against him, it will not be by my agency. That I am his enemy I do not deny, but I tell him now that somewhere amongst us he has another and a more deadly enemy. Let him remember this." He glanced at Nicholas's injured arm. Nicholas made a quick movement. "I do not think your arm is fractured," said Dr. Hart. "You had better let someone look at it. If the skin is broken it will need a dressing, and perhaps a sling. Mrs. Compline will be able to attend to it, I think." He walked out of the room.

Mrs. Compline drew back the sleeve of Nicholas's dressing-gown. His forearm was swollen and discoloured. A sort of blind gash ran laterally across its upper surface. He turned his hand from side to side, wincing at the pain. "Well," said William, "it seems he's right about that, Nick. It can't be broken."

"It's bloody sore, Bill," said Nicholas, and Mandrake was astounded to see an almost friendly glance pass between these extraordinary brothers.

William came forward and stooped down, looking at the arm. "We could do with a first-aid kit," he said, and Jonathan bustled away muttering that Mrs. Pouting was fully equipped.

"It's Hart all right," said William. He turned to contemplate Madame Lisse, who still waited with Chloris and Mandrake in the passage. "Yes," William repeated with an air of thoughtfulness, "it's Hart. I think he's probably mad, you know."

"William," said his mother, "what are you saying? You

have been keeping something from me, both of you. *What do you know about this man?*"

"It doesn't matter, Mother," said Nicholas impatiently.

"It does matter. I *will* know. What have you found out about him?"

"Sandra," cried Hersey Amblington, "don't. It's not that. Don't, Sandra."

"Nicky, my dear! You know! You've guessed." Mrs. Compline's eyes seemed to Mandrake to be living fires in her dead face. She, like Nicholas, looked at Madame Lisse. "I *see*," she said. "You know too. You've told my son. Then it is true."

"I don't know what you're talking about, Mother," said Nicholas querulously.

"Nor I," said Madame Lisse, and her voice was shriller than Mandrake could have imagined it. "This is ridiculous. I have said nothing."

"Hersey," said Mrs. Compline, "do you see what has happened?" She put her arms round Nicholas's neck and her hand, with agonised possessiveness, caressed his shoulder. "Nicky has found out and threatened to expose him. He has tried to kill Nicholas."

"Look here," William demanded, "what *is* all this?"

"It's a complete and miserable muddle," said Hersey sharply, "and it's certainly not for publication. Mr. Mandrake, do you mind . . .?"

Mandrake muttered: "Of course," turned away, and shut the door, leaving himself, Chloris Wynne, and Madame Lisse alone in the passage.

"This woman is evidently insane," said Madame Lisse. "What mystery is this she is making? What am I supposed to have told Nicholas Compline?"

Mandrake, conscious of a violent and illogical distaste for Madame Lisse, said loudly: "Mrs. Compline thinks you have told her son that Dr. Hart is the surgeon who operated on her face."

He heard Chloris catch her breath, and whisper: "No, no, it's impossible. It's too fantastic." He heard his own voice trying to explain that Jonathan was responsible. He was conscious in himself of a sort of affinity with Mrs. Compline, an affinity born of disfigurement. He wanted to explain to Chloris that there was nothing in the world as bad as a hideous deformity. Through this confusion of emotions and thought he was aware of Madame Lisse watching him very closely, of the closed door at his back, of the murmur of Mrs. Compline's voice beyond it in Nicholas's room where, Mandrake supposed, her sons listened to the story of Dr. Franz Hartz of Vienna. The truth is, Mandrake was suffering from a crisis of nerves. His experience of the morning, his confession to Chloris, the sense of impending disaster that like some grotesque in a dream, half-comic, half-menacing, seemed to advance upon Nicholas; all these circumstances had scraped at his nerves and wrought upon his imagination. When Jonathan came hurrying along the passage with a first-aid outfit in his hands, Mandrake saw him as a shifty fellow, as cold-blooded as a carp. When Madame Lisse began to protest that she knew nothing of Dr. Hart's past, that Mrs. Compline was insane, that she herself could endure no longer to be shut up at Highfold, Mandrake was conscious only of a sort of wonder that this cool woman should suddenly become agitated. He felt Chloris take him by the elbow and heard her say: " Let's go downstairs." He was steadied by her touch, and eager to obey it. Before they moved away, the door opened and William came stumbling out, followed by Jonathan.

" Wait a bit, Bill," Jonathan cried. " *Wait* a bit."

" The bloody swine," William said. " Oh, God, the bloody swine." He went blindly past them and they heard him run downstairs. Jonathan remained in the doorway. Beyond him, Mandrake saw Hersey Amblington with her arms about Mrs. Compline, who was sobbing. Nicholas, very pale, stood, looking on.

" It's *most* unfortunate," Jonathan said. He shut the door delicately. " Poor Sandra has convinced William that there has been a conspiracy against her. That Hart has made a story of the catastrophe for Madame Lisse, that—oh, you're there, Madame. Forgive me; I hadn't noticed. It's all *too* distressing, Aubrey. Now William's in a frightful tantrum and won't listen to reason. Nicholas assures us he knew nothing of the past but he might as well speak to the wind. We're in the very devil of a mess. It's snowing harder than ever, and what in heaven's name am I to do?"

A loud and ominous booming sound welled up through the house. Caper, finding no one to whom he could announce dinner, had fallen upon an enormous gong and beaten it. Jonathan uttered a mad little giggle.

" Well," he said, " shall we dine?"

IV

The memory of that night's dinner party was to be a strange one for Mandrake. It was to have the intermittent vividness and the unreality of a dream. Certain incidents he would never forget, others were lost the next day. At times his faculty of observation seemed abnormally acute and he observed exactly, inflexions of voices, precise choice of words, details of posture. At other times he was lost in a sensation of anxiety, an intolerable anticipation of calamity, and at these moments he was blind and deaf to his surroundings.

Only six of the party appeared for dinner. Madame Lisse, Mrs. Compline, and Dr. Hart had all excused themselves. Dr. Hart was understood to be in the boudoir where he had gone after his speech in his own defence, and where, apparently at Jonathan's suggestion, he was to remain during his waking hours, for the rest of his stay at Highfold. Mandrake wondered when Jonathan had told the servants. The party at dinner was therefore composed of the less antagonistic elements. Even William's and Chloris's broken engagement seemed a minor dissonance, quite overshadowed by the growing uneasiness of the guests. Nicholas, Mandrake decided, was now in a state of barely suppressed nerves. His injured arm was not in a sling but evidently gave him a good deal of pain, and he made a clumsy business of cutting up his food, finally allowing Hersey Amblington to help him. He had come down with Hersey, and something in their manner suggested that this arrangement was not accidental. " And really," Mandrake thought, " it would be better not to leave Nicholas alone. Nothing can happen to him if somebody is always at his side." Mandrake was now positive that it was Hart who had made the attacks upon Nicholas and himself, and he found that the others shared this view and discussed it openly. His clearest recollection of the dinner party was to be of a moment when William, who had been silent until now, leant forward, his hands gripping the edge of the table, and said: " What's the law about attempted murder?" Jonathan glanced nervously at the servants, and Mandrake saw Hersey Amblington nudge William. " Oh, damn." William muttered, and was silent again. As soon as they were alone, he returned to the attack. He was extraordinarily inarticulate and blundered about from one accusation to another, returning always to the ruin of his

mother's beauty. "The man who did that would do anything,"
seemed to be the burden of his song. "The Œdipus complex
with a vengeance," thought Mandrake, but he was still too
bemused and shaken to crystallise his attention upon William,
and listened through a haze of weary lassitude. It was useless
for Nicholas to say that he had never heard the name of his
mother's plastic surgeon. "Hart must have thought you
knew," William said. "He thought that Mother had told you."

"Rot, Bill," said Nicholas. "You're barking up the wrong
tree. *It's because of Elise Lisse*. The fellow's off his head with
jealousy."

"I'm older than you," William roared out with startling
irrelevancy. "I remember what she was like. She was beautiful. I remember the day she came back. We went to the
station to meet her. She had a veil on, a thick veil. And when
I kissed her she didn't lift it up and I felt her face through
the veil and it was stiff."

"Don't, Bill," Hersey said.

"You heard what she said—what mother herself said. She
said up there in your room: 'Nicky's found out. He's afraid
Nicky will expose him.' God, *I'll* expose him. He's gone to
earth, has he! I'm damn' well going to lug him out and——"

"William!" Jonathan's voice exploded sharply, and Mandrake roused himself to listen. "William, you will be good
enough to pull yourself together. Whether you choose to do
your mother an appalling wrong by reviving for public discussion a tragedy that is twenty years old, is your affair. I do
not attempt to advise you. But this is my house and I am very
much your senior. I must ask you to attend to me."

He paused, but William said nothing, and after a moment
Jonathan cleared his throat and touched his spectacles. Mandrake thought dimly: "Good heavens, he's going to make
another of his speeches."

"Until this evening," Jonathan said, "I refused to believe
that among my guests there could be one—ah—individual who
had planned, who still plans, a murderous assault upon a
fellow-guest. I argued that the catastrophe at the swimming
pool was the result of a mischievous, rather than a malicious
attack. I even imagined that it was possible poor Aubrey had
been mistaken for myself." Here Jonathan blinked behind his
spectacles and the trace of a smirk appeared on his lips. He
smoothed it away with his plump hand and went on very
gravely. "This second attempt upon Nicholas has convinced

me. If that idol, which I may say I have always rather disliked, had fallen, as without a shadow of doubt it was intended to fall, upon his head, it would have killed him. There is no doubt at all, my dear Nick, it would have killed you."

"Thank you, Jonathan," said Nicholas with a kind of sneer, "I think I realise that."

"Well, now, you know," Jonathan continued, "this sort of thing is pretty bad. It's preposterous. It's like some damn' pinchbeck story-book."

"Jo," Hersey Amblington interjected suddenly, "you really can't keep us all waiting while you grizzle about the aesthetic poverty of your own show. We're all agreed it's a rotten show, but at least it has the makings of a tragedy. What are you getting at? Do you think Dr. Hart's out for Nick's blood?"

"I am forced to come to that conclusion," said Jonathan primly. "Who else are we to suspect? Not one of ourselves, surely. I am not breaking confidence, I hope, Nick, when I say that Hart has threatened you, and threatened you repeatedly.

"We've heard all about that," Hersey grunted.

"Ah—yes. So I supposed. Well, now, I am a devotee of crime fiction. I have even dabbled in quite solemn works on the detection of crime. I don't pretend to the smallest degree of proficiency, but I *have* ventured to carry out a little investigation. Nicholas tells me that ten minutes before he so nearly became the victim of that atrocious booby-trap, he left his room and—ah—visited that of Madame Lisse."

"Oh Lord!" Hersey muttered, and Mandrake thought he heard Chloris utter a small contemptuous sound.

"This was, of course, a reckless and foolish proceeding," said Jonathan. "However, it has this merit—it frees Madame Lisse from any imputation of guilt. Because Nick, when he left his room, opened and shut the door with impunity, and was talking to Madame Lisse until he returned to sustain the injury to his arm. Nick tells me he heard the clock on the landing strike the half-hour as he walked down the passage to Madame's room. I had glanced at the drawing-room clock not more than a minute before the crash, and it was twenty to eight. The two clocks are exactly synchronised. As the trap could not have been set until after Nick left his room, that gives us ten minutes for our field of inquiry. Now, at the time of the accident, Aubrey and I were both in the drawing-room. I found him there when I came down, and actually heard him go downstairs some little time before that. I am therefore able to provide Aubrey with an alibi, and I hope he will vouch for me. Now, can any of you do as much for each other?"

"I can for Sandra," said Hersey, "and I imagine she can for me. I was in her room talking to her when Nick yelled, and I'm sure I'd been there longer than ten minutes. I remember quite well that when I passed Nick's door it was half open and the light on. I saw him beyond the door in his room, and called out something."

"I remember that," said Nicholas. "I left the room a very short time afterwards."

"So there was no Buddha on the top of the door *then*," said Jonathan. "I am persuaded that apart from Nick having gone out in safety, proving that the trap was laid later than this, we might rest assured that if the room light was on the trap had not been set. One would be almost certain to see the dark shape on the top of the door if the light was on. I have found out, by dint of cautious inquiries, that there were no servants upstairs at that time. It appears that those members of my staff who were not with Caper in the dining-room were listening to the wireless in the servants' hall. Now, you see, I have done quite well, haven't I, with my amateur detection? Let me see. We have found alibis for Sandra, Hersey, Madame Lisse, Aubrey, and, I hope, myself. What do you think, Aubrey?"

"Eh? Oh, I think it was more than ten minutes before the thud that you came downstairs," Mandrake said.

"Well, now, Miss Chloris," said Jonathan, with a little bend in her direction, "what about you?"

"When it happened I was in my room. I'd had a bath and was dressing. I don't think I can prove I didn't go out of my room before that. But I didn't leave it after I went upstairs except to go into the bathroom next door. When I heard the crash and Nicholas cried out, I put on my dressing-gown and ran into the passage."

Mandrake was roused by a sharp sensation of panic. "What does that thing weigh?" he asked. "The Buddha thing?"

"It's heavy," said Jonathan. "It's solid brass. About twenty pounds, I should say."

"Do you think Miss Wynne could raise an object weighing twenty pounds above her head, and balance it on the top of a door?"

"Nobody's going to worry about whether she could or couldn't," said Nicholas impatiently. "She didn't."

"Quite so," said Mandrake.

"Well," said Chloris mildly, "that's true enough."

"Nobody's asked me for my alibi," said William. "I think it's rather feeble, all this, because, I mean, we know that Hart did it."

"But the point is——" Jonathan began.

"I was in the smoking-room," said William ruthlessly, "listening to the wireless. I suddenly realised I was a bit late and started to go upstairs. I was just about up when Nick let out that screech. I heard you come down, Jonathan, about ten minutes earlier. You spoke to Caper in the hall about drinks at dinner, and I heard you. But that proves nothing, of course. Oh, wait a bit, though. I could tell you what the news was. There's been a reconnaissance flight over . . ."

"Oh, what the hell's it matter?" said Nicholas. "What's the good of talking like little detective fans? I'm sorry to be rude, but while you're all trying to bail each other out, our charming beauty specialist is probably thinking up a new death-trap on the third-time-lucky principle."

"But to try anything else, when he knows perfectly well we suspect him!" Hersey exclaimed. "It'd be the action of a madman."

"He is a madman," said Nicholas.

"I say," said William. "Has anybody done anything about that Buddha? I mean, it's probably smothered in his finger-prints. If we're going to give him in charge . . ."

"But are we going to give him in charge?" asked Hersey uneasily.

"I will," said William. "If Nick doesn't, I will."

"I don't think you can. It's not your business."

"Why not?" William demanded.

Jonathan cut in hurriedly, asking William if he proposed to make his mother's tragedy front-page publicity. The conversation became fantastic. William showed a tendency to shout and Nicholas to sulk. Chloris turned upon Mandrake a face so eloquent of misery and alarm that he instantly took her hand and found more reality in the touch of her fingers, moving restlessly in his grasp, than in anything else that was happening. Jonathan began to explain that he had locked the

Buddha away in his room. He reminded them of the nature of the trap. When Nicholas returned to his room he found the door not quite closed. The room was in darkness as he had left it. He pushed at the door with his left hand. The door resisted him and then gave way suddenly. At the same instant his arm was struck and Madame Lisse screamed. He cried out and stumbled into the room.

Nicholas irritably confirmed this description, and cut in to say he had seen Dr. Hart go into the bathroom adjoining his room and had heard him turn on the taps. " Of course he simply dodged out when he knew I had gone. He was spying on me, I suppose, through the crack of the door. His room's only about fourteen feet away from mine on the opposite side of the passage."

Mandrake, nervously tightening his grip on Chloris's hand, thought with a sort of unreal precision of the guest wing. Mrs. Compline in the front corner room, then Madame Lisse, a cupboard, and Mandrake himself, all in a row, with a bathroom; then William, and then Hart in the corner room at the back, and another bathroom round the corner. Hersey Amblington in the converted nursery beyond. On the other side of the passage, overlooking the central court round which the old Jacobean house was built, were Nicholas's room, opposite William's, and then a bathroom, and an unoccupied room. Nicholas's was diagonally opposed to Hart's. Hart could easily have spied on Nicholas, and Mandrake pictured him turning on the bath taps and then perhaps opening the door to return to his room for something and seeing Nicholas stealing down the passage towards Madame Lisse's door. He pictured Hart as the traditional figure of the suspicious lover, his compact paunch curving above the girdle of his dressing-gown. " He clutched a sponge-bag to his breast and his eye was glued to the crevice," Mandrake decided. Perhaps he saw Nicholas tap discreetly at Madame Lisse's door, or scratch with his finger-nail. Perhaps Nicholas slipped in without ceremony. " And then, what?" Mandrake wondered. A quick sprint down the passage to the niche? A lop-sided shuffle back to Nicholas's room? Did Dr. Hart carry the Buddha under the folds of his dressing-gown? Did he turn on the light in Nicholas's room and climb on the chair? Was his somewhat remarkable face distorted with fury as he performed these curious exercises? No. Try as he might, Mandrake could not picture Hart and the Buddha without investing the whole affair with an improper air of *opéra bouffe*.

He was roused from his reverie by Chloris withdrawing her hand, and by William saying in a loud voice: " You know, this is exactly like a thriller, except for one thing."

" What do you mean, William? " asked Jonathan crossly.

" In a thriller," William explained, " there's always a corpse and he can't give evidence. But here," and he pointed his finger at his brother, " you might say we have the corpse with us. That's the difference."

" Let us go to the library," said Jonathan.

CHAPTER VIII

THIRD TIME LUCKY

I

HERSEY AMBLINGTON and Chloris did not stay long with the party in the library. They went upstairs to visit, severally, Mrs. Compline and Madame Lisse. Jonathan had suggested this move to Hersey.

" I'll go and see how Sandra's getting on, with the greatest of pleasure," Hersey said. " I was going to do so in any case. But I must say, Jo, I don't think the Pirate will welcome my solicitude. What's supposed to be the matter with her?"

" A sick headache," said Jonathan. " The migraine."

" Well, the sight of me won't improve it. Damn the woman; what business has *she* to throw a migraine?"

" Naturally," Nicholas said, " she's upset."

" Why? Because she's afraid her face-lifting friend will make another pass at you? Or because she's all shocked and horrified that we should suspect him? Which?"

Nicholas looked furious but made no rejoiner.

" Would I be any use?" asked Chloris. " I don't mind casting an eye at her."

" Good girl," said Hersey. " Come on." And they went upstairs together.

Hersey found Mrs. Compline sitting by her fire, still wearing the dress into which she had changed for dinner.

"I ought to have come down, Hersey. It's *too* cowardly and difficult for me to hide like this. But I couldn't face it. Now that they all know! Imagine how they would avoid looking at me. I thought I had become hardened to it. For twenty years I've drilled myself, and now, when this happens, I am as raw as I was on the day I first let Nicholas look at me. Hersey, if you had seen him that day! He was only a tiny boy, but he —I thought he would never come to me again. He looked at me as though I were a stranger. It took so long to get him back."

"And William?" Hersey asked abruptly.

"William? Oh, he was older, of course, and not so sensitive. He seemed very shocked for a moment, and then he began to talk as if nothing had happened. I've never understood William. Nicky was just a baby, of course. He asked me what had happened to my pretty face. William never spoke of it. And after a while Nicky forgot I had ever had a pretty face."

"And William, it seems, never forgot."

"He was older."

"I think he's more sensitive."

"You don't understand Nicky. I see it all so plainly. He has got to know this Madame Lisse, and of course she has thrown herself at his head. Women have always done that with Nicky. I've seen it over and over again."

"He doesn't exactly discourage them, Sandra."

"He *is* naughty, I know," admitted Mrs. Compline, dotingly. "He always tells me all about them. We have such laughs together sometimes. Evidently there was something between Madame Lisse and—that man. And then when she met Nicholas, of course, she lost her heart to him. I've been thinking it out. That man must have recognised me. His own handiwork! Twenty years haven't changed it much. I suppose he was horrified and rushed to her with the story. She, hoping to establish a deeper bond between herself and Nicky, told him all about it."

"Now, Sandra, Nicholas himself denies this."

"Of course he does, darling," said Mrs. Compline rapidly. "That's what I've been trying to explain—you don't understand him. He wanted to spare me. It was for *my* sake he threatened this man. It's because of what Hartz did to *me*. But to spare me he let it be thought that it was some ridiculous affair over this woman."

" That seems very far-fetched to me," said Hersey bluntly.

A dull flush mounted in Mrs. Compline's face. " Why," she said, " the woman is on her knees to him already. He has no cause to trouble himself about this Madame Lisse. It's Dr. Hart who's troubling himself."

" But why?"

" Because he has found out that Nicholas knows his real identity and is afraid of exposure. Hersey, I've made William promise that he won't leave Nicholas. I want you to do something for me. I want you to send them both up here. I'm terrified for Nicky."

" But if, as you seem to think, Hart's afraid of exposure, there wouldn't be any point in his attacking Nick. He'd have to polish off the lot of us. We all know now."

But Hersey was up against an inflexible determination, and she saw that Sandra Compline would accept no explanation that did not show Nicholas in an heroic light. Nicholas must be upheld as the pink of courtesy, the wooed but never the wooer, the son who placed his mother above all women—a cross between Hollywood ace and a filial Galahad. She argued no more, but tried to convince Mrs. Compline that however dangerously Hart might have threatened Nicholas he would attempt no more assaults since he now realised that they all suspected him. She left, promising to send the two sons to their mother, and returned to the library.

II

Chloris found Madame Lisse extremely difficult. For one thing, she made not the smallest effort to conceal her boredom when, after tapping at the door, Chloris came into her room. It was impossible to escape the inference that she had suspected someone else. When she saw Chloris, in some subtle way she sagged. " As if," thought Chloris, " she unhooked her mental stays." She was in bed, most decoratively. There was a general impression of masses of tawny lace, from which Madame Lisse emerged in pallor and smoothness. " She *is* lovely," thought Chloris, " but I believe she's bad-tempered." Aloud she said: " I just looked in to see if there was anything I could do for you."

" How kind," said Madame Lisse in an exhausted voice. " There is nothing, thank you."

"Have you got aspirin and everything?"

"I cannot take aspirin, unfortunately."

"Then I can't be of any use?"

Madame pressed the tips of her wonderfully manicured fingers against her shaded eyelids. "Too kind," she said. "No, thank you. It will pass. In time, it will pass. It is an affliction of the nerves, you understand."

"Beastly for you. I'm afraid," said Chloris after a pause, "your nerves had a bit of a jolt. We're all feeling rather temperamental at the moment."

"Where is—what is everybody doing?" Madame Lisse asked with a certain freshening of her voice.

"Well, Lady Hersey's talking to Mrs. Compline, who's pretty poorly too, it seems. Mr. Royal and Aubrey Mandrake are in the library, and William and Nicholas are next door in the smoking-room, holding a sort of family council or something. Dr. Hart's in the boudoir, I believe." Chloris hesitated, wondering if it were possible for her to establish some sort of understanding with this woman who made her feel so gauche and so uncertain of herself. It seemed to her that if any one member of the house-party fully comprehended the preposterous situation, that person must be Madame Lisse. Indeed she might be regarded as a sort of liaison officer between Nicholas and Dr. Hart. "Surely, *surely*," Chloris thought, "she must know for certain if Hart is after Nicholas, and if so, why. Is she lying there, sleeking herself on being a successful *femme fatale*? I believe she really *is* in a funk." And, taking a deep breath, Chloris thought: "I'll ask her." With a sensation of panic she heard her own voice:

"Madame Lisse, please forgive me for asking you, but, honestly, things are so desperate with all of us eyeing each other and nobody really knowing what they're talking about, it would be a ghastly sort of relief to know the worst, so I thought I'd just ask you."

"You thought you would just ask me what, Miss Wynne?"

"It sounds so bogus when you say it out loud."

"I can hardly be expected to understand you unless you say it out loud."

"Well, then. Is Dr. Hart trying to kill Nicholas Compline?"

Madame Lisse did not answer immediately, and for a second or two the room was quite silent. Chloris felt the palms of her hands go damp, and a sensation of panic mounted her brain.

She thought: "This is frightful. My nerve must be going."
And then suddenly: "I wish Aubrey was here."

When Madame Lisse spoke her voice was clear and very
cold: "I know nothing whatever about it."

"But——"

"Nothing, do you hear me? Nothing."

And with a gesture whose violence shocked Chloris, she
gripped the lace at her bosom. "How dare you look at me
like that," cried Madame Lisse. "Leave me alone. Go out of
this room. I know nothing, I tell you. Nothing. Nothing.
Nothing."

III

Jonathan struck his plump hands together and uttered a little
wail of despair. "It's all very well to sit there and tell me
something must be done, but what can I *do*? We've no proof.
Nicholas had better go to bed and lock his door. I shall tell
Nicholas to go to bed and lock his door."

"I'm not worrying so much about Nicholas," said Mandrake. "He'll look after himself. I've no opinion at all of
Nicholas. He hasn't got the nerve of a louse. It's William I'm
thinking about. William's dangerous, Jonathan. He's out for
blood. I don't think Hart'll get Nicholas, but, by God, I
believe unless you do something about it, William will get
Hart."

"But why, why, why!"

"Jonathan, you pride yourself on your astuteness, don't
you? Can't you understand what's happened to William?
Didn't you see his face when they were up there in Nicholas's
room? When their mother had told them that Hart was responsible for her disfigurement? Why, you yourself told me
that when he was a child the disfigurement made an indelible
impression on him. You have always recognised the intensity
of his absorption in his mother. You've seen how readily he's
adopted her extraordinary explanation of Hart's attacks on
Nicholas. You've seen how he's abandoned all his private
rows with Nicholas and come out strong in his defence. Can't
you see that psychologically he's all of a piece. I tell you, the
pent-up repressions of a lifetime have come out for an airing.
William's dangerous."

" Freudian mumbo-jumbo," said Jonathan uneasily.

" It may be, but I don't think you can risk ignoring the possibilities."

" What am I to do?" Jonathan repeated angrily. " Lock up the Complines? Lock up Hart? Come, my dear Aubrey!"

" I think that at least you should have it out with Hart. Tell him flatly that we all think he's the author of these attacks. See what sort of a defence he can make. Then tackle William. You shut him up pretty successfully a little while ago, but there he is in the next room with Nicholas, who's no doubt busily engaged in churning it all up again."

" You've suddenly become wonderfully purposeful, Aubrey. At dinner I thought you seemed half in a trance."

" The look in William's eye has effectually roused me."

" And the touch of Miss Wynne's hand, perhaps?" Jonathan tittered.

" Perhaps. Are you going to tackle Hart?"

"What an odious expression that is: ' Tackle.' Very well, but you must come with me."

" As you please," said Mandrake. They moved towards the door. It opened and Chloris came in. " What's the matter?" Mandrake ejaculated.

" Nothing. At least, I've been talking to Madame Lisse. I suddenly felt I couldn't stand it. So I asked her, flat out, if she knew what Dr. Hart was up to. She turned all venomous and sort of spat at me. I've got a jitterbug. This house gets more and more noiseless every hour. Out there the snow's piling up thicker and thicker. I'm sorry," said Chloris, turning to Jonathan, " but it's suffocating isn't it, to be shut up with something that threatens and doesn't quite come off? It's as if something's fumbling about the passages, setting silly, dangerous booby-traps, something mad and dangerous. Do you know, I keep wishing there'd be an air raid. That's pretty feeble-minded, isn't it?"

" Here," said Mandrake, " you sit down by the fire. What the devil do you mean by talking jitterbugs? We look towards you for a spot of brave young mem-sahib. Do your stuff, woman."

" I'm all right," said Chloris. " I'm sorry. I'm all right. Where were you off to, you two?"

Mandrake explained while Jonathan fussed round Chloris, glad, so Mandrake fancied, of an excuse to postpone the interview with Dr. Hart. He threw a quantity of logs on the fire,

hurried away to the dining-room, and returned with the decanter of port. He insisted on Chloris taking a glass, helped
himself, and, as an afterthought, Mandrake. Hersey came in
and reported her interview with Mrs. Compline. She uttered
a phrase that Mandrake had begun to dread. "I looked out
through the west door. It's snowing harder than ever." Jonathan showed an inclination to settle down to a chat, but Mandrake said firmly that they might now leave Hersey and Chloris
together. He waited for Jonathan, who gulped down his port,
sighed, and got slowly to his feet. In the smoking-room next
door the drone of William's and Nicholas's conversation rose
to some slight and amicable climax, ending in a light laugh
from Nicholas. Perhaps, after all, thought Mandrake, he is
making William see sense. Better not to disturb them. And
he led the reluctant Jonathan by way of the hall, into the green
boudoir.

When he saw Dr. Hart the fancy crossed Mandrake's mind
that Highfold was full of solitary figures crouched over fires.
The door had opened silently, and for a moment Hart was not
aware of his visitors. He sat on the edge of an arm-chair, leaning forward, his arms resting upon his thighs, his hands dang-
ling together between his knees. His head, a little sunken
and inclined forward, was in shadow, but the firelight found
those hands whose whiteness, firm full flesh and square finger-
tips, were expressive of their profession. "They've got a look
of prestige," thought Mandrake, and he repeated to himself,
"professional hands."

Jonathan shut the door, and the hands closed like traps as
Dr. Hart turned and sprang to his feet.

"Oh—er—hallo, Hart," began Jonathan, unpromisingly.
"We—ah—we thought perhaps we might have a little con-
ference."

Hart did not answer, but he turned his head and stared at
Mandrake. "I've asked Aubrey to come with me," said Jonathan quickly, "because, you see, he's one of the—the victims,
and because, as a complete stranger to all of you"—(A complete stranger to Chloris?" thought Mandrake)—"we can't
possibly suspect him of any complicity."

"Complicity?" Hart said, still staring at Mandrake. "No.
No, I suppose you are right."

"Now," said Jonathan more firmly and with a certain brisk-
ness. "Let us sit down, shall we, and discuss this affair
sensibly?"

"I have said all that I have to say. I made no attack upon Mr. Mandrake, and I made no attack upon Nicholas Compline. That I am at enmity with Compline I admit. He has insulted me, and I do not care for insults. If it were possible I should refuse to stay in the same house with him. It is not possible, but I can at least refuse to meet him. I do so. I take advantage of your offer to remain here or in my room until I am able to leave."

"Now, my dear Hart, this really won't do." Jonathan drew up two chairs to the fire and, obeying a movement of his hand, Mandrake sat in one while Jonathan himself took the other. Hart remained standing, his hands clasped behind his back.

"It won't do, you know," Jonathan repeated. "This last affair, this balancing of a Buddha, this preposterous and malicious trap, could have been planned and executed with one object only, the object of doing a fatal injury to Nicholas Compline. I have made tolerably exhaustive inquiries, and I find that, motive apart, it is extremely improbable that any of my guests, excepting yourself, had an opportunity to set the second trap for Nicholas Compline. I tell you this at the outset, Dr. Hart, because I feel certain that if you can advance some proof of your—your innocence, you will now wish to do so." Jonathan struck the arms of his chair lightly with the palms of his hands. Mandrake thought: "He's not doing so badly, after all." He looked at Jonathan because he found himself unable to look at Dr. Hart, and, on a flash of irrelevant thinking, he remembered that a barrister had once told him that if the members of a returning jury studiously averted their eyes from the prisoner, you could depend upon it that their verdict would be "Guilty."

"I do not know when this trap is supposed to have been set," said Dr. Hart.

"Can you tell us what you were doing during the fifteen or twenty minutes before Nicholas Compline cried out?"

Dr. Hart lifted his chin, drew down his brows, and glared at the ceiling. "He's rather like Mussolini," thought Mandrake, stealing a glance at him.

"When Compline returned with you and with his brother," said Hart, "I was in this room. I went to that door and saw you in the hall. I then returned and continued a conversation with Madame Lisse, who left the room some time before I did. I remained here until it was time to dress. I went upstairs at quarter-past seven, and immediately entered my room.

Perhaps it was ten minutes later that I entered my bathroom next to my bedroom. I bathed and returned directly to my room. I had almost completed my dressing when I heard Compline scream like a woman. I heard voices in the passage. I put on my dinner-jacket and went out into the passage, where I found all of you grouped about the doorway to his room."

"Yes," said Jonathan. "Quite so. And between the time of your leaving this room and the discovery of the injury to Nicholas Compline, did you see any other member of the party or any of the servants?"

"No."

"Dr. Hart, do you agree that before you came here you wrote certain letters—I'm afraid I must call them threatening letters—to Nicholas Compline?"

"I cannot submit to these intolerable questions," said Hart breathlessly. "You have my assurance that I have made no attack."

"If you won't answer me, you may find yourself questioned by a person of greater authority. You oblige me to press you still further. Do you know where Nicholas Compline was when the trap was set for him?"

Hart's upper lip twitched as that moth fluttered under the skin. Twice he made as if to speak. At the third effort he uttered some sort of noise—a kind of moan. Mandrake felt acutely embarrassed, but Jonathan cocked his head like a bird, and it seemed to Mandrake that he was beginning to enjoy himself again. "Well, Dr. Hart?" he murmured.

"I do not know where he was. I saw nobody."

"He tells us that he was talking to Madame Lisse, in her room. What did you say?"

Hart had again uttered that inarticulate sound. He wetted his lips and after a moment said loudly: "I did not know where he was."

Jonathan's fingers had been at his waistcoat pocket. He now withdrew them and with an abrupt movement held out a square of paper. Mandrake saw that it was the Charter form which he had found on the previous night in Nicholas's chair. He had time to think: "It seems more like a week ago," as he read again the words that had seemed so preposterous: "You are warned. Keep off."

"Well, Dr. Hart," said Jonathan, "have you seen this paper before?"

"Never," Hart cried out shrilly. "Never!"

"Are you sure? Take it in your hand and examine it."

"I will not touch it. This is a trap. Of what do you accuse me?"

Jonathan, still holding the paper, crossed to a writing-desk in the window. Mandrake and Hart watched him peer into a drawer and finally take out a sheet of note-paper. He turned towards Hart. In his right hand he held the Charter form, in his left the sheet of note-paper.

"This is your acceptance of my invitation for the week-end," said Jonathan. "After the Charter form came into my hands," he smiled at Mandrake, "I bethought me of this note. I compared them and I came to an interesting conclusion. Your letters are characteristically formed, my dear Doctor. You use a script, and it retains its Continental character. The leg of the German 'K' is usually prolonged. Here we have a 'K' in 'kind invitation.' I am looking at the note. Turning to the Charter form we find that the letters are in script, and the 'K' of 'keep' has a leg that is prolonged through the square beneath it. Now, you sat next to Nicholas on his right hand. You passed your forms to him for scoring. Instead of receiving one form from you, he received two—the legitimate Charter, which curiously enough contained the word 'threats,' and this somewhat childish but, in the circumstances, quite significant warning, which you tell us you have never seen before. Now, you know, that simply won't do."

"I did not write it. It—I must have torn two sheets off together. They were stuck together at the top. Someone else had written on the bottom form."

"Ridiculous!" said Jonathan very sharply. He thrust the two papers into his pocket and moved away. When he spoke again, it was with a return to his usual air of pedantry. "No, really, Dr. Hart, that will *not* do. I myself gave out the forms. Nobody could have foretold to whom I would hand this particular block. You are not suggesting, I hope, that a member of the party, by some sleight-of-hand trick, took your block of forms out of your fingers, wrote on the lower form, and returned it without attracting your attention?"

"I suggest nothing. I know nothing about it. I did not write it. Perhaps Compline himself wrote it in order to discredit me. He is capable of anything—of anything. *Ach Gott!*" cried Dr. Hart, "I can endure this no longer. I must ask you to leave me. I must insist that you leave me alone." He clasped his hands together and raised them to his eyes. " I am most unhappy," he said, " I am in great trouble. You do not understand, you are not of my race. I tell you that these accusations mean nothing to me—nothing. I am torn by the most terrible of all emotions and I cannot fight against it. I am near breaking-point. I entreat you to leave me alone."

" Very well," said Jonathan, and rather to Mandrake's surprise he walked to the door. " But I warn you," he said, " if anything should happen to Nicholas Compline, you, and only you, will immediately fall under the gravest suspicion. I firmly believe you tried to kill Nicholas. If there is one more threat, one more suspicious move upon your part, Dr. Hart, I shall take it upon myself to place you under arrest." He made a quick, deft movement, and the next moment Mandrake saw that in his right hand Jonathan held a very small pistol. " A few moments ago," said Jonathan, " I removed this little weapon from my desk. I am armed, Dr. Hart, and I shall see to it that Nicholas Compline also is armed. I wish you goodnight."

IV

Mandrake did not follow Jonathan from the room. Something had happened to him. He had succumbed to an irresistible feeling of pity for Dr. Hart. He had not ceased to believe that Hart was responsible for the attacks on Nicholas; on the contrary, he was more than ever convinced that he was their author. But something in Hart's attitude, in his air of isolation, in the very feebleness of his efforts to defend himself, had touched Mandrake's sympathetic nerve. He saw Hart as a man who had been driven hopelessly off his normal course by the wind of an overwhelming jealousy. The old phrase " Madly in love " occurred to him, and he thought Hart was indeed the victim of an insane passion. He found in himself a burning anxiety to prevent any further attack, not so much for Nicholas Compline's sake as for Hart's. It would be terrible, he thought, if Hart were to kill Nicholas and then by this dreadful consummation of his passion be brought to his right mind, to a full realisation of the futility of what he had done. He felt that he must try to find something to say to this plump figure of tragedy, something that might reach out to him and rouse him as some actual sound will penetrate and

E

dispel a nightmare. Hart had turned away when Jonathan had shut the door, and had flung himself into a chair by the fire and covered his face with his hands. After a moment's hesitation Mandrake crossed to him and touched him lightly on the shoulder. He started, looked up, and said: " I thought you had gone."

" I shall go in a moment. I have stayed because I want to wake you."

" To wake me? How often have I repeated to myself that most futile of all phrases, ' If only it were a dream.' If only I could be certain, *certain*. Then it would not be so bad."

Mandrake thought: " He *is* going to talk to me." He took the chair opposite to Dr. Hart and lit a cigarette. " If only you could be certain?" he repeated.

" That it is all lies, that he is her lover, that she has betrayed me. But when she denies I cannot help half-believing her. I wish so much to believe. And then I see a look of boredom in her eyes, a look of weariness, of contempt. And with that comes the memory of the glances I have surprised between them, and although I know that with each denial, each scene, I injure myself still further, immediately I begin to make new scenes, demand fresh denials. I am caught in the toils of hell. I am so weary of it, yet I cannot be done with it."

" Why did you come here?"

" To prove to myself, one way or the other. To know the worst. She told me he was to be here and said quite lightly: ' Watch us and find out. It is nothing.' And then when I saw him with all the airs of proprietorship, of complacent ownership, *laughing* at me! Do you know what should have been done in my country, if any one insulted me as this man has insulted me? We should have met and it would have been decided once and for all. I should have killed Nicholas Compline."

" In England," said Mandrake, " we find it difficult to believe that in other countries duelling is still regarded as a satisfactory means of settling a difference. A successful duellist would be regarded as a murderer."

" In any case," said Hart, " he would not consent. He is a poltroon as well as a popinjay."

Mandrake thought: " Such glorious words!" Aloud he said: " He has some cause to be nervous, don't you think?"

" Yet in spite of his terror," Hart continued, beating his clenched hands against his forehead, " in spite of his terror, he goes to her room. He waits until he hears me in the bathroom and then he goes to her. This morning he was in her room. I trapped her into admitting it. And now, a few minutes after she leaves me, after she has seen my agony, she keeps another assignation."

" But, you know, in this country, we are not conventional. I mean, we wander about into each other's rooms. I mean, Chloris Wynne and Lady Hersey, for example, both came and saw me. One thinks nothing of it. The modern Englishwoman——"

" In these matters she is not an Englishwoman, and I, Mr. Mandrake, am not an Englishman. We are naturalised, but we do not change our ideas of what is *convenable*. For what reason should she admit him, for what innocent reason? No, it is useless to torture myself further. She has betrayed me."

" Look here, it's none of my business, but if you are so certain, why not make a clean break? Why take a course that must lead to disaster? Let them go their ways. Things can never be as they were. Why ruin your career "—Mandrake stammered over his series of conventional phrases—" and jeopardise your own life over Nicholas Compline? Is he worth it? And, after all, is she worth it? Let her go. You could never be happy with her now. Even if she married you——"

" *Married* me!" cried Hart. " *Married me!* She has been my wife for five years."

v

Mandrake stayed with Hart for a time, hearing a story in which the themes of Madame Lisse's business instinct, her husband's enslavement, and Nicholas Compline's perfidy, were strangely interwoven. Madame, it seemed, had decided that their respective professions, though allied, were in a public sense incompatible. " She felt that as my wife she could not recommend me to her clients. I have always expressed considerable scepticism about the efficacy of face massage and creams. I have even published a short treatise on the subject. She said that to announce our marriage would be to embarrass my prestige with my *clientele*." His voice went on and on in a breathless hurry. He seemed unable to stop. Always he returned to Nicholas Compline, and with each return he rekindled his own fury against Nicholas. The sudden outpouring of a long-suppressed emotion is supposed to bring relief, but Dr. Hart did not appear to take comfort from his self-revelation. He looked wretchedly ill and his nervous distress mounted with his recital. "He really is *not* responsible," Mandrake thought. "I've done no good at all. I'd better clear out." He could think of no suitable speech with which to end the conversation. Ridiculous phrases occurred to him (" Now, you *won't* kill Nicholas, *will* you?") and he wished with all his heart that he could rid himself of the notion that in some way Dr. Hart was making an appeal to him. He pulled himself to his feet. Dr. Hart, his finger pressed against that twitching lip of his, looked up desolately. At that moment, beyond the communicating door into the smoking-room, Nicholas Compline uttered a laugh loud enough to reach the ears of Dr. Hart and Mandrake. Hart sprang to his feet, and for a moment Mandrake thought that he would actually make a blackguard rush into the smoking-room and go for his tormentor. Mandrake grabbed at his arm. They heard Nicholas's voice say " All right," so clearly that he must have crossed the room. There was a discordant burst of static and distorted music from the wireless just inside the door. Hart cried out for all the world as if he had been struck, tore himself away from Mandrake, and flung open the door into the smoking-room.

" *Gott im Himmel*," he screamed out, " must I be tortured by that devilish, that intolerable noise? *Turn it off. I insist that you turn it off!*"

Nicholas appeared in the doorway. " You go to hell," he said pleasantly. " If I choose to listen to the wireless I'll bloody well listen to it." He slammed the door in Hart's face. Mandrake stumbled between Hart and the door. With a string of expletives that rather astonished himself he shouted out instructions to Nicholas to switch off the radio, which was now roaring " Roll Out the Barrel." It stopped abruptly, and William was heard to say: " Pipe down, for God's sake." Nicholas said: " Oh, *all* right. Go to bed, Bill," and Mandrake and Hart stared at each other for some seconds without speaking.

" Dr. Hart," said Mandrake at last, " if you cannot give me your assurance that you will either go to your own room or remain in this one, I shall—I shall lock you in."

Hart sank back into his chair. " I shall do nothing," he said.

" What can I do?" And to Mandrake's unbounded dismay he uttered a loud sob and buried his face in his hands.

" Oh *God*!" thought Mandrake, " this is too much." He tried to form soothing phrases, but was dismayed by their inadequacy, and finally ran out of words. For a moment he watched Dr. Hart, who was now fetching his breath in shuddering gasps and beating his hands on the arms of his chair. Mandrake remembered Jonathan's treatment for Chloris. He went to the dining-room, found a decanter of whisky, poured out a stiff nip, and returned with it to the boudoir.

" Try this," he said. Hart motioned to him to leave it beside him. Seeing he could do no more, he prepared to leave. As an afterthought he turned at the door. " May I give you one word of advice," he said. " Keep clear of both the Complines." And he limped away to the library.

Here he found Jonathan with Hersey Amblington and Chloris. It seemed quite natural to Mandrake to go at once to Chloris and sit on the arm of her chair, it seemed enchantingly natural that she should look up at him with pleasure.

" Well," she said, " any good?"

" None. He's in an awful state. What about the brothers Compline? We could hear snatches of their cross-talk act in there."

" Lady Hersey's been in to see them."

" And I may say," said Hersey, " that I got a surprise. Nick's pulled himself together, it seems, and is doing his best to let a little sense into poor old William."

" He has also been doing his best to drive Dr. Hart into an ecstasy of hatred by not quite tuning in at full volume to a particularly distressing rendering of ' The Beer Barrel Polka,' " said Mandrake, and described the incident. " Possibly this was an essential step in the soothing of William."

" It must have happened after I left," said Hersey.

" I wonder you didn't hear us yelling at each other from here."

" This room is practically sound-proof," said Jonathan.

" It must be. How is Nicholas getting on with William, Lady Hersey?"

" He's not made a great deal of headway, but at least he's trying. They're supposed to go and see their mother, but they don't seem to be very keen on the idea. They said they particularly want to be left to themselves. What do we do now, Mr. Mandrake?"

"It's nearly ten o'clock," said Mandrake. "I'm damned if I know what we do. What do you think, Jonathan?"

Jonathan waved his hands and said nothing.

"Well," Mandrake said, "I suppose we see Nicholas to his room when he wants to go to bed. Do we lock William in *his* room or what?"

"I think we shut up Dr. Hart," said Hersey. "Then William can't get at Dr. Hart and Dr. Hart can't get at Nicholas. Or am I confused?"

"They may not fancy being locked up," Chloris pointed out. "Honestly, it's *too* difficult."

"Jo," said Hersey suddenly, "do you remember the conversation at dinner last night? When we said what we thought everybody would do in a crisis? It seems we were all wrong about each other. We agreed that you, for instance, would talk. You've not uttered a word since you came into this room. Somebody said Mr. Mandrake would be the impractical member of the party, and here he is showing the most superb efficiency. Chloris—I hope you don't mind me calling you Chloris—suggested that Bill would turn up trumps, while his mother was all for Nicholas. Hopelessly incorrect! It looks as if you were right, Jo. We know nothing about each other."

"Jonathan was eloquent in the boudoir," said Mandrake listlessly.

They made disjointed conversation until Nicholas, wearing a dubious expression, came out of the smoking-room. He grimaced at the others and shut the door.

"How goes it?" Hersey asked. "Thumbs up?"

Nicholas, with exaggerated emphasis, mimed: "Thumbs down."

"It's all right," said Jonathan impatiently. "He can't hear."

"He's still pretty bloody-minded," said Nicholas, throwing himself into a chair. "He's left off threatening to beat up the doctor, thank God, but he's gone into a huddle over the fire and does *not* exactly manifest the party spirit. You know how he used to go as a kid, Hersey. All thunderous."

"'Black Bill'?" said Hersey. "I remember. Couldn't you do anything?"

"I've been kicked out," said Nicholas with a sheepish grin. "Hart's gone to bed, I fancy. We heard him snap off the light. So perhaps Bill might work his black dog off on the wireless."

"This is a shocking state of affairs," cried Jonathan. "I suppose we'd better leave him to himself, um?"

"Well, he's not so hot when he's like this. He'll get over it. I think I've persuaded him to keep away from Hart."

"You *think*!"

"I tell you Hart's gone upstairs. Possibly," said Nicholas, showing the whites of his eyes, "he's thought up a really foolproof way of bumping me off."

"My dear Nick, we shall go up with you. I cannot believe, when he knows what we suspect, and I may say in the face of the little speech I made him, that he will attempt—— But, of course," added Jonathan in a fluster, "we must take every precaution. Your door, now——"

"Make no mistake," said Nicholas grimly. "I shall lock my door."

There was a short pause broken by Hersey. "I simply can't believe it," she said abruptly. "It's so preposterous it just isn't true. All of us sitting round like a house-party in a play, waiting for frightfulness. And that booby-trap! A brass Buddha! No, it's *too* much. To-morrow Dr. Hart will apologise to all of us and say he's sorry his sense of fun carried him too far, and he'll explain that in the Austrian Tyrol they all half-kill each other out of sheer *joie de vivre*, and we'll say we're sorry we didn't take it in the spirit in which it was meant."

"A murderous spirit," Jonathan muttered. "No, no, Hersey. We've got to face it. The attack on Nicholas was deliberately planned to injure him."

"Well, what are we going to *do*?"

"At least we could hear the war news," said Mandrake. "It might work as a sort of counter-irritant."

"We'd better not disturb William," said Jonathan quickly.

"I dare say he'll turn it on in a minute," Nicholas said wearily. "He's keen on the news. Shall I ask him?"

"No, no," said Jonathan. "Leave him alone. It's not quite time yet. Would you like a drink, my dear Nick?"

"To be quite frank, Jonathan, I'd adore a very, very large drink."

"You shall have it. Would you ring? The bell's beside you. No, you needn't trouble. I hear them coming."

A jingle of glasses sounded in the hall and the new footman came in with a tray. For the few seconds that he was in the room Chloris and Hersey made a brave effort at conversation. When he had gone Jonathan poured out the drinks. "What about William?" he asked. "Shall we——? Will you ask him?"

Nicholas opened the study door and stuck his head round it. "Coming in for a drink, Bill? No? All right, old thing, but would you mind switching on the wireless? It's just about time for the news and we'd like to hear it. Thanks."

They all waited awkwardly. Nicholas glanced over his shoulder and winked. The study wireless came to life.

"Hands, Knees, and Boomps-a-daisy," sang the wireless robustly.

"Oh, God!" said Mandrake automatically, but he felt an illogical sense of relief.

"Can you stick it for a minute or two?" asked Nicholas. "It's almost news time. I'll leave the door open."

"*Hands, Knees, and Boomps-a-daisy.*"

"I think," said Jonathan, at the third repetition of the chorus, "that I'll just make certain Dr. Hart is *not* in the boudoir." He got up. At the same moment the dance band ended triumphantly: "Turn to your partner and bow-wow-wow."

"Here's the news," said Hersey.

Jonathan, after listen.ng to the opening announcement, went out into the hall. The others heard the recital of a laconic French bulletin and a statement that heavy snow was falling in the Maginot Line sector. The announcer's voice went on and on, but Mandrake found himself unable to listen to it. He was visited by a feeling of nervous depression, a sort of miserable impatience. "I can't sit here much longer," he thought. Presently Jonathan returned and in answer to their glances nodded his head. "No light in there," he said. He poured himself out a second drink. "He's feeling the strain, too," thought Mandrake.

"I wish old Bill'd come in," said Nicholas suddenly.

"He's better left alone," said Jonathan.

"Shall I take him in a drink?" Hersey suggested. "He can but throw it in my face. I *will*. Pour him out a whisky, Jo."

Jonathan hesitated. She swept him aside, poured out a good three fingers of whisky, splashed in the soda, and marched off with it into the smoking-room.

"It is learned in London to-night," said the announcer, "that Mr. Cedric Hepbody, the well-known authority on Polish folk-music, is a prisoner in Warsaw. At the end of this bulletin you will hear a short recorded talk made by Mr. Hepbody last year on the subject of folk-music in its relation and reaction to primitive behaviourism. And now . . ."

Hersey was standing in the doorway. Mandrake saw her first, and an icy sensation of panic closed like a hand about his heart. The red-leather screen at her back threw her figure into bold relief. The others turned their heads, saw her, and, as if on a common impulse, rose at once to their feet. They watched her lips moving in her sheet-white face. She mouthed at them and turned back into the smoking-room. The announcer's voice was cut off into silence.

" Jo," Hersey said. " Jo, come here."

Jonathan's fingers pulled at his lips. He did not move.

" Jo."

Jonathan crossed the library and went into the smoking-room. There was another long silence. Nobody moved or spoke. At last Hersey came round the screen.

" Mr. Mandrake," she said, " will you go in to Jonathan?"

Without a word Mandrake went into the smoking-room. The heavy door with its rows of book-shelves shut behind him.

It was then that Nicholas cried out: " My God, what's happened?"

Hersey went to him and took his hands in hers. " Nick," she said, " he's killed William."

Part Two

CHAPTER IX

ALIBI

I

WILLIAM was sitting in a low chair beside the wireless. He was bent double. His face was between his knees and his hands were close to his shoes. His posture suggested an exaggerated scrutiny of the carpet. If Mandrake had walked in casually he might have thought at first glance that William was staring at some small object that lay between his feet. The cleft in the back of his head looked like some ugly mistake, preposterous rather than ghastly, the kind of thing one could not believe. Mandrake had taken in this much before he looked at Jonathan, who stood with his back against the door into the boudoir. He was wiping his hands on his handkerchief. Mandrake heard a tiny spat of sound. A little red star appeared on the toe of William's left shoe.

"Aubrey, look at this."

"Is he——? Are you sure——?"

"Good God, *look* at him!"

Mandrake had no wish to look at William, but he limped over to the chair. Has any one measured the flight of thought? In a timeless flash it can embrace a hundred images, and compass a multitude of ideas. In the second that passed before Mandrake stooped over William Compline he was visited by a confused spiral of impressions and memories. He thought of William's oddities, of how he himself had never seen any of William's paintings, of how William's mouth might now be open and full of spilling blood. He thought in a deeper layer of consciousness of Chloris, who must have been kissed by William, of Dr. Hart's hands, of phrases in detective novels, of the fact that he might have to give his own name if he was called as a witness. The name of Roderick Alleyn was woven

138

in his thoughts, and over all of them rested an image of deep
snow. He knelt by William and touched his right hand. It
moved a little, flaccidly, under the pressure of his fingers, and
that shocked him deeply. Something hit the back of his own
hand, and he saw a little red star like the one on William's
shoe. He wiped it off with a violent movement. He stooped
lower and looked up into William's face, and that was terrible
because the eyes as well as the mouth were wide open. Then
Mandrake rose to his feet and looked at the back of William's
head and felt abominably sick. He drew away with an involun-
tary sideways lurch, and his club-foot struck against something on the floor. It lay in shadow, and he had to stoop again
to see it. It was a flattish, spatulate object that narrowed to a
short handle. He heard Jonathan's voice babbling behind him:

"It hung on the wall there, you know. I showed it to you.
It came from New Zealand. I told you. It's called a mere*. I
told you. It's made of stone."

"I remember," said Mandrake.

When he turned to speak to Jonathan he found that
Nicholas had come into the room.

"Nick," said Jonathan, "my dear Nick."

"He's not dead," Nicholas said. "He can't be dead."

He thrust Jonathan from him and went to his brother. He
put his hands on William's head and made as if to raise it.

"Don't," said Mandrake. "I wouldn't. Not yet."

"You must be mad. Why haven't you tried——? Leaving
him! You must be mad." He raised William's head, saw his
face, and uttered a deep retching sound. The head sagged
forward again, loosely, as he released it. He began to repeat
William's name. "Bill, Bill, Bill," and walked distractedly
about the room, making strange uneloquent gestures.

"What are we to do?" asked Jonathan, and Mandrake
repeated to himself: "What are we to do?"

Aloud he said: "We can't do anything. We ought to get
the police. A doctor. We can't do anything."

"*Where's Hart?*" Nicholas demanded suddenly. "*Where is
he?*"

He stumbled to the door beyond William, fumbled with the
key and flung it open. The green boudoir was in darkness and
the fire there had sunk to a dead glow.

"By God, yes, where is he?" cried Mandrake.

Nicholas turned to the door into the hall, and on a common

* Pronounced: merry.

impulse Mandrake and Jonathan intercepted him. " Clear out of my way," shouted Nicholas.

" Wait a minute, for Heaven's sake, Compline," said Mandrake.

" *Wait a minute!*"

" We're up against a madman. He may be lying in wait for you. Think, man."

He had Nicholas by the arm and he felt him slacken. He thought he saw something of the old nervousness come into his eyes.

" Aubrey's right, Nick," Jonathan was gabbling. " We've got to keep our heads, my dear fellow. We've got to lay a plan of campaign. We can't rush blindly at our fences. No, no. There's—there's your mother to think of, Nick. Your mother must be told, you know."

Nicholas wrenched himself free from Mandrake, turned away to the fireplace and flung himself into a chair: " For Christ's sake, leave me alone," he said. Mandrake and Jonathan left him alone and whispered together.

" Look here," Mandrake said, " I suggest we lock up this room and go next door where we can talk. Are those two women all right in there? Better not leave them. We'll go back into the library, then." He turned to Nicholas. " I'm terribly sorry, Compline, but I don't think we ought to—to make any changes here, just yet. Jonathan, are there keys in all these doors? Yes, I see."

The door into the boudoir was locked. He withdrew the key, locked the door into the hall, and gave both keys to Jonathan. As he crossed the room to open the library door he felt a slight prick in the sole of his normal foot, and in one layer of his conscious thoughts, cursed his shoemaker. They shepherded Nicholas back into the library. Mandrake found that behind its rows of dummy books the door into the library also had a lock.

They found Hersey and Chloris sitting together by the fire. Mandrake saw that Chloris had been crying. " I'm out of this," he thought. " I can't try to help." And, unrecognised by himself, a pang of jealousy shook him, jealousy of William, who, by getting himself murdered, had won tears from Chloris.

Mandrake, for the first time, noticed that Jonathan was as white as a ghost. He kept opening and closing his lips, his fingers went continually to his glasses, and he repeatedly gave a dry, nervous cough. " I dare say I look pretty ghastly myself," thought Mandrake. Jonathan, for all his agitation, had assumed a certain air of authority. He sat down by Hersey and took her hand.

" Now, my dears," he began, and though his voice shook his phrases held their old touch of pedantry, " I know you will be very sensible and brave. This is a most dreadful calamity, and I feel that I am myself, in a measure, responsible for it. That is an appalling burden to carry upon one's conscience, but at the moment I dare not let myself consider it. There is an immediate problem, and we must deal with it as best we may. There is no doubt at all, I am afraid, that it is Dr. Hart who has killed William, and in my mind there is no doubt that he is insane. First of all, then, I want you both to promise me that you will not separate, and also that when we leave you alone together you will lock this door after us and not unlock it until one of us returns."

" But he's not going for either of us," said Hersey. " He's got nothing against us, surely."

" What had he against William?"

" William had quite a lot against *him*," said Hersey.

" It must have been the radio," Mandrake said to Nicholas. " He nearly went for you when you turned it on."

Nicholas said: " I told him to go to hell and locked the door in his face." He leant his arms on the mantelpiece and beat his skull with his fists.

" You *locked* the door?" Mandrake repeated.

" He looked like barging in. I was sick of it all. Going for me. Screaming out his orders to me! I wanted to shut him up."

" I remember now. I heard you lock it. He must have gone out into the hall and then into the smoking-room through the hall door."

" I suppose so," said Nicholas, and drove his fingers through his hair.

" Look here," Mandrake said slowly, " this makes a difference."

" If it does," Jonathan interrupted him, " we can hear what it is later, Aubrey. Nick, my dear chap, I think you must see your mother. And we," he looked at Mandrake, " must find Hart." They made a plan of action. The men were to search the house together, leaving the two women in the library with the doors locked on the inside. Nicholas said that his service automatic was in his room. They decided to go upstairs at once and get it. " Bill had his," Nicholas said, and Jonathan said they would take it for Mandrake.

Hersey offered to go with Nicholas to his mother, and Chloris insisted that she would be all right left by herself in the library. " She's a good, gallant girl," thought Mandrake, " and I'm in love with her." He gave her shoulder a pat and thought how out of character his behaviour was.

" Come on," said Hersey.

The library door shut behind them and they heard Chloris turn the key in the lock. The hall was quiet, a dim, hollow place with a dying fire and shadows like the mouths of caverns. Bleached walls faded like smoke up into darkness; curtains, half-seen, hung rigidly in the entrance. Pieces of furniture stood about with a deadly air of expectancy.

Jonathan's hand reached out and a great chandelier flooded the hall with light. The party of four moved to the stairs. Mandrake saw Jonathan take out his pistol. He led the way upstairs and switched on the wall lamps. Hersey and Nicholas followed him, and Mandrake, lifting his club-foot more quickly than he was wont to do, brought up the rear. The nail in his right shoe still pricked him, and he was dimly irritated by this slight discomfort. Up the first flight to the half-way landing where the stairs divided into two narrower flights, of which they took the one that turned to their left. Up to the top landing, where the grandfather clock ticked loudly. Here they paused. Hersey took Nicholas's arm. He squared his shoulders and, with a gesture that for all its nervousness was a sort of parody of his old swagger, brushed up his moustache and went off with her to his mother's room. Mandrake and Jonathan turned to the right and walked softly down the passage.

They found Nicholas's automatic where he had told them to look for it, in a drawer of his dressing-table. William's Nicholas had said, was in his room, beside a rucksack containing his painting materials.

" His room's next door to Hart's," whispered Jonathan. " If he's there, he'll hear us go in. What shall we do?"

" We can't leave stray automatics lying about, Jonathan. Not with a homicidal lunatic at large."

" Come on, then."

William's room was opposite his brother's. Mandrake stood on guard in the passage while Jonathan, looking extraordinarily furtive, opened the door by inches and crept in. There was no light under Hart's door. Was he there behind it, listening, waiting? Mandrake stared at it, half-expecting it to open. Jonathan came back carrying a second automatic. He led the way into Mandrake's room.

" If he's in there, he's in the dark," said Mandrake.

" Quiet! You take this, Aubrey. Nicholas should have had his," whispered Jonathan. " He should have come here first."

" Are they loaded? I couldn't know less about them."

Jonathan examined the two automatics. " I think so. I myself . . ." his voice faded away and Mandrake only caught odd words: ". . . last resort . . . most undesirable . . ." He looked anxiously at Mandrake. " The safety catches are on, I think, but be careful, Aubrey. We must not fire, of course, unless something really desperate happens. Let him see we are armed. Wait one moment."

" What is it?"

A curious smile twisted Jonathan's lips. " It occurs to me," he whispered, " that we are at great pains to defend ourselves, Nicholas, and three of the ladies. We have quite overlooked the fourth."

" But—do you think? Good Heavens, Jonathan——"

" We can do nothing there. It is an abstract point. Are you ready? Let us go, then."

Outside Hart's door they paused. William's automatic sagged heavily in the pocket of Mandrake's dinner-jacket. Nicholas's automatic was in his right hand. His heart thumped uncomfortably, and he thought: " This is *not* my sort of stuff. I'm hating this."

The latch clicked as Jonathan turned the handle. " If it's locked," thought Mandrake, " do we break it in or what?"

It was not locked. Jonathan pushed the door open quietly, slipped through, and switched on the light. The room was orderly and rather stuffy. Dr. Hart's trousers were hung over the back of a chair, his underclothes were folded across the seat, his shoes neatly disposed upon the floor. These details caught Mandrake's eye before he saw the bed, which contained Dr. Hart himself.

II

Apparently he was fast asleep. He lay on his back, his mouth was open, his face patched with red, and his eyes not quite shut. The whites just showed under the lashes, and that gave him so ghastly a look that for a fraction of a second Mandrake's nerves leapt to a conclusion that was at once dispelled by the sound of stertorous breathing.

Jonathan shut the door. He and Mandrake eyed each other and then, upon a common impulse, approached closer to the sleeping beauty-doctor. Mandrake was conscious of a great reluctance to waken Hart, a profound abhorrence of the scene that must follow the awakening. His imagination called up a picture of terrified expostulations or, still worse, of a complete breakdown and confession. He found himself unable to look at Hart, his glance wandered from Jonathan's pistol to the bedside table, where it was arrested by a small chemist's jar half-full of a white crystalline powder, and by a used tumbler, stained with white sediment. "Veronal?" wondered Mandrake, who had once used it himself. "If it is I didn't know it made you look so repellent. He must have taken a big dose."

How big a dose Dr. Hart had taken only appeared when Jonathan tried to wake him.

Under other circumstances Jonathan would have cut a comic figure. First, keeping his own pistol pointed at the sleeping doctor, he called his name. There was no response, and Jonathan repeated his effort, raising his voice, finally to a cracked falsetto. "Hart, Dr. Hart! Wake up!"

Hart stirred, uttered an uncouth sound, and began to snore again. With an incoherent exclamation, Jonathan pocketed his pistol and advanced upon the bed.

"Look out," said Mandrake, "he may be foxing."

"Nonsense!" said Jonathan crisply. He shook Hart by the shoulder. "Never heard of such a thing," said Jonathan furiously. "Dr. Hart! Wake up."

"A-a-ah? *Was haben Sie . . .*" The prominent eyes opened and stared into Jonathan's. The voice tailed away, the eyes became bored and closed again. There followed a slightly ridiculous scene, Jonathan scolding and shaking Hart, Hart mumbling and sagging off into a doze. Finally Jonathan, his face pink with vexation, dipped a towel in the water jug and slapped the doctor's cheeks with it. This did the trick. Hart shuddered and shook his head. When he spoke again his voice was normal.

"Well," said Dr. Hart, " what in Heaven's name is all this? What now? May I not sleep, even! What now?"

He turned his head and saw Mandrake. "What are you doing with that thing in your hand?" he demanded. "Do not point it at me. It's a firearm. What has happened?" Mandrake fidgeted uneasily with the automatic, and curled the toes of his right foot in an attempt to avoid that pestilent shoe nail. Hart rubbed the back of his hand across his mouth and shook his head vigorously.

Jonathan said: " We are armed because we have come to speak with a murderer."

Hart uttered a sound of exasperation. " Mr. Royal," he said, " how often am I to explain that I know nothing about it? Am I to be awakened at intervals during the night to tell you that I was in my bath?"

" What, again!" Mandrake ejaculated.

" Again? *Again!*" shouted Hart. " I do not know what you mean by again. I was in my bath at the time it was done. I know nothing. I did not sleep all last night. For weeks I have been suffering from insomnia, and to-night I have taken a soporific. If I do not sleep I shall go mad. Leave me alone."

" There is the body of a murdered man downstairs, Doctor Hart," said Mandrake. " I think you must stay awake a little longer to answer for it."

Hart sat up in bed. His pyjama jacket was unbuttoned, and the smooth whiteness of his torso made a singularly disagreeable impression on Mandrake. Hart was fully awake now, on his guard, and sharply attentive.

" Murdered?" he repeated, and to Mandrake's astonishment he smiled. " I see. So he has done it after all. I did not think he would go so far."

" What the devil are you talking about?" Jonathan demanded.

" He is killed, you say? Then I am speaking of his brother. I guessed that the brother set that trap. A booby-trap you call it, do you not? He betrayed himself when he reminded them of the tricks they played in their childhood. It was obvious the lady still loved her first choice. He was attractive to women." He paused and rubbed his lips again. Jonathan and

Mandrake found nothing to say. "How was it done?" asked Hart.

Jonathan suddenly began to stutter. Mandrake saw that he was beside himself with rage. He cut in loudly before Jonathan had uttered a coherent phrase:

"Wait a moment, Jonathan." Mandrake limped nearer to the bed. "He was killed," he said, "by a blow on the head from a stone club that hung with other weapons on the wall of the smoking-room. He was bending over the wireless. His murderer must have crept up behind him. No, Jonathan, wait a minute, please. A short while before he was killed, Doctor Hart, we were all in the library, and we heard him turn on the radio. You will remember that the smoking-room is between the library and the green sitting-room, the room that you were in, alone. You will remember that it communicates with both these rooms and with the hall. With the exception of Mr. Royal, who did not enter either of the other two rooms, none of us left the library after we heard the wireless until Lady Hersey went in and found him there—murdered."

The uneven patches of red in Hart's cheeks were blotted out by a uniform and extreme pallor.

"This is infamous," he whispered. "You suggest that I— *I* killed him." With a movement of his hand Mandrake checked a further outburst from Jonathan.

"I could not," said Hart. "The door was locked."

"*How do you know?*"

"After you had gone, I tried it. He had turned that intolerable thing on again. I could not endure it. I admit—I admit I tried it. When I found it locked I—I controlled myself. I decided to leave that room of torture. I came up here and to bed. The door was locked, I tell you."

"The door from the hall into the smoking-room was not locked."

"I did not do it. There must be some proof. It is the brother. The brother hated him as much as I. It is a pathological case. I am a medical man. I have seen it. He had stolen the mother's love and the girl still adored him."

"Doctor Hart," said Mandrake, "it is not Nicholas Compline who is dead. It is his brother, William."

In the silence that followed, Mandrake heard a door, some distance down the passage, open and close. He heard voices, a footfall, somebody coughing.

"*William,*" repeated Hart, and his hands moved across his

chest, fumbling with his pyjama coat. "*William* Compline?
It cannot be William. It *cannot*."

III

They did not have a great deal of trouble with Dr. Hart after
that. He seemed at first to be completely bewildered and (the
word leapt unbidden into Mandrake's thoughts) disgusted.
Mandrake found himself quite unable to make up his mind
whether Hart was bluffing, whether his air of confusion, his
refusal to take alarm, and his obstinate denials were false or
genuine. He seemed at once to be less panic-stricken and more
hopeless than he was when he believed, or feigned to believe
that the victim was Nicholas. He also seemed to be profoundly
astonished. After a few minutes, however, he roused himself
and appeared to consider his own position. He gave them
quite a clear account of his movements from the time Mandrake left him alone in the green boudoir, until he fell asleep.
He said that he had taken some minutes to recover from his
breakdown in Mandrake's presence. He was fully roused by
tentative noises from the wireless, not loud but furtive. He
found these sounds as intolerable to his raw nerves as the
defiant blasts that preceded them. They must have affected
Hart, Mandrake thought, in much the same way as he himself
was affected by stealthy groping in chocolate boxes at the
play. The intermittent noises continued, snatches of German
and French, scraps of music, muffled bursts of static. Hart
imagined Nicholas Compline turning the dial-control and
grinning to himself. At last the maddened doctor had rushed
to the communicating door and found it locked. He had
not, he seemed to suggest, meant to do more than expostulate
with Nicholas, turn off the wireless at the wall switch and leave
the room. However, the locked door checked him. He merely
shouted a final curse at Nicholas and after a minute or two
decided to fly from torment. He switched off the lights in the
boudoir and went upstairs. As he crossed the hall to the foot
of the stairs he passed the new footman with his tray of
glasses. He said the man saw him come out of the boudoir
and that he was about half-way up the first flight when the
man returned from the smoking-room and moved about the
hall. He was still in the hall, locking up, when Hart reached
the half-way landing and turned off to the left-hand flight.

" He will tell you," said Hart, " that I did not enter the smoking-room."

" You could very easily have finished your work in the smoking-room before the man came," Jonathan said icily. " You could have returned to the boudoir and come out when you heard the man crossing the hall."

Mandrake, by a really supreme effort of self-control, held his tongue. He wanted with all his soul to cry out: " No! Don't you *see*, don't you *see* . . .?" He knew Jonathan was wrong, off the track altogether. He was amazed at Jonathan's blindness. Yet because he felt certain that somewhere, beyond his own reach, lay the answer to Hart's statement, he said nothing. Better, he thought, to wait until he had that answer.

" His skull is fractured, you say?" Hart's voice, more composed than it had been since their last interview, roused Mandrake to listen. " Very well, then. You must lock up the room. The weapon must not be touched. It may have the assassin's fingerprints. The door into the hall must be examined by the police. A medical practitioner must be found. Naturally I cannot act in the matter. My own position . . ."

" You!" Jonathan ejaculated. " Great merciful heavens, sir. . . ."

Again Mandrake interrupted. " Doctor Hart," he asked, " suppose the rest of the party agreed, would you be prepared, in the presence of witnesses, to look at the body of William Compline?"

" Certainly," said Hart promptly. " If you wish, I will do so, though it can serve no purpose. In view of your preposterous accusations I will not prejudice myself by making an examination, but I am perfectly ready to look. But, I repeat, you must immediately procure a medical man and communicate with the police."

" Have you forgotten that we're isolated?" And repeating the phrase which he had learned to dread, Mandrake added: " It's snowing harder than ever."

" This is most awkward," said Hart primly.

Jonathan burst incontinently into a tirade of abuse. Mandrake had never, until that day, seen him put out of countenance, and it was a strange and disagreeable experience to hear his voice grow shrill and his speech incoherent. His face scarlet, his small mouth pouted and trembled, and behind those blind glasses of his Mandrake caught distorted glimpses of congested eyeballs. Without a trace of his usual precision he poured out a stream of accusations. "In my house," he kept repeating, "in my house." He ordered Hart to admit his guilt, he predicted what would happen to him. In the same breath he reminded him of Mrs. Compline's ruined beauty, of his threats to Nicholas and of Mandrake's immersion. His outburst had the curious effect of steadying Hart. It was as though that house could hold only one hysterical middle-aged man at a time. Finally, Jonathan flung himself into a, chair, took out his handkerchief, saw a dark stain upon it, and with singular violence hurled it from him. He looked at Mandrake and perhaps he read astonishment and distaste in Mandrake's face, for when he spoke again it was with something of his old manner.

"You must forgive me, Aubrey. I'm exceedingly upset. Known that boy all his life. His mother's one of my oldest friends. I beg of you, Aubrey, to tell me what we should do."

Mandrake said: "I think, if Dr. Hart consents, we should leave him and lock the door after us."

"If I did not consent," said Hart, "you would still do so. One thing I shall ask of you. Will you arrange that someone, Lady Hersey perhaps, explains my present dilemma to my wife. If you permit, I should like to speak to her."

"His wife? *His wife!*"

"Yes, yes, Jonathan," said Mandrake. "Madame Lisse is Madame Hart. We can't go into it now. Do you agree to these suggestions?"

Jonathan waved his hands and, taking this as an assent, Mandrake went to the bedside table and picked up the chemist's jar. "I'll take charge of this, I think," he said. "Is it veronal?"

"I most strongly object, Mr. Mandrake."

"I thought you would. Coming, Jonathan?"

He dropped the jar into his pocket and led the way to the door. He stood aside allowing Jonathan to go out before him. He removed the key from inside the door. The last thing he saw before closing the door was Dr. Hart, his hands on his chest, staring after him. Then he stepped back over the threshold, pulled to the door, and locked it.

"Jonathan," he said, "somewhere or another we've gone incredibly wrong. Let's find Nicholas. We've got to talk."

I·V

Nicholas, wearing an expression that reminded Mandrake of a nervous colt, stood at the end of the passage outside his mother's door. He hurried to meet them.

" Well," he whispered, " for God's sake, what's happened? What's wrong?"

" At the moment, nothing," said Mandrake.

" But I heard Jonathan shouting. Hart's in his room, then? Why have you left him?"

" He's locked up. Come downstairs, Compline. We've got to talk."

" I'm deadly tired," said Nicholas suddenly. And indeed he looked exhausted. " It was pretty ghastly, telling my mamma, you know."

" How is she?" asked Jonathan, taking Nicholas's arm. They moved towards the stairs.

" Hersey's with her. She's all to blazes, to be quite frank. She's got it into her head that it all hangs on—you know. What he did to her face. She thinks it's because of what Bill said about it. I couldn't do anything much. Of course she's— God, it sounds a rotten thing to say, but you know how things are—she's—in a sort of way—glad it's not me. That makes me feel pretty foul, as you may imagine. I'd better tell Hersey it's safe for her to come out when she wants to."

He put his head in at his mother's door and gave this message. They went downstairs to the library. Chloris was sitting very upright in her chair with her hands pressed together in her lap.

" All right?" Mandrake asked.

" Me? Yes; all right. It's nice to see you again. What's happened?"

Jonathan gave Chloris and Nicholas an account of the interview. It was an accurate narrative until he came to Hart's story. Then his indignation seemed to get the better of him, and abandoning Hart's statement altogether, Jonathan talked excitedly of preposterous evasions, trumped-up alibis, and intolerable hardihood. Seeing that Chloris and Nicholas grew more and more anxious and bewildered, Mandrake waited until Jonathan had exhausted his store of phrases and then cut in with an explicit account of Hart's movements according to himself.

" A monstrous conglomeration of lies!" Jonathan fumed.

" I don't think we can altogether dismiss them, Jonathan. I take it that we none of us doubt his guilt, but I'm afraid it's not going to be easy to get over that business of his meeting the footman—supposing, of course, that the man confirms Hart's story. There must *be* an explanation, of course, but——"

" My good Aubrey," cried Jonathan, " of course there's an explanation. When he encountered Thomas—that's the fellow's name, Thomas—it was all over. That's your explanation."

" Yes, but it isn't, you know. Because it was after Thomas came in with the drinks that we heard William turn up the wireless."

There was a rather stony silence, broken by Jonathan. " Then he came downstairs and slipped into the smoking-room."

" But he says Thomas stayed in the hall."

" *He says, he says.* The answer is that he waited in the shadows on the stairs until Thomas left the hall."

" Do you remember," Mandrake asked the other two, " the sequence of events? You, Compline, came out of the smoking-room, leaving your brother—where?"

" He was over by the fire, I think. He wouldn't talk much, but I remembered he did say he was damned if Hart was going to stop him getting the news. It wasn't quite time for it. I'd heard Hart switch off the light in the boudoir and I said he'd evidently gone, so it'd be all right. I didn't want to hear the damn news myself and I'd told you I'd pipe down, so I came away."

" Exactly. As I remember, you came in and shut the door. Later, when you opened it and called out to him about the news, could you see him?"

" No. The screen hid him. But he grunted something and I heard him cross the room."

" Right. And a moment later he turned on the wireless."

" I maintain," said Jonathan, " that it was Hart we heard in there. Hart had murdered him, and when he heard Nick ask for the news he turned it on and got out of the room."

" By that time Hart, according to himself, had met Thomas coming with the tray, had got some way up the stairs and had seen Thomas re-enter the hall. It was only a matter of a minute or two after Thomas left that Lady Hersey went into

the smoking-room. Does that give Hart time to return and do
—what he did?"

"It was longer than that," said Jonathan; "the news had
run for some minutes before Hersey went in."

"But . . ." Chloris made a sudden movement.

"Yes?" asked Mandrake.

"I suppose it's no good, but a wireless does take a little
time to warm up. Could Dr. Hart have switched it on, after
—after he'd—after it was over, and then hurried out of the
room so that it would sound like Bill tuning in? Do you see
what I mean?"

"By heaven!" Nicholas said, "I believe she's got it."

"No," said Mandrake slowly. "No, I'm afraid not. The
wireless was still warm. It was only a few minutes since it had
been switched off. Even when they're cold they don't take
longer than fifteen to twenty seconds, I fancy. For that idea
to work, Hart would have had to switch it on before Thomas
came in with the drinks, and we didn't hear a thing until after
Thomas left. And, what's more, it gives a still smaller margin
of time for the actual crime. It would have to be done after
you, Compline, left your brother, and before Thomas appeared
with the glasses. Remember he had to leave the boudoir by
the door into the hall, enter the smoking-room by *its* door into
the hall, seize his weapon, steal up—I'm sorry, but we've got
to think of these things, haven't we?—do what he did, turn
on the radio, return to the boudoir and come out of it again in
time for Thomas to see him."

"It takes much longer to describe these things than to do
them," said Jonathan.

"No," said Chloris, "I think Aubrey's right, Mr. Royal. It
doesn't seem to fit."

"My dear child, you can't possibly tell."

"What do you think, Nicholas?" This was the first time
Chloris had spoken to Nicholas. He shook his head and
pressed the palms of his hands against his eyes.

"I'm sorry," he said, "but I'm no good. Just about all in."

Mandrake suppressed a feeling of irritation. He found
Nicholas in sorrow as difficult to stomach as Nicholas in good
form. He realised that his impatience was unkind and his feeling of incredulity unjust. Nicholas *was* upset. He was white
and distraught, and it would have been strange if he had not
been so affected. Mandrake realised with dismay that his own
annoyance arose not from Nicholas's behaviour but from the

compassionate glance that Chloris had given him. "Good heavens," Mandrake thought, "I'm a pretty sort of fellow!" And to make amends to h.s conscience he joined Chloris and Jonathan in urg.ng Nicholas to go to oed. Hersey Amblington came in.

"Your mother's a little calmer, Nick," she said. "But I'm afraid she's not likely to sieep. Jonathan, are there any aspirins in this house? I haven't got .ny."

"I—I really don't know. I never use them. I can ask the servants. Unless any of you——"

Nobody had any aspirins. Mandrake remembered Dr. Hart's veronal and groped in his pocket.

"There's this," he said. "Hart had taken as much or more than was good for him and I removed it. It's got the correct dosage on the label. It's a veronal preparation, I think, and is evidently a proprietary sample of sorts. The kind of thing they send out to doctors. Would it do?"

"It couldn't hurt, could it? She could try a small doze. I'll see, anyway."

Hersey went away and returned in a few minutes to say that she had given Mrs. Compline half the amount prescribed. Nicholas offered to go up to his mother, but Hersey said she thought it better not to disturb her.

"She locked her door after me," Hersey said. "She's quite safe and I hope she'll soon be asleep."

Hersey asked for an account of the interview with Hart, and Mandrake gave it to her. She listened in silence to the story of Thomas and the encounter in the hall.

"What about the Pirate?" she asked suddenly. "Is she enjoying her beauty sleep under a good dollop of her own skin food, or does she know what's happened?"

"If you mean Madame Lisse," said Nicholas, with a return to his old air of sulkiness, "I've told her. She's frightfully upset."

"That's just too bad," said Hersey.

"She's Hart's wife," said Mandrake drearily. "Haven't we told you?"

"*What?*"

"Don't ask me why it was a secret. Something to do with face-lifting. It's all too fantastically involved. Perhaps you knew, Compline?"

"I didn't know. I don't believe it," said Nicholas dully, and nothing, Mandrake thought, could have shown more clearly the shock of William's death than the amazing apathy with which this news was received. They discussed it half-heartedly and soon returned to the old theme.

"What I can't understand," said Chloris, "is *why* he did it. I know Bill had talked wildly about exposing him, but after all *we* knew about the Vienna business too. He couldn't hope to frighten us into silence."

"I think he's mad," said Nicholas. "I think it was simply that last outburst of anger at the wireless that sent him off at the deep end. I think he probably went into the room with the idea of screaming out at Bill as he had already screamed at me. And I think he had a sort of hysterical crisis and grabbed the nearest weapon and——" He caught his breath in a sort of sob, and for the first time Mandrake felt genuinely sorry for him. "That's what I think," said Nicholas, "and you can imagine what it feels like. I'd deliberately goaded him with the wireless. You heard me, Mandrake." He looked from one to another of his listeners. "How could I know? I suppose it was a silly thing to do, a rotten thing to do, if you like, but he'd been pretty foul with his threats and his booby-traps. It was me he was after, wasn't it? How could I know he'd take it out on old Bill? How could I know!"

"Don't, Nick," said Hersey. "You couldn't know."

Mandrake said: "You needn't blame yourself. You've got it wrong. Don't you see, all of you? He came in at the hall door. William was sitting with his back to the door, bending over the radio. All Hart could see from there was the back of his tunic and the nape of his neck. A few minutes before, he had heard you, Compline, tell him face to face that you were going to use the radio if you wanted to. A few seconds later both Hart and I heard you say: 'Oh, *all* right. Go to bed, Bill.' There, when he entered the room, was a man in uniform bending over the controls. The only light in the room was over by the fireplace. Don't you understand, all of you? When he struck at William Compline he thought he was attacking his brother."

v

"Aubrey, my dear fellow," said Jonathan, "I believe you are right. I am sure you are right. It is quite masterly. An admirable piece of reasoning."

" It doesn't get us over the hurdle, though," said Mandrake.
" He's been too clever for us. You'll have to talk to that man,
Jonathan. If he saw Hart go upstairs and remained in the hall
for any length of time afterwards, Hart's got an alibi that we're
going to have a devilish job to break. What's the time?"

" Five past eleven," said Chloris.

" They won't be in bed yet, will they? You'd better send for
him, Jo," said Hersey.

Jonathan fidgeted and made little doubtful sounds. " My
dear Jo, you'll have to tell the servants some time."

" I'll go and speak to them in the servants' hall."

" I wouldn't," said Hersey. " I'd ring and speak to them
here. I think we ought to be together when you talk to
Thomas. After all," said Hersey, " I suppose if we can't break
Dr. Hart's alibi, we're all under suspicion."

" My dear girl, that's utterly preposterous. Please remember
we were all together in this room when William produced the
war news on the wireless. Or, which I think more likely, when
Hart produced it."

" No," Mandrake said. " We've tried that. It won't work.
Jonathan, you went into the hall after the news began. Was
Thomas there then?"

" No," shouted Jonathan angrily, " of course he wasn't.
The hall was empty and there was no light in the boudoir. I
crossed the hall and went into the downstairs cloakroom.
When I returned it was still empty."

" Then perhaps his story about Thomas . . ."

" For heaven's sake," cried Hersey, " let's ask Thomas.

After a good deal of demurring, Jonathan finally rang the
bell. Caper answered it, and accepted the news of sudden
death and homicide with an aplomb which Mandrake had
imagined to be at the command only of family servants in
somewhat dated comedies. Caper said " Indeed, sir?" some
five or six times with nicely varied inflexions. He then went in
search of Thomas, who presently appeared wearing the air of
one who has crammed himself hastily into his coat. He was
a pale young man with damp waves in his hair. Evidently he
had been primed by Caper, for he was not quite able to conceal a certain air of avidity. He answered Jonathan's questions
promptly and sensibly. Yes, he had met Dr. Hart in the hall
as he brought up the tray. Dr. Hart came out of the boudoir
as Thomas walked up the passage and into the rear of the hall.
He was quite positive it was the boudoir. He noticed that the

lights were out. He noticed light coming from under the door into the smoking-room. Before Thomas entered the library, Dr. Hart had reached the stairs and had turned on the wall switch belonging to the stair lamps. When Thomas came out of the library, Dr. Hart had reached the visitors' room flight. Thomas stayed in the hall. He locked the front doors, made up the fire and tidied the tables. In answer to a question from Mandrake he said that he heard music from the radio in the smoking-room.

" What sort of music?" asked Mandrake.

" Beg pardon, sir?"

" Did you recognise the music?"

" 'Boomps-a-daisy,' sir," said Thomas unhappily.

" Well, go on, go on," said Jonathan. " You went away then, I suppose."

" No, sir."

" What the devil did you do with yourself, hanging about the hall?" demanded Jonathan, who was beginning to look extremely uneasy.

" Well, sir, excuse me, sir, I—I . . ."

" You *what*!"

" I went through the movements, sir. 'Hands, knees,' in time to the music, sir. I don't know why, I'm sure, sir. It just came over me. Only for a minute like, because the music only lasted a very short time, sir, and then it was turned off."

" Cavorting about the hall like a buck-rabbit!" said Jonathan.

" I'm sure I'm very sorry, sir."

For a moment Jonathan seemed to be extraordinarily put out by this confession of animal spirits on the part of Thomas, but suddenly he made one of his quick pounces and cried out triumphantly: " Aha! So you were dancing, Thomas, were you? An abrupt attack of *joie de vivre*? And why not? Why not? You were intent upon it, I dare say. Turning this way and that, eh? I suppose it would take you right across the hall. I'm not very familiar with the dance, I must confess, but I imagine it's pretty lively, what?"

" Yes, sir. Rather lively, sir."

" Rather lively," repeated Jonathan. " Quite so. You'd be so taken up with it, I dare say, that you wouldn't notice if somebody came into the hall, um?"

" Beg pardon, sir, but nobody came into the hall, sir. The music-stopped and the news started and I went back to the servants' sitting-room, sir, but nobody came into the hall while I was there."

" But, my good Thomas, I—I put it to you, I put it to you, that while you were clapping your hands and slapping your knees and all the rest of it, it would have been perfectly easy for someone to cross the hall unnoticed. Come now!"

" Look here, Thomas," said Mandrake. " Let's put it this way. Somebody *did* come downstairs while you were in the hall. This person came downstairs and went into the smoking-room. Don't you remember?"

" I'm very sorry, sir, to contradict you," said Thomas, turning a deep plum colour, " but I assure you they didn't. They couldn't of. I was close by the smoking-room door, sir, and facing the stairs. What I mean to say, I just 'eard, heard, the tune, sir, and I'm sure I don't know why, I did a couple of hands, knees, and boomps; well, for the fun of it, like."

" Thomas," Mandrake said, " suppose you were in a court of law and were asked to swear on the Bible that nobody was in the hall from the time you came out of the library until the time you went back to your own quarters? What about it?"

" I'd swear, sir."

" There's nothing to be gained by going on with this," Aubrey," said Jonathan. " Thank you, Thomas."

" Thank you, sir," said Thomas, and retired.

" There's only one explanation," said Nicholas. " He must have come back after that chap went back to his quarters."

" All the way downstairs and across the hall?" said Mandrake. " I suppose it's possible. In that case he avoided running into Jonathan, and did the whole thing while that short news bulletin was being read. It was all over and he'd bolted when Lady Hersey went into the smoking-room and turned off the radio. It's a close call."

He bent down and slipped a finger inside his shoe. " Damn!" he said. " Does any one mind if I take off my shoe? I've got a nail sticking into my foot."

He took off the shoe and noticed how they all glanced at his sound foot and away again quickly. He groped inside the shoe. " There it is," he muttered; " a damn' great spike of a thing."

" But there's something in the sole of your shoe," said Chloris. " Look."

Mandrake turned the shoe over. " It's a drawing pin," he said.

" There's *some* explanation," said Nicholas with a real note

of despair in his voice. " He's upstairs there, lying in his bed,
by God, and laughing at us. Somehow or other he worked it.
During the news. It must have been then. Somehow or other.
When I think about it I'm sure it was Bill who worked the
wireless. I know you'll say it was easy for anybody to grunt
and cross the room, but somehow, I can't explain why, I believe it was Bill—it sort of *felt* like Bill."

" Ssh!" said Hersey suddenly. " Listen!"

They stared at her. Her hand was raised and her head tilted.
Into a profound silence that fell upon them came a wide,
vague drumming. The shutters of the library windows creaked.
As they listened, the room was filled with that enveloping outside noise.

" It's beginning to rain," said Jonathan.

CHAPTER X

JOURNEY

I

THEY had exhausted themselves arguing about the gap in
Hart's story. They had said the same things over and over
again. They longed to go to bed, and yet were held prisoner
in their chairs by a dreadful lassitude. They kept telling
Nicholas to go to bed, and he kept saying that he would go.
They spoke in low voices to a vague background of drumming
rain. Mandrake felt as if it was William himself who kept
them there, William who, behind locked doors, now suffered
the indignities of death. He could not help but think of that
figure in the chair. Suppose, with those stealthy changes,
William's body was to move? Suppose they were to hear,
above the murmur of rain, a dull thud in the room next door?
Nicholas, too, must have been visited by some such thoughts,
for he said: " I can't bear to think of him—can't we—can't
we?" And Mandrake had to explain again that they must not
move William.

" Do you think," he asked Jonathan, " that with this rain
the roads will be passable in the morning? What about the
telephone? Is there any chance that the lines will be fixed up?"

There was a telephone in the library, and from time to time

they had tried it, knowing each time that it was useless. "If the roads are anything like passable," Mandrake said, "I'll drive into Chipping in the morning."

"You?" said Nicholas.

"Why not? My club foot doesn't prevent me from driving a car, you know," said Mandrake. This was one of the speeches, born of his deformity, which he sometimes blurted out and always regretted.

"I didn't mean that," said Nicholas. "I'm sorry."

"Why shouldn't I go?" asked Mandrake, looking from one to another. "Even if we can't break Hart's alibi, I suppose none of you will suspect me. After all, I *was* shoved in the pond."

"I keep forgetting that complication," said Jonathan.

"I don't," Mandrake rejoined warmly.

"We ought none of us to forget it," said Chloris. "It's the beginning of the whole thing. If *only* you'd gone on looking out of the pavilion window, Nicholas."

"I know. But I was half-undressed and hellish cold. I just saw it was Mandrake and answered his wave. If only I had looked out again!"

"I've not the least doubt about what you'd have seen," Mandrake rejoined. "You'd have seen that infamous little man come up in a flurry of snow from behind the pavilion, and you'd have seen him launch a sort of flying tackle at my back."

"I've made a complete hash of everything," Nicholas burst out. "You're all being very nice about it, I know, but the facts stare you in the eye, don't they? I know what you're thinking. You're thinking that if I hadn't baited Hart this would never have happened. Well, let him get on with it, by God. He's messed it up three times, hasn't he? Let him have another pot at me. I shan't duck."

"Nick," said Hersey, "don't show off, my dear. Are we never to register dislike of anyone for fear they go off and murder our near relations? Don't be an ass, my dear old thing. Since we are being candid, let's put it this way. Dr. Hart was crossed in love and he couldn't take it. You did the crossing. I don't say I approve of your tactics, and, as I dare say you've noticed, I don't admire your choice. But, for pity's sake, don't go all broken-with-remorse on us. You've got your mother to think of."

"If anybody other than Hart is to blame," said Jonathan, "very clearly it is I."

"Now, Jo," said Hersey roundly, "none of that from you. You've been a very silly little man, trying to rearrange people's lives for them. This is what you get for it, and no doubt it'll be a lesson to you. But it's no good putting on that face about it. We must be practical. We've got a man whom we all believe to be a murderer, locked up in his room, and as we don't seem to be very good at bringing it home to him the best thing we can do is to accept Mr. Mandrake's offer and to hope that in the morning he will be able to reach a telephone and find us a policeman."

"Hersey, my dear," said Jonathan with a little bob in her direction, "you are perfectly right. Nick and I must bow to your ruling. If Aubrey can and will go, why then go he shall."

"I thought," said Mandrake, "that I'd try to reach the rectory at Winton St. Giles. You see, there's rather a super sort of policeman staying there, and as I know him . . ."

"Roderick Alleyn?" Chloris cried out. "Why, of course!"

"I thought I'd put the whole thing before him. I thought that when I got upstairs I'd write it all down, everything I can remember from the time I got here. I don't know what the regulations are, but if I show what I've written to Alleyn, at least if *he* can't do anything he'll advise *me* what to do."

"I think we should see your notes, Aubrey."

"Of course, Jonathan. I hope you'll be able to add to them. It seems to me that when you write things out they have a way of falling into place. Perhaps when he reads our notes we may see a still wider gap in Hart's alibi. I think we should concentrate on the time Jonathan was in the downstairs cloakroom and the moment or two after Jonathan returned and before Lady Hersey went into the smoking-room. I think we shall find that the gaps are there all right. If we don't, perhaps Alleyn will."

"I'm afraid I don't believe he will," said Chloris slowly. She reached out her hand and touched Mandrake's arm. "Don't think I'm crabbing your idea. It's a grand idea. But somehow, I can't tell you how I hate to say it, somehow I don't believe we will find a big enough gap. I don't think there is one."

"I won't have that," said Jonathan loudly, "there's plenty of time. There must be."

He stood up and the others rose with him. At last they were going to bed. With dragging steps and heavy yawns they moved uncertainly about the room. The men had a last drink.

Desultory suggestions were made. Nicholas, with a return of nervousness which contrasted strangely with his recent mood of heroic despondency, started an argument about leaving Hart's door unguarded. Hart might try to break out, he said. Mandrake pointed out that if they kept their own doors locked it wouldn't much matter if he did. He, as much as they, was a prisoner in the house. " Anyway," added Mandrake, " we're not going to sleep through a door-smashing incident, I suppose. Here's your automatic, by the way, Compline." And for the life of him Mandrake couldn't resist adding: " You may feel more comfortably if you have it at your bedside." Nicholas took it quite meekly.

" Well," he said in a small desolate voice, " I may as well go up, I suppose." He looked towards the locked door into the smoking-room and Mandrake saw his rather prominent eyes dilate. " He offered to swap rooms with me," said Nicholas. " Decent of him, wasn't it? In case Hart tried anything during the night, you know. Of course, I wouldn't have let him. I'm glad we sort of got together a bit this evening." He looked at his hands and then vaguely up at Jonathan. " Well, good-night," said Nicholas.

" We'll come up with you, Nick," said Hersey, and linked her arm in his.

" Will you? Oh, thank you, Hersey."

" Of course we shall," said Chloris. " Come on, Nick."

Jonathan and Mandrake followed, and as Mandrake, weary to death, limped up those stairs for the last time on that fatal day, he thought, and detested himself for so thinking: " He *would* go up between the two women. I bet he's got hold of Chloris's hand." Jonathan said good-night on the half-way landing and turned off to his own wing. Only then did it occur to Mandrake that since his flare-up with Hart, Jonathan had been unusually quiet. " And no wonder," he thought. " They can say what they like, but after all if he hadn't thrown his fool party . . ."

They went with Nicholas to his room. Moved by an obscure mixture of contrition and genuine sympathy, Mandrake shook hands with him and instantly regretted it when Nicholas, with tears in his eyes, kissed the two women and said in a broken voice: " Bless you. I'll be all right. Good-night."

" Good-night," said Hersey in the passage and stumped off to her room.

F

"Good-night," said Chloris to Mandrake, and then, rather defiantly: "Well, I *am* sorry for him."

"Good-night," said Mandrake, "so am I."

"You do look tired. We've all forgotten about your horrid plunge. You won't tackle those notes to-night?"

"I think so. While it's still seething, don't you know?"

"Well, don't treat the subject surrealistically or we'll none of us be able to contradict you. You ought not to have had all these games thrust upon you. Are you all right?"

"Perfectly all right," said Mandrake. "But I approve of you feeling sorry for me."

So Chloris gave him a kiss, and in a state of bewildered satisfaction he went to his room.

II

It was one o'clock when he laid down his pen and read through his notes. At the end he had written a summary in which he attempted to marshal the salient facts of the three assaults. He re-read this summary twice.

"1. The incident of the Charter form. Hart wrote the message because he, and only he, handed his papers on to Nicholas. The letters resemble those in his note to Jonathan. The incident followed his picking a quarrel with Nicholas after dinner. N.B.—get an account of quarrel from Jonathan, who was the only witness.

"2. The incident by the pond. Motive apart, Nicholas didn't shove me over because he recognised me through the window and in any case knew I was wearing the cape. Besides he saved my life by throwing in the inflated bird. William didn't because he arrived at about the same time as Nicholas and had come down the terrace-steps. Nicholas saw him come. Chloris didn't because she didn't. Jonathan arrived after Chloris, catching her up when she was nearly there. He had seen Hart leave by the front drive. Hart arrived by a path that comes out behind the pavilion. I had my back turned to him. He had seen Nicholas, wearing a cape that is the double of mine. I had the hood over my head. N.B.—who was the woman who came out of the house as far as the terrace? (Footprints in snow.) She may have seen who threw me overboard. If so, why hasn't she spoken? Her prints were close to the others. A small foot. Could she have gone down the steps inside my footprints? Madame Lisse's window overlooks the terrace. Hart habitually wears a cape.

" 3. The booby-trap. Hart is the only member of the party who hasn't an alibi. Jonathan's alibi depends on me. I can't remember exactly how long he was in the drawing-room before the crash, but anyway why should Jonathan want to kill Nicholas? Hart must have set the booby-trap.

" 4. The murder. On re-reading these notes I find that Madame Lisse, Lady Hersey and Mrs. Compline have not got alibis. Madame Lisse and Mrs. Compline could have come downstairs and entered the smoking-room by the boudoir. But if either of them did it, how did she leave? Thomas was in the hall when William turned on the radio and remained there until the news. I suppose the Lisse or Mrs. Compline might have actually hidden in the room and slipped out when Lady Hersey came to fetch Jonathan, but it seems more likely that they could have managed to dodge both Thomas and Jonathan. Mrs. Compline is out of it. No motive. Madame Lisse had no motive in killing Nicholas, so if she did it she recognised William and her motive here . . ."

At this point Mandrake, remembering that the others would read his summary, lost his nerve and scored out the next three lines and the preceding words from " No Motive " onwards. He then read on.

" Nicholas didn't do it because some time after he left the smoking-room, the wireless was switched on. This must have been done by William or conceivably by his murderer. We didn't see him although the door was open. The screen hid him. But someone did cross the room and turn on the wireless.

" Lady Hersey went in with the drink and of course, theoretically, could have killed William, and then come and called Jonathan. No motive.

" Hart came out of the boudoir and was seen by Thomas as he brought the drinks. When Thomas reappeared a few seconds later, Hart was on the stairs. No time to go back and kill William in the interim. He didn't return before the news because Thomas remained in the hall until then and because William turned on ' Boomps-a-daisy ' after Hart had gone. If Hart killed William, it was after Thomas left the hall. Could he have done it in the time and avoided meeting Jonathan?

" Jonathan himself left the library after the news began and returned before Hersey took in the drink. He says he crossed the hall to and from the cloakroom and saw nobody. Could Hart have dodged him? Possible.

"This seems to be the only explanation."

Here the summary came abruptly to an end. Mandrake sat very still for perhaps a minute. Then he took out his cigarette case, put it down unopened, and reached again for his pen. He added six words to his summary:

"Could Hart have set another booby-trap?"

When he lifted his hand he saw that he had left a small red stain on the paper. He had washed his hands as soon as he came upstairs, but his mind jumped with a spasm of nausea to the memory of the red star that had fallen from William's mouth. Then he remembered that when he took out his cigarette-case he had felt a prick and there, sure enough, on the tip of his middle finger was a little red globule. He felt again in his pocket and found the drawing-pin that had penetrated the sole of his shoe. He put it on the paper before him. Across the back of the drawing-pin was a dry white ridge.

He heard William's voice speaking gravely in the drawing-room: "*Very* thick oil paint."

He put the drawing-pin in a match-box and locked the box in his attaché case, together with the Charter form which he had got from Jonathan.

Then he went to bed.

III

It was some time before he slept. Several times he came to the borderland where conscious thought mingles fantastically with the images of the subconscious. At these moments he saw a Maori mere, like Damocles' sword, suspended above his head by a hair which was fixed to the ceiling by an old drawing-pin. "It *might* hold," said William, speaking indistinctly because his mouth was full of blood. "It *might* hold, you know. I use *very* thick oil paint." He couldn't move because the folds of the Tyrolese cape were wrapped round his limbs. A rubber bird, wearing a god-like leer, bobbed its scarlet beak at him.

"It's snowing harder than ever," said the bird, and at that precise moment Hart cut the hair with a scalpel. "*Down* she comes, by Jupiter," they all shouted, but Chloris, with excellent intentions, kicked him between the shoulder-blades and he fell with a sickening jolt back into his bed, and woke again to hear the rain driving against the window-pane.

At last, however, he fell into a true sleep, and was among the first of the seven living guests to do so. Dr. Hart was the very first. Long before the others came upstairs to bed, Dr. Hart's dose of proprietary soporific had restored his interrupted oblivion and now his mouth was open, his breathing deep and stertorous.

His wife was not so fortunate. She heard them all come upstairs, she heard them wish each other good-night, she heard door after door close softly, and imagined key after key turning with a click as each door was shut. Sitting upright in bed in her fine nightgown she listened to the rain, and made plans for her own security.

Hersey Amblington, too, was wakeful. She kept her bedside lamp alight and absent-mindedly slapped " Hersey's Skin Food " into her face with a patent celluloid patter. As she did this she tried distractedly to order her thoughts away from the memory of a figure in an armchair, from a head that was broken like an egg, and from a wireless cabinet that screamed " Boomps-a-daisy." She thought of herself twenty years ago, afraid to tell her cousin Jonathan that she would marry him. She thought of her business rival and wondered quite shamelessly if, with the arrest of Hart, Madame Lisse would carry her piratical trade elsewhere. Finally, hoping to set up a sort of counter-irritant in horror, she thought about her own age. But the figure in the chair was persistent, and Hersey was afraid to go to sleep.

Chloris was not much afraid. She had not seen William. But she was extremely bewildered over several discoveries that she had made about herself. The most upsetting of these was the discovery that she now felt nothing but a vague pity for Nicholas, and an acute pity for William. She had never pretended to herself that she was madly in love with William but she had believed herself to be very fond of him. It was Nicholas who had held her in the grip of a helpless attraction, it was from this bondage that she had torn herself on a climax of misery. She believed that when Nicholas had become aware of his brother's determined courtship, he had set himself to cut William out. Having succeeded very easily in this project he had tired of her and, in the meantime, he had met Elise Lisse. She thought of the letter in which she broke off her engagement to Nicholas, and with shame of the new engagement to

his brother; of how every look, every word that was exchanged between them, for her held only one significance;
its effect upon Nicholas, of the miserable satisfaction she had
known when Nicholas showed his resentment, of the exultation
she had felt when, again, he began to show off his paces before
her. And now it was all over. She had cried a little out of pity
for William and from the shock to her nerves, and she had seen
Nicholas once and for all as a silly fellow and a bit of a
coward. A phrase came into her thoughts: " So that's all
about the Complines." With an extraordinary lightening of
her spirits she now allowed herself to think of Aubrey Mandrake. " Of Mr. Stanley Footling," she corrected herself. " It
ought to be funny. Poor Mr. Stanley Footling turning as
white as paper and letting me in on the ground floor. It isn't
funny. I can't make a good story of it. It's infinitely touching
and it doesn't matter to me, only to him." And she thought:
" Did I take the right line about it?" She had gone to her
room determined to break Dr. Hart's alibi, but a whole hour
had passed and not once had she thought of Dr. Hart.

Jonathan Royal clasped his hot-water bag to his midriff and
stared before him into the darkness. If the top strata of his
thoughts had been written down they would have read something like this: " It's an infernal bore about Thomas but there
must be some way out of it. Aubrey is going to be tiresome, I
can see. He's half inclined to believe Hart. *Damn* Thomas.
There must be some way. An ingenious turn, now. My
thoughts are going round in circles. I must concentrate. What
will Aubrey write in his notes? I must read them carefully.
Can't be too careful. This fellow, Alleyn. What will he make
of it? Why, there's motive, the two attempts, *our* alibis—he
can't come to any other conclusion. *Damn* Thomas."

Nicholas tossed and turned in the bed his brother had
offered to take. He was unaccustomed to consecutive or
ordered thinking, and across his mind drifted an endless pro-
cession of dissociated images and ideas. He saw himself and
William as children. He saw William going back to school
at the end of his holidays. Nicholas and his tutor had gone in
the car to the station. There was Bill's face, pressed against
the window-pane as the train went out. He heard Bill's adoles-
cent voice breaking comically into falsetto: " She'd like it to
be you at Penfelton and me anywhere else. But I'm the eldest.
You can't alter that. Mother will never forgive me for it." He
saw Chloris the first time she came to Penfelton as William's

guest for a house-party. " Mother, will you ask Chloris Wynne? She's my girl, Nick. No poaching." And lastly he saw Elise Lisse, and heard his own voice: " I never knew it could be like this. I never knew."

Sandra Compline laid down her pen. She enclosed the paper in an envelope and wrote a single word of direction. Outside on the landing the grandfather clock struck two. She wrapped her dressing-gown more closely round her. The fire was almost dead and she was bitterly cold. The moment had come for her to get into bed. The bedclothes were disordered. She straightened them carefully, and then glanced round the room which was quite impersonal and, but for the garments she had worn during the day, very neat. She folded them and put them away, shivering a little as she did so. She caught sight of her face in the glass and paused before it to touch her hair. On an impulse, she leant forward and stared at the reflection. Next, she moved to the bedside-table and for some minutes her hands were busy there. At last she got into bed, disposed the sheet carefully, and drew up the counterpane. Then she stretched out her hand to the bedside-table.

IV

It was an isolated storm that visited Cloudyfold that night. Over the greater part of Dorset the snow lay undisturbed, but here in the uplands it was drilled with rain, and all through the night hills and trees suffered a series of changes. In the depths of Jonathan's woods, branches, released from their burden of snow, jerked sharply upwards. From beneath battlements of snow, streams of water began to move and there were secret downward shiftings of white masses. With the diminution of snow the natural contours of the earth slowly returned. Towards dawn in places where there had been smooth depressions sharp furrows began to take form, and these were sunken lanes. In Deep Bottom, beneath the sound of rain was the sound of running water.

The guests, when at last they slept, were sometimes troubled in their dreams by strange noises on the roofs and eaves of the house where masses of snow became dislodged and slid into gutters and hollows. The drive and the road from Highfold down into Cloudyfold village and up into the hills began to find themselves. So heavy was the downpouring of rain that by dawn the countryside was dappled with streaks of heavy greys and patches of green. When Mandrake woke at eight o'clock his windows were blinded with rain and through the rain he saw the tops of evergreen trees, no longer burdened with snow.

He breakfasted alone with Jonathan, who told him that already he had seen some of the outdoor staff. His bailiff had ridden up from his own cottage on horseback and had gone out again on a round of inspection. Jonathan had told him of the tragedy. He had offered to ride over Cloudyfold. It meant twelve miles at a walking pace supposing he did get through.

"If I stick," said Mandrake, "he can try. If I'm not back in three hours, Jonathan, he had better try. What sort of mess is the drive, did he say?" The Bewlings, it seemed, had been down to the front gates and reported that the drive was "a masterpiece of muck," but not, they thought, impassable. You could get over Cloudyfold on a horse, no doubt, but a car would never do it.

"How about the road down to the village?" asked Mandrake.

"That's in better case, I understand."

"Then if I got through Deep Bottom I could drive down to Cloudyfold village and telephone from there to the rectory at Winton St. Giles?"

"The lines may be down between the village and Winton. They go over the hills. I think it most probable that they are down. As far as the Bewlings went they found nothing the matter with my own line."

"Can't I get to Winton St. Giles by way of the village?"

"A venture that is comparable to Chesterton's journey to Birmingham by way of Beachy Head, my dear Aubrey. Let me see. You would have to take the main road east, turn to your right at Pen-Gidding, skirt Cloudyfold hills and—but Heaven knows what state those roads would be in. From Pen-Gidding there are only the merest country lanes."

"I can but try."

"I don't like it."

"Jonathan," said Mandrake, "do you like the idea of leaving William Compline's body in your smoking-room for very much longer?"

"Oh, my dear fellow, no. No, of course not. This is horrible, a nightmare. I shall never recover from this week-end, never."

"Do you think one of the Bewling brothers could come with

me? If I did come to a standstill it would be helpful to have someone, and if I don't he could direct me."

"Of course, of course. If you must go." Jonathan brightened a little and began to make plans. "You must take a flask of brandy, my dear boy. James Bewling shall go with you. Chains now. You will need chains on your wheels, won't you?"

"There's not by any chance a police-station at Cloudyfold village?"

"Good gracious, no. The merest hamlet. No, the nearest constable, I fancy, is at Chipping, and that's beyond Winton St. Giles."

"At any rate," said Mandrake, "I think I'd better see Alleyn first. I only hope he'll consent to run the whole show and come back with me, but I suppose I shall run into an entanglement of red-tape if I suggest such a thing."

"Dear me, I suppose so. I scarcely know which prospect is more distasteful—the Chipping constabulary or your terrifying acquaintance."

"He's a pleasant fellow."

"Very possibly. Perhaps I had better send for old James Bewling before he plunges out of doors again."

Jonathan rang the bell, which was answered by Thomas, who was unable to conceal entirely an air of covert excitement. He said that the Bewlings were still in the house and in a minute or two James appeared, very conscious of his boots.

"Now, James," said Jonathan, "Mr. Mandrake and I want your advice and assistance. Dry your legs at the fire and never mind about your boots. Listen."

He unfolded Mandrake's project. James listened with his mouth not quite shut, his eyes fixed upon some object at the far end of the room, and his brows drawn together in a formidable scowl.

"Now, do you think it is possible?" Jonathan demanded.

"Ah," said James. "Matter a twenty miles it be, that road. Going widdershins like, you see, sir. She'll be fair enough so furr as village and a good piece below. It's when she do turn in and up, if you take my meaning, sir, as us'll run into muck and as like as not, slips, and as like as not if there bean't no slips, there'll be drifts."

"Then you *don't* think it possible, James?"

"With corpses stiffening on the premises, sir, all things be possible to a man with a desperate powerful idea egging him on."

"My opinion exactly, Bewling," said Mandrake. "Will you come with me?"

"That I will, sir," said James. "When shall us start?"

"Now, if you will. As soon as possible." And as he spoke these words Mandrake was moved by a great desire for his venture. Soon he would meet Chloris again, and to that meeting he looked forward steadily and ardently, but in the meantime he must be free of Highfold for a space. He must set out in driving rain on a difficult task. It would be with bad roads and ill weather that he must reckon for the next hour or so, not with the complexities of human conduct. His eagerness for these encounters was so foreign to his normal way of thinking that he felt a sort of astonishment at himself. "But I don't like leaving her here. Shall I wait until she appears and suggest that she comes with us? Perhaps she would not care to come. Perhaps I have embarrassed her with my dreary confidences. She might be afraid I'd go all Footling at her on the drive." He began to horrify himself with the notion that Chloris thought of him as under-bred and over-vehement, a man whom she would have to shake off before he became a nuisance. He went upstairs determined that he would not succumb to the temptation of asking her to go with him, met her on the top landing, and immediately asked her.

"Of course I'll come," said Chloris.

"It may be quite frightful. We may break down completely."

"At least we'll be out of all this. I won't be five minutes."

"You'll want layers of coats," cried Mandrake. "I'll get hold of old James Bewling and we'll have the car round at the front door as soon as he's found me some chains."

He went joyfully to his own room, put on an extra sweater, a muffler and his raincoat. He snatched up the attaché case containing his notes, the drawing-pin and the Charter form. He remembered suddenly that the others were to have gone over the notes before he took them to Alleyn. Well, if they wanted to do that they should have got up earlier. He couldn't wait about half the morning. They would have plenty of chances to argue over his account when he came back with Alleyn. Now for the car.

But before he went out of doors he found Jonathan and nerved himself to make a request. The thought of revisiting the smoking-room was horrible, but he had promised himself that he would do so. He half hoped Jonathan would refuse,

but he did not. " I won't come with you, that's all. Don't ask
it. Here are the keys. You may keep them. I simply can
not accompany you."

" I shan't touch anything. Please wait by the door."

He was only a few minutes in that room. They had thrown
a white sheet over the chair and what was in it. He tried not
to look at that, but he was shaken when he came out and said
good-bye quietly to Jonathan.

He went out by the west door and walked around the back
of the house to the garages. The whole world seemed to be
alive with the sound of rain and wind. Much of the snow
lying in exposed places had gone, everywhere it was pocked
and crenellated. From the eaves of Highfold it hung in strange
forms that changed continually and tapered into falling water.

Using his stick vigorously, Mandrake reached the garages to
find James Bewling, assisted by his brother, engaged in fitting
chains to the car wheels. They seemed to Mandrake to be incredibly slow about this. The chains were improvised arrange-
ments and one set kept slipping. At last, however, they were
ready and he prepared to drive out.

" They'll hold now, certain sure. Lucky we had 'em," said
James. " Us'll need 'em up along, never fear. Now then, sir,
if you be agreeable I reckon car's ready to start. Us've filled
her up with petrol and water and there's hauly-chains and
sacks in the back."

" Come on then," said Mandrake.

James climbed in the back. As they left the garage his
brother bawled at them: " If 'er skiddles, rush 'er up." He
drove round to the front doors and found Chloris there. The
collar of her heavy coat was turned up, and she had a gay
scarf tied round her head so that he saw her face as a triangle.
It was a very white triangle and her eyes looked horror-
stricken. As soon as she saw the car she stumbled down the
steps, and, leaning against the wind, ran round to the pas-
senger's door. Before he could get it open she was struggling
with the handle and in a moment had scrambled in beside him.

" What now?" asked Mandrake.

" I'd better tell you before we start, but Mr. Royal says we're
to go anyway. Another ghastliness. Mrs. Compline. She's
tried to kill herself."

v

Mandrake turned with his hands on the driving-wheel and gazed at her. James Bewling cleared his throat stertorously.

"Please start," said Chloris, and without a word Mandrake engaged his first gear. To the sound of slapping chains, driving wind and rain, and with a cold engine, they moved across the wide sweep and round the west side of the house.

"She did it herself," said Chloris. "One of the maids went up with her breakfast and found the door locked. The house-keeper thought she ought not to be disturbed, but the maid had seen lamplight under the door when she went up with early tea. So they told Mr. Royal. It seemed queer, you see, for the lamps to be going after it was light. In the end they decided to knock. It was just after you went out. They knocked and knocked and she didn't answer. By that time Nicholas was there and in an awful state. He insisted on Mr. Royal forcing the door. She'd left a note for him—for Nicholas. There's been a frightful scene, it seems, because Mr. Royal said Nicholas should give the note to somebody. He won't let Nicholas keep it, but he hasn't read it himself. I don't know what was in the note. Only Nick knows. She's unconscious. They think she's dying."

"But—how?"

"The rest of that sleeping draught and all the aspirins she'd got. She'd told Lady Hersey she had no aspirins. I suppose she wanted to get as much as possible. You'd feel sorry for Nicholas if you could see him now."

"Yes," said Mandrake sombrely. "Yes, I do feel sorry for Nicholas now."

"He's gone to pieces. No more showing-off for poor old Nick," said Chloris with a catch in her voice. "There couldn't be any doubt at all that it was suicide, and he agreed that Dr. Hart should be asked to see her. Pretty queer, wasn't it? They all agree that he murdered Bill, and yet there he was working at artificial respiration and snapping out orders with everybody running round obeying them. I think the world's gone mad or something. He's given me a list of things we're to get at the chemist's in Chipping. It's not far beyond Winton St. Giles. I could take the car on if you like while you see Mr. Alleyn. And the police surgeon. We've got to try and find him, but the important thing is to get back as quickly as possible."

" Does Hart think . . .?"

" I'm sure he thinks it's pretty hopeless. I wasn't in the room. I waited by the door for orders. I heard him say something about two hundred grains of veronal alone. He was barking out questions to Lady Hersey. How much had she given? How dared she give it. If it wasn't so frightful it'd be funny. She's in a pretty ghastly state herself. She feels she's responsible."

" I took the stuff away from Hart," said Mandrake. " God, that's a touch of irony for you! I was afraid he might try something on himself."

" You needn't go all remorseful," said Chloris quickly. " Dr. Hart said the aspirin alone would have been disastrous. I heard him say that to Lady Hersey."

They had reached the woods, where the drive ran between steep banks. Here the surface, no longer gravelled, was soft, laced with runnels of water, and littered with broken twigs and with clods of earth that had carried away from the banks. In one place there was a miniature landslide across their route. Mandrake drove hard at it in second gear and felt his back wheels spin and then grip on the chains.

" That's a taste of what we may expect in Deep Bottom, I suppose," he called to James Bewling.

" 'Twill be watter down-along, I reckon, sir."

" If we stick . . ." Chloris began.

" If we stick, my dear, they can damn' well produce a farm animal to lug us out on the far side."

" It's dogged as does it," said Chloris.

Beyond Highfold woods, the drive, where it crossed the exposed parklands, was furrowed and broken by pot-holes. James Bewling remarked that he and Thomas had been telling the master for a matter of ten years that he did ought to lay down a load of metal. The rain drove full on the windscreen, checking the wiper, splaying out in serrated circles and finding its way in above the dashboard. The thrust of the wind made the car fight against Mandrake's steering. He drove cautiously towards the edge of Deep Bottom, peering through the blear of water. He recognised in himself an exhilaration, and this discovery astonished him, for he had always thought that he loathed discomfort.

Snow still lay in Deep Bottom. When they reached the lip

of the hollow and looked down, they saw the drive disappear under it and rise again on the far side like a muddy ribbon.

"She's be gone down a tidy piece," said James. "Not above two foot now, I reckon, but happen thurr'll be watter underneath. Happen us'd do better with sack over radiator, sir."

Mandrake pulled up and James plunged out with his sack. Mandrake stumbled after him. He didn't want to sit in the car while James fixed up the sack. He wanted to be knowledgeable and active. He tied the sacking over the radiator cap, using his handkerchief to bind it. He looked critically at the way James had tied the corners of the sack. Swinging his heavy boot briskly, he came back to the car, smiling through the rain at Chloris. The warmth in her returning glance delighted him and he innocently supposed that it was inspired by his activity. It was the glance, he told himself, of the female, approving, dependent, and even clinging. He would never know that Chloris was deeply touched, not because she saw him as a protector, but because suddenly she read his thoughts. And from that moment, in her wisdom, she let herself be minded by Mandrake.

The car began its crawl down into Deep Bottom.

"For a tidy ten yurr and more," said James Bewling in the back seat, "my wold brother Thomas and me been telling master as 'ow 'ee did oughter put a dinky lil' bridge across this yurr bottom. Last winter 'er was in a muck with ranging torrents and floods. Winter afore, 'er fruz. Winter afore that 'er caved in sudden." Here the car lurched in and out of a pot-hole and James was thrown about in the back seat. "Winter afore that 'er flooded again. Bean't no proper entrance to gentleman's 'state, us tells 'un. Ay, and us tells bailiff tu. Pull over to your right, sir, by this yurr puddlesome corner or us'll sink to our bottoms."

The front wheels plunged deep into a welter of slush. The back wheels churned, gripped, skidded and gripped again. Now they were into the snow, with James Bewling roaring: "To tha right and rush 'er up." The bonnet dipped abruptly and a welter of snow spurted over the windscreen. Mandrake leant out of the driving window and took the whipping rain full in his eyes. "Keep 'er going, sir," yelled James.

"I'm in a blasted hole or something. Come *up*."

The car moved bodily to the left, churned, crept forward in a series of jerks and stopped. "Doan't stop in-gine fur Lawk's sake," James implored, and was out and up to his knees. He disappeared in the rear of the car.

"What's he doing?" asked Mandrake. "He's on your side.

Chloris looked out on her side. "I can only see his stern. He seems to be stuffing something under the back wheel. Now he's waving. He wants you to go on."

Mandrake engaged his bottom gear, pulled out his choke a fraction, and tried. The car gripped somewhere, wallowed forward and stuck again. James returned for his shovel and set to work in front of the bonnet. Mandrake got out, leaving instructions with Chloris to keep the engine going. The noise of the storm met him like a physical blow, and the drive of rain on his face numbed it. He struggled round to the front of the car and found James shovelling with a will in three feet of snow. Mandrake wore heavy driving gloves, and set to work with his hands. In the centre the snow was still frozen, but at the bottom it had turned to slush and the earth beneath was soft and muddy. The front wheels had jammed in a cross-gut which, as they cleared it, began to fill with water. James roared out something that Mandrake could not understand, thrust his shovel into his hands, and plunged away behind the car. Mandrake toiled on, looking up once to see Chloris's face pressed anxiously against the windscreen. He grinned, waved his hand, and fell to again with a will. James had returned, dragging two great boughs after him. They broke them up as best they could, filled in the gut with smaller branches, and thrust the remaining pieces in front of the rear wheels.

The inside of the car seemed a different world, a world that smelt of petrol, upholstery, cigarettes and something that both Mandrake and Chloris secretly realised was peculiar to James Bewling, an aftermath of oilskin, elderly man, and agricultural activities. Mandrake slammed the door, sounded his horn as a warning to James, and speeded up his engine.

"Now then, you old besom," Mandrake apostrophised his car, "up with you." With a great crackling of branches, an ominous sinking and a violent lurch, they went forward and up, with James's voice raised to an elderly screech, sounding like a banshee in the storm. The chains bit into firmer ground. They were going uphill.

"That's the first hurdle over, I fancy," said Mandrake. "We'll wait for James at the top."

In the rectory at Winton St. Giles, Chief Detective-Inspector

Alleyn put his head round the study door and said to his wife:
" I've been looking out of the top windows at the summit of
Cloudyfold. I wouldn't be surprised if it's raining over there.
What do you say, Rector?"

The Reverend Walter Copeland turned his head to look out
of the window. The lady behind the large canvas muttered to
herself and laid down her brushes.

" Rain?" echoed the rector. " It's still freezing down here.
Upon my word, though, I believe you're right. Yes, yes, undoubtedly it's pouring up round Highfold. Very odd."

" Very odd indeed," said Mrs. Alleyn grimly.

" My angel," said her husband. " I apologise in fourteen
different position. Rector, for pity's sake resume your pose."

With a nervous start the rector turned from the window,
clasped his hands, tilted his fine head, and stared obediently
at the top left-hand corner of the canvas.

" Is that right?"

" Yes, thank you," said the lady. Her thin face, wearing a
streak of green paint across the nose, looked round the side of
the canvas at her husband.

" I suppose," she said with a surprising air of diffidence,
" you wouldn't like to read to us?"

" Yes, I would," said Alleyn. He came in and shut the door.

" Now that's really delightful," said Mr. Copeland. " I hope
I'm not a bad parish priest," he added, " but it *is* rather
pleasant to know that there can be no more services to-day—
Dinah and I had matins all to ourselves you know—and that
for once the weather is *so* bad that nobody is likely to come
and visit me."

" If I were on duty," said Alleyn, looking along the book-
shelves, " I should never dare to make those observations."

" Why not?"

" Because, if I did, as sure as fate I'd be called out into the
snow, like a melodrama heroine, to a particularly disagreeable
case. However," said Alleyn, taking down a copy of *North-
anger Abbey*, " I'm not on duty, thank the Lord. Shall we
have Miss Austen?"

" This yurr be Pen-Gidding," said James Bewling. " Just to
right, sir. We'm half-way theer. A nasty stretch she'll be
round those thurr hills, and by the looks of her thurr's bin
no rain hereabouts."

" What's the time?" asked Chloris.

Mandrake held out his wrist. "Have a look."

She pushed up his cuff. "Ten past eleven."

"With any luck we'll be ringing the rectory doorbell before noon."

CHAPTER XI

ALLEYN

I

"NICHOLAS," said Madame Lisse, "come here to me."

He had been staring through the windows of the green sitting-room at the rain, which still came down like a multitude of rods, piercing all that remained of snow on the drive, filling the house with a melancholy insistence of sound. After she had spoken, though not immediately, he turned from the window and slowly crossed the room.

"Well?" he asked. "Well, Elise?"

She reached out her hand to him, touching his wrist, compelling him with her fingers to come nearer to her. "I am deeply grieved for you. You know that?" she said.

He took the hand and rubbed it between his two palms as if he hoped to get some warmth from it. "If she goes," he said, "I've no one else, no one at all but you." He stood beside her, still moving her fingers between his hands and peering at her oddly, almost as if he saw her for the first time. "I don't understand," he said. "I don't understand."

Madame Lisse pulled him down to the footstool beside her chair. He yielded quite obediently.

"We have got to think, to plan, to decide," said Madame Lisse. "I am, as I have said, deeply grieved for you. If she does not live it will be a great loss, of course. Your mother having always favoured you, one is much puzzled that she should despair to extremity at the death of your brother. For myself I believe her action should rather be attributed to a morbid dread of publicity about the misfortune to her beauty." Madame Lisse touched her hair with the tips of her fingers. "The loss of beauty is a sufficient tragedy, but to that she had become resigned. Your brother's threat to expose Francis, as well as the shock she sustained on recognising Francis, no doubt unhinged her. It is very sad." She looked down at the top of his head. It was a speculative and even a calculating glance. " Of course," she said, " I have not seen her letter." Nicholas's whole body seemed to writhe. " I can't talk about it," he muttered.

" Mr. Royal has taken it?"

" Yes. In case—he said . . ."

" That was quite sensible, of course."

" Elise, did you know it was Hart who did it—to her—in Vienna?"

" He told me on Friday night that he had recognised her."

" My God, why didn't you tell me?"

" Why should I? I was already terrified of the situation between you. Why should I add to your antagonism? No, my one desire was to suppress it, my one terror that she should recognise him and that we should be ruined." She clenched her hands and beat the arms of her chair. " And now what am I to do! It will all come out. That he is my husband. That you are my lover. He will say terrible things when they arrest him. He will bring me down in his own ruin."

" I swear you won't suffer." Nicholas pressed his face against her knees and began to mutter feverish endearments and reassurances. " Elise—when it's over—it seems frightful to speak of it—everything different, now. Elise—alone together. *Elise?*"

She stopped him at last, pressing her hands on his head.

" Very well," she said. " When it's all over. Very well."

II

Dr. Hart leant back on his heels, looked at the prostrate figure on the mattress, bent forward again and slapped the discoloured and distorted face. The eyes remained not quite closed, the head jerked flaccidly. He uttered a disconsolate grunt, turned the figure on its face again, and placed his hands over the ribs. Sweat was pouring down his own face and arms.

" Let me go on," said Hersey. " I know what to do."

He continued three or four times with the movements of artificial respiration, and then said suddenly: " Very well. Thank you. I have cramp."

Hersey knelt on the floor.

" It is so long," said Hart, " since I was in general practice. Twenty-three years. I cannot remember my poisons. The stomach should be emptied—that is certain. If only they can return soon from the chemist. If only they can find the police surgeon!"

"Is there any improvement?" asked Jonathan.

Hart raised his shoulders and arms and let them fall.

"Oh dear, oh dear!" cried Jonathan, and wrung his hands. "What possessed her?"

"I cannot understand it. It is the other son to whom she gave her devotion."

Hersey raised her head for a moment to give Dr. Hart a very direct stare. "Do not stop or hesitate," he said at once, "steady rhythmic movements are essential. Where is the other son now?"

"Nicholas is downstairs," Hersey grunted. "We thought it better to keep him out of this. All things considered."

"Perhaps you are right." He knelt again, close to Sandra Compline's head, and stooped down. "Where is that woman? That Pouting, who was to prepare the emetic, and find me a tube. She is too long coming."

"I'll see," said Jonathan and hurried out of the room.

For a time Hersey worked on in silence. Then Hart took the patient's pulse and respiration. Jonathan came panting back with a tray covered by a napkin. Hart looked at the contents. "A poor substitute," he said. "We can but try. It will be better perhaps if you leave us, Mr. Royal."

"Very well." Jonathan walked to the door, where he turned and spoke in a high voice. "We are trusting you, Dr. Hart, because we have no alternative. You will remember, if you please, that you are virtually under arrest."

"Ah, ah!" Hart muttered. "Go away. Don't be silly. Go away."

"Honestly!" said Hersey, and then: "You'd better go, Jo."

Jonathan went, but no farther than the passage, where he paced up and down for some ten minutes. It is a peculiarity of some people to sing when they are agitated or annoyed. Jonathan was one of these. As, with mincing steps, he moved about his guest-wing passage, he hummed breathily, "Il Etait Une Bergère," and beat time with his finger-tips on the back of his hand. Past the niche in the wall where the brass Buddha had stood, as far as the grandfather clock, and back down the whole length of the passage, he trotted, with closed doors on each side of him and his figure passing in and out of shadows. Once he broke off his sentry-go to enter Hart's room, where he stood at the window, tapping the pane, breathily humming, staring at the rain. But in a moment or two he was back and down the passage, pausing to listen outside Mrs. Compline's door, and then on again to the grandfather clock. Hersey found him at this employment when she came out. She took his arm and fell into step with him.

"Well, Jo," said Hersey, and her voice was not very steady, "I'm afraid we're not doing much good. At the moment nothing's worked."

"Hersey, she *must* recover. I—I can't believe—what's happening to us, Hersey? What's happening?"

"Oh, well," said Hersey, "it'll be worse in the air raids. Dr. Hart's doing his best, Jo."

"But *is* he? Is he? A murderer, Hersey. A murderer, to stand between our dear old friend Sandra and death! What an incredible—what a frightful situation!"

Hersey stood stock-still. Her hand closed nervously on Jonathan's arm and she drew in a long breath. "I don't believe he is a murderer," she said.

Jonathan pulled his arm away as violently as if she'd pinched it.

"My dear girl," he said loudly, "don't be a fool. Great Heaven . . .!" He checked himself. "I'm sorry, my dear. I was discourteous. You will forgive me. But to suggest that Hart, *Hart*, who has scarcely attempted to conceal his guilt——"

"That's not true, Jo. I mean, if he did it he managed to provide himself with an alibi that none of us can easily break."

"Nonsense, Hersey. We *have* broken it. He committed his crime after William had turned on the news or else he himself turned it on and waited his chance to dart out of the room."

"Yes, I know. Why didn't you run into him?"

"Because he took very good care to avoid me."

"He seems to have done a tidy lot of dodging," said Hersey dubiously. Jonathan uttered an exasperated noise.

"What has come over you, Hersey? You agreed that he had done it. Of course he did it. Of course he killed William. Killed him brutally and deliberately, believing him to be his brother. Aubrey has made that much clear."

"I don't believe he did it," Hersey repeated, and added shakily, "after all, it's not an easy thing to say. I don't enjoy facing the implication. But I——"

" *Don't say it again*," whispered Jonathan, and took her by
the wrists. " Who else? Who else? What has come over you?"

" It's seeing him in there, working over Sandra. Why, I
believe he'd even forgotten he was accused until you reminded
him just now. It's the one or two things that he's said while
I've been in there. I don't think he was saying them to me so
much as to himself. I believe he's got an idea that if he can
save Sandra it'll atone, in a queer sort of way, for what he
did to her beauty."

" Good God, what rubbish is this? He wants to save her
because he thinks he'll impress us, as it seems he has impressed
you, with his personal integrity. Of course he doesn't want
Sandra to die."

" If he was guilty of murdering her son? That's not good
reasoning, Jo. Sandra would be one of the most damaging
witnesses against him."

" You must be demented," Jonathan said breathlessly, and
stood looking at her and biting his fingers. " What does all this
matter? I suppose you agree that whoever set the booby-trap
committed the murder? Only Hart could have set the booby-
trap. But I'll not argue with you, Hersey. You're distracted,
poor girl, distracted as we all are."

" No," said Hersey. " No, Jo, it's not that."

" Then God knows what it is," cried Jonathan, and turned
away.

" I think I heard him," said Hersey. " I must go back."

In a moment she had gone and Jonathan was left to stare
at the closed door of Sandra Compline's room.

III

" Only five more miles to go," said Mandrake. " If the
snow's frozen hard all the way I believe we'll do it."

They were in a narrow lane. The car churned, squeaked
and skidded through snow that packed down under the wheels,
mounted in a hard mass between the front bumpers and the
radiator, and clogged the axles. Their eyes were wearied with
whiteness, Mandrake's arms and back ached abominably,
James Bewling had developed a distressing tendency to suck
his teeth.

" Queer though it may seem in these surroundings," said
Mandrake, " the engine's getting hot. I've been in bottom

gear for the last two miles. Chloris, be an angel and light me a cigarette."

" Down hill now, sir, every foot of her," said James.

"That may or may not be an unmixed blessing. Why the *hell* is she sidling like this? What happened to the chains? Never mind. On we go."

Chloris lit a cigarette and put it between his lips. "You're doing grand, dearie," she said in Cockney.

" I've been trying to sort things out a little for a quick news bulletin when we get there, always adding the proviso, *if* we get there. What's best to do? Shall I, while you push on to the chemist, tell Alleyn in a few badly-chosen words, as few as possible, what's happened, and shall we implore him to come back at once, reading my notes on the way?"

" I suppose so. Perhaps he'll insist on our going on to Great Chipping for the local experts. Perhaps he won't play."

" It's a poisonous distance to Great Chipping. He can ring up. Surely the lines won't be down all over this incredibly primitive landscape. We *must* get back with the things from the chemist." The rear of the car moved uncannily sideways. "She's curtsying again. Damn, there's a bad one. *Damn.*"

They were nearly into the hedgerow. Mandrake threw out his clutch and rammed on the brake. " I'm going to have a look at those chains."

" Don't 'ee stir, sir," said James. " I'll see."

He got out. Chloris leant forward and covered her face with her hands.

" Hallo," said Mandrake. " Eye-strain?" She didn't answer, but some small movement of her shoulders prompted him to put his arm about them and then he felt her trembling. " I'm so sorry," he said, " so terribly sorry. Darling Chloris, I implore you not to cry."

" I won't. I'm not going to. It's not what you think, not sorrow. Though I am terribly sorry. It must be shock or something. I've been so miserable and ashamed about the Complines. I've so wanted to be rid of them. And now— look how it's happened. It was foul of me to get engaged to Bill on the rebound. That's what it was, no denying it. And I knew all the time what I was up to. Don't be nice to me, I feel like a sweep."

" I can't be as nice as I'd like to because here, alas, comes Mr. Bewling. Blow your nose, my sweet. There'll always be an England where there's a muddy lane, a hoarding by a cowslip field, and curates in the rain. Well, James, what have you discovered?"

"Pesky chain on off hind-wheel's carried away, sir. Which is why she's been skittering and skiddling the last mile or so."

"No doubt. Well, get in, James, get in, and I'll see if I can waddle out of the hedgerow. On mature consideration, perhaps you'd better watch me."

James hovered over the now familiar process of churning wheels, short jerks and final recoveries. He stood within view of Mandrake and made violent gyratory movements with his hands, while an enormous drop swung from the tip of his nose.

"I have never responded in the smallest degree to rustic charm," said Mandrake. "All dialects are alike to me. James seems to me to be an extremely unconvincing piece of *genre*. What does he mean by these ridiculous gestures?"

"He means you're backing us into the other ditch," said Chloris, blowing her nose. "Oh, do be careful. Don't you see, he's steering an imaginary wheel."

"His antics are revolting. Moreover, he smells. There, you unspeakable old grotesque, is that right?"

James, capering in the snow and unable to hear any of this, innocently nodded and grinned.

"I think you're beastly about him," said Chloris, "he's *very* kind."

"Well, he can get in again. Here he comes. Are you right, James? Have a cigarette."

"No, thankee, sir," said James, breathing hard. "I've never smoked one of they since I was as high as yer elber. A pipe's my fancy, sir, and that be too powerful a piece of work for the lady."

"Not a bit, James," said Chloris. "Do have a pipe. You've earned it."

James thanked her, and soon the inside of the car smelt of nothing but his pipe. For some little time they lurched down the lane in silence, but presently Mandrake leant his head towards Chloris and said in a low voice: "I hope you won't mind my mentioning it, but I never expected to lose my heart to a blonde. The darker the better hitherto, I assure you. Not pitch-black, of course. White faces and black heads have been my undoing."

"If you're trying to cheer me up," Chloris rejoined, "you've hit on an unfortunate theme. I went ashen for Nicholas, and I certainly can't revoke for you."

"There!" cried Mandrake triumphantly. "I should have known my instinct was not at fault. You idiot, darling, why did you? Oh, all right, all right. What's the time?"

"It's five minutes to twelve. We shan't be there by midday after all."

"We shan't be much later, I swear. I wonder—— Have you ever known any one who took an overdose of a sleeping-draught?"

"Never. But we had something about them in my home-nursing course. I've been trying to remember. I think they're all barbitones, and I think the lecturer said that people who took too much sank into a coma and might keep on like that for hours or even days. You had to try and get rid of the poison and rouse them. I—I think it's terribly important that we should be quick. Dr. Hart said so. Aubrey, we've got so much to say when we get there, and so little time for saying it."

"I've tried to get it down to some sort of coherent form."

"When you made your notes, did you think of anything new, anything that would help to explain about William?"

Mandrake did not answer immediately. They had reached a stretch of road where the snow was less thick and was frozen hard. They had left the Cloudyfold hills behind and to their right, and had come into a level stretch between downlands and within sight of scattered cottages, each with its banner of smoke, the only signals of warmth in that cold countryside. Hedges broke through the snow, like fringes of black coral in an immobile sea. There was no wind down here, and the trees, lined with snow, made frozen gestures against a sky of lead. Mandrake was visited by the notion that his car was a little world which clung precariously to its power of movement, and he felt as if he himself fought, not against snow and mud, but against immobility. He wrenched his thoughts round to Chloris's question.

"If you open that attaché case you'll find the notes," he said. "Would you get them out? I don't know if you can read in this state of upheaval. Try."

Chloris managed to read the notes. They crept on with occasional wallowings in softer snow, and presently James Bewling said that the next turn in the road would bring them within sight of the spire of Winton St. Giles parish church, and Mandrake himself began to recognise the countryside and distant groups of trees that he had passed on his way from

Winton to Cloudyfold. That was on Thursday. And as he arrived at this point, through the open driving window came the faintest echo of a bell.

"Good Lord!" he thought, "it's Sunday. Suppose they're all in church. James," he called out, "what time is morning service at St. Giles?"

"Ah. Rector do set most store by early service," James rejoined. "She be at eight. T'other's at half-past ten. Reckon he'll have it to hisself this morning."

"That's all right, then. But what's that bell?"

"Rector do ring bell at noon."

"The Angelus," said Mandrake. Chloris looked up from her papers, and for a little while they listened to that distant clear-cold voice.

"They're friends of yours, aren't they?" said Chloris.

"The Copelands? Yes. Dinah's beginning to be quite a good actress. She's going to play in my new thing, if the blitz-krieg doesn't beat us to it. I suppose it won't seem odd to you, but for at least twelve hours I haven't thought about my play. What do you make of the notes?"

"There are some things I didn't know about, but not many." Chloris caught her breath. "You say at the end: 'Could Hart have set a second booby-trap.' Do you mean could he have done something with that frightful weapon that would make it fall on . . .? Is that what you mean?"

"Yes. I can't get any further, though. I can't think of any-thing."

"A 'Busman's Honeymoonish' sort of contraption? But there are no hanging flower-pots at Highfold."

"Well, if you can think of anything! I must tell you I went into the room before we left. I looked all round, trying to see if some little thing was out of order in the arrangement of the room, unusual in any way. I—didn't enjoy it. I couldn't see anything remotely suggestive of booby-traps. The ceiling's a high one. Anyway, how could Hart have dangled a stone weapon from the ceiling?"

As soon as these words had fallen from his lips, Mandrake experienced a strange fore-knowledge of how they would be answered. So vivid was this impression that when Chloris did speak, it was to him exactly as though she echoed his thoughts.

"Are you so certain," she said, "that it must be Dr. Hart?"

And he heard his own voice answer, as if it spoke to a given cue: "I thought I was. Aren't you?" She didn't reply, and a moment later he said with an air of conviction: " It must be. Who else?" And as she still kept silence: "Who else?"

" Nobody, I suppose. Nobody, of course."

" If it was anybody else the original booby-trap goes unexplained. We know that only Hart could have set it. Don't we?"

" I suppose so. Although, reading your notes, mightn't it be just possible that one of the alibis——? It's your evidence."

" I know what you mean, but it's beyond all bounds incredible. Why? Not a motive in the wide world! Besides I can't believe it. It's monstrous."

" Yes, I know. Well, then, what about a second booby-trap? The detective stories tell you to look for the unusual, don't they?"

" I don't read them," said Mandrake, with some slight return to his professional manner. " However, I *did* look for the unusual."

" And found nothing?"

" And found nothing. The room had a ghastly air of interrupted normality."

They were ploughing through a small drift. The snow yielded, mounted in a wall in front of the radiator, and splashed across the windscreen. They felt a familiar and ominous quiver and in a moment had come to a standstill.

" Out comes wold shovel agin," said James cheerfully. " She's not a bad 'un this time, sir."

Mandrake backed out of the drift, and again James set to work.

" There's one detail," said Mandrake. " That for some reason annoys me. No doubt; there's nothing in it."

" What's that?"

" You saw it. Do you remember the drawing-pin in the sole of my shoe? I picked it up in the smoking-room. There's dried paint on it, and it's the same as the ones that are stuck in the lid of William's paint box."

" I'm afraid I don't see . . ."

" I said there was nothing in it. The only thing is, why should William have had a drawing-pin in the study? He did no painting at Highfold."

" Yes, he did," Chloris contradicted. " At least, he did a drawing of me yesterday before lunch. It was while he was doing it that we had our row. And the paper was pinned down to a bit of board. And he dropped one of the pins."

" Oh," said Mandrake flatly. " Well, you might add that to the notes. That's a flop, then. What do we think of now?"

" Well, I can't think of anything," said Chloris hopelessly.

" What the devil," said Mandrake, " is that old mountebank doing?"

James Bewling, having cleared a passage in front of the car, had, with great difficulty, climbed the bank under the buried hedgerow and now stood waving his arms and pointing down the road. Mandrake sounded his horn, and James instantly plunged down the bank and across the intervening snowdrift to the car. He climbed into the back seat, shouting excitedly as he came.

" Road's clear, down-along," shouted James. " There's a mort of chaps with shovels and one of they scrapers. On 'ee go, sir, us'll be there in ten minutes."

" Thank God!" said Mandrake and Chloris sincerely.

IV

Dinah Copeland trudged down the side path and pressed her face against the french window, instantly obscuring it with her breath. Alleyn put down his book and let her in.

" You *do* look wholesome," he said.

" Did you hear me ring the Angelus?" she demanded. " Was it all right, Daddy?"

" Very nice, my dear," said the rector out of the corner of his mouth, " but I mustn't talk. Mrs. Alleyn's doing my bottom lip."

" I've finished," said Troy.

" For the morning?"

" Yes. Would you like to look?"

Dinah kicked off her snow-boots and hurried round the easel. Troy grinned at her husband, who upon that signal joined her. She thrust her thin arm in its painty sleeve through his, and with Dinah they looked at the portrait.

" Pleased?" Alleyn asked his wife.

" Not so bad from my point of view, but what about Dinah?"

" It's heaven," said Dinah emphatically.

" Not quite what the church-hen ordered, I'm afraid," Troy murmured.

" No, thank the Lord. I *was* wondering if by any chance

you'd gone surrealist and would mix Daddy up with some nice symbols. I've got rather keen on surrealism since I've been working with Aubrey Mandrake. But now I see it I'm quite glad you haven't put in any egg shells or phallic trimmings."

"*Dinah!*"

"Well, Daddy, everybody recognises the frightful importance—all right, darling, I won't. I do wish my young man was here to see it," said Dinah. "Daddy, aren't you glad we scraped acquaintance with Mr. Alleyn over our murder?"

"I'm very glad, at all events," said Troy. "Do you know this is the only time since we were married that he's let me meet any of his criminal acquaintances?" She laughed, squinted at her work, and asked: "Do you think it's all right, Roderick?"

"I like it," said Alleyn gravely.

The rector, who wore the diffident simper of the subject, joined the group at Troy's easel. Alleyn, gripping his pipe between his teeth and humming gently to himself, began to roll up and put away his wife's tubes of paint. She lit a cigarette and watched him.

"For a long time," said Troy, " he endured my paint-box in silence, and then one day he asked me if dirt was an essential to self-expression. Since then it's got more and more like the regulation issue for investigating officers at C.I."

"Whereas before it was a test case for advanced students at Hendon. I found," said Alleyn, " characteristic refuse from Fiji, Quebec, Norway, and the Dolomites. Hallo! What's that?"

"What's what?" asked Troy.

"There's a car struggling outside in the church lane."

"*Church lane!*" Dinah ejaculated. " It must be driven by a lunatic if its come from anywhere round Cloudyfold. They've cleared the lane up to the first turning, but above that it's thick snow. Your car must have come in from the main road, Mr. Alleyn. It'll very soon have to stop."

"It has stopped," said Alleyn. " And I fancy at your gate. Oh, dear me!"

"What's the matter with you?" asked his wife.

"By the pricking of my thumbs! Well, it can't be for me, anyway."

"Somebody's coming up the side path," cried Dinah, and a moment later she turned an astonished face upon the others. " It's Aubrey Mandrake."

" Mandrake?" said Alleyn, sharply. " But he ought to be on the other side of Cloudyfold."

" It can't be Mandrake, my dear," said the rector.

" But it *is*. And the car's driven away. Here he comes. He's seen me and he's coming to this window." Dinah stared at Alleyn. " I think there must be something wrong," she said. " Aubrey looks—different."

She opened the french window, and in another moment Aubrey Mandrake walked in.

" Alleyn!" said Mandrake. " Thank God you're here. There's been a most appalling tragedy at Highfold and we've come to get you."

" You detestable young man," said Alleyn.

v

" So you see," Mandrake said, " there really was nothing for it but to come to you."

" But it's *not*," Alleyn protested piteously, " it's really *not* my cup-of-tea. It's the Chief Constable's cup-of-tea, and old Blandish's. Is Blandish still the Superintendent at Great Chipping, Rector?"

" Yes, he is. This is an appalling thing, Mandrake. I—I simply can't believe it. William Compline seemed such a nice fellow. We don't know them very well, they're rather beyond our country at Penfelton, but I liked what I saw of William."

" Mrs. Compline's in desperate case. If we don't get back quickly . . ." Mandrake began. And to Alleyn cut in crisply: " Yes, of course." He turned to Mr. Copeland. " I've forgotten the name of your Chief Constable, sir."

" Lord Hesterdon. Miles and miles away to the north, and if, as Mandrake says, the telephone wires over Cloudyfold are down, I'm afraid you won't get him."

" I'll get Blandish if I have to wade to Great Chipping," Alleyn muttered " May I use your telephone?"

He went into the hall.

" I'm sorry," said Mandrake. " He's livid with rage, isn't he?"

" Not really," said Troy. " It's only his pretty little ways. He'll do his stuff, I expect. He'll have to be asked, you know, by the local police. C.I. people don't as a rule just nip in and take a case wherever they happen to be."

"Red tape," said Mandrake gloomily. "I guessed as much. Murderers can ramp about country houses, women can kill themselves with overdoses of veronal, well-intentioned guests can wallow in and out of snow-drifts in an effort to help on an arrest, and when, after suffering the most disgusting privations, they win home to the fountain-head, it is only to become wreathed, Laocoön-like, in the toils of red tape."

"I don't think," said Troy, "that it will be quite as bad as that." And Dinah, who was listening shamelessly at the door, said: "He's saying: 'Well, you'll have to ring up C.I., blast you.' "

"Dinah, darling," said her father, "you really mustn't."

"It's all right," said Dinah, shutting the door. "He's cursing freely and asking for Whitehall 1212. When do you think your girl friend will get back, Aubrey?"

"She'll have to beat up the Little Chipping chemist. We only remembered it was Sunday when we heard your bell."

"That was me," said Dinah. "Mr. Tassy is our chemist, and he lives over his shop, so that'll be all right. The road from here to Chipping has been cleared pretty well, but I hear there are masses of frightful drifts beyond on the way to Great Chipping. So I don't see how you'll get the police-surgeon or Mr. Blandish."

"If you'll excuse me," said Troy, "I believe I'll pack my husband's bag."

"Then you think he'll come?" cried Mandrake.

"Oh yes," said Troy vaguely, "he'll come all right."

She went out, and as the door opened they heard Alleyn's voice saying: "I haven't got a damn' thing. I'll ring up the local chemist and get some stuff from him. Is Dr. Curtis *there*? At the Yard? Well, get him to speak to me. You'd better find out . . ." The door shut off the rest of his remarks.

"Daddy," said Dinah, "hadn't we better give Aubrey a drink?"

"Yes, yes, of course. My dear boy, forgive me; of course, you must be exhausted. I'm so sorry. You must have a glass of sherry. Or——"

"You'd better have a whisky, Aubrey. It's almost lunchtime, so why not eat while you're waiting? And if you can't wait for Miss Wynne, when she comes we can at least send something out to the car. I'll bustle them up in the kitchen. Bring him along to the dining-room, Daddy."

She hurried out, and met Alleyn in the hall. "I'm so sorry,"

Alleyn said. " Nobody could want to go away less than I do,
but here's Blandish gibbering at Great Chipping with a cracked
water-tank in his car and a story of drifts six feet deep between
us and him. He's going to get hold of a doctor, commandeer
a car, and ginger up the road-clearing gang, but in the meantime he wants me to go ahead. I've rung up my atrocious
superior, and he's all for it, blast his eyes. May Troy stay on
as we originally planned, and finish her portrait?"

" Of course. We'd never forgive you if you put her off
her stroke. I say, this *is* a rum go, isn't it?"

" Not 'alf," said Alleyn. " It's a damned ugly go by the sound
of it."

" Awful. You wife's upstairs."

" I'll find her."

He ran to his dressing-room and found his wife on her knees
before a small suit-case.

" Pyjamas, dressing-gown, shaving things," Troy muttered.
" I suppose you'll be there to-night, won't you? What'll you
do for all those things in the case bag? Squirts and bottles
and powders, and stuff for making casts?"

" My darling oddity, I can't think. At least, I've got a
camera, and I've rung up the chemist at Chipping. Miss Wynne
was in the shop. He's going to give her some stuff for me—
iodine and what-not. Can you lend me a soft brush, darling?
One of the sort you use for water-colour. And scissors? And
some bits of charcoal? For the rest, I'll have to trust to Fox
and Co. getting through by train. They're looking out a route
now. It'll be detecting in the raw, won't it? Case for the
resourceful officer."

" I'm a rotten packer," said Troy, " but I think that's all
you'll want."

" My dear," said her husband, who was at the writing-table
helping himself to several sheets of notepaper and some
envelopes, " almost you qualify for the rôle of clever little
wife."

" You go to the devil," said Mrs. Alleyn amiably.

He squatted down beside her, looked through the contents
of the suit-case, refrained from improving on the pack and
from saying that he did not think it likely he would need his
pyjamas. " Admirable," he said. " Now I'd better swathe myself in sweaters and top-coats. Give me a kiss and say you're
sorry I'm going out on a beastly case."

" Did you ever see such a change in any one as appears in

the somewhat precious Mandrake?" asked Troy, hunting in his wardrobe.

"It takes murder to mould a man."

"Do you think the statement he's written is dependable?"

"As regards fact, yes, I should say so. As regards his interpretation of fact, I fancy it wanders a bit. For a symbolic expressionist he seems to have remained very firmly wedded to a convention. But perhaps that's the secret of two-dimensional poetic drama. I wouldn't know. Is that a car?"

"Yes."

"Then I must be off." He kissed his wife, who was absently scrubbing at her painty nose with the collar of her smock. She looked at him, scowling a little.

"This is the worst sort of luck," said Alleyn. "It was being such a good holiday."

"I hate these cases," said Troy.

"Not more than I do, bless you."

"For a different reason."

"I'm so sorry," he said quickly. "I know."

"No, you don't, Rorry. Not squeamishness, nowadays, exactly. I wish Br'er Fox was with you."

She went downstairs with him and saw him go off with Mandrake, his hat pulled down over his right eye, the collar of his heavy rain-coat turned up, his camera slung over his shoulder and his suit-case in his hand.

"He looks as if he was off on a winter sports holiday," said Dinah. "I don't mean to be particularly callous, but there's no denying a murder *is* rather exciting."

"Dinah!" said her father automatically.

They heard the car start up the lane.

CHAPTER XII

RECAPITULATION

I

ALLEYN sat in the back seat and read through Mandrake's notes. He was parted from Mr. Bewling by a large luncheon basket provided by Dinah Copeland. "We'll open it," said Chloris Wynne, "at our first breakdown. If The Others overheard me saying that I dare say they won't let us have a breakdown so that they can collar the lunch."

"What *can* you mean?" asked Mandrake.

"Don't you know about The Others?" said Chloris in a sprightly manner. "They're the ones that leave nails and broken glass on the road. They hide things when you're in a hurry. They've only got one arm and one leg each, you know. So they take single gloves and stockings, and they're frightfully keen on keys and unanswered letters."

"My God, are you being whimsical?" Mandrake demanded, and Alleyn thought he recognised that particular shade of caressing rudeness which is the courtship note among members of the advanced intelligentsia. He was not mistaken. Miss Wynne made a small preening movement.

"Don't pretend you're not interested in The Others," she said. "I bet they take the top of your fountain-pen often enough." She turned her beautifully arranged head to look at Alleyn. "Bleached," he thought automatically, "but I dare say she's quite a nice creature."

"Do they ever get into Scotland Yard, Mr. Alleyn?" she asked.

"Do they not! They are the authors of most anonymous letters, I fancy."

"There!" she cried. "Mr. Alleyn doesn't think I'm whimsical." He saw, with some misgivings, that Mandrake had removed his left hand from the driving wheel, and reflected, not for the first time, that affairs of sentiment will flourish under the most unpropitious circumstances. "But she's rattled all the same," he thought. "This brightness is all my eye. I wonder how well she knew the young man who is dead."

His reflections were interrupted by James Bewling, who cleared his throat portentously.

" Axcuse me, sir," said James. " I bin thinking."

" Indeed?" said Mandrake apprehensively. " What's the matter, James?"

" I bin thinking," repeated James. " Being this yurr is a lethal matter, and being this gentleman is going into the thick of it with his eyes only half-open like a kitten, and being he'll be burning in his official heart and soul to be axing you this and axing you that, I bin thinking it might be agreeable if I left the party along to Ogg's Corner."

" Whatever do you mean, James?" asked Chloris. " You can't just walk out into a snowdrift from motives of delicacy."

" It's not so bad as that, Miss. My wold aunty, Miss Fancy Bewling, bides in cottage along to Ogg's Corner. Her's ninety-one yurs of age and so cantankerous an old masterpiece as ever you see. Reckon her'll be pleased as punch to blow me up at her leisure until Mr. Blandish and his chaps comes along, when I'll get a lift and direct 'em best way to Highfold."

" Well, James," said Mandrake, " it's not a bad idea. We'll be all right. I know the way, and we've ploughed a sort of path for ourselves. What do you think, Mr. Alleyn?"

" If there's any danger of Blandish missing his way," said Alleyn, " I'd be very glad to think you were there, Bewling."

" Good enough, sir. Then put me down if you please, souls, at next turning but one. Don't miss thicky little twiddling lane up to Pen Bidding, Mr. Mandrake, sir, and be bold to rush 'er up when she skiddles."

So they dropped him by his aunt's cottage, and it seemed to Alleyn that Miss Wynne watched him go with some regret. She said that Mandrake might despise James, but she considered he had shown extraordinary tact and forbearance. " He must have died to know more about the disaster," she said, " but he never so much as asked a leading question."

" We talked pretty freely without him having to bother," Mandrake pointed out. " However, I agree it was nice of James. Is there anything you want to ask us, Alleyn? By dint of terrific concentration I can manage to keep the car on its tracks and my mind more or less on the conversation."

Alleyn took Mandrake's notes from his pocket, and at the rustle of paper he saw Chloris turn her head sharply. Something about the set of Mandrake's shoulders suggested that he, too, was suddenly alert.

"If I may," said Alleyn, "I should like to go over these notes with you. It's fortunate for me that you decided to make this very clear and well-ordered summary. I'm sure it gives the skeleton of events as completely as possible, and that is invaluable. But I should like with your help to clothe the bones in a semblance of flesh."

This was spoken in what Troy called "the official manner," and it was the first Chloris and Mandrake had heard of this manner. Neither of them answered, and Alleyn knew that with one short speech he had established an atmosphere of uneasy expectation. He was right. Until this moment Chloris and Mandrake had wished above all things for the assurance that Alleyn would take charge. Now that, with a certain crispness and a marked change of manner he had actually done so, each of them felt an icy touch of apprehension. They had set in motion a process which they were unable to stop. They were not yet nervous for themselves, but instinctively they moved a little nearer to each other. They had called in the Yard.

"First of all," said Alleyn, "I should like to go over the notes, putting them into my own words to make quite sure I've got hold of the right ends of all the sticks. Will you stop me if I'm wrong? The death of this young man, William Compline, occurred at about ten minutes past ten yesterday evening. He was sitting in a room which communicates with a library, a small sitting-room, and a hall. Just before the discovery of his body, the library was occupied by his host, Mr. Jonathan Royal, by Lady Hersey Amblington, by Miss Chloris Wynne, by Mr. Aubrey Mandrake, and by Mr. Nicholas Compline. The small sitting-room had been occupied by Dr. Francis Hart, but on his own statement and that of the footman, Thomas, it appears that Dr. Hart left the sitting-room—you call it a boudoir, I see—at the same time as Thomas came into the hall with a grog tray which he took into the library. That was some minutes after Nicholas Compline had left his brother and joined the party in the library, and quite definitely before you all heard the wireless turned on in the smoking-room. The wireless was turned on after the drinks came in. You agreed you would like to hear it, and Nicholas Compline opened the door and called out to his brother. A screen hid William, but Nicholas heard someone cross the room, and a moment later the wireless struck up 'Boomps-a-daisy.'"

" That's it," said Chloris. " Nick left the door open."

" Yes. You endured the dance music, and in a minute or so the news came on the air. At about this moment Mr. Royal went out to reassure himself that Dr. Hart was not in the boudoir. He states that he did not enter the boudoir, but saw there was no light under the door. He visited a cloakroom, and, having met no one in the hall, returned before the news ended."

" Yes."

" All right. Well, now, I understand that the wireless had been in use not long before. It's not likely, then, that the music was delayed by any warming-up process?"

" No," said Chloris. " I thought of that, but it seems that the radio had been switched on all the time and wouldn't need to warm up. As soon as Bill turned the volume control it'd come up."

" As soon as the volume control was turned at all events," said Alleyn, " and it must have been turned."

" By William," said Mandrake, " or his murderer. Exactly."

" And you see," Chloris added, " we *asked* for it, and it was at once turned on. By *Somebody*."

" Yes. We now come to the curious episode of the dancing footman. The music follows Thomas's re-entry into the hall when he saw Dr. Hart on the stairs. Therefore, it seems, Dr. Hart did not turn up the volume control. Now it appears that Thomas, arrested by the strains of a composition known as ' Boomps-a-daisy,' was moved to dance. As long as the music continued, Thomas, a solitary figure in the hall, capered, clapped his hands, slapped his knees, and stuck out his stern in a rhythmic sequence. When the music stopped, so did Thomas. He left the hall as the news bulletin began. Then we have Mr. Royal's short excursion, and, lastly, some minutes later, Lady Hersey Amblington, carrying a tumbler, walked from the library into the smoking-room, reappeared in the doorway, returned into the smoking-room and switched off the radio. She then called out to her cousin, Mr. Royal, who joined her. Finally she came back to the library and summoned you, Mr. Mandrake. You went into the smoking-room and found William Compline there, dead. It was somewhere about this time that you trod on a drawing-pin which stuck in the sole of your shoe."

" Yes."

" The instrument used by the assailant," said Alleyn, with

a private grimace over the police-court phrase, " seems to have been a Maori mere which was one of a collection of weapons hanging on the smoking-room wall. Which wall?"

" What? Oh, on the right from the library door. There's a red leather screen inside the door, and this unspeakable club was just beyond it."

" I see you've given me a very useful sketch-plan. Would you mark the position on the wall? I'll put a cross, and you shall tell me if it's in the right place."

ɔris took the paper and showed it to Mandrake, who slowed down, glanced at it, nodded, and accelerated. James Bewling had got hold of a set of chains in Chipping, and the wheels bit well into their old tracks.

" Right," said Alleyn. " During this time, two members of the party were upstairs. They were Mrs. Compline and Madame Lisse, who you tell me is actually Mrs. Francis Hart." He paused. Neither Chloris nor Mandrake spoke.

" That's right, isn't it?"

" Yes," said Chloris, " that's it."

" As far as we know," said Mandrake unwillingly.

" As far as we know," Alleyn agreed. " At all events we know that neither of them could have come downstairs while Thomas was there. If it was anybody other than William Compline who turned up the wireless this person must have entered the room after Nicholas Compline left it and remained there until after Thomas left the hall. If, on the other hand, it was William himself who turned up the wireless, his murderer must have entered the room after Thomas left the hall, and made his getaway before Lady Hersey went in with the drink."

" Avoiding Jonathan Royal," added Mandrake. " Don't forget he crossed the hall twice."

" Oh," said Alleyn vaguely. " I hadn't forgotten that. Now, before we leave these, the crucial periods as I see them, I pause to remind myself that the communicating door between the smoking-room and the boudoir was locked on the smoking-room side."

" Yes," said Mandrake. " I ought to have said, I think, that there is nowhere in the smoking-room where anybody could hide. The screen's no good because of the door into the library. I think I'm right in saying the murderer must have come in by the hall door."

" It looks like it," Alleyn agreed. " Avoiding the dancing footman and Mr. Royal."

" Somebody could hide in the hall," said Chloris suddenly. " We'd thought of that."

" There's still the dancing footman. He defines the periods when it would have been possible for the murderer to enter or leave the smoking-room."

" Yes," agreed Mandrake. " Thomas continued his antics until the music stopped, and that leaves a margin of a few minutes before Lady Hersey entered the room. The boudoir's no good because the door was still locked. I know that."

" Then," said Chloris slowly, " doesn't it look as if the crucial time is the time when the murderer *left* the room. Because whether he worked the wireless or not he could only have got away after Thomas had left the hall."

" Top marks for deduction, Miss Wynne," said Alleyn.

" It's a grim notion," said Mandrake suddenly, " to think of us all sitting there calling for the news. If it was Hart, imagine him having to pull himself together and turn up the wireless ! "

" Don't ! " said Chloris.

Alleyn had, with some difficulty in the jolting car, made a series of marginal notes. He now glanced up and found Chloris leaning her arm along the front seat and looking at him.

" I'd like to get Lady Hersey's movements fixed in my head," he said. " She went into the smoking-room with the drink, disappeared round the screen, returned to the doorway, said something you couldn't hear, disappeared again, and called out to Mr. Royal, who then joined her. Finally she re-entered the library and asked you, Mandrake, to go to your host."

" That's it." Mandrake changed down and crawled the car over its own skid marks. Chloris drew in her breath audibly. " It's all right," he said. " No trouble this time." But Alleyn, who had been watching her, knew that it was not their progress that had scared her. She looked quickly at him and away again. " Lady Hersey," she said, " is an old friend of the Complines. She's terribly nice and she's been absolutely marvellous since it happened. She was helping Dr. Hart with Mrs. Compline. She couldn't be more sorry and upset about it all."

These somewhat conventional phrases were shot out at nobody in particular, and were followed by an odd little pause.

" Ah," Alleyn murmured, " those are the sort of touches

that help to clothe the bare bones of a case. We'll collect some more, I hope, as we go along. I'm working backwards through your notes, Mandrake, and arrive at the booby-trap. A heavy brass Buddha, of all disagreeable objects, is perched on the top of a door so that when the door is opened it is bound to fall on the person who pushes the door. The room is Nicholas Compline's and it is upon his arm the Buddha falls. This trap was set, you say, during a visit Compline paid to Madame Lisse. You've worked out a time check on two clocks, the grandfather clock at the top of the stairs and the drawing-room clock which agrees with it. On this reckoning it appears that the trap was set some time between half-past seven, which struck as Nicholas Compline left his room, and a minute or so past twenty-to-eight when you heard him cry out as the Buddha struck his arm. You suggest that you have found alibis during this period for everybody but Dr. Hart who was in the bathroom. Lady Hersey gives Mrs. Compline her alibi, Mr. Royal gives you yours, Mandrake. Can you return the gesture?"

"I can say that I think he arrived in the drawing-room some little time before the crash."

"Ten minutes before?"

"I feel sure it must have been. I—we were talking. Yes, it must have been at least ten minutes."

"There's no way by which you could come a little nearer to it? For example, did he light a cigarette when he came into the room?"

"Let me think. No. No, I don't believe he did. But I did. I'd forgotten to bring my case down and I was helping myself to one of his when he came into the room. I remember that," said Mandrake, and Alleyn saw the back of his neck go red, "because I felt——" He stopped and made rather a business of adjusting his windscreen-wiper which at that moment was not needed.

"Yes?"

"What? Oh, I merely felt, very stupidly, a little embarrassed." Mandrake's voice trailed off and then he said loudly: "I was not born into the purple, Mr. Alleyn. Until a few years ago I lived in the odour of extreme economy, among people who waited to be invited before they smoked other people's cigarettes."

"I should call that a sign of courtesy rather than penury," said Alleyn, and received a brilliant smile from Miss Wynne.

"Well, you lit your cigarette, then. That's a help. Was it still going when you heard Nicholas Compline yell?"

"Was it, now? Yes. Yes, I remember throwing it in the fire before I went upstairs, but it was almost smoked out, I'm sure. Yes, I'm sure of that."

"Good. Well, now, Madame Lisse's alibi is vouched for by Nicholas Compline and looks pretty well cast-iron. William Compline was in the smoking-room listening to the news bulletin. He heard Mr. Royal speak to the butler in the hall, and was prepared to give the gist of the bulletin which does not come on until 7.30."

"Surely that's of academic interest only," said Mandrake, "considering what happened to William Compline."

"You are probably quite right, but you know what police-men are. Dr. Hart has no alibi. Wait a bit, I must count up. Who haven't I got? Oh, there's you, Miss Wynne."

"I haven't got one," said Chloris quickly. "I was in my room and I had a bath next door and I changed. But I can't prove it."

"Oh, well," said Alleyn, "it'd be an odd state of affairs if everybody could prove all the things they hadn't done every minute of the day. Is there to be no privacy, not even in the bathroom? That leaves Lady Hersey Amblington."

"But she was with Mrs. Compline," said Mandrake. "Nicholas saw her go past his door on her way to Mrs. Compline's room. It's there in the notes. We've been over that."

"Have we? Then I've got myself into a muddle no doubt. Lady Hersey gives Mrs. Compline an alibi. Does Mrs. Compline do as much for Lady Hersey? I mean did Mrs. Compline agree that Lady Hersey was in her room from 7.30 until the alarm?"

"Well, she—well, I mean she wasn't there when we talked about alibis. Lady Hersey saw her afterwards and may have spoken about it then."

"But actually nobody else questioned Mrs. Compline about it?"

"No, but of course it's all right. I mean it's out of the question that Lady Hersey——"

"I expect it is," said Alleyn. "But you see just at the moment we're dealing with hard facts, aren't we? And the actual fact, which may be of no importance whatever, is that Lady Hersey vouches for Mrs. Compline but Mrs. Compline doesn't happen to have corroborated her account. Is that it?"

"She can't," said Chloris. "She can't, now. She may never . . ."

"We won't jump that fence," said Alleyn, "until we meet it."

II

So far the return journey had not presented many difficulties. The new set of chains worked well and Mandrake kept to his own tracks where the snow had packed down hard and was already freezing over again. They ran into desultory flurries of snow, but the rain had not crossed Cloudyfold. Beyond the hills the sky was still terraced with storm clouds, prolonged at their bases into down-pouring masses, as if some Olympian painter had dragged at them with a dry brush.

At Alleyn's suggestion they broached Dinah's luncheon hamper, and he continued his examination of Mandrake's notes in an atmosphere of ham and hard-boiled egg, plying Chloris with food and both of them with questions.

"The oddest thing about this beastly business," he said, "seems to be your plunge in the pond, Mandrake. You say here that Dr. Hart had the best chance of bringing it off unobserved, and that he saw Compline leave the house wearing Mr. Royal's cape, which is the double of your cape which incidentally seems to be Hart's cape. Having absorbed those fancy touches, I learn that Nicholas Compline saw you through the window of the pavilion where he was undressing in order to plunge into the ornamental waters in pursuance of a wager. He recognised you and you exchanged waves. Then comes your plunge attended by the Compline brothers, Hart, Miss Wynne, and Mr. Royal, in that order. Again Mrs. Compline, Madame Lisse and Lady Hersey are absent. The first two breakfasted in their rooms. Lady Hersey says she was in the smoking-room. I understand you have read these notes, Miss Wynne?"

"Yes."

"Have you formed any theory about the footprints which Mandrake says he saw in the snow? The small prints that led out to the top of the terrace from the house and returned to the house, suggesting that the person who made them stood on the terrace for a time at a spot from which she—apparently it must have been a woman—had a full view of the pond and the pavilion."

"I?" said Chloris. "Why, I've thought a lot about it ever since Aubrey told me, but I'm afraid I've no ideas at all. It might have been one of the maids, even, though I suppose that's not very likely."

"Did you notice these prints as you went down?"

"I'm not sure. I stood on the top of the terrace for a bit and noticed Aubrey's and some other big footprints—William's they must have been—and I thought I might walk down inside them, do you know? I've got a sort of feeling I did notice something out of the tail of my eye. I've got a sort of after-flavour of having fancied there must be someone else about, but it's much too vague to be useful. On the way back I was too concerned about Aubrey to notice."

"Were you?" asked Mandrake with unmistakable fervour. Alleyn waited philosophically through an exchange of inaudible phrases, and remarked on the air of complacency that characterises persons who have arrived at a certain stage of mutual attraction.

"The smoking-room is on that side of the house, isn't it?" he said at last.

"Yes," agreed Chloris uncomfortably, "but so are the visitors' rooms upstairs."

"Do they overlook the lake and pavilion?"

"Madame Lisse's room doesn't," said Mandrake. "I asked Jonathan that, and he said some tall evergreens on the bank would be in the way. I imagine they'd interrupt Mrs. Compline's view too."

"And you definitely connect these three strange events? You feel certain that the same person is behind all of them?"

"But—yes," said Chloris blankly. "Of course we do. Don't you?"

"It looks like it, certainly," said Alleyn absently.

"Surely," said Mandrake acidly, "it would be too fantastic to suppose there has been more than one person planning elaborate deaths for Nicholas Compline during the week-end?"

"For Nicholas Compline," Alleyn repeated. "Oh, yes. It would, wouldn't it?"

"I assure you I had no enemies at Highfold. I'd never met a single one of the guests before."

"Quite so," said Alleyn mildly. "Going back still farther

we come to the first hint of trouble, the rather childish message on the Charter form which you say Dr. Hart handed to Nicholas Compline, together with a form that had been correctly filled in. 'You are warned. Keep off.' You say that there is no question of any one else handing this paper to Compline."

" No possibility of it. Nicholas simply took the paper from Hart," said Mandrake, " and on looking at it, found this second one underneath. Hart's explanation was that he must have torn two papers off at once. Nicholas didn't say at the time what was on the paper, but he was obviously very much upset and later that evening he told Jonathan he thought he ought to go. The following day, and good God it's only yesterday, he actually tried to go and nearly drowned himself in a drift."

" Yes. And that completes the skeleton." Alleyn folded the notes and put them in his pocket. " As they used to say in Baker Street: ' You are in possession of the facts.' I'd like a little news about the people. You say that with the exception of your host you had met none of them before. That's not counting Miss Wynne, of course."

" Yes, it is," said Chloris, and with an air of great demureness she added: " Aubrey and I are complete strangers."

" I don't suppose I shall know her if I meet her again." Alleyn sighed as Mandrake once more removed his left hand from the driving-wheel. " He will resent everything I say to her," thought Alleyn, " and she will adore his resentment. Blow!" However, he introduced the subject of motive, which Mandrake, in his notes, had dealt with allusively, unconsciously supposing the reader would be almost as familiar as himself with the relationships of the eight guests to each other and to their host. In a very short time he discovered that these two were quite ready to talk about Madame Lisse and Lady Hersey, about Mrs. Compline and Dr. Hart, and about William's fury when he discovered that Hart was the author of his mother's disfigurement. They were less ready to discuss in detail Hart's enmity to Nicholas, though they never tired of stressing it. Hart had threatened Nicholas. Nicholas had goaded Hart until he completely lost control of himself. That was the burden of their song. It was on account of Nicholas's attentions to Madame Lisse, they said. When Alleyn asked if Nicholas knew that Madame Lisse was Madame Hart they said they hadn't asked him, and Chloris added, with a new edge to her voice, that it was highly probable. Alleyn said mildly that it appeared that Nicholas had acted like a fool. " He seems to have baited Hart to the top of his bent and at the same time been rather frightened of him."

" But that's Nicholas all over," said Chloris. " It was exactly that. The small boy tweaking the dog's tail. That's Nicholas." Mandrake cut in rather hurriedly, but Alleyn stopped him. " You know Compline well, Miss Wynne?" She took so long to answer that he was about to repeat the question which he was certain she had heard, when, without turning her head, she said : " Yes. Quite well. I was engaged to him. You'd better hear all about it, I suppose."

" I can't see . . ." Mandrake began, but this time it was Chloris who stopped him : " It hasn't anything to do with it, I know, but I think Mr. Alleyn would rather see for himself."

" An admirable conclusion," said Alleyn lightly, and he heard without further comment the story of the two engagements. When she had finished he made her a little speech, saying he was sorry under such tragic circumstances to be obliged to pester her with questions. Nothing could have been more uncomfortable than their reception of this simple offer of sympathy. Their silence was eloquent of embarrassment. Chloris did not turn her head, and when Alleyn caught sight of Mandrake's face in the driving glass it was scarlet and scowling.

" You needn't bother," said Chloris in a high voice. " I wasn't in love with William. Didn't you guess that? As I have already explained to Aubrey I did it on the rebound from Nicholas." In spite of herself her voice lost composure and she ended up shakily : " That doesn't say I'm not terribly sorry. I liked old Bill. I liked him tremendously."

" I liked him too," said Mandrake. " He was an oddity, wasn't he?" Chloris nodded, and Alleyn thought that in making this unemphatic comment on William Compline, Mandrake had shown sureness of touch and a certain delicacy of understanding. He went on quietly : " He would have interested you, I believe, Alleyn. He was one of those people who speak a thing almost at the same time as they think it, and, as he had a curious simplicity about him, some of the things he said were odd and disconcerting. He was quite like his brother to look at. The shape of his head——" Mandrake stumbled a little and then went on rather hurriedly. " From behind, as I explained in those notes, it was difficult to tell them apart. But they couldn't have been more unlike in temperament, I should say."

"And he painted?"

"Yes. I haven't seen any of his works."

"They were queer," Chloris said. "You might like them, Aubrey. They might be quite your cup-of-tea, but most people thought his pictures too embarrassingly bad. I must say I always felt rather shy when I saw them. I never knew what to say."

"What are they like?" asked Alleyn.

"Well, a bit as if a child had done them, but not quite like that."

"*Very* thick oil paint," said Mandrake under his breath.

"Why, have you see one?" asked Chloris in astonishment.

"No. He told me. He said it rather quaintly. If there was something childlike in his painting it must have come from himself."

"Yes, that's true," said Chloris, and they began quite tranquilly to discuss William. Alleyn wondered how old they were. Miss Wynne was not more than twenty, he thought, and he remembered a critique of one of Mandrake's poetic dramas in which the author had been described as extremely young. Perhaps he was twenty-six. They were fortified with all the resilience that youth presents to an emotional shock. In the midst of murder and attempted suicide, they had managed not only to behave with address and good sense, but also to fall in love with each other. Very odd, thought Alleyn, and listened attentively to what they had to say about William Compline. They were discussing him with some animation. Alleyn was pretty sure they had almost forgotten his presence. This was all to the good, and a firm picture of the murdered and elder Compline began to take form. With owlish gravity Chloris and Mandrake discussed poor William's "psychology" and decided that unconscious jealousy of Nicholas, a mother-fixation, an inferiority complex, and a particularly elaborate Œdipus complex were at the bottom of his lightest action and the sole causes of his violent outburst against Hart. "Really," said Mandrake, "it's the Ugly Duckling and Cinderella themes. Extraordinarily sound, those folk tales." "And of course the painting was simply an effort to overcome the inferiority complex—er, on the pain-pleasure principle," added Chloris uncertainly. Mandrake remarked that Mrs. Compline's strong preference for Nicholas was extremely characteristic,

but of what Alleyn could not quite make out. However, he
did get a clear picture of two unhappy people dominated by
the selfish, vain, and, according to the two experts in the
front seat, excessively oversexed Nicholas. Shorn of intellectual garnishings it was still a sufficiently curious story. One
phrase of Chloris's struck him as being particularly illuminating. " I would have liked to be friends with her," she said,
" but she hated me from the beginning, poor thing. First because I was engaged to Nick, and secondly and even more
violently because, as she made herself suppose, I jilted him
for William. I think she knew well enough that Nick hadn't
been exactly the little gent, but she wouldn't let herself believe
that he could do anything that wasn't perfect. For her he
just *had* to be heroic, don't you know, and she had a fantastic
hatred for anyone who made him look shabby."

" Did she know about *l'affaire Lisse*, do you suppose?"
asked Mandrake.

" I don't know. I dare say he kept it dark. He could be
pretty quiet about his philanderings when it suited him. But
even if she did know, I believe she would have taken it as a
perfectly natural obsession on Madame Lisse's part. In her
eyes Nicholas was really rather like one of those Greek gods
who lolled about on clouds and said ' I'll have *that* one!' "

Alleyn coughed, and Miss Wynne became aware of him.
" I suppose," she said, " you think it revolting of us to talk
about them like this."

" No," he said, " I would find a show of excessive distress
much more disagreeable."

" Yes, I know. All the same it's pretty ghastly not being
able to get back quicker. I suppose you can't rush her up a
bit, Aubrey, can you? It's terribly important that Dr. Hart
should get these things. I mean, in a sort of way, everything
depends on us."

" I'm banging along as fast as I dare. There's Pen-Gidding
ahead. We're making much better time. Look, there's the
rain still over the Highfold country. We'll be running into
it again soon. If I stick in Deep Bottom it's only about half
a mile from the house."

" Return to horror," said Chloris, under her breath.

" Never mind, my dear," whispered Mandrake. " Never
mind."

" There's one thing that strikes me as being very odd,"
Alleyn said, " and that is the house-party itself. What per-

suaded your host to collect such a gang of warring elements under his roof? Or didn't he know they were at war?"

"Yes," said Mandrake, "he knew."

"Then why . . .?"

"He did it on purpose. He explained it to me on the night I arrived. He wanted to work out his æsthetic frustration in a flesh-and-blood medium."

"Good Lord!" Alleyn ejaculated, "how unbelievably rum."

III

There was no wind over Cloudyfold that afternoon, but the rain poured down inexorably. By half-past two the rooms at Highfold had begun to assume a stealthy dimness. The house itself, as well as the human beings inside it, seemed to listen and to wait. Highfold was dominated by two rooms. Behind the locked doors of the smoking-room William Compline now sat as rigidly as if he had been made of iron, his hands propped between his feet and his head fixed between his knees. In the principal visitor's room his mother lay in bed, breathing very slowly, scarcely responding now to Dr. Hart when he slapped the face he had marred twenty years ago, or when he advanced his own white face close to hers and called her name as if he cried for admittance at the door of her consciousness. Hersey Amblington, too, cried out to her old friend, and three times Nicholas had come. It had been difficult for Nicholas to obey Hart and call loudly upon his mother. At first his voice cracked grotesquely into a sobbing whisper. Hart kept repeating: "Loudly. Loudly. To rouse her, you understand. She must be roused." And Hersey: "If she hears it's you, Nick, she may try. You must, Nick, you must." Mrs. Pouting in her sitting-room, and Thomas in the hall, and Caper in the pantry, and Madame Lisse in the green boudoir, and Jonathan Royal on the stairs had all heard Nicholas shout as though across a nightmare of silence: "*Mother! It's Nicholas! Mother!*" They had all waited, listening intently, until his voice cracked into silence and they became aware once more of the hard beat of rain on the house. Jonathan, from his place on the stairs, had heard Nicholas leave his mother's room and cross the landing. He had seen him stop at the stairhead, raise his clasped hands to his lips, and then, as if some invisible cord had been released, jerk forward until his head rested on his arms across the balustrade. Jonathan started forward, but at the sound of harsh sobbing paused and finally stole downstairs, unseen by Nicholas. He crossed the hall, and after some hesitation entered the green boudoir.

Between Hersey Amblington and Dr. Hart there had arisen a curious feeling of comradeship. Hersey had proved herself to be an efficient nurse, obeying Hart's instructions without question or fuss. There were certain unpleasant things that could be attempted and between them they had made the attempts. Hart had not pretended to any experience of veronal poisoning. " But the treatment must be on general common-sense lines," he said. " There we cannot go wrong. Unfortunately there has not been the response. We have not eliminated the poison. If only they would return from the chemist!"

" What's the time now?"

" Nearly two o'clock. They should have returned."

He bent over the bed. Hersey watched him and in a minute or two she said: " Am I mistaken, Dr. Hart, or is there a change?"

" You are not mistaken. The pupils are now contracted, the pulse is 120. Do you notice the colour of the finger nails, a dusky red?"

" And her breathing."

" It is gravely impeded. We shall take the temperature again. God be thanked that at least this old Pouting had a thermometer."

Hersey fetched the thermometer and returned to the window where she waited, looking through rain across the terrace and down to the bathing-pool. Cypress trees had been planted at intervals along the terrace and one of these hid the far end of the pool and the entrance to the pavilion. " She could not have seen Mandrake go overboard," thought Hersey, " but she could have seen him leave the house and go down." And she looked at the wardrobe where yesterday she had found a wet coat.

" The temperature is 102.8°," said Hart. " It has risen two points. Well, we must try the emetic again, but I am afraid she is now quite unable to swallow."

Hersey rejoined him, and again they worked together to no avail. After a time she suggested that he should leave her in charge. " You've eaten nothing and you haven't sat down since they brought you here hours ago. I can call you if there's any change." Hart glanced up with those prominent eyes of his and said: "And where should I go, Lady Hersey? To my room? Should I not be locked up again? Ever since I came to the patient I believe there has been someone on guard in the passage or on the stairs. Is that not so? No, let me remain here until the car returns. If they have brought a medical man I shall go back to my cell."

"I don't believe you killed William Compline," Hersey said abruptly.

"No? You are a sensible woman. I did not kill him. There is no doubt, I am afraid, that the condition is less satisfactory. She is more comatose. The reflexes are completely abolished. Why do you look at me in that fashion, Lady Hersey?"

"You seem to have no thought for your own position."

"You mean that I am not afraid," said Dr. Hart, who was again stooping over his patient. "You are right. Lady Hersey, I am an Austrian refugee and a Jew who has become a naturalised Briton. I have developed what I believe you would call a good nose for justice. Austrian justice, Nazi justice, and English justice. I have learned when to be terrified and when not to be terrified. I am a kind of thermometer for terror. At this moment I am quite normal. I do not believe I shall be found guilty of a murder I did not commit."

"Do you believe," asked Hersey Amblington after a long pause, "that the murderer will be arrested?"

"I do believe so." He straightened his back, but he still watched his patient.

"Dr. Hart," Hersey said harshly, "do you think you know who killed William Compline?"

"Oh, yes," said Hart, and for the first time he looked directly at her. "Yes. I believe I know. Do you wish me to say the name?"

"No," she said. "Let us not discuss it."

"I agree," said Dr. Hart.

IV

Down in the green sitting-room Jonathan Royal listened to Madame Lisse. An onlooker with a taste for irony might have found something to divert him in the scene, particularly if he liked his irony laced with a touch of macabre. A nice sense of the fitness of things had prompted Madame to dress herself in black, a dead crepey black that gloved her figure with adroitness. She looked and smelt most expensive. She had sent a message to her host by Mrs. Pouting, asking for an interview. Jonathan, fresh from seeing Nicholas Compline's breakdown on the upstairs landing, eyed his beautiful guest with a certain air of wariness.

"It is so kind of you to see me," said Madame Lisse. "Ever since this terrible affair I have felt that of all our party you would remain the sanest, the best able to control events, the one to whom I must instinctively turn."

Jonathan touched his glasses and said that it was very nice of her. She continued in this strain for some time. Her manner conveyed, as an Englishwoman's manner seldom conveys, a sort of woman-to-man awareness that was touched with camaraderie. With every look she gave him, and her glances were circumspect, she flattered Jonathan, and although he still made uncomfortable little noises in his throat, and fidgeted with his glasses, he began to look sleek and into his own manner there crept an air of calculation that would have astonished his cousin Hersey or Chloris Wynne. He and Madame Lisse were very polite to each other, but there was a hint of insolence in their civility. She began to explain her reasons for keeping her marriage to Hart a secret. It had been her idea, she said. She had not wished to give up her own business which was a flourishing one, but on the other hand Dr. Hart, before they met, had, under his own name, published a book in which he exposed what he had called the "beauty-parlour racket." "The book has had considerable publicity and is widely associated with his name," she said. "It would have been impossible for me as his wife to continue my business. Both of us would have appeared ridiculous. So we were married very quietly in London and continued in our separate ménages."

"An ambiguous position," Jonathan said with a little smile.

"Until recently it has worked quite well."

"Until Nicholas Compline was transferred to Great Chipping, perhaps?"

"Until then," she agreed, and for a time both of them were silent while Jonathan looked at her steadily through those blank glasses of his. "Ah, well," said Madame Lisse, "there it is. I was quite powerless. Francis became insanely jealous. I should never have allowed this visit, but he guessed that

Nicholas had been asked and he accepted. I had hoped that Nicholas would be sensible, and that Francis would become reassured. But, as it was, both of them behaved like lunatics. And now the brother and the disfigured mother too, perhaps— it is too horrible. I shall blame myself to the end of my life. I shall never recover from the horror," said Madame Lisse, delicately clasping her hands, " never."

" Why did you wish to speak to me?"

" To explain my own position. When I heard last night of this tragedy I was shattered. All night I stayed awake thinking —thinking. Not of myself, you understand, but of that poor gauche William, killed, as it seems, on my account. That is what people will say. They will say that Francis mistook him for Nicholas and killed him because of me. It will not be true, Mr. Royal."

At this remarkable assemblage of contradictory data, Jonathan gaped a little, but Madame Lisse leant towards him and gazed into his spectacles, and he was silent.

" It will not be true," she repeated. " Do not misunderstand me. There can be no doubt who struck the blow. But the motive—the motive! You heard that unfortunate young man cry out that all the world should learn it was Francis who ruined his mother's beauty. Why did she try to kill herself? Because she knew that it was on her account that Francis Hart had killed her son."

Jonathan primmed his lips. Madame Lisse leant towards him. " You are a man of the world," said this amazing lady, " you understand women. I felt it the first time we met. There was a *frisson*—how shall I describe it. We were *en rapport*. One is never mistaken in these things. There is an instinct." She continued in this vein for some time. Presently she was holding one of Jonathan's hands in both her own, and imperceptibly this state of affairs changed into Jonathan holding both hers in one of his. Her voice went on and on. He was to understand that she was the victim of men's passions. She could not help it. She could not stop Nicholas falling in love with her. Her husband had treated her exceedingly ill. But the murder had nothing to do with her or with Nicholas. There were terrible days ahead, she would never recover. But, and here she raised Jonathan's hand to her cheek, he, Jonathan, would protect her. He would keep their secret. " What secret?" cried Jonathan in alarm. The secret of Nicholas's infatuation. Her name need never be brought into the picture. " You ask the impossible!" Jonathan exclaimed. "My dear lady, even if I——" She wept a little and said it was evident he did not return the *deep, deep* regard she had for him. She swayed very close indeed and murmured something in his ear. Jonathan changed colour and spluttered: "If I could . . . I should be enchanted, but it is beyond my power." He wetted his lips. "It's no good," he said, "Mandrake knows. They all know. It's impossible."

While he still glared at her they both heard the sound of a car coming slowly up the last curve of the drive.

CHAPTER XIII

EXAMINATION

I

ALLEYN went alone to the smoking-room. On their arrival Mandrake had gone at once to find Jonathan, and had returned to say he would be down in a minute or two. "And in the meantime," Mandrake said, "I am deputed to show you anything you want to see. I suppose—I mean I've got the keys . . ." Alleyn thanked him, took the keys, and let himself into the smoking-room. He drew back the curtains from the windows and a very cold light discovered the body of William Compline. The greenstone blade lay on the floor about two feet from William's left shoe. The striking edge was stained. There was a short thong round the narrow grip. Alleyn had seen Maori meres in New Zealand museums and had reflected on the deadly efficiency of this beautifully shaped and balanced weapon. "The nearest thing," he murmured as he bent over it, "to the deadly Gurkha kukri that is possible in stone, and that only in the extremely hard and tough New Zealand greenstone. Unless this expert is a lunatic, there'll be no prints, of course." He looked very closely at the wireless. It was an all-wave instrument made by a famous firm. There were five bakelite control knobs under the dial. From left to right the knobs were marked Brilliance, Bass, Tuner, Wave-Band and Volume. The screws that attached them were sunk in small holes. The tuner control, placed above the others, was formed by a large quick-turning knob from the centre of which a smaller knob for more delicate tuning projected. The main switch was on the side facing the boudoir door. Alleyn noted the position of the tuning indicator and reflected that if a time check was needed he could get one from the B.B.C. He turned from the wireless to a writing-desk that stood against the same wall, between two windows. Above this desk was hung an array of weapons, a Malay kriss, a boomerang, a Chinese dagger, and a Javanese knife; the fruits, thought Alleyn, of some Royal tour through the East to Oceania. An empty space on the extreme left of the group suggested the position of the mere, and an unfaded patch on the wall gave a clear trace of its shape. It had been in full view of William as he sat fiddling with the radio controls and had hung immediately above and back from the volume control. This conjured up a curious picture. Was William so absorbed in the radio that he did not notice his assailant take the weapon from its place on the wall? That was scarcely credible. Had his assailant removed the weapon some time previously? Or did William notice the removal and see no cause for alarm? In that case the assailant could surely not have been Hart, since William's antagonism to Hart was so acute that it was impossible to imagine him regarding such a move with anything but the deepest suspicion. Had Hart, then, previously removed the mere? But when? Before Mandrake spoke to him in the boudoir? Not afterwards, because William was there with Nicholas, who locked the communicating door in Hart's face. Again he looked from the volume control to the space on the wall and wondered suddenly if Hart's ignorance of radio could possibly be assumed. But suppose Hart removed the mere? He had not been present at dinner. Had he taken it while the others were dining? Alleyn turned from the wall to the desk, a small affair with two drawers, one of which was not quite closed. He opened it with his finger-nail. Inside were a number of small pads. " Charter forms, by gum," Alleyn muttered.

He had brought with him the parcel ordered by telephone from the chemist. He opened it and transferred the contents to his own attaché case. Among them were two pairs of tweezers. With these he took the Charter pads one by one from the drawer and laid them out on the desk. There were nine, and most of them were complete with their own small pencils. At the back of the drawer he found a number of india-rubbers.

" A little dreary labour," he thought, " should no doubt be

expended. Later, perhaps." And, taking great pains not to touch the pads, he transferred them, together with the pencils and india-rubbers, to an empty stationery box he found in another drawer. This he placed in his attaché case. He then moved on from the desk towards the library door. A four-fold red leather screen stood in front of the library door. It almost touched the outside wall and extended to an angle some five or six feet out into the room. Alleyn went round it and faced the door itself, which was in the corner of the room. The door-knob was on his right. He unlocked it, glanced into the library, and shut it again. As he stooped to the lock he noticed a small hole in the white paint on the jamb. It resembled the usual marks left by wood-rot. The one tool of his trade that Alleyn had about him was his pocket lens. He took it out, squatted down, squinted through it at the hole. He fetched a disgruntled sigh and moved to the fireplace. Above the mantelpiece the wall was decorated with an old-fashioned fishing-rod, complete with reel. Beneath it hung a faded photograph in an Oxford frame. It presented a Victorian gentleman wearing an ineffable air of hauteur and a costume which suggested that he had begun to dress up as Mr. Sherlock Holmes, but, suddenly losing interest, had gone out fishing instead. With some succees, it seemed, as from his right hand depended a large languid trout, while with his left hand he supported a rod. Across this gentleman's shins, in faded spidery letters, was written the legend: "Hubert St. John Worthington Royal, 1900. 4½ lbs. Pen-Felton Reach." This brief but confusing information was supplemented by a label which hung from the old rod. "With this rod," said the label dimly, " and this fly—an Alexandra—I caught a four-and-a-half pounder above Trott's Bridge in Pen-Felton Reach. It now enters an honourable retirement. H. St. J. W. Royal, 1900."

"Well done, H. St. J. W. R.," said Alleyn. "Would you be Jonathan's papa, now, or his grandpapa? Not that it matters. I want to have a look at your reel."

It appeared that somebody else had been interested in the reel. For whereas the rod and the reel itself had escaped the attention of Jonathan's housemaids, the mass of rolled line was comparatively free from dust, and, although on one side this roll of line was discoloured and faded, the centre and the other side were clean and new-looking. Alleyn saw that the loose end of the line that hung down had a clean cross-section. He caught this end in his tweezers, pulled out a good stretch of line, cut it off with Troy's nail scissors, which he had pocketed before leaving, and put it away in another envelope. Mandrake was an observant fellow, he thought, but evidently he had missed the trout line.

Alleyn now examined the fireplace, and, looking at the dead ash in the grate, sighed for his case bag and his usual band of assistants. It had been a wood fire, and in burning out had missed the two side logs, which had fallen apart, showing their charred inner surfaces. Between these was a heap of ash and small pieces of charcoal. Alleyn squatted down and peered through his pocket lens at this heap without disturbing it. Lying across the surface, broken at intervals, but suggesting rather than forming a thread-like pattern, trailed a fine worm of ash. It was the ghost of some alien substance that had been thrown on the fire not long before it died out. Alleyn decided to leave the ash for the moment and continued his prowl round the room. The door into the library was a massive affair, felted, and lined, on the library side, with shelves and dummy books, bearing titles devised by some sportive Royal.

" I fancy the radio'll have to blast its head off before you'd hear much of it in the library," thought Alleyn. " Damn, I'd like to try. Better not, though, till I've printed the knobs and trimmings."

He hunted over the floor, using his torch and pressing his fingers into the pile of the carpet. He found nothing that seemed to him to be of interest. He completed his examination of the room and returned at last to the body of William Compline.

Alleyn's camera was a very expensive instrument. He had brought it with him to make records of his wife's work during its successive stages. He now used it to photograph William Compline's body, the area of floor surrounding his feet, his skull, the mere, the wireless cabinet, the ash in the fireplace, and the library door jamb. " In case," he muttered, " Thompson and Co. don't get through to-night." Detective-Sergeant Thompson was his photographic expert.

Having taken his pictures, he stood for a time looking down at William. " I don't imagine *you* knew anything about it." And he thought: " Life's going to be pretty cheap when summer comes, but you've caught a blitzkrieg of your own, and so for you it's different. You've conjured up the Yard, you poor chap. You've cranked up the majesty of the law, and by the time *your* killer reaches the dock, Lord knows how many

of your friends will be there to give evidence. There ought to
be a moral lurking somewhere round this, but I'm damned if
I know what it is." He replaced the sheet, looked round the
room once more, locked the two inner doors, gathered up
his possessions and went into the hall. As he was locking the
door he heard a sort of male twittering, and turning round saw
on the stairs a small rotund gentleman dressed in plus fours
and wearing thick-lensed glasses.

"I'm so awfully sorry to keep you waiting," said this person.
"Mandrake looked after you?"

"Very well indeed, thank you."

"Yes. He told me you were here," said Jonathan. "I
begged him to—to give you the keys of that terrible room.
I—I find myself very much upset. I'm quite ashamed of myself."

"A very natural reaction, sir," said Alleyn politely. "May
we have a word or two somewhere?"

"Eh? Yes. Yes, of course. Er—in the drawing-room, shall
we? This way."

"I fancy Mandrake and Miss Wynne are in the drawing-
room. Perhaps the library?"

Jonathan nervously agreed to the library, and Alleyn had
a notion that he would have preferred somewhere farther away
from the smoking-room. He saw Jonathan look quickly at
the communicating door and then turn away abruptly to the
fire.

Before anything else," Alleyn said, "I must ask how Mrs.
Compline is. Mandrake will have told you that the local police
are trying to find a doctor. In the meantime, I hope . . ."

"She's very ill indeed," said Jonathan. "That's why you
find me so greatly upset. She—they think she's going to die."

I I

Jonathan was not easy to deal with. He was both restless
and lugubrious, and it was with difficulty that Alleyn contrived to nail him down to hard facts. For five minutes he
listened to a recital in which such matters as Jonathan's affec-
tion for the Complines, his bewilderment, the sacred laws of
hospitality and the infamy of Dr. Hart were strangely mingled.
At last, however, Alleyn managed to pin him down to giving
direct answers to questions based on Mandrake's notes. Jona-

than gave a fairly coherent account of his own talks with Nicholas and laid great stress on the point of Hart's practically admitting that he had written threatening letters. " And in *my* house, Alleyn, in *my* house he had the effrontery to make use of a round-game . . ." Alleyn cut short this lament with a direct question.

" Who is with Mrs. Compline at the moment?"

" Hart!" Jonathan exclaimed. " There it is, you see! Hart! I know it's a most improper, a monstrous arrangement, but what could we do?"

" Nothing else, sir, I'm sure. Is he alone?"

" No. No, my cousin, Lady Hersey Amblington, who is an experienced V.A.D., is there. I spoke to her on my way down. I did not go in. She came to the door. They—ah—they're doing something—I understand you brought—but Hart appears to think she is almost beyond help."

" In that case," said Alleyn, " as soon as it's possible, I should like to see Dr. Hart. At once, if he can leave his patient."

" I don't think he can do so just yet. There's one other thing, Mr. Alleyn." Jonathan's hand went to the inside pocket of his coat. He drew out a long envelope.

" This," he said, " contains the letter she left behind for Nicholas. He has read it, but nobody else has done so. I persuaded him to place it in this envelope in the presence of my cousin, Hersey Amblington, and myself. We have signed a statement to that effect on the outside. I now," said Jonathan, with a small bow to Alleyn, " hand it to you."

" That's very correct, sir," said Alleyn.

" Oh, well, I'm a J.P., you know, and if, as we fear, poor Sandra does not recover . . ."

" Yes, of course. I think I should see Mr. Compline before I open the letter. It's more important at the moment that I should talk to Dr. Hart. Perhaps we had better go upstairs. Dr. Hart may be able to come out for a moment. Will you take me up, please?"

" But—is it absolutely necessary . . .?"

" I'm afraid Mrs. Compline's condition makes it imperative, sir. Shall we go?"

Jonathan pulled at his lower lip, eyed Alleyn over the top of his glasses, and finally made a little dart at him. " In your hands," he chattered, " unreservedly. Come on."

He led the way upstairs. They turned off to the left and

came up to the visitors' wing. Alleyn paused at the stairhead. A little to his right, and facing the stairs, he saw an
empty niche in the wall, and, remembering the plan Mandrake had sketched in the margin of his notes, he recognised
this as the erstwhile perch of the brass Buddha. The men's
rooms, then, would be down the passage. Madame Lisse's,
he remembered, was opposite the stairhead, and Mrs. Compline's next door to the left. Indeed, Jonathan now pointed
to the door of this room, and, with a wealth of finicking gestures, indicated that Alleyn should wait where he stood. "Just
a moment, Alleyn," he mouthed. "Better just—if you don't
mind—one doesn't know . . ."

He tiptoed to the door, and, staring apprehensively at Alleyn,
tapped very gently, paused, shook his head and tapped again.
In a moment or two the door opened. Alleyn saw a tallish
woman, with a well-groomed head and a careful make-up on
a face that wore an expression of extreme distress. Jonathan
whispered, and the lady looked quickly over his shoulder at
Alleyn. "Not now, Jo," she said. "Surely, not now." Jonathan whispered again, and she said with a show of irritation:
"There's no need to do that. *She* can't hear, poor dear."

Alleyn moved towards them. "I'm so sorry," he said, "but
I'm afraid I must see Dr. Hart as soon as possible."

Jonathan said hurriedly and rather ludicrously: "You don't
know Mr. Alleyn, Hersey. My cousin, Lady Hersey Amblington, Alleyn."

"If he's still . . ." Alleyn began, and Hersey said quickly:
"He's done everything possible. I'm afraid he doesn't think
it's going to be any use. He's been rather marvellous, Mr.
Alleyn."

Before Alleyn could reply to this unexpected tribute or to
the petulant little cluck with which Jonathan received it, the
door was suddenly pulled wide open from within and there
stood a heavy, pale man wearing no jacket, his shirt-sleeves
rolled up, his face glistening.

"What *is* all this?" demanded Dr. Hart. "What now!
Lady Hersey, you have no business to stand chattering in door-
ways when perhaps I may need you."

"I'm sorry," said Hersey meekly, and disappeared into the
room. Hart glared at Alleyn. "Well?" he said.

"I'm an officer of Scotland Yard, Dr. Hart. May I speak
to you?"

"Why in God's name haven't you brought a medical man with you. Well, well, come in here. Come in."

So Alleyn went into the room and Hart very neatly shut the door in Jonathan's face.

III

The bed had been moved out from the wall and the light from a large window fell across it and directly upon the face of the woman who lay there. Her eyes were not quite closed, nor was her mouth, which, Alleyn saw, was crooked, dragged down on one side as though by an invisible cord. So strong was the light that, coming from the dark passage, he saw the scene as a pattern of hard whites and swimming blacks, and some moments passed before his eyes found, in the shadows round the bed, a litter of nursing paraphernalia which Hersey at once began to clear away. Alleyn became aware of a slow, deep, and stertorous rhythm, the sound of the patient's breathing.

"Is she deeply unconscious?" he asked.

"Profound coma," said Hart. "I have, I think, done everything possible in the way of treatment. Mr. Mandrake gave me your notes, which, I understand, came from a surgeon at Scotland Yard. They confirmed my own opinion as regards treatment. I am deeply disappointed that you have not brought a medical man with you, not because I believe he could do anything, but because I wish to protect myself."

"Was the stuff from the local chemist no use?"

"It enabled me to complete the treatment, but the condition has not improved. Have you pencil and paper?" demanded Dr. Hart surprisingly.

"I have." Alleyn's hand went to his pocket.

"I wish you to record the treatment. I am in a dangerous position. I wish to protect myself. Lady Hersey Amblington will be witness to my statement. I have administered injections of normal saline, and of Croton oil. Every attempt to obtain elimination—you are not taking notes," said Dr. Hart accusingly.

"Dr. Hart," said Alleyn, "I shall take exhaustive notes in a little while, and you will be given every opportunity to make statements. At the moment I am concerned with your patient. Is there the smallest hope of her recovery?"

" In my opinion, none. That is why . . ."

" I think I understand your position. Has she, at any time since you have attended her, regained consciousness?"

Dr. Hart turned down his shirt sleeves and looked about for his aggressively countrified coat. Hersey at once brought it and helped him into it, and Alleyn found a moment in which to appreciate Dr. Hart's unconscious acceptance of her attention.

" At first," he said, " she could be made to wince by slapping the face. Twice she opened her eyes. The last time was when her son tried to rouse her. Otherwise there has been nothing."

Hersey made a sharp movement and Alleyn said: " Yes, Lady Hersey? You were going to say something, weren't you?"

" Only that she did speak once. Dr. Hart was at the far end of the room, and I don't think he heard her."

" What is this?" said Hart sharply. " You should have told me immediately. When did the patient speak?"

" It was when Nicholas was here. You remember he shouted. You told him to. And he shook her. There was no response, she had closed her eyes again, and you—you sort of threw up your hands and walked away. Do you remember?"

" Of course I remember!"

" Nicholas leant forward and put his hand against her cheek —the disfigured cheek. He did it quite gently, but it seemed to rouse her. She opened her eyes and said one word. It was the faintest whisper. You couldn't have heard."

" Well, well, well, what was this one word?" Hart demanded. " Why did you not call me at once? What was it?"

" It was your name." There was a short silence, and Hersey added: " She didn't speak again."

Alleyn said: " Did you get the impression that she spoke with any intention?"

" I—don't think so. Perhaps she realised Dr. Hart was attending her," said Hersey, and Alleyn thought: " You don't believe that." He moved nearer to the bed and Dr. Hart joined him there. " How long?" Alleyn murmured.

" Not very long, I think."

" Should I fetch Nicholas?" said Hersey.

" Does he wish to return?" asked Hart coolly.

" I don't think so. Not unless—— I promised I would tell him when . . ."

" It will not be just yet, I think."

"Perhaps I'd better tell him that. He's in his room. I shall be there if you want me."

Alleyn opened the door for her. When he moved back into the room, Dr. Hart was stooping over his patient. Without turning his head, but with a certain deepening of his voice, he said: "I would have given much, I would have given something that I have struggled greatly to retain, if by doing so I could have saved this case. Do you know why that is?"

"I think perhaps I might guess."

"Come here, Inspector. Look at that face. For many years I used to dream of those disfigurements, for a long time I was actually afraid to go to sleep for fear I should be visited by a certain nightmare, a nightmare of the re-enactment of my blunder, and of the terrible scene that followed her discovery of it. You have heard, of course, that she recognised me and that the elder son, who has been killed, reacted most violently to her story?"

"I've been given some account of it," said Alleyn without emphasis.

"It is true that I was the Franz Hartz of Vienna who blundered. If I could have saved her life I would have felt it to be an atonement. I always knew," said Dr. Hart, straightening his back and facing Alleyn, "I always knew that some day I should meet this woman again. There is no use in concealing these things from you, Inspector. These others, these fools, will come screaming to you, eager to accuse me. I have refused to discuss my dilemma with any one of them. I am ready to discuss it with you."

Alleyn reflected with faint amusement that this, from a leading suspect, was just as well. He complimented Dr. Hart on his decision, and together they moved away from the bed to a more distant window, where Jonathan's bouquet of everlasting flowers, papery little mummies, still rustled in their carefully chosen vase. And now Alleyn did produce a pocket note-book.

"Before we begin," he said, "is there any possibility that Mrs. Compline will regain consciousness?"

"I should say there is not the remotest possibility. There may be a change. I expect, and your police-surgeon's advice confirms my suspicion, that the respiration may change. I should prefer to remain in this room. We shall conduct the interview here, if you please."

And, while the light from a rain-blurred window imperceptibly thickened and grew cold upon the face of Dr. Hart's patient, he answered Alleyn's questions. Alleyn had had official dealings with aliens for many years. Since the onset of Nazidom he had learned to recognise a common and tragic characteristic in many of them, and that was a deep-seated terror of plain-clothes police officers. Dr. Hart's attitude surprised him very much. As he carried forward his questions he found that in the face of what appeared to be an extremely nasty position Hart showed little nervousness. He answered readily, but with a suggestion of impatience. Alleyn was more than usually careful to give him the official warnings. Hart listened to them with an air of respect, nodding his head gravely but showing no inclination to consider his answers more carefully. If he was indeed innocent he was the ideal witness, but in this case his belief in his own safety was alarming. If he was guilty he was a very cool customer indeed. Alleyn decided to try him a little further.

"It comes to this, then," he said. "You can offer no explanation of how this extra Charter form containing the warning reached Captain Compline. Nor have you any theory as to who pushed Mr. Mandrake into the pond, though you agree that you saw Mr. Compline leave for the pond wearing precisely the same kind of cape. Is that right?"

"It is true that I do not know who pushed Mr. Mandrake into the pond," said Hart slowly. "As for the Charter form, I suggested at the time that I might have torn two forms off together and that the bottom form had been written by somebody else."

"Somebody who made letters reminiscent of your own writing?"

"I have not seen the form. I do not know what was written on it."

"Five words. 'You are warned. Keep off.'"

A dull red crept into those heavy cheeks. For the first time he seemed disconcerted. For the first time Alleyn saw the nervous tic flutter under his lip.

"Dr. Hart," Alleyn said, "of all the people in that room, who had most cause to send such a message to Nicholas Compline?"

"Two people had cause. His brother and myself. His brother had cause. Had he not practised his goat's tricks upon the girl, the brother's fiancée?"

"And only on her?" Hart was silent. "Is it true," Alleyn

asked, " that you had written to Nicholas Compline, objecting to his friendship with your wife and threatening to take certain steps if this friendship continued?"

" Did *he* tell you that?" Hart demanded.

" I haven't seen him yet, but if you wrote such letters he's not likely to keep it a secret."

" I do not deny that I wrote them. I deny that I wrote this ridiculous message. And I object most strongly to the introduction into this affair of matters that concern only myself."

" If they prove to be irrelevant they will not be made public. Dr. Hart, you tell me you have nothing to fear and nothing to conceal from me. At the same time you don't deny that you threatened Nicholas Compline. I must tell you that I've had a very full account of this week-end from a member of your party. I've warned you that your statements, if relevant, may be used in subsequent proceedings. I'm going to ask you certain questions and I shall do my best to check your answers. We shall get on a good deal faster if you don't challenge my questions, but either refuse or consent to give plain answers to them."

There was a pause and then Hart said hurriedly: " Very well, very well. I do not seek to obstruct you. It is only that there is one matter that is most painful to me. Unendurably painful."

" I'm sorry. Do you agree that you were at enmity with Compline?"

" I objected to his behaviour in regard to—my wife."

" Did he know she was your wife?"

" I desired to tell him so."

" But you didn't tell him?"

" No. My wife did not wish me to do so."

" Have you quarrelled with him since you came to Highfold?"

" Yes. Openly. I have not attempted to conceal my mistrust and dislike of him. Would a man who was planning a murder behave in such a manner? Would he not rather simulate friendship?"

Alleyn looked at the pale face with its twitching lip. " If he he was in full command of his emotions, no doubt he would attempt to do so." Hart found no answer to this, and he went on: " Did you meet any one on your way from the house to the pond?"

" No."

"I have had a very brief look at that part of the garden. You went by a path that comes out at the back of the pavilion?"

"Yes."

"What did you see as you came round the pavilion?"

"I heard shouts and I saw William Compline, Nicholas Compline, Miss Wynne and Mr. Royal gesticulating on the edge of the pond."

"Yesterday evening when you came upstairs to dress, did you see anybody after you went to your room?"

"Nobody."

"Have you ever touched the brass Buddha that injured Nicholas Compline?"

"Never. But—wait a moment—yes. Yes, my God, I have touched it."

"When?"

"It was the first night. We went up to our rooms. I remember I drew back because I did not wish to accompany Nicholas Compline, who walked a little ahead with his brother. Mr. Royal drew my attention to this Buddha. He asked me if I knew anything of Oriental art. As an excuse to delay I feigned an interest. I reached out my hands and touched it. Compline made some remark on the obesity of the Buddha. It was an insult to me. Whenever he could insult me he did so. So I have touched it."

"Coming back to last night. Will you describe your movements from the time you entered the green boudoir until the time you went upstairs for the last time?"

Hart did this, and his description tallied with Mandrake's note. "I felt I could not dine with them. They suspected me. It was an intolerable situation. I spoke to Mr. Royal, and he suggested that I remain in that room. When, as I have told you, I finally left it, it was for the first time. I went straight to my room. The footman saw me."

"Had you been into the smoking-room at any time yesterday?"

"I do not think so. That insufferable machine was there. In the morning he had driven me crazy with it. First one horrible noise, then another, and all of them distorted. I cannot endure radio. I have a radio-phobia. I did not go into the room at all yesterday."

"But you have been there at some time?"

"Oh, yes. The first night we played this Charter game in that room."

"Will your describe the room to me?"

"Describe it? But you have seen it? Why should I?"

"I should like you to do so if you will."

Hart stared at Alleyn as if he was insane and began a laborious catalogue. "First then, if you must have it, there is this detestable radio close to the boudoir door. When I think of the room I think of the radio by which it is made hideous. There are English leather chairs. There is a red leather screen. There are pictures, English sportings, I think. And photographs, very old and faded. There is such a photograph above the mantelpiece of an old fellow with a fish. He wears an absurd costume. There is also hanging on the wall a fishing-rod. Surely this is a great waste of time, Inspector?"

"Are you a fisherman?"

"*Gott im Himmel*, of what importance is it whether I fish or do not fish! I do not fish. I know nothing of fishing." Hart stared irritably at Alleyn and then added: "If I lose my temper you will forgive me. I have heard of the efficiency of Scotland Yard. No doubt there is some reason which I do not follow for these questions of interior decoration and fishing. I can tell you little more of the room. I did not particularly observe this room."

"The colour of the walls?"

"A light colour. A neutral colour. Almost white."

"And the carpet?"

"I cannot tell you—dark. Green, I think. Dark green. There are, of course, three doors. The one into the boudoir was locked by Nicholas Compline after I requested that he should not use that machine of hell."

"What else did you see on the walls?"

"What else? Ah, the weapons, of course. Mr. Royal drew our attention to the weapons, I remember, on Friday night. It was before dinner. Some of the men were in the room. He described the travels of his father in the antipodes where he collected some of them. He showed me——"

"Yes, Dr. Hart?"

Hart paused with his mouth open and then turned away. "I have just remembered," he muttered. "He took down the stone club from the wall, saying it was—I forget—a Polynesian or New Zealand native weapon. He gave it to me to examine. I was interested. I—examined the weapon."

"Both the mere and the Buddha?" said Alleyn, without particular stress. "I see."

I V

It was twenty to four when Alleyn finished with Dr. Hart. Hart made another examination of his patient. He said that her condition was "less satisfactory." Her temperature had risen and her respiration was more markedly abnormal. Alleyn would have been glad to escape from the rhythm of deep and then shallow breaths, broken by terrible intervals of silence. Hersey Amblington returned, and Hart said he thought that Nicholas should be warned of the change in his mother, and she went to fetch him. Obviously Hart expected Alleyn to go. He had told him there was no possibility of Mrs. Compline's regaining consciousness before she died, but Alleyn did not feel justified in acting upon this assurance. He remained standing in shadow at the far end of the room, and Hart paid no more attention to him. The rain drove in sighing gusts against the closed windows, and found its way in through the open ones, so that Alleyn felt its touch upon his face. A vast desolation filled the room, and still there came from the bed that sequence of deep breath, shallow breath, interval, and then again, deep breath, shallow breath.

The door opened and Hersey Amblington came in with Nicholas.

Alleyn saw a tall young man in uniform who carried his left arm in a sling. He noticed the lint-coloured hair, the blankly good-looking face with its blond moustache and faintly etched lines of dissipation, and he wondered if normally it held any trace of colour. He watched Nicholas walk slowly towards the bed, his gaze fixed, his right hand plucking at his tie. Hersey moved forward a chair, and without a word Nicholas sat beside his mother. Hersey stooped over the bed and presently Alleyn saw that she had drawn Mrs. Compline's hand from under the sheets and laid it close beside Nicholas. It was so flaccid it seemed already dead. Nicholas laid his own hand over it, and at the touch broke down completely, burying his face beside their joined hands and weeping bitterly. For several minutes Alleyn stood in the shadow, hearing the wind and rain, the sound of distorted breathing, and the heavy sobs of Nicholas Compline. Then there was a lessening of sound. Hart moved to the head of the bed, looked at Hersey, and nodded. She had laid her hand on Nicholas's shoulder, but before he raised his head Alleyn had slipped out of the room.

It was darkish now, in the passage, and he almost collided with Jonathan Royal, who must have been standing close to the door. Jonathan had his finger to his lips. As they faced each other there they heard Nicholas, beyond the closed door, scream out: "Don't touch her, you——! Keep your hands off her. If it hadn't been for you she'd never have done it."

"My God!" said Jonathan in a whisper. "What now? What's he doing to her?"

"Nothing that can hurt her," said Alleyn.

CHAPTER XIV

INTERROGATION

I

At five o'clock the telephone in the library rang out. Alleyn, who was there, answered it. It was a police call from London for himself, and he took it with the greatest satisfaction. The Yard reported that Detective-Inspector Fox, together with a surgeon, a finger-print expert, and a photographer, had left London at three o'clock and would reach Pen-Felton by way of a branch line at 7.30. The Chipping constabulary had arranged for a car to bring them on to Highfold.

"I'm damn' glad to hear it," said Alleyn warmly. "I'm here with a couple of bodies and seven lunatics. D'you know what's happened to the Chipping people?"

"They got stuck somewhere, sir, and had to walk back. We'd have reported before, but the line's only just fixed."

"The whole thing's damn' silly," said Alleyn. "We might be marooned in Antarctica. Anyway, thank heaven for Fox and Co. Good-bye."

He hung up the receiver, drove his hands through his hair, and returned to Mandrake's notes. As a postscript, Mandrake had added a sort of tabulated summary:—

	If the Murderer mistook William for Nicholas				If the Murderer recognised William	
	Motive	Opp. 1st attempt	Opp. 2nd attempt	Opp. 3rd attempt	Motive	Reason for other attempts
Dr. Hart	Yes	Yes	Yes	Booby-trap?	Yes	Made against Nicholas
Nicholas Compline	—	—	—	—	None	None
Jonathan Royal	None	Possibly	Improbable	Yes?	None	None
Lady Hersey	None	Yes	Yes?	Yes	None	None
Mrs. C.	None	Yes	No	Yes	?	None
Aubrey Mandrake	None	Yes!	No	No	None	None
Madame Lisse	None	Yes	No	Yes	?	None
Chloris Wynne	None	No	Yes	No	None	None

Alleyn shook his head over the last name. "Industrious Mr. Mandrake! But he's not to be trusted there," he thought. "We have a young woman who has been jilted by Nicholas, who attracted her. As soon as she engages herself to William, who does not attract her, Nicholas begins to make amorous antics at her all over again. A wicked young woman might wish to get rid of William. A desperate young woman might wish to get rid of Nicholas. And is it *quite* impossible that Miss Wynne darted down to the pond before making her official arrival with Jonathan? Perhaps it is. I'll have to go down to that pond." He lit a cigarette and stared dolefully at the row of "yes's" against Hart. "All jolly fine, but how the devil did he rig a booby trap that neither Nicholas nor William noticed? No, it's not a bad effort on Master Mandrake's part. But I fancy he's made one error. Now, I *wonder.*" And, taking up his pen, he put a heavy cross against one of Mandrake's entries. He wandered disconsolately about the library, and finally, with a grimace, let himself into the smoking-room. He went straight to the radio, passing behind the shrouded figure in the chair. This time he did not draw back the curtains from the windows, but turned up the lights and used his torch. The wireless cabinet stood on a low stool. Alleyn's torch-light crawled over the front surface and finally came to rest on the bakelite volume control, which he examined through his lens. He found several extremely faint lines inside of the screw-hole. There were also some faint scratches across the surface outside the hole, making tracks in a film of dust.

The stillness of the room was interrupted by a small murmur of satisfaction. Alleyn got out his pair of tweezers, and introduced them delicately into the hole in the volume control. Screwing his face into an excruciating grimace, he manipulated his tweezers and finally drew them out. He squatted on the carpet quite close to the motionless folds of white linen that followed so closely the frozen posture of the figure they concealed that an onlooker might have been visited by the horrid notion that William imitated Alleyn and, under his shroud, conducted a secret scrutiny of the carpet. Alleyn had laid an envelope on the carpet, and on its surface he dropped the minute fragment he had taken in his tweezers. It was scarcely larger than an eyelash. He peered at it through his glass.

" Scarlet. Feather, I *think*. And a tiny scrap of green," said Alleyn. And whistling soundlessly, he sealed his find up in the envelope.

Next he peered into the crevice between the large and small tuning controls. " Not so much as a speck of dust," he muttered, " although there's plenty in the screw-hole. There's the actual shaft which rotates, of course. It's reminiscent of a pulley." He found one or two scratches on the surface of the tuning control. It was just possible through the lens to see that each of these marks had a sharp beginning and a gentler tail, suggesting that some very fine pointed object had struck the surface smartly and fallen away. Alleyn re-examined the carpet. Below the wall where the mere had hung, and a little to the right, he found one or two marks that he had missed on his first examination. They occurred beneath the small desk that stood under the weapons. Here the pile of the carpet was protected and thick. Across its surface, running roughly parallel with the wall, were a series of marks which, when he examined them through his glass, looked like the traces of some sharp object that had torn across the surface of the pile. In one place he found a little tuft of carpet that had become detached. He photographed this area, fenced it in with chairs, and returned to the library.

Here he found a young footman with a tea-tray.

" Is that for me?" Alleyn asked.

" Yes, sir. I was to ask if there was anything further you required, sir."

" Nothing, at the moment, thank you. Are you Thomas?"

" Yes, sir," said Thomas with a nervous simper.

" I'd like a word with you." Alleyn poured out a cup of tea. " Still keen on Boomps-a-daisy?"

Thomas did not answer, and Alleyn glanced up at him.

" Never want to hear it again s'long as I live, sir," said Thomas ardently.

" You needn't regret your burst of good spirits, you know. It may be very valuable."

" Beg pardon, sir," said Thomas, " but I don't want to be mixed up in nothing unpleasant, sir. I've put my name down, sir, and I'm waiting to be called up. I don't want to go into the army, sir, with an unpleasantness hanging over me, like."

Alleyn was only too familiar with this attitude of mind and was careful to reassure Thomas.

" There ought to be no unpleasantness about furthering the cause of justice, and that's what I hope you may be able to do. I only want you to repeat an assurance you have already given Mr. Royal and Mr. Mandrake. I'm going to put it this way, and I hope you'll agree that it couldn't be put more candidly. Would you be prepared to swear that between the time you passed through the hall to the library and the time when you left off dancing, Dr. Hart could *not* have entered the smoking-room?"

" Yes, sir, I would."

" You've thought it over carefully, I expect, since Mr. Royal spoke to you last night."

" I have indeed, sir. I've been over and over it in my brain till I can't seem to think of anything else. But it's the same every time, sir. Dr. Hart was crossing the hall when I took the tray in, and I wasn't above a few seconds setting it down, and when I come out, sir, he was half-way up the stairs."

" Was there a good light on the stairs?"

" Enough to see him, sir."

" You couldn't have mistaken somebody else for Dr. Hart?"

" No, sir, not a chance, if you'll excuse me. I saw him quite distinct, sir, walking up with his hands behind his back. He turned the corner and I noticed his face looking sort of—well, it's difficult to describe."

" Try," said Alleyn.

" Well, sir, as if he was very worried. Well, kind of frantic, sir. Haunted almost," added Thomas with an air of surprising himself. " I noticed it particular, sir, because it was just the same as he looked when he was walking in the garden yesterday morning."

Alleyn's cup was half-way to his lips. He set it down carefully.

" Did you see Dr. Hart in the garden yesterday morning? Where abouts?"

" Behind that bathing-shed—I mean that pavilion, sir. We'd heard about the bet Mr. William Compline had on with his brother, sir, and I'm afraid I just nipped out to see the fun, sir. One of the maids kind of kidded me on, if you'll excuse the expression, sir."

" I'll excuse it," said Alleyn. " Go on, Thomas. Tell me exactly what you did see."

" Well, sir, I knew Mr. Caper wouldn't be all that pleased if he knew, so I went out by the east wing door and walked round to the front of the house by a path in the lower gardens. It comes out a little way down the drive, sir."

" Yes."

" I dodged across the drive, sir, and up through the trees towards the terrace. I was just above the pavilion, sir, and I looked down and there was the doctor gentleman, with his hands behind his back, walking towards the rear of the pavilion. I'd seen him go out by the front door before I left, sir. Mr. Royal saw him off."

" Did you continue to watch him?"

" No, sir, not for long. You see, while I was looking at him I heard a splash and a great to-do, and I ran on to where I could see the pond, and there was Mr. Nicholas throwing in one of them floating birds and yelling for help, and Mr. Mandrake half drowning in the pond and Mr. William running down the steps, with the young lady and Mr. Royal just crossing the terrace. But the doctor must have come along as quick as he could, sir, because he got there just as they hauled Mr. Mandrake out."

"Did you see any one else on the terrace? A lady?"

"No, sir." Thomas waited for a moment, and then said: "Will there be anything further, sir?"

"I fancy not, Thomas. I'll get that down in writing and ask you to sign it. It'll do very nicely indeed to go on with."

"Thank you, sir," said Thomas primly, and withdrew.

II

"Dr. Hart," Alleyn muttered after a long cogitation. "Opportunity for first attempt." He altered the entry in Mandrake's tables and rang the bell. It was answered by Caper, a condescension that Alleyn imagined must have been prompted by curiosity. He divided butlers into two classes, the human and the inhuman. Caper, he thought, looked human.

"You rang, sir?" said Caper.

"To send a message to Mr. Nicholas Compline. I don't want to worry him too much, but I should like to see him if he's free."

"I'll make inquiries, sir," said Caper. Inhuman butlers, Alleyn reflected, always ascertained.

"Thank you. Before you go, I'd like your opinion on the footman."

"On Thomas, sir?"

"Yes. I expect he's told you all about his interviews with Mr. Royal."

"He has mentioned them, sir."

"What's your opinion of him?"

Caper drew down his upper lip, placed Alleyn's cup and saucer on the tray, and appeared to deliberate. "He's not cut out for service, sir," he said finally. "In a manner of speaking he's too high-spirited."

"Ah," Alleyn murmured, "you've heard about Boomps-a-daisy."

"I have, sir. I was horrified. But it's not that alone, not by any means. He's always up to something. There's no harm in the lad, sir. He's a nice, open, truthful lad, but not suitable. He'll do better in the army."

"Truthful," Alleyn repeated.

" I should say exceptionally so, sir. Very observant and bright in his ways, too."

" That's a useful recommendation."

" Will that be all, sir?"

" Not quite." Alleyn waited for a moment and then looked directly at Caper. " You know why I'm here, of course?"

" Yes, sir."

" There is no doubt whatever that Mr. William Compline has been murdered. This being so, it appears that his murderer is now at large in this house. I am sure that the members of Mr. Royal's staff will want to give us all the help they can in a difficult and possibly even a dangerous situation."

" I'm sure we'll all do our duty by the master, sir," said Caper, and if this was not a direct answer Alleyn chose to regard it as one. He began, very delicately, to probe. He believed that the servants in a large household have a seventy per cent working knowledge of everything that happens on the other side of the green baize door. This uncanny awareness, he thought, was comparable to the secret communications of prisoners, and he sometimes wondered if it was engendered in the bad old days of domestic servitude. To tap this source of information is one of the arts of police investigation, and Alleyn, who did not care overmuch for the job, sighed for Inspector Fox, who had a great way with female domestics. Fox settled down comfortably and talked their own language, a difficult task and one which it was useless for Alleyn to attempt. Caper had placed him in Jonathan's class, and would distrust and despise any effort Alleyn made to get out of it. So he went warily to work, at first with poor results. Caper remembered speaking to Mr. Royal in the hall before dinner on the previous evening. Mr. Royal ordered the wine for dinner and asked the time, as there was some question of letting the port settle after it was decanted. It was twenty-five minutes to eight. It would be about five minues later that Caper heard somewhere upstairs a heavy thud, followed by a shout from Mr. Nicholas. Mr. Royal had gone to the big drawing-room when he left Caper. Alleyn tried for an account of the quarrel between Hart and Nicholas Compline on Friday night after dinner. Caper said he had heard nothing of it. Alleyn groped about, watching his man, and at last he found an opening. Caper, true to his class, disliked foreigners. Something in the turn of his voice when Hart's name was introduced gave Alleyn his cue.

"I suppose," Alleyn said, "Dr. Hart and Madame Lisse have often visited Highfold?"

"No, sir. Only once previously. We had a ball in aid of the Polish refugees, and they both attended. That was in December, sir."

"Has Mr. Royal visited them?"

"I believe so, sir. I believe Mr. Royal dined with Mrs. Lisse, if that is the lady's name, not long after the ball. I understand the doctor was present on that occasion. Shortly afterwards he presented Mr. Royal with That Garment, sir."

"The Tyrolese cape?"

"Exactly so, sir," said Caper, after closing his eyes for a second.

"It wouldn't be right, then, to say that the entire party was well known to the staff?"

"No, sir. Her ladyship and Mrs. Compline and the two young gentlemen are old friends of Mr. Royal's, and Mr. Mandrake has often visited."

"He's an old friend of Mr. Royal's too, then?"

"I understand there is some business connection, sir," said Caper, and a kind of quintessence of snobbery overlaid the qualification.

"Did it strike you that it was a curiously assorted party?" Alleyn ventured. "Mr. Royal tells me you've been with him since you were a boy. Frankly, Caper, have you ever known another week-end party quite like this one?"

"Frankly, sir," said Caper, coming abruptly into the open, "I haven't." He paused for a moment, and perhaps he read a friendly interest in Alleyn's face. "I don't mention the hall out of the hall as a rule, sir," he said, "but, as you say, this is different. And I will say that Mrs. Pouting and myself never fancied them. Never."

"Never fancied who, Caper?"

"The foreigners, sir. And what's been seen since they came hasn't served to change our opinion."

With a certain distaste, Alleyn recognised his opening and took it. "Well, Caper, what *has* been seen? Hadn't you better tell me?"

Caper told him. There had been stories of Dr. Hart and Madame Lisse, stories that had percolated from Great Chipping. Caper digressed a little to throw out dark references to the Fifth Column and was led back gently to the burden of his song. There had been other stories, it seemed, of visits in the dead of night from Dr. Hart to Madame Lisse, and Mrs. Pouting had given it as her opinion that if they were not married they ought to be. From this it was an easy step to Nicholas. It was "common knowledge" said Caper, that Mr. Nicholas was paying serious court to Madame Lisse. "If it had been the elder brother she'd have taken him, sir, and it's the opinion of some that if poor Mr. William had come along first it would have been another story." It was obvious that Nicholas passed the test of the servants' hall. Caper said they were always very pleased to hear he was coming. The impression Alleyn had got from Mandrake and Chloris Wynne was of a vain, shallow fellow with a great deal of physical attraction for women. The impression he had got from his own brief glimpse of Nicholas was of a young man bewildered and dazed by a profound emotional shock. Jonathan, when he spoke coherently, had sketched a picture of a somewhat out-of-date rip. Caper managed to suggest a spirited grandee. Mr. William, he said, was the quiet one. Strange in his ways. But Mr. Nicholas was the same to everybody, always open-handed and pleasant. He was very well liked in the district. Alleyn led him back to Madame Lisse, and soon discovered that Mrs. Pouting and Caper believed she was out to catch Nicholas. That, in Caper's opinion, was the beginning of the trouble.

"If I may speak frankly, sir, we'd heard a good deal about it before Mrs. Lisse came. There was a lot of talk."

"What did it all add up to?"

"Why, sir, that the lady was taken up with this Dr. Hart until she saw something a good deal better come along. Mrs. Pouting says . . ."

"Look here," said Alleyn, "suppose you ask Mrs. Pouting to come in for a moment."

Mrs. Pouting was fetched and proved to be a large, capable lady with a good deal of jaw and not very much lip. With her entrance it became clear that the servants had determined that Madame Lisse and Dr. Hart, between them, were responsible for the whole tragedy. Alleyn recognised very characteristic forms of loyalty, prejudice and obstinacy. Jonathan and his intimate friends were not to be blown upon, they had been deceived and victimised by the foreigners. The remotest suggestion of Jonathan's complicity was enough to set Mrs.

Pouting off. She was very grand. Her manner as well as her skirts seemed to rustle, but Alleyn saw that she was big with a theory and meant to be delivered of it.

"Things have been going on," said Mrs. Pouting, "which, if Mr. Royal had heard of them, would have stopped certain persons from remaining at Highfold. Under this very roof, they've been going on."

"What sort of things?"

"I cannot bring myself . . ." Mrs. Pouting began, but Alleyn interrupted her. Would it not be better, he suggested, for her to tell him what she knew, here in private, than to have it dragged out piecemeal at an inquest. He would not use information that was irrelevant. Mrs. Pouting then said that there had been in-goings and out-comings from "Mrs. Lisse's" room. The housemaids had made discoveries. Dr. Hart had been overheard accusing her of all sorts of things.

"What sorts of things?" Alleyn repeated patiently.

"She's a bad woman, sir. We've heard no good of her. She's treated her ladyship disgracefully over her shop. She made trouble between Mr. Nicholas and his young lady. She's out for money, sir, and she doesn't care how she gets it. I've my own ideas about what's at the bottom of it all."

"You'd better tell me what these ideas are, Mrs. Pouting."

Caper made an uncomfortable noise in his throat. Mrs. Pouting glanced at him and said: " Mr. Caper doesn't altogether agree with me, I believe. Mr. Caper is inclined to blame *him* more than *her*, whereas I'm quite positive it's *her* more than *him*."

"What is?"

"If I may interrupt, sir," said Caper, "I think it would be best for us to say outright what's in our minds, sir."

"So do I," said Alleyn heartily.

"Thank you, sir. Yesterday evening, after the accident with the brass figure, Dr. Hart came downstairs and sat in the small green room, the one that opens into the smoking-room, sir. It happened that Mrs. Pouting had gone into the smoking-room to see if everything was to rights there, the flower vases full of water and the fire made up and so on. The communicating door was not quite closed and . . ."

"I hope it will be clearly understood," Mrs. Pouting struck in, " that I had *not* realised anybody was in the boudoir. I was examining the radio for dust—the maids are *not* as thorough as I could wish—when quite suddenly, a few inches away, as it seemed, I heard Dr. Hart's voice. He said: 'Let them say what they like, they can prove nothing.' And Mrs. Lisse's voice said: 'Are you sure?' I was very awkwardly placed," continued Mrs. Pouting genteelly. "I scarcely knew what to do. They had evidently come close to the door. If I made my presence known they would think perhaps that I had heard more and—well, really, it was very difficult. While I hesitated they began to speak again, but more quietly. I heard Mrs. Lisse say: 'In that event I shall know what to do.' He said: 'Would you have the courage?' and she said: 'Where much is at stake, I would dare much.' And then," said Mrs. Pouting, no longer able to conceal her relish for dramatic values, "*then*, sir, he said, almost admiringly, sir: '*You devil, I believe you would.*' And she said: 'It's not *I would*, Francis, it's *I will*.' Then they moved away from the door and I went out. But I repeat now what I said shortly afterwards to Mr. Caper: she sounded murderous."

III

"Well," said Alleyn, after a pause, "that's a very curious story, Mrs. Pouting." He looked from one to the other of the two servants, who still kept up their air of contained deference. "What's your interpretation of it?" he asked.

Mrs. Pouting did not reply, but she slightly cast up her eyes and her silence was ineffably expressive. Alleyn turned to Caper.

"Mrs. Pouting and I differ a little, sir," said Caper, exactly as if they had enjoyed an amiable discussion on the rival merits of thick and thin soup. "Mrs. Pouting, I understand, considers that Dr. Hart and Mrs. Lisse are adventurers who were working together to entrap Mr. Nicholas Compline, but that Dr. Hart had become jealous and that they had fallen out. Mrs. Pouting considers that Mrs. Lisse took advantage of Dr. Hart's two attempts on Mr. Nicholas to kill Mr. William and make it look as if Dr. Hart had done it, mistaking him for his brother. With a mercenary motive, sir."

"Extremely Machiavellian!" said Alleyn. "What do you think?"

"Well, sir, I don't know what to think, but somehow I can't fancy the lady actually struck the blow, sir."

"That," said Mrs. Pouting vigorously, "is because you're

a man, Mr. Caper. I hope I know vice when I see it," she added.

"I'm sure you do, Mrs. Pouting," said Alleyn absently. "Why not?"

Mrs. Pouting clasped her hands together, and by that simple gesture turned herself into an anxious human creature. "Whether it's both of them together or her alone," she said, "they're dangerous, sir. I know they're dangerous. If they'd heard me telling you what I have told you——! But it's not for myself, sir, but for Mr. Royal, that I'm worried. He's made no secret of what he thinks. He says openly that Dr. Hart (though why Doctor when he's no more than a meddler with Heaven's handiwork, I'm sure I don't know)—that Dr. Hart struck down Mr. William and that he'll see him hanged for it, and there they both are, free to deal another blow."

"Not quite," said Alleyn. "Dr. Hart, at his own suggestion, is once more locked in his room. I said I'd see Mr. Compline next, Caper, but I've changed my mind. Will you find out of Madame Hart is disengaged?"

"*Madame Hart!*" they both said together.

"Ah, I forgot. You haven't heard that they are man and wife."

"His wife!" whispered Mrs. Pouting. "That proves I'm right. She wanted to be rid of him. She wanted to catch the heir to Penfelton. That's why poor Mr. William was killed, and if the man is hanged for it, mark my words, Mr. Caper, she'll marry Mr. Nicholas."

And with this pronouncement, delivered with sibylline emphasis, Mrs. Pouting withdrew, sweeping Caper away in her train.

Alleyn noted down the conversation, pulled a grimace at the result and fell to thinking of former cases when the fantastic solution had turned out to be the correct one. "It's the left-and right theory," he thought. "A. wishes to be rid of B. and C. A. murders B. in such a fashion that C. is arrested and hanged. Mrs. Pouting casts Madame for the rôle of A. A murderess on the grand scale. What do murderesses on the grand scale look like?"

The next moment he was on his feet. Madame Lisse had made her entrance.

Nobody had told Alleyn that she was a remarkably beautiful woman, and for a brief moment he experienced the strange feeling of awed astonishment that extreme physical beauty may bring to the beholder. His first conscious thought was that she was lovely enough to stir up a limitless amount of trouble.

" You sent for me," said Madame Lisse.

" I asked if I might see you," said Alleyn. " Won't you sit down?"

She sat down. The movement was like a lesson in deportment, deliberately executed and ending in stillness, her back held erect, her wrists crossed on her lap.

" I wonder," thought Alleyn, " if William ever wanted to paint her." With every appearance of tranquillity she waited for him to begin. He took out his note-book and flattened it on his knee.

" First," he said, " I think I should have your name in full."

" Elise Lisse."

" I mean," said Alleyn, " your legal name. Madame. That should be Elise Hart, I understand." And he thought: " Golly! That's shaken her!" For a moment she looked furious. He saw the charming curve of her mouth harden and then compose itself. After a pause she said very sedately: " My legal name. Yes, of course. I do not care to use it and it did not occur to me to give it. I am separated from my husband."

" Ah, yes," said Alleyn. " Legally separated?"

" No," she said placidly. " Not legally."

" I hope you will forgive me if I ask you questions that may seem irrelevant and impertinent. You are under no obligation to answer them: I must make that quite clear, and perhaps I should add that any questions which you refuse to answer will be noted."

This uncompromising slice of the official manner seemed to have very little effect on Madame Lisse. She said: " Of course," and leant a little towards him. He got a whiff of her scent and recognised it as an expensive one.

" You are separated from your husband, but one supposes, since you go to the same house-parties, that it is an amicable arrangement."

There was a considerable pause before she answered: " Not precisely. I didn't care for accepting the same invitation but did so before I knew he had been invited."

" Were his feelings in the matter much the same as yours?"

" I can't tell you," said Madame Lisse. " I think not."

" You mean that you have not discussed the matter with him?"

" I don't enter into discussions with him if I can avoid doing so. I have tried as far as possible to avoid encounters."

Alleyn watched her for a moment and then said: " Did you drive here, Madame Lisse?"

" Yes."

" In your own car?"

" No. My—my husband drove me. Mr. Royal unfortunately made the suggestion and I couldn't very well refuse."

" Could you not? I should have thought you might have found a way out."

She surprised him by leaning still farther forward and putting her hand on the arm of his chair. It was a swift intimate gesture that brought her close to him.

" I see I must explain," said Madame Lisse.

" Please do," said Alleyn.

" I am a very unhappy woman, Mr.—— I do not know your name."

Alleyn told her his name and she managed to convey with great delicacy a suggestion of deference. " Mr. Alleyn. I didn't know—I am so sorry. Of course I have read of your wonderful cases. I'm sure you will understand. It will be easy to explain to you, a relief, a great relief to me." Her fingertips brushed his sleeve. " There are more ways than one," Alleyn thought, " of saying: ' Dilly, dilly, dilly, come and be killed.' " But he did not answer Madame Lisse, and in a moment she was launched. " I have been so terribly unhappy. You see, although I had decided I could no longer live with my husband, it wasn't possible for either of us to leave Great Chipping. Of course it is a very large town, isn't it? I hoped we would be able to avoid encounters but he has made it very difficult for me. You will understand what I mean. He is still devoted to me."

She paused, gazing at him. The scene was beginning to develop in the best tradition of the French novel. If the situation had been less serious and she had been less beautiful he might have found it more amusing, but he had a difficult job to do and there are few men who are able to feel amusement at overwhelming beauty.

" He has haunted me," she was saying. " I refused to see him but he lay in wait for me. He is insane. I believe him to

be insane. He rang me up and implored that I should allow
him to drive me to Highfold. I consented, hoping to bring
him to reason. But all the way here he begged me to return
to him. I said that it was impossible and immediately he began
to rave against Mr. Nicholas Compline. Nicholas Compline
and I have seen a good deal of each other and he, my husband,
became madly jealous of our friendship. I am a lonely woman,
Mr. Alleyn, and Mr. Compline has been a kind and chivalrous
friend to me. You do believe me, don't you?" said Madame
Lisse.

Alleyn said: "Is it true that sometime ago you gave a
dinner party to which you invited your husband and Mr.
Royal, who, by the way, did not know Dr. Hart was your
husband?"

He saw her eyes turn to flint but she scarcely hesitated: "It
was my one attempt," she said, " to try and establish friendly
relations. I hoped that they would take pleasure in each
other's company."

"By gum!" thought Alleyn, "You've got your nerve about
you."

"Madame," he said, "I am going to ask you a very direct
question. Who, do you think, committed this murder?"

She clasped her hands over the arm of his chair. "I had
hoped," she whispered, "that I might be spared that question."

"It is my duty to ask it," said Alleyn solemnly.

"I must refuse to answer. How can I answer? I loved
him once."

By this remarkable statement Alleyn learned that if, as Mrs.
Pouting considered, Dr. and Madame Hart were joint adventurers, the lady displayed a most characteristic readiness to
betray her partner when the necessity arose.

"You will understand," he said, "that I must question each
member of the party about his or her movements on three
occasions. The first is the occasion when Mr. Mandrake was
thrown into the bathing pool. Where were you at that time,
Madame Lisse?"

"In bed, in my room."

"Was anybody else in your room?"

"I believe a maid came in with my breakfast. I remember
it was a very little while after she left the room that I heard
voices on the terrace beneath my window and not long after
that I was told of the accident."

"Who told you, please?"

She waited for a moment, and then, very delicately, shrugged her shoulders.

"It was Mr. Compline," she said. "You will think it strange that I permitted the visit, but I have adopted the English custom in such matters. He was agitated and felt that he must warn me."

"Warn you?"

"Of this exhibition on the part of my husband."

"Suppose," said Alleyn, "that I told you I had convincing evidence that your husband was not responsible for this affair. What would you say?"

For the first time she looked frightened, and for a moment she had no answer to give him. Her hands were clenched and her arms rigid. "I am afraid that I should not believe you," she said. "It is horrible to have to say such things. I find it unbearable. But one must protect oneself, and other innocent persons."

Alleyn was beginning to get a sort of enjoyment out of Madame Lisse.

"I am to understand," he said, "that it was a very unusual event for Mr. Compline to pay you such an informal visit?"

"The circumstances were extraordinary."

"Were they extraordinary when he again visited you at half-past seven that same evening?"

"Of course. I had asked him to come. I was most anxious to see him alone. By that time I was convinced that my husband meant to do him an injury. My husband had told me as much." Perhaps Alleyn looked a little incredulous, for she said quickly: "It is quite true. He said that he had come to the end of his endurance and could not trust himself. I was terrified. I warned Mr. Compline and begged him to be careful. When he left me I looked after him and I saw that horrible figure fall from the top of his door. His hand was almost on the door. I screamed out and at the same moment it struck his arm. It might have killed him."

"No doubt," said Alleyn, who had already taken possession of the Buddha. "Then you and Mr. Compline were together from the time he left his room and walked down the passage to yours, until he returned and received his injury?"

"Yes. He has told me he came straight to my room."

"You were together," Alleyn repeated slowly, "the whole time?"

Again he thought he had frightened her. Again there was

an odd little pause before she said: "Yes, certainly. I never left my room until he went."

"And did he?"

"He?" she said readily. "Oh no, *he* didn't, of course. I had to send him away in the end."

There was something here, Alleyn felt sure, that she had concealed from him, but he decided to leave it for the moment, and went on to the time of the murder. Again Madame Lisse had been in her room. "I was in agony. I suffer from the *migraine* and this was a terrible attack, brought on, no doubt, by nervous suspense. I went to bed before dinner and remained there until I was told of the tragedy."

"Who told you of the tragedy, Madame?"

"Nicholas Compline. He broke it to me after he had told his mother."

"And what was your reaction?"

"I was horrified, of course." She leant back again in her chair and it seemed to him that she marshalled a series of sentences she had previously rehearsed. "At first I thought it was a mistake, that he had meant to kill Nicholas, but then it dawned upon me that it was William's threats to expose him that had driven him to do it. I realised that it had nothing to do with me, nothing at all. No other explanation is possible."

"You believe that it was impossible that William could be mistaken for Nicholas?"

"Of course. They were not so alike. Even the backs of their heads. There was a small thin patch in William's hair, just below the crown of his head."

"Yes," said Alleyn, watching her trembling lips. "There was."

"Whereas Nicholas has thick hair, like honey. And the nape of William's neck—it was——" She caught her breath and her voice seemed to die on her lips.

"You must have observed him very closely," said Alleyn.

CHAPTER XV

DOCUMENT

I

ALLEYN'S interview with Nicholas was an uncomfortable affair. They had not been together for two minutes before he realised that he had to deal with a man who had pretty well reached the end of his tether. Nicholas was bewildered and dazed. He answered Alleyn's questions abruptly and almost at random. Even when the question of the murderer's identity was directly broached, Nicholas merely flared up weakly like a damp squib, and went out. Alleyn became insistent and Nicholas made an effort to concentrate, saying that Hart must have done it and escaped after Thomas left the hall. When Alleyn asked if he thought it was a case of mistaken identity, he said he did and spoke incoherently of the two earlier attempts. "It was me all along," he said, "that he was after. I thought at first Bill's fiddling about with the radio had sent him off his head, but Mandrake pointed out that Hart must have come in by the door from the hall, and that leaning over like that, the back of Bill's head and tunic would look like mine. And he must have heard me tell Bill to go to bed."

"When was that?"

Nicholas passed his hand across his eyes, pressing down with his finger-tips. "Oh, God," he said, "when was it? I can't sort of think. It was when Hart turned bloody-minded over the radio. He and Mandrake were in the room they call the boudoir. He opened the door and raised hell about the wireless. I slammed the door in his face, and Mandrake yelled out that I was to turn off the radio. I got suddenly fed up with the whole show. I said to my brother something like: 'Oh, all right, the wireless is no go. Get to bed, Bill.' Mandrake and Hart must have heard. I turned the radio down to a whisper. We didn't say anything and I suppose he thought Bill did go away. I heard him switch off the light. He must have done it as a blind or something, to make us think he had gone."

"Was that long afterwards?"

"I don't know. I heard Mandrake go out. It was after that."

"Did you and your brother not speak at all?"

"Yes. When, as I thought, I heard Hart go, I said it was all right now if Bill wanted to use the wireless. He was furious with Hart, you know. We both were, but I saw I'd been making a fool of myself. I was suddenly sick of the whole thing. I tried to calm Bill down. He'd turned pretty grim and wouldn't talk. I hung about a bit and then I came away."

"Can you tell me exactly what he was doing when you left?"

Nicholas went very white. "He was sitting by the fire. He didn't look up. He just grunted something, and I went into the library."

"Did you shut the door?" Alleyn had to repeat this question. Nicholas was staring blankly at him. "*I* don't remember," he said at last. "I suppose so. Yes, I did. They all began asking me about my brother. Whether he was still livid with Hart, kind of thing. I sort of tried to shut them up because of Bill hearing us, but I think I'd shut the door. I'm sorry, I'm not sure about that. Is it important?"

"I'd like an exact picture, you know. You are certain, then, that the door was shut?"

"I think so. Yes, I'm pretty sure it was."

"Do you remember exactly at what moment Mr. Royal left the library?"

"How the devil should I remember!" said Nicholas with a sort of peevish violence. "He can tell you that himself. What *is* all this?" He stared at Alleyn and then said quickly: "Look here, if you're thinking of Jonathan . . . I mean it'd be too preposterous. Jonathan! Good God, he's our greatest friend. God, what *are* you driving at!"

"Nothing in the world," said Alleyn gently. "I only want facts. I'm sorry to have to hammer away at details like this."

"Well, all I can tell you is that some time during the news bulletin Jonathan went into the hall for a minute or two."

"The read leather screen in the smoking-room was stretched in front of the door, as it is now?"

"I suppose so."

"Yes. To get back to the wireless. You tell me that you turned it down after the outburst from Dr. Hart. Did you look closely at it?"

"Why the hell should I look closely at it," demanded Nicholas, in a fury. "I turned it down. You don't peer at a wireless when you turn it down."

"You turned it *down*," Alleyn murmured. "Not off. Down."

"You've grasped it. Down," said Nicholas, and burst into hysterical laughter. "I turned it down, and five minutes later somebody turned it up, and a little while after that Hart murdered my brother. You're getting on marvellously, Inspector."

Alleyn waited for a moment. Nicholas had scrambled out of his chair and had turned away, half-weeping, half-laughing. "I'm sorry," he stammered, "I can't help it. He's in there, murdered, and my mother—my mother. I can't help it."

"I'm sorry, too," said Alleyn. "All this insistence on detail must seem unbearably futile, but I promise you it has its purpose. You see, this is unhappily a police matter, a matter, if you can stomach the phrase, of serving justice, and in that cause very many things must be sacrificed, including the nerves of the witnesses."

"I'm all to pieces," Nicholas mumbled. "I'm no good. It must be shock or something." His voice died away in a trail of inaudibilities. ". . . can't concentrate . . . enough to send you mad . . ." He pulled out his handkerchief and retired to the window where he blew his nose very violently, caught his breath in a harsh sob, and stared out at the teeming rain, beating his uninjured hand on the sill. Alleyn waited for a little while and presently Nicholas turned and faced him. "All right," said Nicholas. "Go on."

"I've nearly done. If you would rather, I can wait . . ."

"No, no. For God's sake, get it over."

Alleyn went back to the incidents of the pond and the Buddha, and at first learnt nothing new from Nicholas. He had seen Mandrake through the pavilion window and they had waved to each other. He had then turned away and gone on with the dismal business of undressing. He had heard the sound of a splash but had not immediately looked out, thinking that Mandrake might have thrown something into the pond. When he did go out to the rescue he had seen nobody else, but the assailant would have had time to dodge behind the pavilion. He had not noticed any footprints. When Hart came upon the scene, Nicholas had already thrown the serio-comic lifebelt into the pond. As for his escape from the brass Buddha, it had fallen out exactly as Madame Lisse had described it. He had felt the door resist him and then give way suddenly. Almost simultaneously with this, he started back and immediately afterwards something had fallen on his forearm. "It's damned sore," said Nicholas querulously, and didn't need much persuasion to exhibit his injury which was sufficiently ugly. Alleyn said it should have a surgical dressing and Nicholas, with considerable emphasis, said he'd see Hart in hell before he let him near it.

"Madame Lisse watched you as you walked down the passage?"

It appeared that he had glanced back and seen her in the doorway. He said that but for this distraction he might have noticed the Buddha, but he didn't think he would have done so. Alleyn asked him the now familiar questions. Had he gone straight to her room on leaving his own and had they been together the whole time?

"Yes, the whole time," said Nicholas, and looked extremely uncomfortable. "We were talking. She wanted to see me, to warn me about him. I hope to heaven you'll keep her name out of this as much as possible, Alleyn."

Alleyn blandly disregarded this.

"You heard nothing suspicious? No noise in the passage outside?"

"We did, as a matter of fact. I thought it was somebody at the door. It was a very slight sound. We sort of—sensed it. You don't want to get a wrong idea, you know," said Nicholas. "I suppose you've heard how he's made life hideous for her. She told me all about it." For the first time Alleyn saw a wan shadow of Nicholas's old effrontery. He stroked the back of his head and there was a hint of complacency in the gesture. "I wasn't going to be dictated to by the fellow," he said.

"What did you do?" Alleyn inquired. Nicholas began to stammer again, and Alleyn had some little trouble in discovering that he had taken cover behind a screen while the lady looked into the passage.

"So, in point of fact, you were not together the whole time?"

"To all intents and purposes we were. She was away only for about a minute. Of course what we had heard was Hart going past the door with that blasted image in his hands. I suppose when Elise looked out he was in my room. She'll tell you it was only for a minute."

Alleyn did not tell him that in giving her account of their meeting, Madame Lisse had made no mention of this incident.

II

Before he let Nicholas go, Alleyn asked him, as he had asked Hart, to give a description of the smoking-room. Nicholas appeared to find this request suspicious and distressing and at first made a poor fist of his recital. "*I* don't know what's in the ghastly place. It's just an ordinary room. You've *seen* it. Why do you want to ask me for an inventory?" Alleyn persisted, however, and Nicholas gave him a list of objects, rattling it off in a series of jerks: "The wireless. Those filthy knives. There are seven of them and the thing that did it"—he wetted his lips—"hung on the left. I remember looking at it while we were talking. There were some flowering plants in pots, I think. And there's a glass-topped case with *objets d'art* in it. Medals and miniatures and things. And sporting prints and photographs. There's a glass-fronted cupboard with china and old sporting trophies inside, and a small bookcase with *Handley Cross* and *Stonehenge* and those sorts of books in it. Leather chairs and an occasional table with cigars and cigarettes. I can't think of anything else. My God, when I think of that room I see only one thing and I'll see it to the end of my days!"

"You've given me a very useful piece of information," Alleyn said. "You've told me that when you left your brother, the Maori mere was still in its place on the wall."

Nicholas stared dully at him. "I hadn't thought of it before," he said. "I suppose it was."

"Are you quite certain?"

Nicholas passed his hand over his eyes again. "Certain?" he repeated. "I thought I was, but now you ask me again I'm not so sure. It might have been when Bill and I were in the smoking-room in the morning. What were we talking about? Yes. Yes, we were talking about Mandrake in the pond. Yes, it *was* in the morning. Oh, hell, I'm sorry. I can't swear it was there in the evening. I don't think I looked at the wall, then. I can't remember."

"There's only one other thing," Alleyn said. "I must tell you that Mr. Royal has given me the letter that was found in your mother's room."

"But," said Nicholas, "that's horrible. It was for me. There's nothing in it—can't you—must you pry into everything! There's nothing in it that can help you."

"If that's how it is," said Alleyn, " it will go no further than the inquest. But I'm sure you will see that I must read it."

Nicholas's lips had bleached to a mauve line. "You won't understand it," he said. "You'll misread it. I shouldn't have given it to them. I should have burnt it."

"You'd have made a really bad mistake if you'd done that." Alleyn took the letter from his pocket and laid it on the desk.

"For God's sake," Nicholas said, "remember that when she wrote it she was thinking of me and how much I'd miss her. She's accusing herself of deserting me. For God's sake, remember that."

"I'll remember," Alleyn said. He put the letter aside with his other papers and said that he need keep Nicholas no longer. Now that he was free, Nicholas seemed less anxious to go. He hung about the library looking miserably at Alleyn out of the corners of his eyes. Alleyn wrote up his notes and wondered what was coming. He became aware that Nicholas was watching him. For some little time he went on sedately with his notes, but at last looked up to find, as he expected, those rather prominent grey eyes staring at him.

"What is it, Mr. Compline?" said Alleyn quietly.

"Oh, nothing. It's just—there doesn't seem anywhere to go. It gets on your nerves wandering about the house. This damned mongrel rain and everything. I—I was going to ask you where he was."

"Dr. Hart?"

"Yes."

"He's locked up at the moment, at his own request."

"So long as he *is* locked up. Mandrake and Hersey seem to have gone silly over him. Because he attended my mother! God, she was at his mercy! Hart! The man who ruined her beauty and had just murdered her son. Pretty, wasn't it! How do I know what he was doing to her."

"From what Lady Hersey tells me his treatment was exactly what the doctor I spoke to prescribed. I'm sure you need not distress yourself by thinking that any other treatment would have made the smallest difference."

"Why didn't Mandrake get here sooner! They wanted the stuff from the chemist urgently, didn't they? What the hell was he doing! Nearly four hours to go sixty miles! My mother was dying and the best they could do was to send a bloody little highbrow cripple with a false name."

"A false name!" Alleyn ejaculated.

"Yes. Didn't Jonathan tell you? He told me. He's as common as dirt, is Mr. Aubrey Mandrake, and his name's Footling. Jonathan put me up to pulling his leg about it, and he's had his knife into me ever since."

The door opened, and Aubrey Mandrake looked in.

"Sorry," he said, "I didn't know you were still engaged."

"We've finished, I think," said Alleyn. "Thank you so much, Mr. Compline. Come in, Mr. Mandrake."

III

"I only came in," said Mandrake, "to say Lady Hersey is free now, if you want to see her. She asked me to tell you."

"I shall be glad to see her in a minute or so. I just want to get my notes into some sort of order. I suppose you can't do shorthand, can you?"

"Good heavens, no," said Mandrake languidly. "What an offensive suggestion."

"I wish I could. Never mind. I've been going through your notes. They're of the greatest help. You haven't signed them, and I'll get you to do so, if you don't mind."

"I don't mind, of course," said Mandrake uneasily "but you must remember they're based on hearsay as well as on my own observation."

"I think you've made that quite clear. Here they are."

He gave Mandrake his pen and pressed the notes out flat for him. It was a decorative affair, the signature, with the tail of the y in "Aubrey" greatly prolonged and slashed forward to make the up-stroke of the M in "Mandrake." Alleyn blotted it carefully and looked at it.

"This is your legal signature?" he said, as he folded the notes.

When Mandrake answered, his voice sounded astonishingly vicious. "You've been talking to the bereaved Nicholas, of course," he said. "It seems that even in his sorrow he found a moment for one of his little pleasantries."

"He's in a condition that might very well develop into a nervous crisis. He's lashing out blindly and rather stupidly. It's understandable."

"I suppose he told you of the incident at dinner? About my name?"

"No. What was the incident at dinner?"

Mandrake told him. " It's too squalidly insignificant and stupid, of course," he ended rapidly. " It was idiotic of me to let it get under my skin, but I happen to object rather strongly to that particular type of wholesome public-school humour. Possibly because I did not go to a public-school." Before Alleyn could answer, he went on defiantly: " And now, of course, you are able to place me. I'm the kind of inverted snob that can't quite manage to take the carefree line about my background. And I talk far too much about myself."

"`I should have thought," said Alleyn, " you'd have worked all that off with your writing. But then I'm not a psychologist. As for your name, you've had the fun of changing it, and all I want to know is whether you did it by deed poll or whether I've got to ask for the other signature."

" I haven't, but I'm going to. ' The next witness was Stanley Footling, better known as Aubrey Mandrake.' It'll look jolly in the papers, won't it?"

" By the time this case comes off, the papers won't have much room for fancy touches, I believe," said Alleyn. " If you don't mind my mentioning it I think you're going to find that your particular bogey will be forgotten in a welter of what we are probably going to call ' extreme realism.' Now write your name down like a good chap, and never mind if it is a funny one. I've a hell of a lot to do."

Mandrake said with a grin: " How right you are, Inspector," and re-signed his notes. " All the same," he added, " I could have murdered Nicholas." He caught his breath. " How often one uses that phrase! Don't suspect me, I implore you. I could have, but I didn't. I didn't even murder poor William. I liked poor William. Shall I fetch Lady Hersey?"

" Please do," said Alleyn.

IV

Motive apart, Lady Hersey was, on paper, the likeliest suspect. She had opportunity to execute both attempts, if they had been attempts, as well as the actual murder. During the long journey in the car Alleyn had found his thoughts turning to this unknown woman, as a figure which, conjecturally, might be the key-piece in a complicated pattern. In all police investigations there is such a figure and sometimes, but not always, it is that of the criminal himself. Though none of the interviews had disclosed the smallest hint of a motive in Lady Hersey's case, he was still inclined to think she occupied a key position. She was the link common to the Complines, Jonathan Royal, and the two Harts. " The one person who could have done it," Alleyn muttered, " and the one person who didn't want to." This was an inaccurate statement but it relieved his feelings. The case was developing along lines with which Alleyn was all too familiar. He had now very little doubt as to the identity of William Compline's murderer, and also very little substantial proof to support his theory or to warrant an arrest. The *reductio ad absurdum* method is not usually smiled upon by the higher powers at New Scotland Yard, and it can be a joyous romping-round for defending counsel. Alleyn knew that a bungling murderer can give more trouble than a clever one. " And the murderer of William Compline is a bungler if ever there was one," he thought. He was turning over Mrs. Compline's letter to her son when he heard Lady Hersey's voice on the stairs. He hesitated, returned the letter to his pocket and fished out the length of line he had cut from the reel in the smoking-room. When Hersey Amblington came in he was twisting this line through his long fingers and when he rose to greet her it dangled conspicuously from his hands.

" I'm sorry if I've kept you waiting, Mr. Alleyn," she said. " There were things to do upstairs and nobody else to do them."

He pushed forward a chair and she sat down slowly and wearily, letting her head fall back against the chair. A sequence of fine lines appeared about her mouth and eyes, and her hands looked exhausted. " If you're going to ask me to provide myself with three nice little alibis," said Hersey, " you may as well know straight away that I can't do it. I seem to remember reading somewhere that that makes me innocent and I'm sure I hope it's true."

" It's in the best tradition of detective fiction, I understand," said Alleyn with a smile.

" That's not very comforting. Am I allowed to smoke?"

Alleyn offered her his case and lit her cigarette for her, dropping his length of fishing line over her wrist as he did so. He apologised and gathered it into his hand.

" Is that a clue or something?" asked Hersey. " It looks like fishing-line."

" Are you a fisherman, Lady Hersey?"

" I used to be. Jonathan's father taught me when I was a child. He's the old party in the photograph in that ghastly room next door."

" Hubert St. John Worthington Royal who caught a four-and-a-half pounder in Pen-Felton Reach?"

" If I wasn't so tired," said Hersey, " I'd fall into a rapture over your powers of observation. That's the man. And the rod on the wall is his rod. Now I come to think of it, your bit of string looked very much like his line."

Alleyn opened his hand. Without moving her head or her hands she looked languidly at it.

" Yes," she said, " that's it. It's been looped back from the point of the rod to the reel for years." She looked up into Alleyn's face. " There's something in this, isn't there? What is it?"

" There's a lot in it," Alleyn said slowly. " Lady Hersey, will you try to remember, without straining at your memory, when you last saw the line in its customary position."

" Friday night," said Hersey instantly. " There was an old cast on it, shrivelled up with age, and a fly. I remember staring at it while I was trying to fit in a letter in that foul parlour-game of Jo's. It was the cast that caught the famous four-and-a-half pounder. Or so we've always been told."

" You went into the smoking-room last night some little time before the tragedy, but when the two brothers were there?"

" Yes. I went in to see if they had calmed down. That was before the row over the radio."

" You didn't by any chance look at the old rod then?"

" No. No, but I did at lunch time. Just before lunch. I was warming my toes at the fire and I stared absently at it as one does at things one has seen a thousand times before."

" And there was the line looped from the tip to the reel?"

Hersey knitted her brows and for the first time her full attention seemed to be aroused. " Now you ask me," she said, " it wasn't. I remember thinking vaguely that someone must have wound it up to something."

" You are positive?"

" Yes. Yes, absolutely positive."

" Suppose I began to heckle you about it?"

" I should dig my toes in."

" Good!" said Alleyn heartily, and wrote it down.

When he looked up Hersey's eyes were closed, but she opened them and said: " Before I forget or go to sleep there's one thing I must say. I don't believe the face-lifter did it."

" Why?" asked Alleyn without emphasis.

" Because I've spent a good many hours working for him up there in Sandra Compline's room. I like him, and I don't think he's a murderer, and anyway I don't see how you can get over the dancing footman's story." Alleyn dropped the coil of fishing line on the desk. " That little man's no killer," Hersey added. " He worked like a navvy over Sandra, and if she'd lived she'd have done her best, poor darling, to have him convicted of homicidal lunacy. He knew that."

" Why are you so sure she would have taken that line?"

" Don't forget," said Hersey, " I was the last person to see her alive. I gave her a half-doze of that stuff. She wouldn't take more, and she said she had no aspirin. I suppose she wanted—wanted to make sure later on. Nick had broken Bill's death to her. She seemed absolutely stunned, almost incredulous if that's not too strange a word to use. Not sorrowful so much as horrified. She wouldn't say anything much about it, although I did try gently to talk to her. It seemed to me it would be better if she broke down. She was stony with bewilderment. But just as I was going she said: ' Dr. Hart is mad, Hersey. I thought I could never forgive him, but I think my face has haunted him as badly as it has haunted me.' And then she said: ' Don't forget, Hersey, he's out of his mind.' I haven't told any one else of this. I can't tell you how strange her manner was, and how astonished I was to hear her say all that so deliberately when a moment before she had seemed so confused."

Alleyn asked Hersey to repeat this statement and wrote it down. When he had finished she said: " There's one other thing. Have you examined her room?"

" Only superficially. I had a look round after Compline went out."

" Did you look at her clothes?" asked Hersey.

" Yes."

" The blue Harris tweed overcoat?"

" The one that is still very damp? Yes."

" It was soaking wet yesterday afternoon, and she told me she hadn't stirred out of the house all day."

V

Alleyn opened Mrs. Compline's letter to her son in the presence of Jonathan Royal, Nicholas Compline, and Aubrey Mandrake. He did not read it aloud, but he showed it to Mandrake and asked him to make a copy. While they waited in an uncomfortable silence Mandrake performed this office, and at Alleyn's request re-sealed the original in a fresh envelope across the flap of which Jonathan was asked to sign his name. Alleyn then tied a string round the envelope and sealed the knot down with wax from his chemist's parcel. He said that he would be obliged if Jonathan and Nicholas would leave him alone with Mandrake. Jonathan seemed perfectly ready to comply with this request, but Nicholas treated them to a sudden and violent outbreak of hysteria. He demanded that the letter should be returned, stormed at Alleyn, threatened Hart, and at last, sobbing breathlessly, flung himself into a chair and refused to move. As the best means of cutting this performance short, Alleyn gathered up his possessions and, followed by a very much shaken Mandrake, moved to the green boudoir. Here he asked Mandrake to read over the copy of the letter.

"My Darling," Mandrake read, "you must not let this make you very sad. If I stayed with you even for the little time there would be left to me, the memory of these terrible days would lie between us. I think that during these last hours I have been insane. I cannot write a confession. I have tried, but the words were so terrible I could not write them. What I am going to do will make everything clear enough, and the innocent shall not suffer through me. Already Hersey suspects that I went out of the house this morning. I think she knows where I went. I cannot face it. You should have been my eldest son, my darling. If I could have taken any other way —but there was no other way. All my life, everything I have done has been for you, even this last terrible thing is for you, and, however wicked it may seem, you must always remember that. And now, darling, I must write down what I mean to do. I have kept the sleeping powders they took from that man's room and I have an unopened bottle of aspirins. I shan't feel anything at all. My last thoughts and my last prayers are for you. Mother. I sign this with my full name, because you will have to show it. SANDRA MARY COMPLINE."

CHAPTER XVI

ARREST

I

Alleyn had asked Mandrake to say nothing of the contents of the letter. " Under ordinary circumstances," he said, " I would have had another officer with me when I opened it. I want you to fix the contents firmly in your mind, and I want you to be prepared, if necessary, to swear that it is the original letter which I have sealed in this envelope, the letter which I opened in your presence and from which you made this copy. All this may be quite unnecessary, but as the most detached member of the party I thought it well to get your assistance. I'll keep the copy, if you please."

Mandrake gave him the copy. His hand shook so much that the paper rattled and he muttered an apology.

" It's horrible," Mandrake said. " Horrible. Mother love! My God!" He stared at Alleyn. " This sort of thing," he stammered, " it can't happen. I never dreamed of this. It's so much worse—it's ever so much worse."

Alleyn watched him for a moment. " Worse than what?" he asked.

" It's real," said Mandrake. " I suppose you'll think it incredible, but until now it hasn't been quite real to me. Not even," he jerked his head towards the smoking-room door, " not even—that. One works these things out in terms of an æsthetic, but for them to *happen*——! God, this'll about kill Nicholas."

" Yes."

" To have it before him for the rest of his life! I don't know why it should affect me like this. After all, it's better that it should end this way. I suppose it's better. She's ended it. No horrible parade of justice. She's spared him that. But I can't help suddenly *seeing* it. It's as if a mist had cleared, leaving the solid reality of a disfigured woman writing that letter, mixing the poison, getting into bed, and then, with God knows what nightmare of last memories, drinking it down."

Mandrake limped about the room, and Alleyn watched him.
" At least," said Mandrake, " we are spared an arrest. But
Nicholas saw the letter. He *knew*."

" He still insists that Dr. Hart killed his brother."

" Let me see the copy of that letter again."

Alleyn gave him the copy, and he muttered over the phrases.
" What else can it mean? ' You should have been my eldest
son.' ' Hersey suspects.' ' I cannot face it.' ' Everything I
have done has been for you.' What else but that she did it?
But I can't understand. Why the other two attempts? It doesn't
make sense."

" I'm afraid it makes very good sense," said Alleyn.

II

From five o'clock until seven Alleyn worked alone. First
of all he inspected the Charter blocks, handling them with
tweezers and wishing very heartily for Bailey, his finger-print
expert. The blocks were made of thinnish paper, and the
impression of heavily pencilled letters appeared on the surface
of the unused forms. The smoking-room waste-paper baskets
had been emptied, but a hunt through a rubbish bin in an
outhouse brought to light several of the used forms. The rest,
it appeared, had been thrown on the fire by the players after
their scores had been marked. Mandrake had told him that
after the little scene over the extra form Jonathan had suddenly suggested that they play some other game, and the
Charter pads had been discarded. By dint of a wearisome
round of questions, Alleyn managed to identify most of the
used forms. Dr. Hart readily selected his, admitting placidly
that he had used " threats " as a seven-square word. Alleyn
found the ghost of this word on one of the blocks, which he
was then able to classify definitely as Hart's. The doctor had
used a sharp pencil and had pressed hard upon it, so that the
marks persisted through two or three of the under papers.
But neither on his used form nor on the rest of the pages did
Alleyn find the faintest trace of the words: " You are warned,
keep off." This was negative evidence. Hart might have been
at pains to tear off that particular form and fill it in against
the card back of the block, which would take no impression.
At this stage Alleyn went to Jonathan and asked if he had a
specimen of Hart's writing. Jonathan at once produced Hart's

note accepting the invitation to Highfold. Alleyn shut himself up again and made his first really interesting discovery.
The writing in the note was a script that still bore many foreign
characteristics. But in his Charter form Dr. Hart had used
block capitals throughout, though his experimental scribblings
in the margin were in his characteristic script. Turning to
the warning message, which was written wholly in script,
Alleyn discovered indications that the letters had been slowly
and carefully formed, and he thought that it began to look
very much like the work of someone who was familiar with
Hart's writing and had deliberately introduced these characteristic letters.

Of the other players an exhaustive process of inquiry and
comparison showed that Mrs. Compline, Hersey, Nicholas and
Jonathan had written too lightly to leave impressions, while
William's and Mandrake's papers had been burnt after being
marked. Alleyn could find no trace of the message on any
of the blocks. At last he began to turn back the pages of
each one, using his tweezers and going on doggedly, long after
the faintest trace had faded, to the last leaf of each block. At
the third block about half-way through he made his discovery.
Here, suddenly, he came upon the indented trace of those five
words, and a closer inspection showed him that the page before
the one so marked had been torn away. Owing to its position
the perforations had not been followed, and when he fitted the
crumpled message to the torn edge the serrations tallied. This,
then, was the block upon which the message had been written,
and it was not Dr. Hart's block. He turned back to the first
pages and gave a little sigh. They held no impressions. Alleyn
got a picture of the writer hurriedly using the mass of pages
as a cover, scribbling his message on the central leaf and
wrenching it free of the pad. Either this writer had written his
legitimate Charters with a light hand, or else he had torn
away the additional pages that held an impression. The pad
had belonged neither to William nor to Mandrake, for theirs
bore marks that Mandrake himself had identified. Two of
the remaining pads were marked by certain faint traces, visible
through the lens, and these, he thought, must have been used
by Madame Lisse and Chloris Wynne, whose finger-nails were
long and pointed.

" Not so bad," he murmured, and, whistling softly, put the
Charter pads away again.

He went up to Mrs. Compline's room, taking the not very willing Mandrake with him.

" I like to have a witness," he said vaguely. " As a general rule, we work in pairs over the ticklish bits. It'll be all right when Fox comes, but in the meantime you, as an unsuspected person, will do very nicely."

Mandrake kept his back turned to the shrouded figure on the bed, and watched Alleyn go through the clothes in the wardrobe. Alleyn got him to feel the shoulders and skirts of a Harris tweed overcoat.

" Damp," said Mandrake.

" Was it snowing when you went down to the pond?"

" Yes. My God, were they *her* footsteps? She must have walked down inside my own as Chloris suggested."

Alleyn was looking at the hats on the top shelf of the wardrobe.

" This is the one she wore," he said. " It's still quite wettish. Blue tweedish sort of affair, with a salmon fly as ornament. No, two flies. A yellow and black salmon fly, and a rather jaded trout fly. Scarlet and green—an Alexandra. That seems excessive, doesn't it?" He peered more closely at the hat. " Now, I wonder," he said. And when Mandrake asked him peevishly what he wondered, sent him off to find the maid who had looked after Mrs. Compline. She proved to be a Dorset girl, born and bred on the Highfold estate, a chatter-box, very trim and bright and full of the liveliest curiosity about the clothes and complexions of the ladies in Jonathan's party. She was anxious to become a ladies' maid, and Mrs. Pouting had been training her. This was the first time she had maided any visitors to Highfold. She burst into a descriptive rapture over the wardrobes of Madame Lisse and Miss Wynne. It was with difficulty that Alleyn hauled her attention round to the less exciting garments of Mrs. Compline. The interview took place in the little passage, and Alleyn held the tweed hat behind his back while the little maid chattered away about the wet coat.

" Mrs. Compline hadn't worn that coat before, sir. She arrived in a burberry like you see at the shooting parties, and when they took a walk on the first evening she wore it again, sir. It was yesterday morning she took out the tweed. When the two gentlemen was going to have that bet, sir," said the little maid, turning pink. " I was in madam's room, sir, asking what I should put out for her to wear, when poor Mr. William called out in the passage, 'It's worth a tenner to see him do it.' She seemed very upset, sir. She got up and went to the door and looked after him. She called out, but I don't think he heard her, because he ran downstairs. She said she didn't require me. So I went out, and she must have followed him."

"When did you see her again?"

"Well, after a minute or two, I saw her go downstairs wearing that coat, sir, and a tweed hat, and I called Elsie, the second housemaid, sir, and said we could slip in and make Mrs. Compline's bed and do her room. So we did. At least——" Here the little maid hesitated.

"Yes?" Alleyn asked.

"Well, sir, I'm afraid we *did* look out of the window because we knew about the bet. But you can't see the pond from that window on account of the shrubs. Only the terrace. We saw the poor lady cross the terrace. It was snowing very hard. She seemed to stare down towards the pond, sir, for a little while, and then she looked round and—and Elsie and I began to make the bed. It wasn't above two minutes before she was back, as white as a sheet and trembling. I offered to take away her wet coat and hat, but she said: 'No, no, leave them,' rather short, so Elsie and I went out. By that time there was a great to-do down by the pond, and Thomas came in and said one of the gentlemen had fallen in."

"And while Mrs. Compline was on the terrace, nobody joined her or appeared near her?"

"No, sir. I think Miss Wynne and poor Mr. William must have gone out afterwards, because we heard their voices down there just before Mrs. Compline got back."

"Well done," said Alleyn. "And this," he showed her the tweed hat, "is this the hat she was wearing?"

"That's it, sir."

"Looks just the same?"

The little maid took it in her hands and turned it round, eyeing it in a thoughtful bird-like manner. "It's got two of those feathery hooks," she said at last. "Funny kind of trimming, *I* think. Two."

"Yes?"

"It only had one yesterday. The big yellow and black one."

"Thank you," said Alleyn, and quite fluttered her by the fervency of his smile.

III

Detective-Inspector Fox and Detective-Sergeants Bailey and Thompson arrived at seven o'clock in a hired car from Pen-Gidding. Alleyn was delighted to see them. He set Bailey to work on the brass Buddha, the Charter forms, the Maori mere, and the wireless cabinet. Thompson photographed all the details that Alleyn had already taken with his own camera. And at last the body of William Compline was taken away from the arm-chair in the smoking-room. There was a ball-room at Highfold. It had been added incontinently to the east side by a Victorian Royal, and was reached by a short passage. Here, in an atmosphere of unused grandeur and empty anticipation, Sandra Compline lay not far removed from the son for whom she had not greatly cared. Alleyn heard Jonathan issuing subdued but emphatic orders for flowers.

Fox and Alleyn went together to the library.

"Sit down, Br'er Fox," said Alleyn. "Sorry to have hauled you out, but I'm damn' glad to see you."

"We had quite a job getting here," said Fox, taking out his spectacle case. "Very unpleasant weather. Nasty affair this, sir, by the looks of it. What's the strength of it? Murder followed by suicide, or what?"

"There's my report. You'd better take a look at it."

"Ah," said Fox. "Much obliged. Thank you." He settled his spectacles rather far down his nose and put on his reading face. Fox had a large rosy face. To Alleyn his reading expression always suggested that he had a slight cold in the head. He raised his sandy eyebrows, slightly opened his mouth and placidly absorbed the words before him. For some time there was no sound but the crackle of turning leaves and Fox's breathing.

"Um," he said when he had finished. "Silly sort of business. Meant to look complicated, but isn't. When do we fix this customer up, Mr. Alleyn?"

"We'll wait for Bailey, I think. I'd like to arrest on a minor charge, but there isn't the smell of an excuse so far."

"Assault on Mr. Mandrake?"

"Well," said Alleyn, "we might do that. I suppose I haven't gone wrong anywhere. The thing's so blasted obvious I keep

wondering if there's a catch in it. We'll have to experiment, o
course, with the business next door. Might do that now, i
Bailey's finished. They've taken that poor chap out, haven'
they? All right. Come on, Foxkin."

They went into the smoking-room. Bailey, a taciturn office
with an air of permanent resentment, was packing away hi
fingerprint apparatus, and Thompson had taken down hi
camera.

" Finished?" asked Alleyn. " Get a shot of the ash in th
grate all right?"

" Yes, sir," said Thompson. " Made a little find there, Mr
Alleyn. Bailey spotted it. You know this trace in the ash, th
sort of coil affair?"

" Yes."

" Well, sir, it's what you said all right. String or cord or
something. There's a bit not quite burnt out up at the back
Charred-like, but still a bit of substance in it. Seems as if i
was green originally."

" We'll have it," said Alleyn. " Good work, Bailey. I missed
that."

The mulish expression on Sergeant Bailey's face deepened
" We had a 500 watt lamp on it," he said. " Looks as if
someone'd chucked this string on the fire and pulled those two
side logs over it. They must have fallen apart, and the stuff
smouldered out slowly. Tough, fine-fibred stuff, I'd say.
Might be silk. It finishes with a trace of structureless, fairly
tough black ash that has kept its form and run into lumps.
What's the next job, sir?"

" We'll have to get their prints. I don't for a moment
suppose they'll object. I warned Mr. Royal about it. Thank
the Lord I shan't have to use any of the funny things they
brought me from the chemist. Anything to report?"

" There's a couple of nice ones on that brass image affair,
sir. Latent, but came up nicely under the dust. Same as the
ones on the stone cosh. There's something on the neck of
the cosh, but badly blurred. As good a set as you'd want on
the blade."

" What about the wireless?"

" Regular mix-up, Mr. Alleyn, like you'd expect. But there's
a kind of smudge on the volume control." Bailey looked at
his boots. " Might be gloves," he muttered.

" Very easily," said Alleyn. " Now, look here. Mr. Fox

and I are going to make an experiment. I'll get you two to
stay in here and look on. If it's a success I think we might
stage a little show for a select audience." He squatted down
and laid his piece of fishing-line out on the floor. " You might
just lock the door," he said.

IV

" This is a big house," said Chloris, " and yet there seems
nowhere to go. I've no stomach for the party in the drawing-
room."

" There's the boudoir," Mandrake suggested.

" Aren't the police overflowing into that?"

" Not now. Alleyn and that vast red man went down to
the pond a few minutes ago. Now they've gone back into the
smoking-room. Let's try the boudoir."

" All right, let's."

They went into the boudoir. The curtains were closed and
the lamps alight. A cheerful fire crackled in the grate. Chloris
moved restlessly about the room and Mandrake intercepted a
quick glance at the door into the smoking-room. " It's all
right," he sad. " William's gone, you know, and the police
seem to have moved into the library." There was a sudden
blare of radio on the other side of the door, and both Mandrake and Chloris jumped nervously. Chloris gave a little
cry. " They're in there," she whispered. " What are they
doing?"

" I'll damn' well see!"

" No, don't," cried Chloris, as Mandrake stooped to the
communicating door and applied his eye to the keyhole.

" It's not very helpful!" he murmured. " The key's in the
lock. What can they be doing. God, the noise! Wait a
minute."

" Oh, do come away."

" I'm quite shameless. I consider they are fair game. One
can see a little past the key, but only in a straight line. Keyhole lurking is not what it's said to be in eighteenth-century
literature. Hardly worth doing, in fact. I can see nothing but
that red screen in front of the door into the library. There's
no one . . ." he broke off suddenly. " What is it?" Chloris said,
and he held up his hand warningly. The wireless was switched

off. Mandrake got up and drew Chloris to the far end of the boudoir.

"It's very curious," he said. "There are only four of them. I know that, because I saw the others come. There's Alleyn and the red man and two others. Well, they've all just walked out of the library into the smoking-room. *Who the devil turned on the radio?*"

"They must have gone into the library after they turned it on."

"But they didn't. They hadn't time. The moment that noise started I looked through the keyhole and I looked straight at the door. Why should they turn on the wireless and make a blackguard rush into the library?"

"It's horrible. It sounded so like . . ."

"It's rather intriguing, though," said Mandrake.

"How you *can*!"

He went quickly to her and took her hands. "Darling Chloris," he said, "it wouldn't be much use if I pretended I wasn't interested, would it? You'll have to get used to my common ways, because I think I might want to marry you. I'm going to alter my name by deed poll, so you wouldn't have to be Mrs. Stanley Footling. And if you think Mrs. Aubrey Mandrake is too arty we could find something else. I can't conceive why people are so dull about their names. I don't suppose deed polls are very expensive. One could have a new name quite often, I dare say. My dear darling," Mandrake continued, "you're all white and trembly, and I really and truly believe I love you. Could you possibly love me, or shan't we mention it just now?"

"We shan't mention it just now," said Chloris. "I don't know why, but I'm frightened. I want to be at home, going to my W.R.E.N. classes, and taking dogs for walks. I'm sick of horrors."

"But you won't mix me up with horrors when you get back to your lusty girl friends, will you? You won't say: 'There was a killing high-brow cripple who made a pass at me during the murder'?"

"No. Honestly, I won't. I'll ask you to come and stay, and we might even have a gossip about the dear old days at Highfold. But at the moment I want my mother," said Chloris, and her lower lip trembled.

"Well, I expect you'll be able to go quite soon. I fancy the police have finished with you and me."

There was a tap on the door and Detective-Sergeant Bailey came in.

"Excuse me, sir," he said sombrely. "Chief Inspector Alleyn's compliments, and he'd be obliged if you'd let me take your fingerprints. Yours and the young lady's. Just a matter of routine, sir."

"Oh," said Chloris under her breath, "that's what they always say to reassure murderers."

"I beg pardon, Miss?"

"We should be delighted."

"Much obliged," said Bailey gloomily, and laid his case down on a small table. Mandrake and Chloris stood side by side in awkward silence while Bailey set out on the table a glass plate, two sheets of paper, some cotton wool, a rubber roller, a fat tube, and a small bottle, which, when he uncorked it, let loose a strong smell of ether.

"Are we to be anæsthetised?" asked Mandrake with nervous facetiousness. Bailey gave him a not very complimentary stare. He squeezed some black substance from the tube on to the plate and rolled it out into a thin film.

"I'll just clean your fingers with a drop of ether, if you please," he said.

"Our hands are quite clean," cried Mandrake.

"Not chemically," Bailey corrected. "There'll be a good deal of perspiration, I dare say. There usually is. Now, sir. Now, Miss."

"It's quite true," said Chloris, "There is a good deal of perspiration. Speaking for my self, I'm in a clammy sweat."

Bailey cleaned their fingers and seemed to cheer up a little. "Now, we'll just roll them gently on the plate," he said, holding Mandrake's forefinger. "Don't resist me."

Chloris was making her last fingerprint, and Mandrake was cleaning the ink off his own fingers, when Fox came in and beamed upon them.

"Well, well," said Fox. "So they're fixing you up according to the regulations? Quite an ingenious little process, isn't it, sir?"

"Quite."

"Yes. Miss Wynne won't care for it so well, perhaps. Nasty, dirty stuff, isn't it? The ladies never fancy it for that reason. Well, now that's very nice," continued Fox, looking at Chloris's prints on the paper. "You wouldn't believe how difficult a simple little affair like this can be made if people resist the pressure. Never resist the police in the execution of their duty. That's right, isn't it, sir?" Bailey looked inquiringly at him. "In the drawing-room," said Fox in exactly the same tone of voice. Bailey wrote on the papers, put them away in his case, and took himself and his belongings out of the room.

"The Chief," said Fox, who occasionally indulged himself by alluding to Alleyn in this fashion, "would be glad if you could spare him a moment in about ten minutes' time, Mr. Mandrake. In the library, if you please."

"All right. Thanks."

"Do I stay here?" asked Chloris in a small voice.

"Wherever you like, Miss Wynne," rejoined Fox, looking mildly at her. "It's not very pleasant waiting about. I dare say you'll find the time hangs rather heavy on your hands. Perhaps you'd like to join the party in the drawing-room?"

"Not much," said Chloris, "but I can tell by your style that I'm supposed to go. So I'd better."

"Thank you, Miss," said Fox simply. "Perhaps Mr. Mandrake would like to go with you. We'll see you in the library then, in about ten minutes, sir. As soon as Bailey has finished in the drawing-room. He'll give you the word when to come along. You might quietly drop a hint to Mr. Royal and Mr. Compline to come with you, if you don't mind."

He held the door open, and Mandrake and Chloris went out.

v

"Well, Br'er Fox," said Alleyn, looking up from the library desk, "did that pass off quietly?"

"Quite pleasantly, Mr. Alleyn. Bailey's in the drawing-room now, doing the rest of the party. I unloosed the doctor. It seemed silly him being up there behind a lock a moron could fix in two minutes. So he's in with the rest. His good lady doesn't much fancy being printed."

Alleyn grinned. "The expression 'his good lady' as applied to La Belle Lisse-Hart," he said, "is perfect, Fox."

"I put the young couple in with the others," Fox continued. "I've got an idea that Mr. Mandrake was a bit inquisitive about what we were doing in the smoking-room. He kept looking over at the door, and when he saw I'd noticed he looked away again. So I told him to come along and bring the other two with him as soon as we tip him the wink. You want independent witnesses, I suppose, sir?"

" Yes. What about Lady Hersey?"

" I haven't said anything. We can fetch her away when we want her."

" We'll send Bailey to fetch her away, fetch her away, fetch her away," Alleyn murmured under his breath. And then: " I've never felt less sympathy over a homicide, Br'er Fox. This affair is not only stupid but beastly, and not only beastly but damn' cold-blooded and unnatural. However, we must watch our step. There's a hint of low cunning in spite of the mistakes. I hate the semi-public reconstruction stunt—it's theatrical and it upsets all sorts of harmless people. Still, it has its uses. We've known it to come off, haven't we?"

" We have so," said Fox sombrely. " I wonder how Bailey's getting on with that mob in there."

" See here, Fox, let's make sure we've got it right."

Fox looked benignly at his chief : " It's all right, sir. You've worked it out to a hair. It can't go wrong. Why, we've tried it half a dozen times."

" I meant the case as a whole."

" You've got your usual attack of the doubts, Mr. Alleyn. I've never seen a clearer case."

Alleyn moved restlessly about the room. " Disregard those two earlier farces and we've still got proof," he said.

" Cast-iron proof."

" In a funny sort of way it all hangs on this damned cheerful fellow Thomas. The dancing footman. He defines the limit of the time factor and the possible movements of the murderer. Add to this the ash, H. St. J. W. R.'s fishing-line, the stuff on the wireless, and William's drawing-pin, and there's your case."

" And a very pretty case, too."

" Not so pretty," Alleyn muttered. And then: " I've never asked for your views on this war, Foxkin."

Fox stared at him. " On the war? Well, no, sir, you haven't. My view is that it hasn't started."

" And mine. I believe that in a year's time we shall look back on these frozen weeks as on a strangely unreal period. Does it seem odd to you, Fox, that we should be here so solemnly tracking down one squalid little murderer, so laboriously using our methods to peer into two deaths, while over our heads are stretched the legions of guns? It's as if we stood on the edge of a crackling landslide, swatting flies."

" It's our job."

" And will continue to be so. But to hang someone—now! My God, Fox, it's almost funny."

" I see what you mean."

" It's nothing. Only one of those cold moments. We'll get on with our cosy little murder. Here comes Bailey."

Bailey came in carrying his gear.

" Well," said Alleyn, " have you fixed that up?"

" Yes, sir."

" Any objections?"

" The foreign lady. She didn't like the idea of blacking her fingers. Or that's what she said. Gave quite a bit of trouble in a quiet way."

" And the rest of the party?"

" Jumpy," said Bailey. " Not saying much for stretches at a time and then all talking at once, very nervous and quick. Mr. Royal and Compline seem unfriendly to the doctor and keep looking sideways at him. He's the coolest of the lot, though. You'd think he wasn't interested. He doesn't take any notice of the lady except to look at her as if he was surprised or something. Will you see the prints, Mr. Alleyn?"

" Yes, we'll look at them and check them with what you found on the rest of the stuff. It won't be very illuminating, but it's got to be done. Then we'll have those four in here, and try for results. It'll do no harm to keep them guessing for a bit. Come on, Fox."

VI

" What's the time?" asked Nicholas. Hersey Amblington looked at her wrist-watch. " A quarter-past eight."

" I have explained, haven't I," said Jonathan, " that there's a cold buffet in the dining-room?"

" You have, Jo," said Hersey. " I'm afraid none of us feels like it."

" I am hungry," Dr. Hart observed. " But I cannot accept the hospitality of a gentleman who believes me to be a murderer." Jonathan made an angry little noise in his throat.

" My dear Doctor Hart," Hersey ejaculated, " I really

shouldn't let a point of etiquette hold you off the cold meats. You can't starve."

"I expect to be released to-morrow," said Hart, "and a short abstinence will be of no harm. I habitually over-eat." He looked at his wife, who was staring at him with a sort of incredulous wonder. "Do I not, my dear?" asked Dr. Hart.

Nicholas moved to her side. She turned to him and very slightly shrugged her shoulders.

"It is strange," continued Dr. Hart, "that when my wife would not acknowledge our relationship I was plagued with the desire to make it known. Now that it is known I take but little satisfaction in the privilege."

Nicholas produced a cliché. "There is no need," he said stiffly, "to be insulting."

"But whom do I insult? Not my wife, surely. Would it not be more insulting to deny the legal status?"

"This is too much," Jonathan burst out, but Hersey said: "Oh, let it go, for pity's sake, Jo."

"I cannot expect," said Madame Lisse, "that Lady Hersey will neglect to find enjoyment in my humiliation."

"I don't see that you are particularly humiliated."

"A husband who has committed the most . . ." began Madame Lisse, but Dr. Hart interrupted her.

"Do you know what she has said, this woman?" he demanded of nobody in particular. "She has told me that if she knew of a grain of evidence against me she would use it. I tell you this—if I was accused of the murder of this poor simpleton and if she, without doing harm to herself, could speak the word that would hang me, she would speak it. This is the woman for whom I have tortured myself. You are all thinking it is not nice to make a scene by speaking of her, it is not what an English gentleman would do. You are right. I am not English and I am not a gentleman. I am an Austrian peasant with a little of the south in my veins, and I have suddenly awakened. I am angry when I remember all the idiotic sorrow that I have wasted on this cold and treacherous wife."

"*You bloody murderer!*" Nicholas burst out, and Madame Lisse seized his arm.

"No," she said, "no, Nicholas. For my sake."

"For all our sakes," said Mandrake suddenly, "let's have no more scenes." And a kind of murmur, profoundly in agreement, came from Hersey, Chloris, and Jonathan. Dr. Hart smiled and made a little bow. "Very well. By all means, no more scenes. But *you*," he pointed a short white finger at Nicholas, "will have cause to remember what I have said."

The door opened and Bailey looked in. "Mr. Alleyn's compliments, sir," he said to Jonathan, "and he'd be glad to see you if you're free." His glance travelled to Mandrake and Nicholas. "Thank you, gentlemen," he said, and held open the door. The three men went out. "Mr. Alleyn would be obliged if the rest of the party stayed where they are," said Bailey. "Sergeant Thompson is on duty in the hall."

He closed the door gently, leaving the three women and Dr. Hart together.

VII

"Before we go any further," said Alleyn, "I must explain that we have arrived at a definite conclusion in this case. It is therefore my duty to tell you that the questions I shall now put to you are of importance and that your answers may possibly be used in evidence. I have asked you to come into the library in order that we may go over the events immediately preceding the discovery of Mr. William Compline's body in the next room. I have not asked those members of the party who were upstairs to be present. They cannot help us. I have left Miss Wynne out of the experiment. Her part was entirely negative and there is no need to distress her. I'm afraid that we shall have to ask Lady Hersey to come in, but I thought that first of all I should explain to you, sir, and to Mr. Compline, exactly what we mean to do. You have all heard of police reconstructions. This very short experiment may be regarded as a reconstruction, and if we are at fault in the smallest detail we ask you to put us right. That's all quite clear, I hope. Now I must ask you if you have any objection to helping us in this way."

"Do you mean," asked Jonathan, "that you want us to do everything we did last night?"

"Yes, if you will."

"I'm—I'm not sure that I recollect precisely the order of events."

"Mr. Mandrake and Mr. Compline will, I hope, help you."

"God, I can remember!" said Nicholas.

"And I," said Mandrake. "I think I remember."

"Good. Then, will you help us, Mr. Royal?"

"Very well," said Jonathan, and Mandrake and Nicholas said they too were ready to help.

"We'll begin," said Alleyn, "at the moment when Lady Hersey had returned from the smoking-room where she had talked for a time with you, Mr. Compline, and with your brother. Mr. Mandrake is in the green boudoir beyond, talking to Dr. Hart. Lady Hersey has left the two brothers together. The door into the boudoir is now locked on the smoking-room side. The door from here into the smoking-room is shut, as you can see. Right, Fox."

Fox went out.

"Will you please take up your positions?" said Alleyn. "Mr. Mandrake, you are not here yet. Mr. Compline, you are in the next room. Sergeant Bailey is there, and I'll get you to tell him as well as you can remember, exactly where you were and what you and your brother did."

Alleyn opened wide the door into the smoking-room. The red leather screen still hid the interior, which seemed to be very dimly lit. Nicholas hung back, white and nervous.

"Not too pleasant," he muttered, and then: "It wasn't dark like that."

"The small shaded lamp by the fireside is turned on," said Alleyn. "There are no bulbs in the other lamps."

"Why?" Nicholas demanded.

"Because we've removed them," said Alleyn blandly. "Will you go in?"

From behind the screen Bailey gave a slight cough. Nicholas said: "Oh, all right," and went into the smoking-room. Alleyn shut the door. At the same moment Fox came in with Hersey Amblington. Evidently he had explained the procedure because she went straight to a chair opposite Jonathan's and sat down. "That's what I did when I came in," said Hersey. "I'd left Nicholas and William in the smoking-room and I came here by way of the hall. Is that what you wanted to know, Mr. Alleyn?"

"The beginning of it," said Alleyn. "What next?"

"In a few minutes," said Jonathan. "Aubrey came in. He went to that chair on the far side of the fire. Miss Wynne was sitting there."

Alleyn looked at Mandrake who at once walked to the chair. "I'd come directly from the boudoir by way of the hall, leaving Dr. Hart alone in the boudoir," he said.

"And then?"

" We discussed the situation," said Hersey. " I reported that I'd left the two brothers talking quite sensibly, and then Mr. Mandrake told us how Dr. Hart and Nicholas had had a row over the wireless and how Nicholas had slammed the door, between the boudoir and the smoking-room in Dr. Hart's face."

" Next?"

" We talked for perhaps a minute and then Nicholas came in." She looked from Jonathan to Mandrake. " It wasn't longer, was it?"

" I should say about a minute," Mandrake agreed.

Fox tapped on the door into the smoking-room. There was a pause. Hersey Amblington caught her breath in a nervous sigh. Mandrake heard his own heart beat in the drums of his ears.

The door opened slowly into the smoking-room and Nicholas stood on the threshold, his face like parchment against the dim scarlet of the screen. Bailey came past him and sat in a low stool just inside the door.

" Did you come straight in?" Alleyn asked Nicholas.

" I don't know. I expect I did."

" Does any one else remember."

" I do," said Mandrake. " I remember, Compline, that you came in and shut the door. I suppose you paused for a moment with your hand on the knob."

" It is agreed that Mr. Compline shut the door?" Alleyn asked.

" Yes, yes, yes," Jonathan cried out shrilly. " It was shut."

" Then will you please go on?" said Alleyn quietly.

" Will somebody be very kind," said Nicholas in a high voice, " and tell me precisely what I did next? It would be a pity if I stepped off on the wrong foot, wouldn't it?"

" We may as well keep our tempers, Nick," said Hersey. " You made a face as if to say Bill was still pretty tricky. I did ' Thumbs up? ' and you did ' Thumbs down,' and then you sat in that chair by the door and we talked about Bill. After a bit Jo offered you a drink."

" Agreed?"

" Agreed," said Mandrake. Jonathan uttered an impatient sound and added very querulously : " Yes. Oh yes." Nicholas said : " Oh, by all means, agreed," and laughed.

" There's the chair," said Alleyn.

Nicholas dropped into the armchair on the opposite side of the door from Bailey's stool.

"Jonathan asked me to ring for drinks," said Mandrake,
"but before I could do so we heard a clink of glasses in the
hall and . . ."

He stopped short. Fox had opened the door into the hall
and in the complete silence that followed they all heard the
faint jingling of glasses.

Thomas came in with the grog tray.

He set it on the table and went out, shutting the door behind
him.

"He is now tidying the hall," said Alleyn.

"I'm not enjoying this," said Hersey Amblington loudly.
"I'm hating it."

"It will not be much longer," said Alleyn. Mandrake heard
his own voice saying: "But it *is* horrible. We're creating it
all over again. It's as if we were making something take form
—in there."

"Oh, *don't*," Hersey whispered.

"There's no one in the smoking-room," said Alleyn, and
he spoke with unexpected emphasis. "The other doors are
locked. There is no one in there. Please go on. Did you have
your drinks?"

Nobody answered. At last Mandrake forced himself to
speak: "Jonathan poured them out and then he said: 'What
about William?'"

"One moment. You should be at the table, then, Mr.
Royal."

Jonathan went to the table. Mandrake's voice went on:
"He said: 'What about William?' meaning would he like a
drink, and Compline stuck his head in at the door and sang
out: 'Coming in for a drink, Bill?'"

"May we see that, Mr. Compline?"

Nicholas reached out and opened the door. He made an
attempt to speak, boggled over it, and finally said: "I asked
him to come in. I think he sort of grunted. Then I asked him
to turn on the news. Jonathan and Mandrake had suggested
that we might listen to it."

"What exactly did you say?"

"I can't remember the precise words."

"I can," said Mandrake. "Or pretty nearly. You said:
'D'you mind switching on the wireless? It's time for the news
and we'd like to hear it.' Then there was a slight pause."

Nicholas said: "I waited and heard someone walk across
the floor and I called out: 'Thanks.'"

Another heavy silence fell upon the room. Fox stood motionless by the door into the hall, Bailey by the door into the smoking-room, Alleyn close to Jonathan by the table.

" And then?" Alleyn asked.

" And then we heard the wireless," said Mandrake.

Bailey's hand moved.

And in the empty smoking-room a voice roared:

> " . . . out the barrel,
> Roll out the barrel again."

Jonathan Royal screamed out an oath and backed away from the table, his hand to his mouth.

He was almost knocked over. Nicholas had stumbled to-wards the door where he was checked by Bailey. He struck at Bailey, turned, and made for the door into the hall where Alleyn barred the way. Nicholas mouthed at him.

" Steady," said Alleyn. Nicholas stretched out his uninjured arm, pointing back to the empty room: " I didn't touch it," he gabbled, " I didn't touch it. Hart did it. It's the second booby-trap. Don't look at me like that. You can't prove anything against me." He fell back a pace. Alleyn made a move and Nicholas sprang at him. Bailey and Fox closed in on Nicholas Compline.

CHAPTER XVII

DEPARTURE

I

THE rain fell steadily over Highfold all through that night. When in the dead light of dawn Alleyn shaved and washed in the downstairs cloakroom, the house still drummed faintly to the inexorable onslaught of the rain. At five o'clock the Great Chipping police had telephoned to say they were coming through by the Pen-Gidding road and that an ambulance was already on its way. At half-past five Nicholas Compline lifted a blotched face from his arm and, breaking a silence of six hours, told Fox he wished to make a statement. At six o'clock

Dr. Francis Hart had an interview with Alleyn. He arrived fully dressed and said that with the permission of the authorities he would attempt to drive home by the long route. " My wife has asked me to take her with me," he said. " I have agreed to do so if you allow." Alleyn consented readily. Dr. Hart then made him a formal speech, causing him acute embarrassment by many references to the courtesy and integrity of the British police.

" Never for a moment," said Dr. Hart, " was I in doubt of the issue. As soon as I heard of William Compline's death I knew that it must be his brother."

" You seem to have been the only member of the party who refused to be bamboozled by fancy touches," said Alleyn. " Why were you so certain?"

" I understand my wife," said Dr. Hart simply. He clasped his hands over his waistcoat, frowned judicially, and continued: " My wife is extremely mercenary, and an almost perfect egoist. She was in love with Nicholas Compline. That I perceived, and with that knowledge I tortured myself. She loved him as much as she could love any one other than herself, and obviously he was quite determined to have her. Whether she was his mistress or not I am unable to decide, but in any case my own suspicious attitude and the scenes I created so continually must have been very irksome. I have no doubt he wished her to break with me and if possible obtain a divorce. That, of course, she would refuse to do. A young man with little money would never persuade her to embark on a damaging scandal. But a young man with a large estate and fine prospects—how different! No doubt she told him so. I do not believe she was aware of his guilt, still less that she was a partner in his crime. She would never risk such a proceeding. No. She thought I killed William Compline and that when I was hanged she would wait for a discreet period and then marry his brother. She will now strain every nerve to disassociate herself with the brother."

" I'm afraid," said Alleyn grimly, " that she will *not* succeed."

" Of course not. But if you interview her she will try to persuade you that his motive was purely mercenary and that she was the victim of his importunities. She will also offer to return to me."

Alleyn glanced up quickly. " No," said Dr. Hart. " I have recovered from that sickness. She would have betrayed me.

In our last interview before the crime she told me that if any-thing happened to Compline she would accuse me. I said she would not have the courage and she replied that where much was at stake she would dare much. I felt as a man might feel if some possession he had treasured was suddenly proved to be worthless. I have lost all desire for my wife."

" You have been very frank," said Alleyn after a pause. " When this is all over what do you mean to do?"

" I am a surgeon. I think in a little while there will be a need for many surgeons in England. Perhaps, who knows, I may do more admirable work than the patching-up of faded women's faces." Dr. Hart pulled at his lips with his short white finger. " All the same," he said, " I wish I had been able to save her life."

" It would have been no great service, you know."

" I suppose not." He held out his hand. " Good-bye, Chief Inspector," he said, and bowed stiffly from the waist. Alleyn watched him go, an almost arrogantly foreign figure in his English tweeds. A little while later he heard a car drive round the house. Bailey came in to say that Madame Lisse wished to see him before she left. Alleyn grimaced. " I'm engaged," he said. " Tell her Mr. Fox will see her. I think she'll say it doesn't matter."

II

At half-past six Mandrake and Chloris came into the library with their top-coats over their arms, and asked if they too might leave Highfold.

" Yes," Alleyn said. " You'll be asked to attend the inquest, you know, so I'll have to keep in touch with you."

" I know," Mandrake agreed, " we'd thought of that. When will it be?"

" Wednesday, I should think."

" Jonathan's asked us to stay but we thought we'd like to go up to London for a slight change of scene. We might look in at the rectory. The road'll be all right now. Can we take a message for you?"

Alleyn gave his message. Mandrake and Chloris still hung off and on.

" We also thought," said Mandrake at last, " that we'd like

a few of the worst knots unravelled by a master hand. Or doesn't one ask?"

" What knots?" said Alleyn with a smile.

" Well," said Chloris, " why Aubrey was shoved in the pond, for one. Did Nicholas shove him?"

" He did."

" But he recognised Aubrey."

" Because he recognised him."

" Oh."

" But," said Mandrake. " We'd worked that out quite differently. After the evidence of the footprints and her letter, we decided that Mrs. Compline had followed out to stop Nicholas taking the plunge and had thought I was William gloating, and, on a wave of long pent-up resentment, had shoved me overboard."

" And then," said Chloris, " we thought that when she heard Bill was dead she'd gone out of her mind and imagined that in some way she had killed him. That's how we read the letter."

" It's a very ingenious reading," said Alleyn with the ghost of a smile, " but it doesn't quite fit. How could she have gone down the steps without you seeing her? And even suppose she did manage to do that, she would have had a very clear view of you as you stood facing the pond. Moreover she watched William go downstairs. And finally she had a full account of the whole affair afterwards and heard you being brought upstairs and all the rest of it. Even if she had pushed you overboard she must have very soon heard of her mistake, so how on earth could she think she'd killed William?"

" But the letter?" said Chloris.

" The letter is more tragic and less demented than you thought. The evidence of the footprints tells us that Mrs. Compline stood on the terrace and looked down. A few moments later a housemaid saw her return, looking terribly upset. I believe that Mrs. Compline saw her son Nicholas make his assault upon you, Mandrake. At the time she may have thought it a dangerous piece of horseplay, but what was she to think when she heard him declare that Hart had done it, believing the victim to be Nicholas himself? And what was she to think when the booby-trap was set and again Nicholas accused Hart? Don't you think that, through the hysteria she displayed, ran some inkling of the truth? Last of all, when

Nicholas went to her last night and told her William had been killed *in mistake for himself*, what was she to think then? With her secret knowledge how could she escape the terrible conclusion? Her adored son had murdered his brother. She made her last effort to save him and the legend she had made round his character. She wrote a letter that told him she knew and at the same time accused herself to us. She could not quite bring herself to say in so many words she had killed her son, but Nicholas understood—and so did we."

" I never thought," said Mandrake after a long silence, " that Nicholas did it."

" I must say I'd have thought you'd have guessed. Compline gave you the cape, Mandrake, didn't he? He looked out of the pavilion window and recognised you as you came down. He might have been looking at himself when you stood there in the other cloak. I think at that moment he saw his chance to bring off his tom-fool idea."

" What tom-fool idea?"

" To stage a series of apparent attempts on his own life based on an idea of mistaken identity. He planted that idea in all your heads. He insisted on it. He shoved you in and rescued you and then went about shouting that Hart had tried to drown him. Evidently he'd some such plan in his head on the first night. Hart had written threatening letters and Compline followed up by writing himself a threatening message with a rather crude imitation of Hart's handwriting. Once we'd proved Hart didn't write the message on the Charter form it was obvious only Nicholas could have done so. Perhaps he chucked you that cape deliberately. Before the bathing incident he knew where you all were and no doubt he watched Hart set off alone down the drive. If the plan failed there wasn't much harm done. Next he staged his own flight over country that he knew damned well was impassable. If nobody had gone with him he'd have come back half-drowned in snow and told the tale. Next he rigged up his own booby-trap, choosing a moment when you were all changing in your rooms. He hadn't bargained on Madame Lisse looking after him as he went down the passage. He was going to kick the door open and let the brass Buddha fall on the floor. But knowing that she was watching he had to go a bit further than was comfortable, and he mucked up the business. He chose the Buddha because he'd seen Hart handle it the night before. He chose the Maori mere for the same reason, but he smudged Hart's prints when he used it. He himself wore gloves, of course."

" But the wireless?" asked Chloris.

" Do you remember that Hart had complained bitterly of the wireless? That appears in Mandrake's most useful and exhaustive notes. Compline knew Hart loathed radio. After the fiasco at the pond he shut himself up in the smoking-room, didn't he, until he was turned out by William who wanted to make his drawing. And discordant noises were heard? He was always at the radio? Yes, well, he was making himself very familiar with that wireless set. Do you remember the fishing rod above the mantelpiece in the smoking-room?"

" Yes," they said.

" Complete with fly and cast and green line?"

" Yes."

" Well, when we came on the scene there was no fly and the line had been freshly cut. On the screwhole on the volume control I found a number of almost invisible scratches, all radiating outwards. I also found some minute fragments of red and green feather. The card on the rod tells us that the late Mr. St. J. Worthington Royal used that red-and-green fly when he caught his four-and-a-half pounder. There were other marks on the double tuning control which, at its centre, was free of dust. In the jamb of the door into the library there was a hole which accommodated the drawing-pin Mandrake picked up in the sole of his shoe. You say that William dropped one of his drawing-pins in the smoking-room. I fancy Nicholas found and used it. In Mrs. Compline's tweed hat I found two flies, one red-and-green, rather the worse for wear. The maid who looked after her swears there was only one, a yellow-and-black salmon fly, when she arrived. Who went straight to his mother's room after the murder? Right," said Alleyn answering their startled glances. " Well, yesterday evening we experimented. We found that if we used a length of fishing-line with a fly attached but without a cast, we could hook the fly in the screw-hole of the volume control, pass the green line under the wave band and over the tuning control axis which served as a sort of smooth-running pulley, and fix the other end of the line to the library door jamb with a drawing-pin. When you tweaked the line the hook pulled the volume control from zero to fairly loud, the line playing over the tuning control, which we had set in such a way that the slight pull turned it to the station. As the hook in the screw-hole reached the bottom of the circuit it fell out, and the wireless was giving tongue."

There was a long silence, broken at last by Mandrake. " But anybody could have fixed it," said Mandrake.

" Only after William was dead. He would have seen it when he was tuning, wouldn't he? But this is the place, I see, to introduce Thomas, the dancing footman. Thomas set a limit to the time when the murderer departed. Incidentally, he also proved, by a little excursion, that Hart couldn't have shoved you in the pond. Thomas was Nicholas Compline's undoing. If it hadn't been for Thomas we would have had a job proving that Hart didn't do exactly what Nicholas said he did : creep in by the door from the hall into the smoking-room and kill William. The mistaken identity stunt had to be supported by an approach from the rear. That was why Nicholas locked the door into the boudoir. But as things stood it was perfectly clear from the start that only Nicholas could have benefited by the wireless alibi. Mr. Royal, whose trip into the hall looked rather fishy, left the library after the wireless started, and Dr. Hart would have gained nothing whatsoever by the trick since he was alone for the entire time. Lady Hersey who had no motive, is the stock figure of the thriller-fiction— the all-too-obvious suspect. Moreover the trout-line device would have been of no use to her either, since she went in after the noise started."

"What *exactly* did he do, though?" asked Chloris.

" He killed his brother, rigged the wireless trick, came out and shut the door. Later, he opened the door, held a one-sided conversation with William, asked for the news, tweaked the string which he had pinned to the door jamb, and waited, with God knows what sensations, for someone to go into the smoking-room."

" What happened to the line?"

" You will remember, Mandrake, that while you and Mr. Royal were together by the body, Nicholas came in. He had shut the door after him and was hidden from you by the screen. He had only to stoop and pull the line towards him. The drawing-pin had jerked away and he had no time to hunt for it. The line was in heavy shadow and the same colour as the carpet. It throws back well towards the screen when the trick is worked. He gathered it up and put it on the fire when he got the chance. You left him by the fire for a moment, perhaps?"

"He asked us to leave him to himself."

"I'll be bound he did. But a trout line doesn't burn without leaving a trace, and we found its trace in the ashes."

"I see," said Mandrake.

"I can't help thinking about his mother," said Chloris. "I mean, it was Nicholas she adored."

"And for that reason she killed herself. At the inquest you will hear the letter she wrote. Mandrake has already seen it. She hoped to save Nicholas by that letter. While seeming to make a confession it tells him that she knew what he had done. No wonder he was upset when he read it. It was her last gesture of love—a very terrible gesture."

"I think," said Chloris shakily, "that he truly was fond of her."

"Perhaps," said Alleyn.

The library door opened and Hersey's face, very pale and exhausted, looked in. "Is it an official party?" she asked. Alleyn asked her to come in: "I have already been over a good deal of this with Lady Hersey and with Mr. Royal," he explained, and to Hersey: "I have not got as far as your visit with Nicholas Compline to his mother."

"Oh, yes. You asked me last night to tell you exactly what he did and I couldn't remember very clearly. That's why I've come in. I've remembered what happened after he'd tried to tell her about William. I'm afraid it's quite insignificant. He seemed frightfully upset, of course, and I suppose in a ghastly sort of way he was. He didn't make her understand, and turned away. I had to tell her. I knelt by her bed and put my arms round her. We were old friends, you know. I told her as best I could. I remember, now, hearing him walk away behind me and I remember that in the back of my head I was irritated with him because he seemed to be fidgeting about by the wardrobe. He must have been in a pretty awful state of mind. He was swinging the wardrobe door, I thought. I supposed he didn't know what he was doing."

"I think he knew," said Alleyn. "The tweed hat was on the top shelf of the wardrobe. He was getting rid of a green-and-red Alexandra trout fly."

III

" Wasn't that rather a mad thing to do?" asked Hersey wearily when Alleyn had explained about the trout fly.

" Not quite as mad as it sounds. The hook was not an easy thing to get rid of. He couldn't burn it or risk putting it in a waste-paper basket. He would have been wiser to keep the hook until he could safely dispose of it, or merely leave it on the mantelpiece, but no doubt he was possessed by the intense desire of all homicides to rid himself of the corpus delicti. In the shock of William's death his mother would have been most unlikely to notice a second and very insignificant trout fly in her hat-band."

" And that's all," said Mandrake after a long silence.

" That, I think, is all. You would like to go now, wouldn't you?"

" Shall we go?" Mandrake asked Chloris.

She nodded listlessly but didn't move. " I think I should go if I were you," said Alleyn, looking very directly at Mandrake.

" Come along, darling," Mandrake said gently. They bade good-bye to Hersey and Alleyn and went out.

" ' Darling '?" murmured Hersey. " But it means nothing, nowadays, does it? Why do you want to get rid of them, Mr. Alleyn?"

" We're expecting the police car and the ambulance. It won't be very pleasant. You would like to get away too, I expect, wouldn't you?"

" No, thank you," said Hersey. " I think I'll stay with my cousin Jo. He's pretty well cut up about this, you know. After all, he gave the party. It's not a pleasant thought." She looked at the door into the smoking-room, the door with its rows of dummy books. " Mr. Alleyn," she said, " he's a despicable monster, but I was fond of his mother. Would she perhaps have liked me to see him now?"

" I don't think I should if I were you. We can tell him you've offered to see him and we can let you know later on if he'd like it."

" I must ask you—has he confessed?"

" He has made a written statement. It's not a confession."

" But . . .?"

" I can't tell you more than that, I'm afraid," said Alleyn, and before his imagination rose the memory of sheets of paper covered with phrases that had no form, ending abruptly or straggling off into incoherence, phrases that contradicted each other and that made wild accusations against Hart, against the mother who had accused herself. He heard Fox saying: " I've given him the warning over and over again, but he will do it. He's hanging himself with every word of it." He felt Hersey's gaze upon him, and looking up saw that she was white to the lips. " Mr. Alleyn," she said, " what will happen to Nicholas?" And when he did not answer Hersey covered her face with her hands.

Through the sound of pouring rain Alleyn heard a car coming up the drive and out on the sweep before the house.

Fox came in. " It's our people, Mr. Alleyn?"

" All right," said Alleyn, and he turned to Hersey. " I must go." Hersey walked to the door. He opened it and he and Fox followed her into the hall.

Jonathan was standing there. Hersey went straight to him and he took her by the hands. " Well, dear," said Jonathan, " it—it's time, I think."

Fox had gone to the front door and opened it. The sound of rain filled the hall. A large man in plain clothes came in, followed by two policemen. Alleyn met them and the large man shook hands. Jonathan came forward.

" Well, Blandish," he said.

" Very sorry about this, sir," said Superintendent Blandish. Jonathan made a small waving of his hands and turned back to Hersey.

" All ready for us, Mr. Alleyn?"

" I think so," Alleyn said, and they went into the green sitting-room, shutting the door behind them.

" Hersey, my dearest," said Jonathan, " don't stay out here, now."

" Would you rather I went away, Jo?"

" I—it's for your sake."

" Then I'll stay."

So Hersey saw Nicholas come out between Bailey and Fox, the senior officers keeping close behind him. He walked stiffly with short steps, looking out of the corners of his eyes. His unshaven cheeks were creased with a sort of grin and his mouth was not quite shut. His blond hair hung across his forehead in dishevelled streaks. Without turning his head he looked at his host. Jonathan moved towards him and at once the two men halted.

"I want to tell you," Jonathan said, "that if you wish me to see your solicitors or do anything else that I am able to do, you have only to send instructions"

"There now," said Fox, comfortably, "that'll be very nice, won't it?"

Nicholas said in an unrecognisable voice: "Stop them hanging me," and suddenly sagged at the knees.

"Come along, now," said Fox. "You don't want to be talking like that."

As they went out Jonathan and Hersey saw the ambulance van outside by the police car, and men with stretchers waiting to come in.

I V

"He'd made up his mind to do it somehow, Jo," said Hersey that afternoon. "You mustn't blame yourself too much."

"I do blame myself dreadfully," said Jonathan. He had taken off his glasses and his myopic eyes, blurred with tears, looked childlike and helpless. "It's just as you said, Hersey. I had to learn my lesson. You see I thought I'd have a dramatic party."

"Oh, *Jo*," cried Hersey, with a sob that was almost a laugh. "*Don't.*"

"I did. That was my plan. I thought Aubrey might make a poetic drama out of it. I'm a mischievous, selfish fellow, trying to amuse myself and never thinking—just as you said, my dear."

"I talk too much. I was cross. You couldn't know what was behind it all."

"No. I think perhaps I do these things because I'm a bit lonely."

Hersey reached out her hand and he took it uncertainly between both of his. For a long time they sat in silence, looking at the fire.

V

"What you've got to do," said Mandrake, "is to think about other things. Get a new interest. Me for instance."

"But it isn't over. If it was over it wouldn't be so awful. I've been so mixed up with the Complines," said Chloris. "I wanted to be free of them and now—all this has happened. It sounds silly but I feel sort of lonely."

Mandrake removed his left hand from the driving wheel.

THE END

AGATHA CHRISTIE

The most popular and prolific writer of detective fiction ever known, her intricately plotted whodunits are enjoyed by armchair crime-solvers all over the world. How many of these have *you* read?

THIRD GIRL

MURDER AT THE VICARAGE

ONE, TWO, BUCKLE MY SHOE

CROOKED HOUSE

LORD EDGWARE DIES

A POCKET FULL OF RYE

AFTER THE FUNERAL

THE MYSTERY OF THE BLUE TRAIN

THE PALE HORSE

DEATH IN THE CLOUDS

THREE ACT TRAGEDY

SAD CYPRESS

DEATH ON THE NILE

THE HOLLOW

DEATH COMES AS THE END

CARDS ON THE TABLE

EVIL UNDER THE SUN

THEY DO IT WITH MIRRORS

AT BERTRAM'S HOTEL

4.50 FROM PADDINGTON

A CARIBBEAN MYSTERY

THE LABOURS OF HERCULES

THE CLOCKS

THE MOVING FINGER

MURDER IS EASY

CAT AMONG THE PIGEONS

THE MURDER OF ROGER ACKROYD

N OR M?

THEY CAME TO BAGHDAD

TEN LITTLE NIGGERS

APPOINTMENT WITH DEATH

THE MIRROR CRACK'D FROM SIDE TO SIDE

All available in Fontana Books

NGAIO MARSH

"The finest writer in the English language of the pure, classical, puzzle whodunit. Among the Crime Queens, Ngaio Marsh stands out as an Empress" *Sun* "Her work is as near flawless as makes no odds: character, plot, wit, good writing and sound technique" *Sunday Times* "The brilliant Ngaio Marsh ranks with Agatha Christie and Dorothy Sayers" *Times Lit. Supp.*

SCALES OF JUSTICE

SURFEIT OF LAMPREYS

COLOUR SCHEME

OFF WITH HIS HEAD

VINTAGE MURDER

FALSE SCENT

ENTER A MURDERER

DIED IN THE WOOL

DEATH AND THE
  DANCING FOOTMAN

DEATH AT THE
  DOLPHIN

A MAN LAY DEAD

DEATH IN A WHITE TIE

HAND IN GLOVE

DEATH IN ECSTASY

SINGING IN THE
  SHROUDS

ARTISTS IN CRIME

DEAD WATER

SPINSTERS IN JEOPARDY

All available in Fontana Books

ERIC AMBLER

A world of espionage and counter-espionage, of sudden violence and treacherous calm; of blackmailers, murderers, gun-runners—and none too virtuous heroes. This is the world of Eric Ambler. "Unquestionably our best thriller writer." *Graham Greene* "Ambler is unequalled in his artful reconstruction of the way things seem to happen." *Guardian* "He is incapable of writing a dull paragraph." *Sunday Times* "Eric Ambler is a master of his craft." *Sunday Telegraph*

DIRTY STORY

A KIND OF ANGER

THE NIGHT-COMERS

PASSAGE OF ARMS

THE MASK OF DIMITRIOS

JUDGMENT ON DELTCHEV

THE SCHIRMER INHERITANCE

All available in Fontana Books